AFTER

THE

BLOOM

AFTER THE THE BLOOM

LESLIE SHIMOTAKAHARA

DUNDURN
TORONTO

3655/09

Image credits: hand: shutterstock.com/Elena Ray, blossoms: istock.com/ piyaset
Printer: Webcom

Library and Archives Canada Cataloguing in Publication

Shimotakahara, Leslie, author
    After the bloom / Leslie Shimotakahara.

Issued in print and electronic formats.
ISBN 978-1-4597-3743-3 (paperback).--ISBN 978-1-4597-3744-0 (pdf).--ISBN 978-1-4597-3745-7 (epub)

I. Title.

PS8637.H525A69 2017   C813'.6   C2016-905418-7
                                                     C2016-905419-5

1   2   3   4   5   21   20   19   18   17

Conseil des Arts
du Canada

Canada Council
for the Arts

Canadä

ONTARIO ARTS COUNCIL
CONSEIL DES ARTS DE L'ONTARIO
an Ontario government agency
un organisme du gouvernement de l'Ontario

We acknowledge the support of the **Canada Council for the Arts** and the **Ontario Arts Council** for our publishing program. We also acknowledge the financial support of the **Government of Ontario**, through the **Ontario Book Publishing Tax Credit** and the **Ontario Media Development Corporation**, and the **Government of Canada**.

Care has been taken to trace the ownership of copyright material used in this book. The author and the publisher welcome any information enabling them to rectify any references or credits in subsequent editions.
— *J. Kirk Howard, President*

The publisher is not responsible for websites or their content unless they are owned by the publisher.

Printed and bound in Canada.

VISIT US AT

 dundurn.com | @dundurnpress | dundurnpress | dundurnpress

Dundurn
3 Church Street, Suite 500
Toronto, Ontario, Canada
M5E 1M2

Adrift

1984

One

Their house had always been a wreck. The difference was that back then Rita assumed all houses were like that. Paint on the porch peeling, like old nail polish. Full of boarders, or "guests," as Lily liked to call them; everyone lined up in the cramped hall to use the bathroom at night. The floors of some rooms were so uneven that if Rita closed her eyes, everything seemed to spin gently, the feeling of drunkenness, she'd realize years later.

Cracks in the bricks up one side had gotten worse. Now the whole house looked tilted, about to sink.

It was a bright, hot morning in July. Under normal circumstances, she'd be out for a jog. Instead she was here, squinting up at her childhood home and lingering on the pavement, as if someone had stood her up. Through the yellowed curtains of the house across the street, an old lady peeked out, probably wondering what on earth Rita was doing here, for the second morning in a row, no less. Maybe Rita looked as though she were on a mission to scope the neighbourhood, one of those rich Asians in the slum landlord business.

A little girl ran by, her bright green T-shirt appearing to pulsate with the most amazing greenness, and it seemed impossible that normal life was continuing on — kids were out enjoying the nice weather.

For a blissful moment, Rita felt like she could press the rewind button and slip back, so easily, into thinking that everything was going to be just fine. Of course it was. Lily had antsy feet. And a whimsical heart. She'd wandered off before and had always come back. It was the trademark of women of her generation: despite their veneer of stoicism, deep down anger simmered. They were tired of doing everything for everyone, sick of life as doormats. So from time to time, they blew off steam, hit the road. All mothers did this — or felt like doing this — didn't they? Rita was a mom and she'd felt that way before, as though she were destined to live like the little red hen. It was normal to go on strike, wasn't it?

She closed her eyes and let the darkness take over, not the comforting darkness of sleep, but a deeper, more frightening blackness. The pep talk she'd just been giving herself lost all conviction, sounded as hollow as it was. While it was true that Lily had traipsed off before, she'd always been found within a few hours.

Someone had left a pile of old clothes on the curb. A faded mauve shirt with a crushed-in collar. Baby-doll pumps in dark cherry leather, the round toes scuffed and flattened, like they'd been stepped on. Lily had once worn shoes like that and carried a matching handbag.

A wheezing sound gathered force from somewhere, and it took Rita a moment to realize that it was her own breath — the air shortening, dying in hot bursts in her throat — and all she could think was that maybe it was already too late. A vision swept over her: a small, pallid face touched by a bluish tint, generic and expressionless, the way dead people appeared on TV. She squeezed her eyes tighter and refused to believe that face could be her mother's.

Three days ago, Lily had gone missing. "Missing people with a history of memory problems often go back to the places they used to live," the police officer had said, handing over a FAQ sheet for family members. It seemed this sort of thing happened more often than you'd guess. The cop — a woman, wearing just a trace of nude lipstick — tried to be encouraging, but not overly so. She'd been through the drill before.

Bloor-Lansdowne. Not the poshest part of Toronto, that was for sure. The houses were crammed so close together that they appeared to be falling into each other at uneven heights. Translucent shower curtains turned front porches into makeshift sunrooms, every second house festooned with Christmas lights that never came down. Very little about the neighbourhood had changed since Rita's childhood (beyond the opening of a new strip club). Even the humid air, mixed with the humidity of her own palpitating body, seemed too familiar, oppressive.

What was she supposed to be *doing?* It didn't seem likely that her mother would miraculously stroll by. Yesterday Rita had knocked on the door of the old house. An old tawny-skinned guy had answered. "No," he'd said flatly, when she showed him Lily's photo. He kept saying no in response to all her questions; perhaps he didn't understand English.

Over his shoulder, she could see someone shuffling in the shadows. Peering in, she half expected Grandpa or Aunt Haruko to come into focus, as though for all these years their ghosts had remained right here, keeping the home fires burning. But Aunt Haruko would have never let that grime build up on the windows. Now the place was inhabited by a hodgepodge of sad souls from far-flung, war-torn countries, the mysterious odours of all their foods clashing, blending together in an oily fug.

Unclean.

Yet that was what people had once said about her own family. Rita had never managed to forget the peculiar, withering sensation of being looked at that way. And now, a couple decades later, here she was on the other side of that pitying, judgmental gaze.

Up and down the block and for four blocks in all directions, she'd plastered her bright yellow sheets on phone poles, telephone booths, mailboxes. MISSING PERSON across the top. The photo had been taken on Lily's honeymoon last year. Although only the head portion had been cropped, Rita couldn't help but see the larger image: smiling vivaciously, her mother was perched on the edge of a chaise longue, white foam waves crashing down behind her, pina colada in hand, the tiny pink umbrella as bright as her lipstick. Sixty, she could easily pass for ten years younger. Her dyed black hair fell in loose, permed curls, remarkably similar to the way Rita remembered it as a child.

BACK THEN, LILY would pull Rita onto her lap and tell stories about a faraway land. Glittering green dragons went to war with monster centipedes, which wound their way around mountaintops, like a trail of distant, glowing lanterns. A warrior named Momotaro burst forth from the belly of a peach, and a princess slipped out from the hollow of a bamboo shoot. But it was the strange, sad tale about a fisherman that drifted into Rita's mind now.

One day, when Urashima was out fishing, he met a beautiful sea princess. She lured him to her underwater kingdom, where he stayed for many seasons, seduced by her resplendent riches. At some point, however, their relationship fizzled, as all relationships eventually do. On the day of his departure, the sea princess gave Urashima three presents to remember her by, but she told him not to open any of them until he got home.

When he reached his old village, he noticed the landscape looked different: many more houses had been built on the hillside and new roads had been added out of nowhere. Bewildered, it took him quite some time to find his old house.

All that remained was the stone doorstep.

Beside himself, Urashima didn't know what to do. He opened the first present that the sea princess had given him. Inside was a single white feather. As the lid came off the next box, a cloud of smoke choked him. The third box contained a broken mirror that revealed the wizened face of an old man.

Although there'd been some redemptive aspect to the ending — something about Urashima being transformed into a bird — Rita couldn't really remember that part. The image that had stayed with her was an old Japanese guy, standing on the threshold of his vanished home. Staring into the cracked glass, he was transfixed by a face he barely recognized.

BACK AT HER apartment, she stood by the door for a long time. The sound of her heartbeat blended into the hum of the fridge, punctuated by creaks and laughter from the university kids above her.

Rita felt like a stranger here. She *was* a stranger here, having moved in only last week. Not much unpacking had been done before Lily pulled her disappearing act and everything came to a standstill. Boxes were stacked in the hall. A few had been opened, their contents dumped out. A tangle of bright sweaters lay on the floor, a limp turquoise arm reaching out to her lifelessly. A stable of My Little Pony figures pranced on top of her LP collection — Michael Jackson and Laura Nyro looking up soulfully, enigmatically — and Lite-Brite pieces had rolled all over, caught between the scratched up floorboards like a shattered beer bottle.

The mess that was her life.

All alone, she had no buffer of distractions to take her mind off Lily's disappearance. It intensified an old feeling. She always felt out of it for days after Kristen left on one of her month-long visits to her dad in Vancouver, yet the lulling, biscuity scent of the top of her head stayed behind, her hair still baby soft even though she was six now, grubby paw prints left all over the fridge and mirrors because Rita couldn't bring herself to wipe them away. The solitude — the "me" time — she thought she'd been craving for months oppressed her with its quiet monotony until she would force herself to go to the gym, call up her single girlfriends, get dolled up and go out, drink too many gin and tonics, flirt with some dude who wanted to buy her another, go home with him maybe.

Kids were playing Hacky Sack in the park outside her window, their loose Guatemalan garb flapping like kites in the wind. She thought she recognized the kid with shaggy hair — hadn't he been in her class a few years back? How surprised he'd be to see Mrs. Takemitsu here in Kensington Market. A sudden impulse to sneak up on him, bum a smoke. Her students probably pictured her in some prissy, oatmeal-bland house out in the suburbs, which wasn't that far off from where she'd lived before the divorce. But this was where she'd always belonged, this was where she'd spent her happiest art-school days, amid the incense and rotting garbage and graffiti-covered alleyways. Throughout all those sham years of her marriage, her real self had remained right here, fingernails caked with cyan and sienna.

No doubt Lily would be less than impressed with Rita's new digs. She wouldn't see charm in how the sunlight filtered through the grungy bay window, showing off the stained glass panel. The chipped marble fireplace had been blocked off, unfortunately — it was a fire hazard to let your tenants roast marshmallows, the landlord had said with a laugh — but it would still be perfect for hanging Kristen's stocking up at Christmastime.

If Lily were anywhere to be found, Rita would invite her over for dinner. She'd been meaning to do so for a while. For years, really. Right. Well, better late than never. Tears prickled her eyes. Something — some guilt or bitterness or regret — strangled her breath, the edges of the room fading, blurring. Chicken from the European butcher, rubbed in cumin. A tomato and avocado salad, everything perfectly ripened. She imagined them feasting and drinking wine until their cheeks were flushed and tingly, as though they were the kind of mother and daughter who did this all the time.

THREE DAYS EARLIER, the phone call.

"Rita, is that you? Is your mom there?" It was Gerald, his voice staccato.

"No, why would she be here?" Rita rubbed her eyes and sat up, the alarm clock a fluorescent blue blur. Her glasses slid on. 6:48.

"Lily's gone — I can't find her *anywhere*."

A dull ache spread up the nape of her neck. Queasiness filled her stomach.

It was almost seven, no need to get alarmed. Lily might have just stepped out for milk. Maybe she'd stopped somewhere for a coffee and cruller. Normal people did such things.

Still, Rita skipped her shower. Just brushed her teeth, popped in her contact lenses. Her coffee maker was packed away somewhere, so she cracked open a Coke.

Her little white Dodge Colt made sputtering noises, but it had been doing that for a while now. The drive up Yonge had never been so fast, so quiet, the street like a deserted fairground. Willowdale, what a different world. Wartime bungalows interspersed with pseudohistorical, newer houses and a couple of horrendous hacienda-like mansions. Their house was fairly inconspicuous until you noticed the pair of lion gargoyles that Gerald's first wife had had installed around the door before dying of cancer.

It had been a while since Rita had felt this fear and doom wrapping around her, nuzzling up, like an old pet. Lily was missing and this might be the beginning of one of her bad spells. Maybe this time she wouldn't be okay. Oh, God. It felt so familiar, so horribly familiar. More normal than the state of something resembling happiness that Rita would experience upon driving her daughter to daycare and baking banana bread and standing in front of the chalkboard, thirty bored faces peering at her. Those moments frightened her with their precariousness, their porcelain fragility. What a fake she was. Living in a state of crisis came naturally to her (at least that's what Cal had said at their last marriage-counselling session, right before they'd agreed to throw in the towel). Although Rita didn't entirely agree — surely, the breakdown of their marriage also had to do with his overly close "friendship" with a certain platinum-blond hygienist — she could admit, in retrospect, a grain of truth. It was just easier, in her experience, to assume everything was on the verge of turning to shit.

And now, what did you know? It was actually happening.

Gerald greeted her at the door, his weather-beaten cheeks infused with fiery energy, blondish-white hair flying off in all directions. "The police just got here. Officer Davis and a Chinese guy."

In the kitchen, the Chinese guy introduced himself as Officer Lee. *Pretty hard to remember that name, Gerald.* He had Buddha-chubby cheeks that made him look incredibly young. It was unusual to meet an Asian cop; Rita didn't think she'd ever seen one before. She felt a pang of sympathy over the flack he'd had to take from his family for not going the med-school or MBA route. Officer Davis also appeared young. Muscular build, ice-green eyes, a sandy ponytail. Pretty in a plainish way, if a bit heavyset. She looked bored; they both did. These rookie cops were dragged out to house calls on the hour, placating people about their vandalized sheds and missing dogs — the dull stuff that never led to car chases or drug busts.

"So Mr. Anderberg was telling us about Lily's disappearance," Davis said.

"As I was saying, I woke up real early. Her side of the bed was empty. I thought Lily was just in the bathroom at first, but when she didn't come back, I thought, okay, she's down in the kitchen with a cuppa Ovaltine. You know how she is with her sleep troubles."

"Yeah, it runs in the family." Rita wondered what other sleep habits he'd discovered. According to Cal, she was no better, gnashing her teeth like she was chewing up eggshells.

"So I went down to the kitchen and Lily wasn't there. Searched the entire house, even the garage. That's when I discovered her car's gone."

"What about her purse?" Lee asked.

"Ditto."

"So she went out somewhere."

"In the middle of the night? Why'd she leave without telling me?" Gerald's voice was anguished.

"Look, Mr. Anderberg, let me give it to you straight up." This was Davis now. "In ninety percent of these missing person cases, the person shows up within a day, at a friend's house or something. Went out, forgot to leave a note, that sorta thing. So the first thing for you to do is put together a list of Lily's family and friends and start calling around."

"I'm not familiar with her friends in the Japanese community." Gerald looked over at Rita.

"Me neither. But if you give me Mom's phone book, I'll see who I can recognize."

"That little black book's always in her purse."

Rita stared back at him, an ache forming across her forehead.

"In any case, you folks need to put your heads together," Davis continued.

"Where's Tom?" Rita asked. Stretched out in business class, a Caesar in hand, coasting to the other side of the world, most likely. Her brother had an amazing ability for being unreachable at times like this.

"No idea. Left him a message. Told him to get his butt over here."

Bank and Visa statements fanned across the kitchen table. Davis explained that they'd be monitoring Lily's accounts for withdrawals and credit card charges, which would indicate where she was spending money.

"That could take a while." Gerald sighed. "Lily hardly ever charges anything. For some reason she prefers to pay cash. I'm always getting at her for carrying too much dough around."

He said it like it was just one of his wife's charming idiosyncrasies. The real reason Lily always kept her wallet well stocked, Rita suspected, was that she still lived in fear of being made to evacuate at a moment's notice. Not that she ever talked about the bad old days or even admitted they'd happened.

Camp.

Occasionally, when Rita was little, Grandpa used to tell stories about this place where the sand blew so fiercely that stepping outside was like standing under a shower of pinpricks. "Where was this camp? Were you on vacation?" Rita would ask, although she couldn't understand why anyone would choose to visit such bleakness. The old man wouldn't answer, staring off into space, his cheeks hardened like a walnut shell. As she got older, she came to understand that it had been an internment camp, where all people of Japanese descent had been imprisoned on suspicion of being traitors throughout the war. But Lily insisted she'd never set foot in any such place. *Maybe they sent the farmers and poor people away. Not us. We never left Little Tokyo.*

"D'you consider it unusual behaviour for your mom to go off like this on her own?" Davis said.

The cuckoo clock appeared a welcome hiding spot. Family business was private business, Grandpa had always made clear.

"Mom's just a bit absent-minded."

"Absent-minded how?"

"Forgetful."

"Everyone gets forgetful as they get older." Gerald pulled at a loose thread on his trousers.

"Let's be clear: has Lily ever gone missing for several hours before?"

"Never," Gerald said.

But the officer was looking at Rita.

A pungent odour worked its way into her nostrils, something burnt to a crisp. One of Lily's casseroles hadn't turned out so well. A lot of things hadn't turned out so well, like the state of their family. Rita's face had become hot and prickly; the acrid smell turned her stomach.

She used to live in fear that her friends would find out something was funny with her mom. It was bad enough being Japanese — one of only two Oriental girls at her school and the other girl wasn't at all outgoing or pretty. The last thing she wanted was to be seen as both the Japanese girl *and* the girl with the crazy mother.

"When I was growing up, Mom would get distracted and wander off for maybe half a day, tops. We always knew she was coming back."

"Like she needed some alone time?" Davis said.

"You could say that."

"Fair enough. Every woman needs alone time. Ever find out where she went?"

"Once, when I was a kid, we couldn't find her." Actually, there'd been many times. They smeared together into a dark, murky shape that had left its stain across so many of Rita's childhood memories. "It turned out Mom had wandered past a dry cleaner that must've reminded her of her dad's old shop in Little Tokyo. Guess it stirred up some stuff."

"Stuff? Could you be more specific?" Lee said.

"Stuff about the past. She got confused. About where she was. She thought she was back in her father's store and tried to take over at the cash register, from what I was told."

"What happened?"

"The owner kicked her out. Later, he called our house when he found her crouched in the alley out back, crying. Grandpa was out, so I talked to the guy. I walked over to get her."

"And how was she?"

"By the time I got there, she seemed back to her old self."

"Did she remember what she was doing there?"

"I'm not sure. She was upset, so I didn't push it."

"D'you read in the paper last year about that chick that showed up at a homeless shelter, no purse, no ID, nothing?" Davis's cheeks had turned rosy, almost. "Not even an old lady — young, blond, decent looking. Just walked straight out of her life. Fugue amnesia, they were calling it."

Knife handles protruded from a wood block on the counter. Rita imagined their steel blades narrowed to perfect points.

Weren't the police supposed to be trying to reassure her that Lily was all right — everything would be all right? She'd wandered off before and had always come back, so wasn't the same pattern bound to repeat itself? In a couple hours, Lily would be sitting at this very table, and they'd laugh about the incident and order a pizza. Yet the police weren't acting like everything was fine; they were taking amusement in the possibility that she might be batshit crazy. Sleeping in a homeless shelter or in a ditch on the side of the road. Shame, sharpened by fear, crept around Rita's stomach. The kitchen felt cramped as though there wasn't enough space for them all to stand at the counter or enough air for them all to breathe. Didn't these people have more pressing things to do than hang around yakking?

"I hate to break this up, but maybe you guys should get out there and *find* my mother. I agree she has her problems. That makes it all the more important that you bring her home immediately!"

"We appreciate what you're going through," Davis said. "We'll be on our way just as soon as we've finished interviewing you and Mr. Anderberg."

Rita pinched her lips, not trusting herself to speak. She couldn't afford to alienate the police.

"Well, this is the first I've heard 'bout any of … my wife's memory problems." Gerald looked so blindsided that Rita couldn't help feeling sorry for him.

They'd been married for less than a year. They'd met at a dance for the Electricians Association of Canada, where Lily had been brought as someone else's date, but had somehow managed to hook up with Gerald. Whenever she introduced him to anybody, she liked to emphasize that he was a retired electrical *inspector*, like that made all the difference. Rita thought he seemed like a decent enough guy, if a surprising match for her mother. Funny how after all Lily's years spent preaching the virtues of marrying your own, she'd succumbed to a classic case of yellow fever.

Rita had only partly taken the advice: Cal was Korean, but at least that was Asian. Not that it did jack shit to keep them together.

Poor Gerald. He'd been so eager to get Lily to the altar. How long had they actually dated? He had no idea of the full extent of her ... eccentricities.

"Did your mom ever receive psych treatment?" Lee asked.

It was a question Rita had tossed around with her brother from time to time. Their mother needed help — professional help. Tom never denied the point. But they both knew she'd never go for it, so what were they supposed to do? Have her committed?

"My grandfather considered shrinks on par with witch doctors. Mom just has weak nerves."

"Weak nerves, huh?" Davis laughed. "Nothing that smelling salts won't take care of?"

They wanted to know whether Lily was on any meds. Gerald mentioned some pills she took for her thyroid. They went upstairs to the bathroom to search through the medicine cabinet and then moved on to the bedroom. The pills were nowhere to be found; it seemed she carried them in her purse. Everything of any importance was in that purse: reading glasses, makeup, facial cleanser, half-eaten sandwiches, vitamins. A survival kit, it was her life in miniature.

"Any recent disturbances or fights that might've pushed her to leave?" Davis said.

"'Course not, we're newlyweds."

"Rita, what about you? Anything you can think of?"

"Nothing comes to mind."

"Were you guys close?"

"I don't know. Things have been a bit bumpy since I split with my husband."

"She didn't approve?"

"My mother's pretty old school. It's like, if your husband's not beating you, you should go back and give it another go. Particularly if he happens to be Dental Surgeon of the Year."

Rita still remembered Lily's ecstatic smile when she and Cal had first announced their engagement. All Lily's features had sharpened and jumped up, rosy clouds diffusing across her cheekbones. That hunger in her face. Rita could see she was surprised to discover that her dreamy, dishevelled daughter had it in her, too. That hunger to have a man sweep her off her feet, take care of her. How it had irked Rita to give in: to be brought face to face with this *thing* inside her. This inner weakness she'd been ignoring all her life but, it turned out, she'd inherited from her mother. The truth was that she was just so fucking exhausted. Even back then, she knew she didn't love Cal. She'd never loved Cal. It was a terrible admission. But he'd come along at a time when she was tired of being broke and adrift and her latest show at the co-op had only sold three paintings. What he offered was a chance to sell out, to trade in her sorry existence.

The only thing that could have pleased Lily more would have been Cal's being a doctor.

"My mom pushed me toward dental school, too," Lee said. "She said no good woman would marry a cop."

"Any regrets you don't spend all day in people's mouths?"

"Just that I'm single."

With a hesitant laugh, Rita wondered if this guy might be flirting. It had been a long time since anybody had flirted with her. A sudden rush of emotion, hot moisture bursting behind her eyes — not because she was glad she hadn't lost her groove, but because the moment made her feel strangely close to her mother. As if Lily, having vanished, were all the more present, whispering tips in her ear about how to snag a good man and avoid the deadbeats. "I guess your mom knew best then."

"Asian mothers."

Two

As it started to rain, the windshield turned into a watercolour. Rivulets trickled down, caught flecks of coloured light, smeared into nothing. Cars honked, tires slid across the damp asphalt with a faint sizzling. Everything felt faraway and insubstantial, as if all of Rita's senses had faded to the point they might fail altogether.

The thought that Lily was outside in this made Rita shiver. At least Lily had her car — if that was any comfort. Had she spent the night huddled in the back seat, parked in some dark alleyway? Where *was* she? Why weren't the police doing more to find her?

Maybe she would burst through the door at any minute, lipstick smudged, hair fallen flat, confused about what had happened but unharmed and relieved to be home. Maybe she was there already.

But as soon as Gerald opened the door, it was obvious nothing had changed.

Their living room had aspirations culled from the pages of *Good Housekeeping*. A thick border of ivy and violets had been stencilled along the wall tops; needlepoint cushions adorned the floral chintz sofas. Dishes of potpourri that Gerald's first wife had made herself had long since turned brown and brittle.

Strewn all over the coffee table: notepads, lists, dog-eared copies of the Yellow Pages and White Pages. A pizza box full of crusts. The place was starting to look like a call centre.

There was one trace of Lily's presence, at least: a celadon ceramic dish full of white pebbles covered in water. Branches, leaves, and irises sprung up in an oddly intriguing, asymmetric pattern. Ikebana, Japanese flower arranging. The twilight petals were already wilted; by tomorrow, it would all be dead.

Gerald looked wilted, too, purple-grey pouches under his eyes. For the past three days, they'd been on the phone with neighbours, friends, Lily's dentist, hospitals, homeless shelters. They'd received a good deal of sympathy, but no real information. And no one had a clue how to get in touch with the Japanese ladies she saw once a month at the Nisei Women's Club.

So far, the only thing the police had told them was that Lily had withdrawn six hundred dollars on the day of her disappearance.

"It's a joint account, could've told them that days ago," Gerald said. "They should hand over their badges and lemme do their job!"

While Rita wasn't quite as cynical, she had to admit she had doubts about how high a priority their case was. Officer Davis had mentioned that the Canadian Criminal Code didn't prohibit a person from walking out of her life, provided no crime had been committed.

It was all so confusing. The officers urged them to call everyone under the sun, yet they also wanted a list, complete with addresses and phone numbers. Were they going to contact these people, too? Or would they only call if Lily turned up dead in the trunk of her car?

A press release had been issued. That morning while Rita was on her second Coke, the CBC news announcer devoted all of ten seconds to "Lily Takemitsu Anderberg, a sixty-year-old woman of Japanese descent, five foot four, 110 pounds, last seen at her home in Willowdale on Friday night." The kind of bland filler news that usually didn't even register on your groggy consciousness.

"These things take time," Davis said. "It's important for family not to get overwhelmed. Get rest, eat regular meals, and if you need to, don't feel bad about going back to work."

Rita almost wished it weren't summer break. Toxic armpits, challenging stares, baseball caps on backward. Forget about getting anyone to answer a question about Surrealism; getting them not to throw pencil crayons at each other was enough of a feat. But she liked chatting with the kids about their problems and views on the latest MuchMusic videos, and occasionally a surprisingly good drawing would surface from the sea of hormones. What a welcome diversion all that would be from the silence of Gerald's living room.

From the corner of her eye, she watched him search through the White Pages, his cheeks suffused like overripe tomatoes. You could tell he'd done some hard living in his time, a suspicion that had borne out at his wedding. His friends came in all stripes, but they had one thing in common when Rita asked, "So how do you know Gerald?"

"We met in AA, ten years back."

"Oh, how nice."

An awkward lull. "I'm going to the bar. Can I get you a mineral water or anything?"

So that explained why Gerald was toasting everyone with a goblet of cranberry juice.

Maybe he'd fallen off the wagon since then. Had a reunion with his old friend Jack Daniel's drawn to the surface a dark, violent side? *It's not a crime to walk out of your life.* Maybe Lily had come to her senses and hightailed it. Rita had noticed Davis eying Gerald with suspicion at one point, questioning him about the state of his marriage. Wasn't the husband always the prime suspect?

But the more she thought about it, the less she could see it. The wild flush of Gerald's cheeks was from worry, not rage. Wasn't it? She'd seen the way he looked at Lily with little boy enchantment in his eyes.

Still, you never could tell.

"I'm going to search around upstairs again."

"Sure thing, kiddo."

HER ROOTS WERE growing in. That was the first thing Rita had noticed. Although Lily was usually meticulous about her hair, now a thin, silvery horizon peeked out along her part.

A hand reached out to rub a smudge off Rita's cheek. She'd squirmed away, as though she were a little kid again. Now she thought of that simple, motherly gesture with a pang of longing. Why couldn't she have just stood still, for God's sake?

That was the last time Rita saw her mother, a week ago. Moving day.

Rita had been in a hurry, the rented U-Haul parked outside. She was swinging by to pick up her old boxes, stored in Lily and Gerald's basement. At last, she'd be able to use all those ceramic dishes she'd made back in art school, clay oozing through her fingertips, massaging her palms. How malleable — how full of possibility — life had seemed back then. Cal had never liked the dishes, calling them part of her hippie-dippy phase, and this made unearthing the old treasures all the more fun and delightful.

Maybe Rita had been so excited about her new place that she'd neglected to see her mother was in trouble. More likely, she'd been aware of what was going on but had looked the other way, as she always did, because she couldn't bear to face it.

Burnt brown sugar lingered in the air, sweet and needy. Lily had baked an apple crumble. Yet Rita was busy, her skin covered in sweat and grime, more than her mother could ever wipe away, and she just wanted to grab her boxes and immerse herself in unwrapping wine glasses and popping bubble wrap in the quiet of her new apartment. Besides, as she'd come to tell herself over the years, keeping their relationship on an even keel meant managing their time together very carefully.

Too much chit-chat would only fill her with irritation or worse yet, that gnawing, empty feeling: they'd never see eye to eye on anything. She'd been cheated of that natural mother-daughter closeness.

But Lily had insisted, and as she poured the tea, it sloshed on her hand. Rita sprang up to run the faucet until the water was ice cold. How thin and frail her mother suddenly seemed, her eyes distracted and adrift, lost in some internal landscape that hemmed her in and filled her with a nervous, fluttering energy. It was a look that Rita and Tom had learned to recognize over the years. Whenever they saw it, they both felt an impulse to run.

"You okay, Mom?"

A dip into silence. "Where're you moving to, again?"

"Kensington Market."

"Oh, we used to live not far."

Actually, Margueretta Street was a fair bit farther west.

"We always owned our own house, though," Lily added.

Here we go again, Rita thought. Her slide down the social scale. The shame of being a single mom living in a crappy rental. Next Lily would reminisce about the beautiful Tudor that Rita and Cal had once owned on Golfdale Road, the Mercedes she used to drive, the cottage in Muskoka. The cleaning lady who'd ironed Cal's shirts while Rita pushed her Peg Perego pram past the WASPy neighbours, who probably mistook her for the nanny.

But Lily's eyes remained fixed on the cream wall; it might have been a movie screen and she was waiting for the film to begin. "Before your grandfather bought that house, we moved around quite a bit."

"We did?"

"Oh." Lily had a flush of confusion. "Was that before you were born?"

"I only remember that one house."

"Yeah." Lily nodded a little frantically, like she was trying to convince another person in her head. "The house on Margueretta was the only place we lived."

What memory was she struggling to push from her mind? Memories of the internment? Excitement rose in Rita's gut: she might have been teetering at the top of a roller coaster, wind tearing through her hair, before the inevitable plunge. Though it never came — of course it didn't. Lily's expression smoothed over, as always, everything hidden behind that placid mask.

"Our house was the best on the block. With a bit of money, I could've fixed it up into something special. In that neighbourhood, though, why bother? Not after all the black folks moved in and ruined everything."

"*Mom*. You can't say stuff like that." Strange how being the target of racism had made Lily all the more bigoted, as if pointing fingers at others was the only way she knew how to shield herself. That was the absurd way the world worked.

Yet they were getting away from the real source of Rita's exasperation. A hot tide swept up her neck. "You don't have to be ashamed to talk about it — I *know* what happened, Mom. You were rounded up and thrown in camps, like a bunch of diseased animals!"

"I don't know what you're talking about. And watch your tone."

"Just admit it. You'll feel so much better!"

"Admit what?" The amazing thing was that Lily looked genuinely perplexed, as though a stranger on the street had called out her name, having mistaken her as someone else.

Always this clash of wills. And Lily's signature strategy — surprisingly effective — was to retreat into her shell of proclaimed ignorance. It was taking Rita back, way back. She'd regressed to her teenage self again, hormonally out of whack, living on the verge of glassy tears. The more helpless Lily acted, the more Rita felt it: this cruel, uncontrollable, animalistic urge to tear apart the little world her mother had fabricated out of tissue-paper lies and delusions.

The cuckoo clock let out its mechanized clangs and shrieks, punching the air several times. If she kept this up, she'd never get out of here. Now wasn't the time.

Another time. Maybe. Not.

Like Lily would ever open up about that stuff anyway.

"I have to go, Mom. The truck's due back soon."

A bit of apple crumble, a bit of mother-daughter chit-chat. A bit of screaming. Nothing out of the ordinary.

It wasn't until they were by the door that Rita noticed anything unusual. She was struck by how her mother's eyes had glassed over with a pleading mien.

"You've had a good life, haven't you, dear?"

It was such a funny thing to ask. So sudden and out of character. Why would Lily have asked that? Rita didn't know how to respond.

"I guess so?"

Now she wished she'd taken the time to glance back and examine Lily's face for some clue as to what was going through her mind. The truth was she'd been concerned with nothing more than a quick exit.

THEIR BEDROOM WAS dim and humid, dust glittering in beams of sunlight. It seemed as though it hadn't been inhabited in days; Gerald must have started sleeping in the guest room.

The bedspread, a faded peony print, was a leftover from his first wife. It looked strange next to the yellowed scrolls of Japanese calligraphy. As a kid Rita had fantasized that the scrolls were family heirlooms: the words of their ancestors. When she asked Grandpa who had painted them, however, he said they were by ladies at the Buddhist church. Rita clung to her belief the scrolls were somehow special; it didn't matter that she had no idea what they said. Speaking Japanese would only make things harder on them all, according to Grandpa, so she and Tom only understood a smattering of baby talk, mostly to do with bodily functions — shi-shi, benjo. Yet when she looked at the calligraphy, the dripping black ink communicated a feeling of mystery and enchantment that went beyond words.

Rita could picture her mother perched on the worn, uphol-stered stool in front of the vanity. The circular mirror, aged and foggy in patches, would cast her image back dimly, waveringly. The tabletop was so crowded that things had to be put in shoeboxes. All her perfume bottles with stoppers shaped like diamonds and shepherdesses, tubes of lipstick running the gamut from a barely perceptible nude to blood red. Discontinued shades of coral and copper, nothing ever thrown out. Samples of this and that elixir, unopened silver packets full of promise, saved for a rainy day. So many jars and bottles for Lily to dip her fingertips into, massaging her skin in upward, feathery motions.

She always took special care around her right cheekbone, where the scar had once been. That was why she used to wear her hair like Veronica Lake, the curtain of hair providing some concealment. After fading over the decades, the vestiges of the scar had been removed through plastic surgery, like a dribble of pink wax, wiped clean. Yet Rita would sometimes catch her mother still touching her cheek, her fingertips searching for the ridges of something no longer there. And that was how Rita felt, too. She'd never found out anything about Lily's scar, just one of the many things they'd all learned to pretend was invisible.

Hot prickles of tears. She sank to the bed, head in her hands. The room was rocking, awash in a million clashing perfumes, a floral din. She didn't feel up to being here at all.

Then a framed photo caught her eye. Gap-toothed, rabbit smile, and a little purple barrette peeking out like a glimmer of normalcy. It had been taken last year at Kristen's birthday party.

Yesterday, when they'd talked on the phone, Rita had mentioned nothing about Granny's disappearance. It just seemed better to luxuriate in her daughter's bubbly giggles, something about how scary it'd been to walk across the Capilano Suspension Bridge. The line went fuzzy, the little voice so distant. She wanted Kristen here with her now; she wanted the Care Bear pyjamas and Fruit Roll-Ups stuck to the tabletop. She wanted "Mommy, what makes the rain fall?" and even "Mommy, why can't you and Daddy live together anymore?" But the kid would be full of questions about Granny's vanishing act that Rita couldn't begin to answer, so maybe it was better that Kristen was away for another three weeks. Ugh. Rita only prayed that by the time she got back, everything would be back to normal.

That was the only picture on display. There hadn't been a lot of Kodak moments growing up. Rita's therapist had once asked her to bring in an old photo of her family, but she hadn't been able to find one.

When Rita was little, Lily had been at her best, relatively speaking. Back then, she could be trusted to walk Rita to school and pick her up. She vacuumed and dusted the house while swaying her hips to Billie and Ella and put out little dishes of mints on the front hall vestibule so the place felt more like her idea of a hotel. On hot summer days, she'd stuff tissues into her armpits to protect the pastel fabric of her sleeveless dresses from sweat stains, her dewy face barely an inch from the fan. Bursts of motherliness came over her, and she'd fidget with Rita's pigtails, trying to get them just right, wiping fiercely at her cheek. "You have to look smart because I named you after Rita Hayworth, the most sophisticated lady on earth. Never forget that." But it was Lily who had the star's elegance and ambition — Rita Hayworth back in the days when she was still dark-haired Margarita Cansino, the exotic Mediterranean girl assigned bit parts: an Egyptian beauty, a Russian dancer, a mantrap.

With the caprice of a windstorm, Lily would sometimes flirt with the boarders. There was a prune-faced man named Mr. Dobson, whom she fawned over because he claimed to have been a professor and hoarded shoulder-high piles of books in his room. While reading the newspaper, he'd call out the headlines: "'The Russians Plan to Get There First.' Those damn Russians." As she carried in his tea, his eyes lingered appreciatively. Some days, she'd put a great deal of effort into her appearance, powdering and repowdering her cheek with a great white puff, as if just the right flick of the wrist and wistful smile might make the scar disappear magically. Other days, however, she didn't wear makeup at all, just pulled her hair back in a tight bun that accentuated the glistening pink seam, the exposure of which subdued her spirits. Rita didn't like to see her mother get like that, but it was just her nerves, her weak nerves. Nothing to worry about, according to Grandpa, and he was a doctor.

In the absence of a family photo, the therapist had asked Rita to remember a scene from childhood. What came to mind was an image of them all playing cards.

The sound of the cards shuffling. Grandpa was shuffling them, while explaining the rules of old maid. Their whole family was a bunch of old maids, really. Grandpa hadn't always been an old maid, of course, but his wife had died long before Rita was born. And yet, she wasn't entirely gone because she'd left behind a double: Aunt Haruko, her twin sister. Another old maid, the quintessential old maid. As far as Rita could tell, Aunt Haruko'd never had a boy-friend — not unless you counted Jesus Christ. It was strange to think that Aunt Haruko had once been part of an identical pair, like Mary and Sally Cross in their matching gingham dresses at school. If her grandmother were alive, would the two of them have the same coarsely cut hair and spindly tree bodies? Rita wondered if Grandpa found it unnerving to live with the spitting image of his dead wife.

But two old maids didn't form a pair. They remained just two unusable cards, destined for the reject pile.

Lily's face would light up as she looked down at her hand, regardless of how good or bad her cards were; she knew how to hide her emotions behind that aura of wonder. Cards she wanted you to take protruded slightly. Tom was onto her tactic and it wasn't long before he ducked out of these games anyway. Grandpa, on the other hand, continually fell for it. Only years later, as Rita looked back on those long, rainy afternoons, did she realize there'd been something deliberate about his efforts to lose. He'd always had a soft spot for his daughter-in-law, on account of the fact that his son had aban-doned them all. So if indulging her desire to win at cards made her smile, what could be the harm?

"Oh, I don't mind being the old maid." A soft chuckle.

"The queen of hearts?" Lily plucked the lone card from Grandpa's hand, raising an eyebrow. "It's not a bad sign you'd be left with her."

This was typical of her innuendo. Her hand would brush against Grandpa's arm while clearing away his plate. Once he backed away so suddenly that a knife flew across the room and hit the wall, leaving a dung-brown smear. Their relationship was full of these strained flirtations, punctuated by moments of volatility.

What it came down to was this: Lily needed a man in her life. Her singleness, her old-maid status, seemed unnatural, cruel. Although Kaz had long vanished, his phantom remained behind in the form of her deep loneliness, which she'd transferred over to his father. It didn't take much for her to erupt in a shower of tears and throw herself into Grandpa's arms — his body rigidifying, hands awkward as paddles as they patted the back of her head a few times before pushing her away, gently but firmly. His face turned grey, grief-stricken almost, thanks to whatever she'd whispered in his ear.

ON THE DAY of Lily's disappearance, Tom took his sweet time to show up. He'd been in meetings all morning, hadn't even had a chance to check messages. Or so he said. Rita suspected he'd banked on it being a false alarm. Just wait half a day and Mom would reappear. Unless she didn't.

He plunked his briefcase on the kitchen table, loosened his tie, and ran his hands through his coarse, buzzed hair. Not even a fleck of grey. Although he was forty — six years older than Rita — Tom was often mistaken as her younger brother.

"No sign of Mom, still? She hasn't called? Must've lost track of time at the mall."

True, Lily was a sucker for promotions. But shopping since the crack of dawn? Tom was a little late in the game to breeze in and throw around unhelpful suggestions.

Family stuff didn't fall on him the way it fell on Rita. And he was quite happy to take the back seat. It had been this way for as long as she could remember. Tom had always found convenient reasons not to be around the house: his paper route, his job at the corner store. "It's good for a boy to be independent," Lily had said. And as long as his activities were tied to earning money, Grandpa seemed quite fine with his absence.

Most of the time when they were growing up, Tom wanted nothing to do with Rita. On one sweltering summer afternoon, though, she was allowed a glimpse into his adventures. Carrying her sand pail, she followed him a few blocks to an abandoned apartment building. In the overgrown courtyard was a wishing pond that hadn't held water for years; rotted leaves clogged the paint-chipped bottom. But if you dug through the muck carefully enough, every so often a shiny penny or nickel would be illuminated. So Tom set her little, nimble fingers to work, telling her they were like pirates digging for buried treasure. In the end, they had half a pail of coins, from which her share was enough to buy a cinnamon lollipop. How fiery sweet it had tasted.

Only years later did it occur to her that her brother had given her less than a 5 percent cut of the spoils. The realization made her laugh. Even then, he had a firm grasp of profit margins.

By the time high school rolled around, Tom had moved on to other, more lucrative activities. He had no time for her — no time to torment her even — because he had places to go, games to make. His best friend had a broad forehead and blunt features, as though his face had been carved from a hunk of cheese. That family was rich by neighbourhood standards; they owned two divey bars, where Tom must have gotten his start on the pool tables out back. The sweaty, metallic tang of adrenalin and crumpled bills surrounded him wherever he went. Maybe Kaz would have knocked some sense into him, but not sweet, feeble Grandpa; he was past that stage in his life. Tom could get away with anything.

"So what's the story, guys?" Tom asked.

"The cops just asked a bunch of questions, looked around the house. Left a list of things for *us* to do. God knows what my hard-earned tax dollars are going to!" Gerald stirred his coffee with a clatter.

"I thought Mom was doing so much better these days." Tom looked at Rita.

"Me, too."

"I guess she still has setbacks every so often."

"We have to find her, Tom."

Rita heard her voice cracking, as she let herself be pulled into his embrace, but even the way he patted her back felt mechanical. It wasn't comforting. If her brother looked worried, he didn't look worried enough; there was something hard and concentrated about his expression, as if he were bracing himself for the worst because he'd always known in his heart the worst would one day happen.

"We *will* find her. I'll drive around the neighbourhood and swing by the mall on my way home."

"Already did that," Gerald interrupted.

"Mom'll come back on her own. Any minute."

Tom was just saying what they wanted to hear.

"And what if she doesn't?"

"Well, then. It's out of our control, I guess."

Maybe, deep down, he'd find it a relief if the worst happened. To be free. Free of the fear that next time their mother wouldn't be okay. Free at last of the burdens of family. For reasons Rita had never entirely understood, Tom had long resigned himself to the fact that their family was a losing investment. And what was the point of throwing good money after bad? He could walk away from it all; in his head, maybe he'd already walked away years ago. His powers of self-preservation never ceased to amaze her. Sure, he'd worry about Lily's disappearance, to a point, and then that would be it. He wouldn't move heaven and earth to find her.

If anyone were going to step up, it would have to be Rita.

"So I hear your ma's had memory issues for a while now?" There was an aggressive edge to Gerald's voice, implying that someone should have filled him in a long time ago.

"Sure, she has her ups and downs," Rita said. She could feel the tension running up her brother's neck, the same posture overtaking her own body.

"Must've been hard being a single mom. Bad luck, your father's death."

Rita and Tom exchanged arch looks, his a little sharper than hers. They could imagine how Lily would have spun the story for Gerald, the story of how she'd tragically lost her beloved husband.

"Did she tell you things were peachy 'til Kaz kicked the bucket? That he was a great dad — Father of the Year?" Although Tom wore a bit of a simper, his jaw had tightened. It was the look he'd get while leaning over a pool table.

"You two didn't get along?"

"Never got a chance to find out."

Gerald looked befuddled.

"The guy walked out on us."

"What? I thought he died of a stroke."

Rita glanced at her brother warningly. Why did Gerald have to know about any of that crap? "Yeah, he *did* die of a stroke."

"But that only happened years later. After he'd left us high and dry."

"Oh."

"Yep. Kinda sucks, doesn't it."

"Where'd he go?"

"Moved back to California, apparently. Then, five, six years later, he checked out for good."

"But Lily said —"

"Lily says a lot of things."

"Why'd she lie to me?"

"Don't take it so personal, Gerald. It's what she tells everyone.

Kaz died of a stroke. If it wasn't for that, they'd still be two peas in a pod. Hell, maybe *she* even believes it."

Tom's glum, blindly accepting expression filled Rita with a heavy, bloated feeling. They'd both long given up trying to figure out what made their mother this way.

But Gerald continued to look hurt and confounded.

"Yeah, it sucks." Tom shrugged then straightened up. "But, ya know what? Ya get over it."

In a way Rita envied him; at least he had something to get over. In her case the process of moving on had never been as clear: how could you get over someone you couldn't remember? Kaz had left when she was less than a year old. There weren't even any photos of him around the house to trick her into thinking she recalled some detail — a stubbly jawline, an old cardigan. "What was he *like*, Tom? Did Kaz play ball with you? What kind of car did he drive?" Rita used to ask. Jenny Smart's dad drove a creamy Oldsmobile convertible and smiled like the man in the toothpaste ad and said things like, "Fake it 'til you make it," a phrase he'd learned at a business course in a church basement. But Tom always shook free of Rita's grasp. "He was never around. He was a loser, a bum. I don't *know*."

Lily was no less tight-lipped. And it was dangerous to push her because the mere mention of Kaz's name could presage a plummet in her mood.

Snippets of information Rita had scavenged from eavesdropping on Lily and Grandpa: Kaz had been a man who liked to dance, a man who was good with the ladies; he'd had no respect for the rules; he was a lazy, good-for-nothing bum. They rarely talked about him, beyond a lone comment, quickly averted. Still, it was enough to provide her imagination with a hanger on which she could drape her own images and associations. If Kaz had been a bum, she pictured Marlon Brando in *On the Waterfront*, a man of principles, in his own tragic, sorry-ass way. Or he was like Alan Ladd in *Shane*, full of simmering fury and underlying decency.

"So how did your mom meet this Kaz fellow?" Gerald's arms were tightly crossed, his face lit up in blotchy patches.

"I guess they must've met at camp," Tom said.

"Camp?"

"Yeah, it was just some church camp," Rita blurted.

Although Tom raised an eyebrow, he began nodding, backing her up. "Picnics, canoeing, you know." Amused complicity twitched about his lips. Maybe neither of them was prepared to get too cozy with Gerald Anderberg just yet.

"Hey, I love camping. One of these days, I'm gonna buy us a Winnebago."

"You do that," Tom said.

Heat bloomed over Rita's skin. She tried to get a hold of her breathing, her throat too narrow for all the choppy emotions suddenly surging up. She didn't understand where this urge for secrecy was coming from — the very refusal to talk about the past that had forever irked her about their mother. But what did she and Tom know about what had gone on at camp? For all they knew, it *had* been one big cookout, everyone holding hands around the fire, singing "Kumbaya," or the Japanese equivalent. It was as much a mystery to them as to anyone. They'd just be guessing, spinning tales.

The Desert

1943

Three

At first, he faded into the mountain's shadow. Lily's eyes played tricks on her. That dark presence at the edge of her vision, could it be nothing more than sand and wind and her lonely imagination? The ground was a mess of chalk dust flying up and mixing with the powder on her cheeks, sticky as cake batter. Should she turn around? Cast a flirtatious glance over her shoulder? But that would seem immodest, and she had to leave those days behind.

The farther she walked, the more certain she became that someone was following her. An admirer in the middle of the desert? That meant she still looked pretty — at least, somewhat. The rush of adrenalin jarred her mood from the falling grey skies.

All the barracks looked the same: the same sagging, makeshift steps and filthy mop perched outside, dried laundry stiff and grey, dismal as skinned rabbits. Despite everything, an air of refinement still surrounded Lily, or at least she liked to think so, as she bent down to adjust the tiny buckle on her high-heeled shoe. Really, she just wanted an excuse to look back at her admirer, without making it too obvious, of course.

Oh, God. *Him again.*

She'd seen him gazing at her across the mess hall the other day, a dreamy smile melting across his lips. Before the war, she'd never had to associate with guys of this sort, their hats tied on with scarves, dirt-smeared shirts. They had a different way of standing, boys of that sort, bending their knees as though their toes had sunk into the earth. Her father would have slapped her silly if he'd ever caught her mixing with them. Although, in truth, he was once no different than these peasant boys, these kitchen boys, fresh from Japan.

The guy froze in his tracks. A teasing smile lingered. He knew he'd been caught, and like a little kid about to be punished, he kept on mocking her, daring her to look away.

Everyone was aware they were the ones stirring up trouble. Spreading rumours about sugar vanishing from mess halls, pointing fingers, getting people riled up. *Sure been a long time since we had anything sweet.* Yesterday, another fight broke out and a couple more nisei boys showed up at breakfast with black eyes.

"Why are you following me?"

"I'd like to take your picture."

He must be soft in the head. He didn't have a camera, none of them did. A crude wooden box that looked more like a breadbox was nestled in the crook of his arm.

Salt air, solitude. All she could think about was how desperately she missed the ocean. The sound of the waves whooshing in and out.... They used to go to the ocean often before the war. Her father had a car back then, a black Studebaker, which he needed to make deliveries. Sunday was his day off, and she could still feel the sticky hot seat against the backs of her thighs as he'd look at her with a half-disapproving, half-indulgent smile. "Sit with your legs crossed, young lady. Never forget you're representing the Japanese-American life."

How quickly things could change. No longer was there any such thing as "Japanese-American." And how could she hold on to a shred of dignity with these thugs following her around?

Maybe he'd been watching her for a while now. Every day she was out here, practising her walk. In the last pageant the judges criticized Lily's walk as too American: her stride too long and fluid, too much swing to her hips. They docked her points. The nerve of them. For the next Cherry Blossom Pageant, she had to learn to walk properly in a kimono: slowly, evenly, in small steps — the Japanese way of walking. She should try to turn slowly, showing off the nape of her neck and that petal-soft slip of skin at the top of the back, the only bit of nudity allowed. If she was lucky, she'd have a flatter backside, less inclined to twitch back and forth.

So every day she had to practise her walk, an old pair of pantyhose tied around her thighs under her skirt, binding her legs together in delicate, mincing steps.

With each step, she relived her moment of glory, or near-glory at least. Men of all ages had sat in the front rows, staring with appraising smiles at the girls. Receiving so much attention was novel and intoxicating, and she loved how it continued after the contest was over as the men lingered by the curb waiting for the convertible draped in red, white, and blue bunting to drive through Little Tokyo and part of downtown LA. The queen's crown glittered like shattered glass as Lily sat in the back seat. First runner-up. How tantalizingly close she'd come to wearing that crown.

"Can't I take your picture, miss?"

She shook her head, backing away as he looked inside that strange wooden box — his imaginary camera. Sweat had soaked through her dress in grey blotches, making her all too aware of the astringent smell of her own basting flesh.

"Don't worry. I'm not working for the government. I'm not making a documentary. I just like to take pictures of beautiful things."

"I'm not even supposed to be here." The words flew from her lips with the authority of a headmistress, as though it were all some administrative mistake that her name had been put on the list.

"None of us are *supposed* to be here."

Her cheeks on fire, she turned away. The sun beat down and she continued to walk until everything started to look the same throughout this godawful place. The tarpaper barracks went on and on, block after block. Thirty-six blocks and counting. At the southern end, she saw men — her men — swinging axes to clear the sagebrush. Their chests glistened as they worked with a force that scared her.

It was unsettling to see these once distinguished men reduced to beasts of burden. The stoic, polite behaviour, once said to elevate the Japanese above the other Oriental races, was slipping away, rapid as the windblown sand. Out here no one knew how to behave — or who they even were. Would Mrs. Sato have gotten into a screaming match with that surly Matsumoto boy in the old days? Unheard of. Would bags of sugar vanish in the night, dragged off by God knows whom? A fistful of dollars exchanged for a few burlap bags. *There are bad apples here*, people were whispering.

The ground began to waver and clumps of brush on the horizon reminded her of ocean waves, frozen at an instant.

The art building had to be around here somewhere, but she might have already walked past it, and dust was getting trapped in her eyes and nose and ears. It flew up her skirt, sticking to her thighs, and she couldn't stop thinking how much she missed the ocean.

A fuzzy feeling crept into her head, a great dark pressure expanding across her brain. A wave of light-headedness, sweat dripping down her back. The wind had muted to a strange buzz and everything was moving in a kind of slow motion, like the blades of a fan in those seconds after it's been flicked it off. Her thoughts also ran in circles…. The nerve of him — speaking to her like that. *None of us are* supposed *to be here.* She struggled to hang on; the gritty air forced its way into her lungs. She'd show him. In the next pageant, she'd walk across the stage as delicate as a little boat floating in the breeze.

The sky covered her and she fell to her knees, everything spinning, until the thud of darkness.

YOU DREAM WHEN you faint?

Her vision was being tunnelled while everything faded to black and white, the contrast between light and dark so extreme. Yet she was still here, at camp. She knew by the sickly apple trees, gnarled as the toes of an old man. Then in a flash, like some trick of movie-making or time-lapse photography, everything sped up and the trees were rejuvenated to a sea of cherry blossoms in full bloom, stirring her soul to life — little ballerinas.

Something was pulling under her chin, a peculiar bonnet. She was dressed like a pioneer woman, a rancher's wife, but her husband was nowhere to be seen. She stared down the road at the Inyo Mountains, rising higher than God himself through the haze, and felt the sad presence of the Indians, who used to range across the valley, back before the Spanish ranchers kicked them out. Blood on both sides ended up soaking the sand, so the few survivors called the place Matanzas. Spanish for *massacre*.

Lily scanned the sand at her feet, searching for bloodstains. The wind whipped it up into her eyes as she began to wake up.

BLINKING, SHE LOOKED up: a stubbly chin, eyes darker than her own. In the dream state she was still slipping out of, immersing herself in the grassy, ripe odour of this stranger's body felt oddly lulling. She settled back in the hammock of his arms, awash in a feeling she couldn't quite place.

He carried her through a set of doors down a long white corridor and laid her down on a bed covered in fresh white sheets, the freshest she'd had in months. An artificial meadow smell, intoxicating and familiar. Everything about the room looked very clean and impressive, like the walls were glowing with a fierce white aura.

"She fainted," the guy said.

A stout, iron-haired nurse rushed over with a basin. She began pouring cool water over Lily's wrists.

Now, as he backed away, Lily could see him better: a tall, lanky fellow, perhaps a couple years older than she, twenty maybe. He seemed uncomfortable, hands jammed in his back pockets.

The doctor came over. A small, lithe man with cheeks smooth as pebbles, his lab coat blindingly white. Dr. Takemitsu. Seeing him from a distance, Lily had assumed he was in his forties, but up close there was something younger looking — ageless almost — about his glowing skin, his serious, all-seeing eyes. A hush fell over her stomach. This was her first time in a doctor's office; there were very few doctors in the Japanese-American community. Whenever their wives used to come to the shop, her father's face would light up and he'd give them special treatment, discounting prices, expediting orders. It was more than just the fact that these men were leaders in the community. They were touched by some mysterious, near magical power, holding the health and future of the entire community in their ivory-smooth hands.

"What happened?" Dr. Takemitsu said.

"Girl got too much sun, I guess. I dunno."

"You were following her? Kaz has nothing better to do than chase skirt all day."

"Hey. I was out walking. I happened to see her collapse, so I went over. Okay, Dad?"

"Well, she's lucky he was following her," the nurse said. "Otherwise, she'd still be slumped in the sand."

So his name was Kaz, and he was the doctor's son? Really? His sloppy clothes, his scowling expression…. He wasn't one of the guys she'd seen flipping and swinging girls across the dance floor at the mixers the JACC organized in tinsel-clad mess halls. He wasn't blowing his brass like some would-be Benny Goodman in the bands that everyone and his brother had joined to pass the time.

But upon closer examination, Lily wondered if there wasn't something a bit too clean-shaven about this Kaz fellow, after all. She looked at his smooth, slender hands, and those weren't the fingers of someone used to digging through soil. The soft-gelled wave of his hair appeared at odds with the country-boy image he seemed to be cultivating. The crumpled bandanna around his neck suddenly looked no more real than a costume for a school play, the slight grime on his cheeks like stage makeup.

Kaz. The name had an appealing intensity. Her admirer, her rescuer.... In a flash he'd been redeemed: transformed from some lunatic bumpkin kid into someone important — a leader, a healer, a scion. The sweet rush made her feel that she could be someone else, someone important, too.

"Thank you for bringing me here," she called over.

Kaz's face softened though he remained silent, slouched against the wall. She wanted to ask him what was wrong, baffled by how he could look at the doctor with such hostility. Before she could say anything, he'd slipped out the door without so much as a glance back.

"That boy." Dr. Takemitsu shook his head. "Better watch out for him."

"Why? What do you mean?"

But the doctor had already walked away.

Sitting up, Lily observed that only a few other patients occupied the row of beds. An old woman snored lightly, her long white hair pouring over the pillow. A young man with two black eyes tried to hide himself behind a magazine. Wasn't he June Shigetani's younger brother?

"Bob, is that you?"

He tried to smile, not very successfully. His nostrils had disappeared into a swollen mound.

"My God! What happened to you?"

"It's nothing. Just a scrap over some girl."

He was lying, she suspected. His battered face had nothing to do with a girl.

Before she could question him further, the double doors flew open. In stormed a gaggle of shrieking women. They were carrying a pregnant girl, laid out on an old door being used as a stretcher. Lily half recognized her from the barracks — Esther, wasn't that her name? She was moaning like no tomorrow. The room started to spin again as the salty, raw smell of blood and oozing innards wafted over.

"She slipped!" Esther's sister said. "Rolled down the hill like a watermelon."

Dr. Takemitsu and the nurse sprang into action, stretching the poor girl out on a bed all too close to Lily's. The sheets were soon soaked in watery crimson.

She was amazed by how the doctor remained so calm and in control, swiftly commanding this and that instrument. On the periphery of her vision, giant forceps rested ominously on the table.

Lily clenched her eyes. The room faded in and out, everything drowned out by Esther's cries. Guttural, inhuman cries.

After a while, the noise levelled into a thick hum that insulated the walls of her brain. A story edged its way in, one of the Japanese fairy tales her mother used to tell her.

A poor charcoal maker, who lived up in the mountains, had a beautiful, young wife. Every evening, she insisted on spending a great deal of time alone, shut inside their bedroom closet. Perplexed and rather hurt, he struggled to respect her wishes. One night, when his wife didn't come out for hours, his curiosity got the better of him and he peeked through the crack of the door. All he could see was a gangly crane — naked of all feathers, covered in ruddy, bumpy skin. Lily couldn't remember how or why the woman had been transformed into a bird; the story was dim and fragmented in her mind. All she could recall was that the crane had been holding the last feather plucked from her own behind to weave into an exquisite tapestry that unrolled at her feet.

"You've seen my true body now and must be disgusted," the crane said to the charcoal maker in his wife's voice. "So I must leave you immediately!"

A window flung open and the naked bird made her escape as a thousand other cranes converged in an upsurge of snowy feathers to shelter her.

Look away.

That seemed to be the story's peculiar message. It was wisest to look away from such things: a naked crane weaving its magic, a naked woman pushing life into the world. To see that true body could only spell disaster. Some secrets were best left untouched; Lily had learned that lesson all too well. Her mother's pale, downcast face. The cadence of her words in Japanese like the clink of falling dominoes.

That was the last story her mother had ever told her. Not long after, her mother, like the crane, had disappeared forever.

A shrill cry pierced the air. How much time had gone by? Ten minutes, an hour, a day? The next thing Lily knew, the doctor was beaming at the foot of Esther's bed, holding in his hands a slick, purplish bundle of flesh. A crying baby. And Esther was crying, too, sweat and tears mixed on her florid cheeks. Her sister ran outside to tell their family.

"It's a boy," Dr. Takemitsu said proudly.

"Haruki," Esther whispered, cradling the baby against her breast. "Harry, for short. Thank you for saving my little Harry!"

An hour later the excitement had subsided. Esther and her entourage of visitors had been moved to another room, leaving the doctor with nothing to do except make rounds again.

He paused at Lily's bedside.

"Would Esther have bled to death if it hadn't been for you?"

"We do what we can." He wrapped something around her arm, pumping a small bulb, and as the cuff inflated, it cut off her circulation. Next, he placed a cold metal disk on her chest and slipped a peculiar noose-like instrument into his ears.

"What's that for?"

"Listening to your heart."

So the doctor could hear the wild wings flapping in her chest? The thought made her cheeks burn. "Why did you say I have to watch out for your son?"

"Let's just say that Kaz has a way with the ladies."

"He seems pretty nice to me."

"You don't know him like a father knows his son."

"But he saved me."

How strange that the doctor would malign his own son. Her imagination raced to grasp all the scenarios that might be responsible. Had Kaz stolen the family car and joyously, drunkenly, crashed into a fence? Had he set fire to the house as a kid?

"Young lady, your heart is racing. You have to calm down."

The cool metal sent tingles through her body, while his eyes brushed past, amused, knowing.

Kaz. *Kaz.* His name thrilled her, like the sound of thunder or waves whooshing over her skin. This ne'er-do-well, this doctor's son, this degraded scion. Her rescuer. The metal migrated another inch over. With every passing second, she became more fearful that the doctor could hear the wayward murmurs of her heart.

Four

Some afternoons they took long walks together under the tattered canopy of dead fruit trees. Yellow splotches of brittlebush and spiny hopsage tickled Lily's ankles. She tried to brush against Kaz's side so he'd take her hand, but he seemed oblivious to the opportunity.

He just kept rambling on about his hick dreams. Before the war he'd been driving down the coast, taking pictures of the lush strawberry farms owned by Japanese farmers, salt of the earth. That was what he planned do after the war: buy a farm and start afresh.

"When I think of how those farms had to be sold off or abandoned, I want to kill somebody. That land *belongs* to our people." He spat on the parched, colourless ground.

"Don't you think you could do more good by following in your father's footsteps?"

"Naw, I'm just a med-school flunky. Couldn't even pass the entrance exam. I don't know why the old man deludes himself I'm gonna be a doctor after the war."

"You could be! Why don't you get involved in the JACC? That'd look good on a med-school application."

"I'm no Jackalope. Who appointed them as our leaders anyway? They're just a bunch of college boys the government propped up after they'd dragged all the real leaders off to jail."

Shame spread over Lily. Her father had been one of the men the FBI singled out first as an issei leader, an elder. They'd shown up in the middle of the night when he was in his pyjamas and hadn't even let him change before dragging him in for questioning. Now he was imprisoned someplace far away and hadn't responded to her letters in months. Why wouldn't the JACC do anything to help him?

Japanese American Citizens Confederacy. JACC. It was getting to be a bad word around here. At first, all the nisei guys were members. You had to be a nisei — second generation, Japanese-American — in order to belong. Not surprisingly, the issei didn't like being excluded. Nor did the kibei, that proud group of young men educated in Japan. Apparently, the government considered them the most dangerous, traitorous group of all.

JACCers. Jackalopes. Jackrabbits. Traitors. Lapdogs. The guys who sold the community out. While people once felt privileged to be associated with the JACC, now many were jumping ship. They were worried that next the fingers would be pointed their way with name-calling and raised fists.

Much as she felt terrible about her dad, why did Kaz have to swing so far in the opposite direction? He'd taken a liking to a certain group of kitchen boys who stood around outside the mess hall, immersed in smoke and secrecy. It bothered her that Kaz dressed as though he were part of their gang. Time and time again, she urged him to be more careful. Fantasizing that she alone had the power to reform him, reshape him in his father's image. And then he'd marry her and they'd live in a beautiful white house with a trellis, like all doctors' families, right in the centre of town.

Kaz laughed her warnings off. "What are you so scared of?"

"Are you crazy? You know where they send the troublemakers — a far worse prison."

She'd heard rumours that the uniforms had a giant *X* on the back to make it easier for guards to shoot anyone trying to escape. Her poor father. If anything happened to him, she'd have no one.

"Look around you, Lily. Truth is they're understaffed as hell. If we wanted, we could have the run of the place, easy."

Something crumpled inside her when Kaz talked this way.

"What's wrong, Water Lily? You're crying."

She shook her head, unable to speak.

"You can tell me."

"It's nothing. I'm fine."

He leaned in and their lips brushed, her tears pooling, salty as seawater, in the cleft between their mouths. He kissed her more deeply and her arms reached for his shoulders, as though she were seizing a lifebuoy or a slippery rock.

"CAN'T I TAKE your picture?"

So they were back to this again. "Where's your camera, Kaz?"

He extended the wooden box that was always tucked under his arm.

"That's not a camera. It looks more like a lunch box."

"That's exactly what I want people to think. Can you keep a secret?"

She nodded.

He lifted the lid to expose a black metal dial. "It was easy enough to sneak in this lens and shutter. My friend Shig, who's a carpenter, he made this box from scraps of wood, attaching the lens to an old pipe so the camera can focus." He smiled at her astonishment.

"But … the film? How do you get the film?"

"You'd be surprised. Not everyone who works here agrees with what the government's done. Some people are actually on *our* side."

Someone on staff was sneaking in rolls of film?

From the satchel over his shoulder, Kaz pulled out something that expanded into a peculiar three-legged stand. He perched the camera down on top of it. "C'mon. It's just one picture."

"There's a guard right over there. He can see us!"

"Oh, don't worry about him. We have an understanding."

And it was true: for some reason, the guard looked right past them. Because Kaz was the doctor's son. Surely that must be why they cut him so much slack.

"So, okay then?"

There was something about the way Kaz kept looking at her, as if he alone had the power to create her image by crafting this whole desert mise en scène. Marlene Dietrich in *Morocco*, maybe. Or perhaps he was envisioning her as a more American girl — the spunky prostitute in *Stagecoach*, run out of town by those righteous ladies. She gazed out at the untamed landscape, hoping that she, too, would find her final refuge in John Wayne's brawny arms.

"Smile like you're Miss California."

So she smiled. Blindly, she smiled. For the first time in her life, she wasn't trying to look demure or dainty, she was just responding to the glow of energy on this man's face, bright as the flash of a camera.

AUNT TETSUKO CLOMPED over in homemade geta sandals, which Uncle Mas had fashioned from scraps of wood. She tripped on a knot of sagebrush that poked up between the floorboards. Her hair was pulled up in an old scarf like a cleaning lady. Lily was glad that her father had been spared from seeing his sister go to seed.

The hand on Lily's arm felt like a chicken foot. "Who's this boy you've been seen with?"

Ignoring the question, Lily pushed aside the grey blanket draped across the room like a curtain to partition off a small private space, where she shared a bunk bed with her cousin Audrey. Straw poked up through the crude mattress cover, rustling, itchy against the thighs.

Lily's old bed had had a frilly white bedspread. Her collection of Japanese dolls used to perch on the dresser. She'd had to give them away to hakujin friends — supposedly for safekeeping, but she doubted she'd get them back. They'd had to pack quickly; she'd had to report to the community centre early the next morning, where the bus had come to get them. In the end, she'd just stuffed as many dresses as she could into two pillowcases and dragged them down the street. How she wished she'd brought a pretty blanket or a nice sheet at least.

Aunt Tetsuko followed and clawed her arm again. "Who *is* he? I won't have you running around like some of the silly girls here!"

Youth was in the air — a new spirit of risk and rebelliousness that accompanied fathers and elders being dragged off. You could feel it in the way many of the young people eyed each other adventurously and kissed right out in the open. It terrified folks of Aunt Tetsuko's generation, who'd barely dared to glance at the opposite sex until proper introductions had been made.

"He's Dr. Takemitsu's son. He's taking care of me. I'm going to be his girl."

An exhausted laugh. "Baka! Stupid girl."

"Shush."

They had to be careful not to say anything too loudly because the flimsy partitions between apartments didn't extend as high as the ceiling. Raised voices and grunts of all kinds could be heard; the creaking and moaning of young couples trying to have honeymoons went on and on all night. Lily didn't want her news being broadcast across camp.

She turned away and curled up on the bed, face to the wall. Her aunt's dismissive words continued to gnaw at her. Who could deny that Kaz was chummy with Susie Tadashi and Kei Takahara and who knew who else? And Kei — with her chipmunk cheeks — wasn't even pretty. But he'd taken their pictures, too. A whole album full of other girls. Although Lily tried to pretend it didn't bother her, a lizard was scaling the walls of her stomach.

Darkness fell like a shroud. Coldness seeped into her bones, a numbness that was almost comforting. Aunt Tetsuko was arguing with Uncle Mas in Japanese, her voice barely a crackle above the whoosh. Sand whipped up against the side of their quarters and rocks flew up, hit the walls, made them tremble. Through the cracks in the floorboards, a steady stream of fine white powder sprayed up, settling on everything. The air was soon thick as fog.

A guard's footsteps. His flashlight sent glitter over their window. In front of the barbed wire fence, just beyond the next barrack, the watchtower beamed down its Cyclops light, turning figure eights across the gusty ground.

FRANK ISAKA'S BACK, everyone was saying, all in an uproar. Curious how the name of the president of the JACC — the very name once said with pride, with hope — now left a bitter taste in people's mouths.

Lily tried to stay aloof from all the gossip. It would blow over; it always did. People were being too harsh on Frank. When he came to give talks, she still liked his fresh-faced charisma, his self-assured voice. After hearing him talk, she always felt better, like she was protected, because she was nisei and the JACC would take care of her.

She made her way to the area outside the largest mess hall, where a podium had been set up on a stage bearing the JACC banner. A sizable crowd had gathered, some faces surly, others bright and attentive.

A few years ago, Frank first came to the community's attention. Even in those early days he was fond of slogans. They stood him in good stead in the months leading up to the internment, as the government must have seen it would need some leader to convince the Japanese people to go peacefully. And how eloquently Frank delivered that message: Go calmly, without protest, without fuss. What were those snappy phrases he'd used over and over again? "The end justifies the means." "The greatest good for the greatest number." And in the vast land of America, the Japanese community proved but a small number indeed. At times, his speeches took on an apocalyptic fervour, as though he were a country preacher: "We know that our exodus will be a patriotic sacrifice, and what a sacrifice it will be. But the government should not fear any resistance on our part. Our people will go protesting only one thing — their patriotism to the United States flag.... We shall look at this movement as a grand adventure, of the order that our parents took in pioneering the new country, like the hardy souls of Biblical times...."

His speech today, however, had a less upbeat tone. Frank was talking about how certain "seeds of bitterness" had been planted throughout the community by a handful of "bad apples," who, out of nothing other than boredom and malice, had taken it upon themselves to "stir the pot" at every opportunity. Naturally, he didn't want to say too much, preferring to talk around these "unfortunate incidents."

Of course, everyone knew what he was actually referring to.

An image of Bob's swollen face, the other day at the hospital, flashed in Lily's mind.

"It's up to us to come together as a community, a family." Frank's arms rose in an expansive gesture. "Nisei, issei, kibei — we need to look beyond these superficial divisions. Only then will we win the respect of the American people."

A hush settled over the crowd. Some nisei nodded, their faces aglow, still convinced he was their prophet. Others muttered under their breath and some were hissing, softly at first, yet it grew louder, like steam escaping from a pot.

"What d'you know about what we need to do?" someone shouted out. "You're hardly even here. You're off travelling the country making pretty speeches!"

Frank pretended he hadn't heard or maybe he really hadn't. Nothing could penetrate his shell of confidence, his unbreakable smile.

THE PHOTO SHOWED a girl walking across a windy desert, her face hidden beneath a tangle of hair. Hair blending into ribbons of flying sand. Skin melting in the thick, shimmering heat.

The picture didn't at all match how Lily envisioned herself: if it *was* her, it also wasn't her. Or it was one of the other hers. That faint kaleidoscope of shattered, other selves whirring along the edges of consciousness — so fast, so light, it was difficult to know if they existed at all.

But Kaz said the picture was beautiful. It was hers to keep. More pictures followed. Her face caught in so many varied, fleeting expressions that never quite felt like her own.

Other times, he gave her shots of the landscape: the sultry horizon, its mesmerizing flatness and sudden curves, mountains soaring up into the ink-washed sky.

THE CAMP GOT an order for camouflage nets, so a factory was built overnight.

Lily and the other women were led into an open-air building, twenty feet high. From a massive stand, hemp nets flowed down — giant spiderwebs across the sky. Their task was to weave long scraps of green and beige fabric through the web in zigzag patterns.

Her shoulders ached, her fingers cramped up. Hemp bits snowed down on her cheeks.

"It's crazy," a girl named Sachi said under her breath. "We're not loyal enough to walk in the street, but we're good enough to take the jobs no one else wants?"

"Just be glad you have a job," Mrs. Okada said down the line.

Silence fell over the group. Only the nisei were allowed to work in the net factory, and since their wages were the best in the camp, the issei folks were furious.

Lily tried to focus on her work. A peculiar smell — as though someone had placed a penny in salt water — filled her nostrils. The skyline faded and fell away from her, a swoosh of blue.

When she came to, she was lying on a bench and Mrs. Okada was stroking her forehead. She felt wasted, limp as an overboiled vegetable.

Mrs. Okada and her daughter helped Lily to the doctor's office. Dr. Takemitsu appeared startled but pleased to see them.

"I'm sorry. I don't mean to be such a bother."

"You're not meant to work so hard. You shouldn't be in that factory. I'm going to get you a job in my hospital."

The nurse pressed a glass to Lily's lips and the cool water rushed down her throat, cleansing away the dust and grime. She tried to keep her eyes open while the room spun gently.

"Rest." The doctor's face turned fuzzy, a receding shadow.

He was at her bedside when she awoke: the first thing she saw was the resemblance between father and son. Kaz had the same high cheekbones and slightly near-set eyes. The same stubborn lips. She could see how the years would add charcoal streaks and reconfigure his hairline. The thought of spending her life with him was so enticing that for a moment, she had a strange, misplaced impulse to lean forward and kiss the doctor's lips.

"So I hear Kaz's going to be a doctor."

"Is that what he told you, Lily?"

"That's what *you* told him."

A bemused look, his expression relaxing for just a second. "Let me tell you something about being a doctor. It takes tenacity — stick-to-it-ness. Like the stickiness of good rice."

"Kaz will come through. He'll be the next Dr. Takemitsu."

"You certainly are an optimist. His prospects aren't great. He's flunked the exam twice, and all he seems to care about is dancing and women."

This was the first time Lily had seen the doctor let his guard down. It meant something to her that he felt comfortable talking to her so frankly. "Kaz does seem … kind of lost."

"That's putting it mildly. If it hadn't been for the war, he'd have run off with that jazz singer from San Francisco. I was almost glad when the war struck, if you can believe it, because at least here I can keep an eye on him." A soft, shuddering sigh. "He never was the same after his mother died when he was little."

"I'm so sorry to hear that."

"Kaz's mother was an incredible woman. *She* could have saved him. She was a woman so innocent and pure she never even wanted to get married."

"How did you meet her?"

His face tensed up. Lily worried she'd overstepped, trod on too-intimate territory.

"I met her on the first trip I made back to Japan, after I'd graduated from med school. I went in order to find a wife. The baishaku-nin from my hometown had sent me photographs of picture brides."

"And you selected Kaz's mother."

"Not exactly. I wanted to meet the women in person. I wasn't about to just choose a wife from a photo and send her a ticket to America."

"What was it like going to the matchmaker's studio?"

"Horrible. All the women I'd selected were decked out in their best kimonos, their faces painted white, like geishas. Not one had a face that touched my soul."

"Did you find another baishakunin?"

"No, I'd had it with the old ways. Figured I'd just stay a bachelor for the time being. Then the next morning, as I was walking down the street, a wisp of whiteness caught my eye: a young woman in a simple white dress. She was passing out rice cakes to homeless men and she looked at each dirty face with such gentleness, such love in her eyes. In Japan, beggars are very ashamed; they kneel with their foreheads pressed to the ground. But this girl — Fumiko, I'd later learn her name was — insisted they sit up and eat with dignity. Perhaps she took pity on them because she, too, came from a group that had been hated for centuries, the Kakure Kirishitans. Hidden Christians."

"Christians were hated in Japan?"

"For over three hundred years. Whole communities were rounded up and their ears chopped off. They were made to repent or march hundreds of miles to their place of execution." The doctor shook his head, like he couldn't imagine the horrors. He talked about how this only attracted more converts as the religion was pushed underground. Fumiko's family came from a sect of Hidden Christians who'd secretly worshipped in their homes for generations. "Of course, I didn't discover any of this until later, after I'd gotten up the nerve to actually talk to her."

Warmth spread across Lily's chest as she watched the doctor's face soften and glow. "How did you manage that?"

The doctor told Lily how the next day, he'd caught sight of the girl again. She was wearing the same white dress, this time with a veil over her head, pulled back such that he could glimpse her face. He trailed her for many blocks until they reached the edge of town, where a wooded area began. He followed her deep into the densely packed trees, clambering over rocks and boulders, and he tripped on some giant roots, nearly killing himself. Always that slip of translucent white, like a moth's wings fluttering before him.

At last, he came to a clearing. There were rows of benches where people were seated while more people stood or perched on rocks around the edges. A small choir was gathered in front of the shrine; several priests and nuns were milling about greeting people. The girl in white was at the front with a cluster of people whom the doctor was later introduced to as her family. Several other ladies also had on white veils, including her twin sister, Haruko. As the doctor hung back, one of the priests began leading everyone in Hidden Christian prayers. "Orashio, as they call them. A soft, strange chanting in garbled Latin. The scene touched my heart and I knew that this was the woman I would marry."

Lily thought about how the doctor must have looked that balmy morning in the glade, the sun refracting from the lush leaves, sending flecks of verdant light across his excited cheeks. The girl in white, the girl of his dreams, at the centre of all this beauty and strangeness. Even now, all these years later, his face shone at the memory. *Love. Yes, this is what love looks like*, Lily thought, and she wanted to draw closer to him — impulsively, desperately, like a moth to a votive.

She thought about how her own parents had met; though, their marriage couldn't have been more different. In her earliest memories, she'd always been aware of her mother's brittle moods and deep unhappiness: she'd never wanted to come to America as a picture bride; she'd never wanted to marry a man double her age — a dry cleaner no less. The matchmaker had duped her into it. She'd never adjusted to life away from home. Lily remembered watching her mother standing bewildered in her bedroom, her skirt falling down to her knees, as she struggled with the buttons. Clothes in Japan didn't have buttons, and her fingers would never get used to the awkward motion. Lily had begged her to learn English and turned up the radio full blast in hopes that the English words would sink into her brain, but it hadn't done any good. Her soul just faded away, lost in the memory of some distant koto music....

Whenever she thought about her mother, she felt herself slipping, her chest lurching, the ground loosening beneath her feet. The same feeling she'd had as a child, crouched under the kitchen table. It started gently with just a taunt — Can't this woman get anything right? Can't she even learn to cook pasta? — but then his hand unfurled in a slap and tightened into a fist. The thud of flesh against flesh, followed by her mother's soft, stoic moaning. The beatings always seemed to be set off by some failure on her mother's part to assimilate to American culture. Didn't she realize that the porcelain plate with Eleanor Roosevelt's picture in the centre was meant for hanging on the wall, not eating from? And was it really so difficult to learn to use a knife and fork?

Lily would curl into herself and pray that the release of violence might bring out her father's relaxed, jovial side. Perhaps afterward her mother would clean herself up and her father would ask whether they wanted to go to the ocean for a picnic. The brisk air, the salty sting of tears. Gulls plunging and ascending across the horizon. The ocean scene somehow seemed to wash clean the situation, allowing Lily to forget what had just happened. So during the onslaught of violence, Lily learned to grasp on to these images and anticipate their purifying, lulling effect as she hid under the table and rocked on her haunches.

After her mother had left, her father's drinking got worse, and the rumours spread by women in the community became more vicious by the day. Girls in Lily's class were no longer allowed to associate with her. *Your mother's not coming back. She ran off with a man to Japan!*

Her mother was rumoured to have met her lover on the ship that carried her back to Fukuoka. It was supposed to be just a visit to her ailing father. But that visit had turned into a lifetime of separation.

How different her mother's life might have been if she'd married a man like Dr. Takemitsu. How different Lily's own life could have been, too.

Things got worse. Late at night, her father would stagger around the house calling out for his wife, commanding her to fetch another bottle from the basement. Lily tried to soothe him by bringing whatever he asked for, and later she'd help him out of his clothes as he flopped onto the bed like a dead whale. Some nights he'd throw his sweaty arms around her and at first she thought he was just trying to get his balance, but it soon became clear there was a darker intention running through his body. "My little cherry blossom," he called out, pulling her closer, his words slurring, "you always were so much sweeter than your mother…." She giggled to pretend it was all a joke. By tomorrow he'd sober up and everything would be just fine.

His moods only became more turbulent, however. While preparing dinner, she sensed his eyes following her backside, watching her every move.

Her head felt muddled because she wanted to please him, and if that meant replacing her mother — by cooking his favourite meals, by rubbing his feet — she was willing to try. The more she tried, the more he demanded when he'd come into her room late at night. She didn't want to trust her memories.… That stale breath wafting down her neck in torrents, those callused, apelike hands making her go all soft and buttery, and she knew that what he was doing to her was horrible and disgusting and she wanted it to stop, yet she couldn't afford to enrage him.

Gauzy white curtains hung across her bedroom window. She slept with the window open that summer when she was ten, when it happened a lot. The night breeze caught the translucent fabric and whipped it through the air, making her think of a tormented ghost, and she was able to imagine that it was *her* — it was *her* ghost whipping up a frenzy and flying up to the ceiling and billowing outside.

"Everything all right, Lily? You're awfully quiet."

Blushing, she prayed the doctor couldn't see into her polluted mind. This man — so gentle, so wholesome, so *good* — appeared before her as everything her own father had never been.

"What my son needs is the influence of a good woman."

"A good woman?"

"I've seen how Kaz looks at you and follows you around. He'd listen to you. You could help him."

"What are you so worried about?"

"Kaz's always hanging around those boys. The troublemakers."

"Oh, he isn't close to them."

"Don't delude yourself. I've seen them together."

"He's just a friendly guy. Friendly to everyone."

"If anything happens, I want you to know you can come to me. Anytime. I would be grateful, Lily-san."

She nodded, caught off guard, unsure of what exactly he was asking of her.

"In fact, I'd appreciate it if you'd tell me what's going on with my son, from time to time."

"You want me to ... spy on Kaz?"

"I want you to look out for him. He doesn't have the best judgment, you see."

As she nodded again, heat rushed over her face, warmed by the doctor's bright, approving gaze.

Five

"Don't you think it's weird he's paying so much attention to you?" Audrey sat on the upper bunk, bare feet dangling down, all too close to Lily's nose. "I mean, what makes *you* so special?"

"He's a doctor, okay? I wasn't feeling well. He took care of me. End of story."

Aunt Tetsuko peeked around the curtain, eavesdropping, as usual. "Audrey's right. People'll start talking, ne? I don't want you hanging around the hospital. Understand, Lily?"

"But the doctor said he'll get me a job!"

"Fat chance." Audrey wiggled her toes.

"Think you're too good to work at the net factory now?" Aunt Tetsuko sneered. "Got better things to do, like get ready for beauty pageants? Maybe you should pack your gear and go live in one of the other barracks, with all the other beauty queens!"

Let them mock her all they wanted. Lily didn't care. The doctor had asked for her help, and she'd given her word. The sense of being bound to the Takemitsu family washed over her in waves of comfort and belonging.

Grabbing a sweater, she pushed past her aunt and headed for the door. Crouched behind the barrack, she watched the jackrabbits leap by in the sunset. Their dark buff fur, lightly peppered, blended into the brush. If it weren't for their creamy underbellies and pink, fairy-wing ears, they'd vanish completely.

But it was their ears that made them attuned to predators. Even the babies had amazing survival instincts, born fully furred, their eyes wide open. No need of familial protection at all.

ONE EVENING, IN line outside the latrines, Lily ran into her old friend, Kaoru Inouye. "It's wonderful to see you, Kaoru." They embraced.

"It'd be better running into you out in the real world. But still." A small, forced laugh, hands on ample hips.

"Did you just arrive at Matanzas?"

Kaoru nodded. She said she'd been transferred from another camp in order to be with her father.

"Did you see me in the last pageant?"

"I didn't make it out — had to work that day — but I heard all about it." Kaoru stared at the ground, drawing a spiral with the toe of her boot, setting off a small whirlwind.

No doubt they'd drifted apart in recent years, but Lily was surprised by her friend's cool, unimpressed manner.

"So where do they put a girl like you to work here, Lily?"

"The net factory. For now. You?"

"Outdoor maintenance."

No wonder Kaoru was in a dour mood. Lily had seen the girls out all day in the blistering heat, sweeping up trash and lugging around heavy equipment. "Maybe you'll be transferred to another job one of these days?"

"Huh. Not likely."

Things had been so different when they were little. They were all just Japs, back then. Chubby legs charging back and forth as they walked quickly — and then ran — trying to escape the shower of pebbles and taunting voices of the white boys gathered behind them. The stones getting ever closer. *Chinky chinky Chinaman sitting on a rail! Along came a white man and chopped off his tail!*

How fast they ran through the labyrinth of garbage-filled alleys. They scurried into the basement storage room beneath Kaoru's father's store, rapid as mice. By then, tears were running down Lily's cheeks. Kaoru, by contrast, had an air of toughness. A little sumo wrestler.

"Don't those idiots know we're not Chinks?"

"We're Americans," Lily whispered.

Kaoru's eyebrows sprung up, yet her toughness melted into a fragile sheen. Kaoru wasn't an American. She'd been born in Japan.

It hadn't made much difference when they were kids. Now, on the other hand, Lily sensed something guarded about the way Kaoru looked at her.

"Are you all right, Lily? You're kind of pale."

"I haven't been feeling so well. The heat."

"Oh, Lily, so kirei. The pretty, delicate one."

Vaguely aware she was being mocked, she said nothing.

"Be careful about the friends you're keeping. Kaz Takemitsu, he's a slick one."

"And you're some expert on romance?"

Kaoru's face flinched and Lily wished she could take it back. They waited in silence and by the time their turns came, they might as well have been strangers.

MAYBE KAORU WAS right, though. Some days, Kaz barely glanced at her as he grabbed a seat at a table on the other side of the mess hall, immersing himself in the bright gazes and giggles of so many other girls. Lily wondered what he saw in them, whether they possessed some vital energy or shining kernel of beauty that she lacked. She tried to convince herself that she was his favourite. His father had appointed her as such.

Other times, however, he'd wink at her, as if they shared a special, inner secret. He'd sit down across from her. The ebb and flow of everything around them — snot-nosed babies crying, trays of muddy food drifting by, the sea of dirty faces — all of a sudden none of it seemed real. With Kaz there in front of her, their knees nudged against each other, they might have been a couple of lovestruck American kids on a date at the town diner.

He might not be aware of how much he needed her, but it was only a matter of time.

And then, one day, after Lily had eaten lunch all by herself, Kaz intercepted her outside.

"Hey, there." He squeezed her hand, lowered his voice. "Let's meet up later, okay?"

"Meet up? But … where?"

"The aqueduct. Meet me there tomorrow night after curfew?"

Her heart sped up. The aqueduct was one of the few secluded places where young couples could sneak off for a snatch of privacy and long, hungering kisses in the twilight. But after curfew? "I can't, Kaz. Are you out of your mind?" How on earth did he expect her to sneak past Aunt Tetsuko and the night guards? What kind of girl did he think she was, anyway?

"Relax, you. I just want to spend time with you away from everyone, away from the craziness of this place." He explained that the guards on duty tomorrow night were known to indulge in a boozy poker game. So it wouldn't be too difficult to sneak out.

Despite her indignation, excitement blossomed inside her. So Kaz *had* fallen for her. He wanted to be alone with her after dark.

A moonlight rendezvous. She imagined them hiding in the aqueduct together, as though the land itself had opened up its secrets, drawn them deep into its sinuous troughs and crevices. The brush of his lips, the drumbeat of her heart, his hands running through her hair....

It was crazy — was she actually thinking about going?

"I can't, Kaz."

"You *can*. Tomorrow night, I'll be there waiting."

AT DINNER, SHE hardly ate a thing. She masticated a mouthful of rice, not touching the soggy brown stew. When Jimmy, her little cousin, asked if he could have it, she passed her plate over, but Aunt Tetsuko shook her head.

"You have to eat, Lily. You're getting so thin."

"That's how the judges like it."

Aunt Tetsuko sighed, like she didn't have the heart to speak her mind. "You want to keep fainting?"

Fainting, sleeping, dreaming: in truth, these states of unconsciousness were more pleasant, or more tolerable at least, than the lucid world.

Her real life was about to begin tomorrow night, if only she could muster the nerve.

What if she got caught, though? What would she say? She pictured herself sweating and stammering lies. These days, more folks than ever were being plucked out for interrogation and some never returned. It didn't take much to be labelled a bad apple.

THE NEXT DAY was particularly sweltering, unbearable. By noon, after weaving hundreds of scraps through the giant spiderweb, Lily's fingers were about to fall off. She closed her eyes and thought about Kaz: their meeting that night hovered before her like an island of escape, a cool mirage.

At lunch, Mrs. Okada sat down beside her. "Why does the food here look like dog food?"

"Tastes like dog food, too!" Her son, Johnny, stared at his plate, lumpy grey sauce congealed on the ball of rice.

"It's not so bad with a bit of soy sauce," Lily said.

Johnny stared back, hormones raging through his pimply cheeks. "Nothing disguises the taste of this slop!"

Why did she bother being nice to anyone? People liked you better if you were just as surly as everyone else.

The boy's eyes, full of aggression, darted back to Lily. "I can't eat this slop!" He pushed his plate across the table with such force it landed right in her lap. Horror and laughter poured from his beady eyes. She cringed as the hot muck seeped onto her thighs.

By now people were looking over. There was Kaoru one table over, her lips puckered. A few other girls, who used to go to Lily's school, appeared barely able to contain themselves, too.

Mrs. Okada leaned across the table and cuffed her son's ear. "Now look what you've done — apologize!"

"Why should I?" Johnny stood up. "I want to talk to the cook!"

They were sitting close enough to the kitchen for the staff to hear. Out swaggered Kenny Honda, a stout kibei guy in his mid-thirties, with biceps like ham hocks.

"Who says I can't cook?"

Years ago, Kenny used to be a boxing champion. He was so quick on his feet that he might have had a shot at the big league if he hadn't suffered one bad fight and lost sight in his left eye. Nasty luck. It left him bitter. Now his fighter instincts came out in his temper. He was the ringleader of the group that Kaz had been hanging around far too much.

"You wanna see what's in my pantry? You wanna try cookin' for hundreds from a few bags of rice and some old cans of beans?" His good eye glinted like a dagger while his other eye wandered left of centre, an eerie grey pool.

Johnny refused to sit down. "I've seen you guys unload food from the trucks. There's more in there than just this slop!"

"Come in and look for yourself! Bare shelves. And if that ain't bad enough, stuff's been disappearin' again. Two more bags of sugar vanished last night without a trace."

A kitchen guy appeared behind him. "It's true. We're living among thieves!"

By this point everyone was listening. Kenny was a popular guy; people throughout camp respected him. Tense glances darted across the tables. It wasn't the first time he and his crew had called attention to missing food.

The rumours all started a few months ago when Kenny noticed that a sack of sugar had disappeared. He told his friends, and that got everyone talking. Then cooks in mess halls on other blocks also noticed sugar unaccounted for. And the more people talked, the more the list of vanished items grew: chunks of meat, carrots, potatoes. A vat of chicken casserole must have grown legs and walked off on its own.

Mrs. Okada scanned the room. "But who among us would steal?"

"Let me tell you," Kenny said, more kitchen workers gathering behind him. "You know how the Jackrabbits are always pointing fingers at me, sayin' I'm a bad apple? *They're* the bad apples. They don't give a rat's ass that the camp supervisors are selling our food on the black market!"

A stunned silence settled over the crowd.

"Why should they?" someone shouted.

"You're damn right." Kenny raised a finger in the air. There was something theatrical about all his gestures, as if he were enjoying being back in the ring after all these years, putting on a show for the crowd.

"They're in the pay," Tony Shibuya shouted out. "All the JACC guys are in the pay — they're just a bunch of traitors and lapdogs of this stinking camp administration."

"They're in cahoots with the camp guards, who're selling our food on the black market!"

"Now you've gone too far, Kenny," boomed a voice from across the room. Burt Kondo, a prominent member of the JACC, had stood up, his tall, lean body like a flagpole. "You don't know what you're talking about, so why don't you just shut your trap?"

"And who's gonna make me?" Kenny strolled over.

A hush came over the crowd, and Burt froze. The indignation in his eyes rapidly faded, his skin waxy pale.

"Think you're so kashikoi now?"

"Sure has been a long time since we had anything sweet," another voice piped up.

With a thud in her gut, Lily realized it was Kaz. She couldn't believe it. He'd gotten up behind Kenny, as though they were a pair of hooligans.

"Oh, don't be ridiculous!" said Mrs. Okada. "Our people wouldn't have anything to do with the black market."

"Our people?" Kenny chuckled. "Lady, there ain't no 'our people' in here. There's just you and me and a bunch of Jackalopes who're getting a helluva lot better treatment than you and me. All because they're doing favours."

"You have no idea what you're talking about." Burt shook his head, like he was talking to a couple of feeble-minded children. "You don't know the first thing about how much Frank Isaka's done for our community."

"Oh, Frank Isaka." Kaz made a sour face.

"Where is he?" Kenny said. "He ain't even here — he's off at some fancy conference giving speeches about the grand history of the JACC, full of pretty words about cheerful co-operation, offerin' our boys up for the draft. Can you believe it? He thinks our boys should fight for Uncle Sam while we're all cooped up here!"

A ripple of anger passed through the crowd.

"So what've you got to say to that?" Kenny leaned in at Burt.

"Bakatare is what I say!" Kaz hissed.

Burt continued defending the JACC, but he didn't get very far before Kenny lunged forward and knocked him to the ground. A blur of fists pummelling like rocks down a hill, gaining momentum with every rotation. All the rage that had been pent up in him for years — humiliation layered upon humiliation — was now being taken out on Burt's poor face.

A scream pierced the air. It took several seconds for Lily to realize that it was coming from her own throat, and by then her voice was drowned out by the hooting and hollering of everyone around her.

Six

She pulled the curtain around her bed and curled up, curled into herself. Her thoughts had recoiled to that little cave at the back of her brain. She didn't want to let any images in. That body on the floor — moaning, mewling. So many shining, riveted faces. But Kenny'd had the right idea: he calmly straightened up and began clearing away dishes, as though he were just minding his own business. A bored sigh, heaving shoulders, roll of the eyes. *Show's over.* The crowd scattered as the guards came hollering in. No one dared to point a finger his way. Not even the table of JACCers, not even Burt. At last Dr. Takemitsu arrived to take Burt to the hospital.

Lily edged closer to the wall, sand whipping against its other side. Through the cascade she could hear Aunt Tetsuko's muffled chatter, followed by the tearful whimpering of one of the younger children. Audrey climbed onto the bunk above, softly passing gas. Hard for Lily to believe that these people were her family. They felt more like prison mates in this wasteland, this desert purgatory.

Now more than ever, she knew she had to go to the aqueduct. Kaz had fallen under Kenny's spell so utterly that he wasn't even himself anymore. She needed to protect him, to restore him to his true self. This was what the doctor had asked of her.

At last everyone was snoring. Rising stealthily, she pulled a shawl over her shoulders, tiptoed across the squeaking floorboards, and slipped outside.

The night air was cold and cutting — she'd never been out this late in the desert. Sand was spraying all over her, like a shower of glass shards across the skin. Her eyes adjusted, narrowed to slits, her lashes providing something of a filter. The pain faded to a tingle. At least the haze provided camouflage.

Just as she was about to start running, she sensed movement up ahead. Her heart lurched, pattered madly. It was that loutish, red-haired guard. He'd been watching her since the very first day of her arrival. Herding everyone along toward the registration desk, his arm had jostled against her breast — nothing accidental about it, his stare made clear.

Now he was strolling past the barracks, toes turned outward to accommodate his pork barrel of a belly. Why wasn't he off playing poker, drunk out of his skull?

Pressed flat against the wall, she waited several seconds, sweat trickling down her rib cage. At last, he turned the corner. Still her heart wouldn't stop hammering. Should she turn back? Of course she should. What on earth had she been thinking?

To her surprise, she found herself running ahead. Drawing the shawl over her head, she ran blindly, sticking close to the barrack walls — one dark building after another. The sky stretched open to swallow her up in its infinite blackness. Seconds felt like minutes, minutes like hours. A cramp cut across her abdomen and her legs turned rubbery as they sped across the ground with some force that seemed to come from beyond her own body. Sand blew back in her face and filled her mouth as she gasped for air.

The aqueduct passed along the edge of camp, a thin grey line that wound like a river into the distance. Never had she seen it up close. She paused to examine it in the moonlight: nothing but a dried-up trough. Probably hadn't worked in decades — centuries, maybe. Relic of another time, when the land was moist and abloom.

She searched for Kaz but couldn't see anyone. Where was she supposed to meet him? The aqueduct faded up ahead, obliterated by darkness. Her heart plummeted as she stood at the edge shivering, colder with every passing second.

A flicker in the shadows down the way. Down below. The ember of a cigarette illuminated Kaz's face for a beautiful moment, and relief spread warmly across her chest.

Yet he wasn't alone.

Whispers and muted laughter as she approached.

"My, my, if it isn't our little beauty queen," Kaz said. "I didn't think you'd have the guts to come out here."

As she jumped down, the force of the floor shot up through her ankles. "I was worried about you."

"Aw, ya needn't worry your pretty little head."

A new cockiness came over him as he swung his arm around her shoulder, showing off in front of the guys. One of them was Kenny Honda. What on earth had she walked into?

There was something familiar about the other two faces. She recognized them from the old neighbourhood. Shig Nakane's father used to own an auto repair around the corner from their dry-cleaning shop. Shig's fingernails were black as the inside of a chimney despite having spent the past several months soaping dishes. The other guy was Akira Ogura, the older cousin of one of Lily's old classmates. Well into his thirties, Akira had been working as a bookkeeper while studying to become an accountant, the last she'd heard. He'd always struck her as a pretty straitlaced fellow. She would have thought he'd become a JACC leader. Instead, a subtle defiance glinted in his eyes.

What had become of her romantic rendezvous?

Kaz's demeanour wasn't romantic at all. Welcoming her to their headquarters, he lit a match to reveal tiny words etched with a pen-knife on the wall: Black Dragon Society of Matanzas.

"Black Dragon?"

"They're only the greatest secret society in Japan. High-ranking army officers, cabinet ministers, secret agents, hired killers."

"It's famous for sabotage missions and secret collecting," Akira added.

Kenny smiled. "That's why we're starting a branch here."

"But why? Why would we want to sabotage anything?"

"Look around you, Lily."

"Don't you think the government's made it clear?" Kaz said. "We're the enemy. Time to start acting like it."

"But shouldn't we just co-operate with the authorities, and soon the war'll be over, and we'll all be able to go home?"

"Oh, spare me all that JACC claptrap."

Now Kenny looked irritated. "Why do we need a girl in on it, anyway?"

"A girl can be useful," Kaz said.

Useful. Her lips curled into a smile as she cast her eyes downward. She thought of the doctor's soft touch and the coolness of his stethoscope. His steady, compassionate gaze. She couldn't let him down. Not now. Not ever.

"You can trust me," she whispered.

"Good," Kenny said. "'Cause your boyfriend's been taking some pretty interesting pictures."

"Pictures?"

"Not just pin-up girls, like the kind he takes of you. *Real* pictures. The kind that'll help our cause."

Kaz reached into his satchel. The circle tightened around him as Akira cupped his lighter to create a glow. An array of photographs fanned out in Kaz's palms.

Wizened faces of old people: cracked, smiling bowls of clay. Their gnarled, claw-like hands digging through the soil.

Bean fields the old issei farmers had planted. Mammoth mountains looming above, laughing down on their meagre human efforts.

Massive camouflage nets hanging across the sky, all too familiar, yet also new in their strangeness, their rebirth as images. The shadowy faces of the weavers were barely visible on the other side. Could one of those dim, sad faces be her own?

While these pictures brought tears to Lily's eyes, others filled her with a cold, stark terror. She couldn't believe Kaz had managed to capture all this. Fights breaking out, pale faces strained to the point they looked like moonlit carvings, fists swinging in an arced blur. Men dropping to their knees, punched in the gut, photographed from weird angles. The camera must have been hidden under Kaz's jacket.

These pictures at once beckoned and revolted her, exerting an extraordinary, eerie power. Why did Kaz insist on taking them? They were nothing like the pictures he'd given to her; there was nothing beautiful about these images. It upset her just knowing that they existed, proof of how far they'd all fallen. Her ghostly, nameless self — performing menial labour. Fingers so cramped from all the weaving and tying that she'd soon be an arthritic crone.

"Why, Kaz?" A sob caught in her throat. "What's the point of it all? If anyone ever found them —"

"You don't understand. They're important. After the war's over, after some time's gone by, people'll want to know what happened here. And that's the story my pictures will tell."

"A true record of the internment," Kenny added. "Not just the pretty pictures of us smiling internees that the WRA photographers are sent to take."

"The WRA?"

"The War Relocation Authority. The government. The geniuses responsible for running this place. They've got their propaganda folks cooking up pamphlets. Haven't you noticed?"

So that was who they were. A few weeks back Lily had glimpsed a hakujin woman in a mannish white shirt. Gingery hair, pale, fragile skin, the kind easily prone to redness. She was with a paunchy, bearded guy, his face shaded by a stetson. One of those old-fashioned, workhorse cameras stood on a tripod. They were taking pictures of two little boys playing catch under the dazzling, white-hot sun.

Later that evening, in the barracks, Lily had overheard some girls talking about how the man had told them to smile and let their gratitude shine from their cheeks. They should be grateful for how the United States of America had brought them here to shelter and protect them, he said.

A couple of days later, the guy approached Lily. She could feel his eyes grazing her body as he lingered at some distance, taking in the scene: Lily, Aunt Tetsuko, and Audrey outside the barrack. It was after dinner. They were sitting in a circle on upside-down crates in the umbrella of mauve-grey shadows. Not much in the way of conversation, just the *click-click* of their knitting needles — faster and faster, like high heels on pavement, running away. No one looked up. He didn't seem to get that this was his cue to leave. The man plunked down his camera on a stand.

The nerve of him. He wasn't even going to ask permission? Jumping up, Lily shot him a disdainful glance and tethered in the skein of yarn so quickly she didn't realize her handiwork had fallen to the ground. His hat slanted back to reveal an amused expression. As she stormed inside, the scrap of sweater got caught around the crate and unravelled in so many rapid orange zigzags.

"Don't get me wrong," Kaz said. "Not *all* the WRA photographers are government lackeys. You'd be surprised — some of their politics swing pretty far left. They were New Dealers, back in the day, when they toured the countryside taking pictures of migrant farmers, documenting their crap living conditions. They sympathize with the oppressed. Some of these guys are against the whole internment. It goes against their politics, their humanity."

"You've been getting to know them real well."

Kaz shrugged, as if there were more he could say if he wanted to. "Can't hurt to have friends on all sides."

The female photographer was the one Kaz had befriended. Lily had caught sight of them chatting one afternoon. They were leaned against a barrack, heads close together. The woman was talking animatedly, gesturing in a loose-wristed kind of way. A burst of rich laughter that had a moody undertone. She laughed right from the stomach, like a man. Strange to see on such a birdlike woman.

"That girl — the redhead — is she the one who's been slipping you film?"

"Emily's been helping us out in a number of ways."

"Oh, Kaz. What makes you think she can be trusted?" Lily felt sickened.

"Em can be trusted. One hundred percent."

"The question," Kenny said, "is can *you* be trusted?"

"She can be trusted," Kaz said. "I have faith in her."

THE NEXT TWO nights, Lily hardly slept at all. Her mind was abuzz with images of the aqueduct — the obscene etchings on the wall magnified, looming like billboards of her duplicity, her guilt. What if someone had followed her out there? Her stomach clenched in a horrible inertia, as though she'd eaten something bad but couldn't bring herself to vomit.

She thought about going to the doctor and telling him everything. Maybe that would ease her conscience. Wasn't that what he'd told her — she could come to him for help at any time? The thought of further undermining his opinion of Kaz, however, was just too unpleasant. She wanted him to see that his son wasn't such a bad seed. Besides, what did she have to report? So Kaz had taken a few pictures he shouldn't have. Was it such a big deal, really? Worse things were going on here.

So she said nothing and the days wore on.

Kaz's moods shifted with the winds: one moment cool, trapped in his own thoughts, the next moment balmy, brimming with laughter. His body language was just as unpredictable. His palm brushed against her backside — so innocently, so deliberately — but nothing more would happen. Their kisses were halting, plagued by distractions and interruptions. One minute, he'd be staring at her, wide-eyed, mesmerized, but in a flash she watched his desire fade as his thoughts curled away from her. Caught up in his latest scheme with Kenny.

Each week when he signalled to her they were planning to meet that night, she told herself no, no, she couldn't do this anymore. But come nightfall she went. It was always the same group — their whispers full of big plans. As time went on, she relaxed a little: the extent of their crimes, as far as she could tell, didn't amount to much. Not yet, at least. Oh sure, they bragged from time to time about roughing up some poor JACC boy the night before, but fist fights had been erupting all over camp for months now. Grown men, bored for lack of anything to do, were reduced to gang rivalries reminiscent of the schoolyard.

No, it wasn't the violence that upset Lily; the violence had actually started to seem normal. Kenny's convoluted ideas, on the other hand, made her skin crawl.

At their meetings he always did most of the talking, full of bizarre ideas about corruption and conspiracy. All camp officials were in the pay: everyone from the lowliest guard to the head honcho, Ed Howells himself, whom he imitated, swaggering around, clipboard in hand. Why had their clothing allowance cheques been delayed for months now? "It's obvious," Kenny said. Somebody's pocketed them. And why so little food? Again, Kenny insisted that the camp bosses were to blame. They had a special arrangement worked out with grocers in neighbouring towns. The sugar intended for Matanzas never even made it here. And what about all the tomatoes the internees had planted, row upon row? They couldn't seriously believe they were getting the full harvest. The guards had taken them by the truckload.

"We have to get the word out," Kenny announced, one night.

Kaz nodded. "Let's post bulletins exposing the corruption outside the mess halls. We'll sign each post with 'Black Dragon.'"

But Kenny had bigger fish to fry. "To really get things going, guys, we need to start a union. The Kitchen Workers Union. We can demand better wages. Demand our food back."

"Overthrow the administration."

"Now you're talking." Shig grinned.

"We already have the Matanzas Work Corps, don't we?" Lily said.

The guys sniggered and she tried to laugh, too, as if in on the joke.

"That doesn't count. The Jackalopes set up that sham organization ages ago and it isn't doing squat to protect the workers. We need our own organization. If you can't see that, maybe you shouldn't be with us."

Recently, she'd noticed Akira watching her with distrust. He was smarter and more perceptive than the others.

"So, Lily, are you with us or not?"

"Of course I am."

She sensed he still had reservations, though.

"Well, good then, 'cause there's something we want you to do for us."

"Oh?"

"We'll go over the details later. For now, start familiarizing yourself with this." Akira handed her an envelope.

Reaching inside, she pulled out a pile of newspaper clippings. "JACC Leader Promises Cheerful Co-operation," read one headline. In the photo Frank Isaka was smiling broadly behind a podium, his hand sweeping through the air. There were also some pictures clipped from a high-school yearbook. "Frank Isaka — President of the Debating Club." Already, he'd perfected his suave smile, his well-styled hair.

In another photo, he was lounged back on the school steps, his arm draped around a pretty girl with solemn eyes. Although he was trying to appear easygoing, there was something forced about that smile.

"What do you want me to do with all this?"

"Just read it. Study it." Kaz's hand brushed the small of her back. "We want you to know everything there is to know about Mr. Frank Isaka. Try to get into his mind and figure out what makes him tick."

"Think about how you'd make him fall for you," Kenny added.

"Fall for me?"

"Yeah, fall head over heels, like all the guys do."

A soft, high-pitched ringing filled her ears, rising in tandem with her stuttering heart.

"Like I've fallen for you, of course," Kaz said.

Beneath all the bravado: a drop of tenderness. Her anger thinned. Kaz couldn't help being susceptible to the influence of his low-life friends. *He just needs the influence of a good woman.* Wasn't that what his father had said?

THE SUMMER WORE on, each day at the net factory hotter and longer than the last. The web of scraps seemed to swim before her, slipping through her fingers like swamp weeds.

One morning, the supervisor called Lily to the front. "You no longer work here, my dear."

"What do you mean? I'll work harder —"

"Don't worry, you're not fired. Greener pastures for you. Dr. Takemitsu wants you to report to your new job at the hospital."

Girls down the line cast envious stares, dust peppering their cheeks.

Lily was floating on air as she entered the cool, bright halls of the hospital. She didn't see its shabby, improvised quality: the old floor lamp being used to illuminate the exam table, which wasn't even a real exam table, just a mattress liner draped over a beat-up desk. All she saw was the pristine whiteness of the walls and the doctor's lab coat.

He greeted her in his usual brisk manner.

She thanked him for what he'd done but explained she had no skills as a nurse. Perhaps she could mop and clean. The doctor shook his head, looking amused.

"Then what'll I do?"

"A girl like you surely knows ikebana."

Before the war, Lily used to dabble in it. Her mother had taught her the basics. It came in handy when she was competing in the Cherry Blossom Pageant; the judges were known to favour girls who could showcase their Japanese hobbies. But it had been ages since she'd done a proper flower arrangement, and what would she use out in this wasteland?

The doctor told her to see what she could find outside.

Hardly a bush or bud. Nothing at all lush or elegant. She snipped some brittle branches from an old apple tree, from which she also plucked a couple of wilted blossoms. Some creamy puffs of Indian ricegrass made up the rest of her bouquet.

It was a slow morning at the clinic. The doctor tended to folks suffering from heatstroke while Lily spread out her foliage on the counter. She was surprised to see he had all the right equipment: kenzans in different sizes had been laid out for her to choose from, their brass needles like porcupine backs, alongside a small hatchet knife, steel clippers, a ball of wire, and a shallow ceramic vase.

It was important that the branches appeared to rise from the same stalk, an effect that could be achieved easily enough with a twist of wire. The challenge was to perfect the shape of the uneven triangle. You had to bend the branches without breaking them, sculpting them with your fingertips, treating them like an extension of yourself. Through the delicate bark, you could supposedly intuit the plant's moods and coax the branch to bend accordingly. But Lily never had much of a handle on even her own moods, and these branches were particularly difficult to work with, snapping at the lightest touch.

When the doctor came to check on her, all she had was a pile of broken twigs. Her face burned as he regarded her failed creation.

"We have to get you some real flowers to work with. I bet Mr. Murase would be willing to help."

"Oh, no. He's scary."

Before the war Mr. Murase owned a bustling nursery. Right outside his barrack door, he'd managed to create a garden oasis: the bushes and bulbs he'd brought from home were miraculously flourishing in luscious patches of colour. Yet the old man was fiercely protective of his flowers, enclosing them under a wire blanket at night. Not even the jackrabbits and squirrels dared to feast.

"Let's just say that Mr. Murase owes me a favour. I'll talk to him. It's for the good of my patients to bring a touch of nature inside these sad walls."

Something else was on the doctor's mind; he lingered, awkward as a schoolboy. His capacity to return her own shyness filled her with a sudden, fumbling pleasure.

"So tell me about my son," he finally said.

Lily could see that he had fears and suspicions eating away at him, responsible for sleepless nights. That was the real reason she'd found herself here. That was why he'd created this sham job for her.

"Well, what do you want to know?"

"I have eyes, Lily. Things have been getting worse around here."

"Oh?"

The doctor sighed, disappointed she wasn't being more forthcoming. "Remember what happened to poor Burt Kondo? A broken nose and two broken ribs. And he's not even the worst of what I see these days."

"Those JACC boys can be pretty arrogant."

"All I care is that Kaz's staying out of all that nonsense."

He wanted to know, yet he didn't want to know. The truth hovered between them, a balloon of warm, quivering air.

How she longed to tell the doctor everything. Burt's beating was the least of it. It was more than just talk now — Kenny knew how to rally the troops. Word had gotten out about the Kitchen Workers Union, and a surprising number of folks wanted in.

"Everything will blow over. Kaz'll be just fine. After the war, he'll get back on track. You'll see."

"You certainly see the good in people, Lily-san."

She smiled, but was he complimenting her at all?

The doctor wasn't going to let it drop. "What I'm asking is whether Kaz's been involved in anything I should be worried about."

When she didn't reply, bewilderment clouded his eyes. "I thought I could depend on you, Lily."

"You *can* depend on me." And the words began tumbling from her lips, mixed with gasps and sobs.

ONE NIGHT WHEN she arrived at the aqueduct, there were no conspiring voices. No taunts, no posturing, no male laughter. Kaz was all alone, slouched against the curved cement, a cigarette dangling from his lips, smoke swirling about his hair.

When he looked up — his eyes smiling, gleaming deviously — her heart tripped over itself. She could see what he was thinking. *It's time.* There was a tautness to his jaw, a tight energy coiled in his knees, a dewy sheen on his forehead. The pungent, fiery whiff of whiskey on his breath. She felt she could smell every hair on his body: the essence of sage and sweat and sex. It wasn't the first time Lily had arrived at this place, where men start to resemble panthers. Kaz ran his hands up the nape of her neck, more rough than gentle, and she wanted him to look at her like he really saw her, but his eyes remained cloudy slits.

Strangely enough, Lily found his remoteness alluring — proof that he'd crossed this threshold many times before. The jazz singer he'd almost run away with. All that "chasing skirt," as Dr. Takemitsu had put it. Pangs of jealousy cut across her brain, feeding that bottomless pit inside her, her need to make him entirely her own.

"I … love you."

His hands continued moving up her thighs, scrunching up her skirt.

His silence hurt her, yet she pushed it aside. He'd come around. She'd make him come around. She stared at the full moon, mesmerized by its brightness, its roundness, as his hands kept exploring and her mind drifted up toward the vast, jewel-studded sky.

As his fingers moved lower, one moment arousing her, the next moment hurting her a little, her thoughts were scattered, adrift. Images of the doctor began flooding her mind. She pictured him standing on the edge of the aqueduct, looking down at them — approvingly? mirthfully? jealously? — and as she craned her neck back, their eyes locked. Kaz became rougher, grabbing her hips, flicking his belt buckle, but she didn't mind because it reminded her how far he'd fallen from his father's dreams. And that was where she came in. By redeeming Kaz, she'd win his father's love: two men, simply versions of the same man, in love with her…. How she luxuriated in that thought, as though becoming Kaz's girl was just a pleasant side effect of what she'd been craving all along: the doctor's love. She imagined the years peeling off his skin, restoring it to the smooth clarity of Kaz's, and it was both their faces kissing her now, the one superimposed upon the other, flickering back and forth, moment to moment.

The doctor. Kaz. The doctor. Kaz.

Seven

When she woke up, an ache stretched across her hip bones. As she pushed hair from her eyes, a veil of sand streamed onto her pillow and she rubbed the granules between her fingertips, rejoicing in their lovely, frictive texture. Warm memories of last night washed over her.

What did she expect Kaz would do when he saw her at breakfast? A tender glance, a knowing smile? Some simple display of possessiveness? A flurry of attentive gestures? Whatever Lily had in mind, she expected, at the very least, that he'd sit with her.

But he was already at a table of girls. She took the only seat available at the end. He didn't even get up. Barely looked at her. Didn't come over and take her hand. He seemed perfectly content to sit next to Linda Itabe, who kept flicking her glossy ponytail and erupting in giggles.

Hurt and confusion clouded Lily's brain, fuzzy from lack of sleep. Sand was falling from her hair onto her lap, but it no longer seemed like proof of anything.

And yet the following day when Kaz came to her, Lily couldn't bring herself to turn him away. He appeared out of nowhere in the late, shadow-filled afternoon as she was practising her walk down a secluded alley. Without even turning around, she sensed his footsteps behind her. A brief interval of hesitation — as though he'd had second thoughts and wanted to pull away from her — and then it was too late; he'd locked his arms around her rib cage, burying his mouth in the nape of her neck, enclosing her in his cloud of earthy sweatiness.

"You sure you wouldn't rather be doing this with Linda Itabe?"

"Relax, Lily. It's better we keep things between us secret." His hands were riding up her breasts.

She pushed them back down. "Secret? Why?"

"Black Dragon, of course." His hiss barely a whisper. "Kenny and I have big plans in the pipeline."

Black Dragon. He acted like it was all so important, rather than just a bunch of bored guys acting big to pass the time. Still, it was a relief to know he trusted her. Of all the girls he could have chosen to draw into his inner circle, he'd chosen her.

Some days, she'd squirm and protest — what if someone saw them and Aunt Tetsuko found out? — but he would grab her wrists and laugh, whispering that she wanted everyone to find out, didn't she? His fingers shoved into her mouth, daring her to bite and make him scream.

Other times, though, Kaz had a tender side. He'd come to her early in the morning, when she was doing ikebana. He slipped in through the back entrance of the hospital, so nobody would see him. The doctor had given her a little room there, barely larger than a storage closet. Glistening pink light streamed in through the tiny window and danced in mottled dots over her branches and leaves and blossoms, everything spread out on the bare mattress. Thanks to Mr. Murase, her supply was always stocked with a handful of roses, carnations, or lilies. And Kaz brought other things he'd foraged: tiny green apples touched with a hint of blush cloud, branches that sloped up at such elegant angles, constellations of bright yellow blossoms shooting up like a starry night. Even withered leaves and petals could be used; nature on the verge of dying was often more beautiful than at the height of its bloom.

She let him undress and caress her body, finger each tiny mole and scar. She sensed his soul hungering for more, at moments like this. *What Kaz needs is the influence of a good woman.* Her thoughts drifted to the doctor, a stone's throw down the hall. Kaz hoisted her onto the bed, and the leaves and branches scratched cryptic patterns across her thighs, backside.

"Do you think your father knows about us?"

"Knows what?"

"That we've gone this far?"

His hands stopped moving, turned clammy. "Why'd you have to bring him up at now of all times?"

"I can't help it." She wanted the doctor to think well of her.

"I don't care if he does!"

Mocking, tittering whispers. The voices might have been coming from behind her, like she was sitting on a bus and eavesdropping on the conversations of strangers. Yet as she listened, it turned out they weren't strangers — these voices were gossiping about her, laughing at her, laden with malicious, schoolgirl glee. "She thinks she's such a good girl, but what a joke, what a hussy!" "She wants both father and son, you know she does!" "Does she even know who's touching her now? Whose fingers are opening up our little Cherry Blossom Queen, petal by petal?"

Lily tried to block it all out by humming a tune in her head.

"Don't even think about winning my father's approval. I gave up on that a long time ago."

Kaz's anger gradually dissipated under her trembling, coaxing fingers. Tears of longing and confusion stinging her eyes.

KENNY WAS GETTING edgy. Things weren't moving fast enough. Lily didn't know what the guy had to complain about; people were lining up to join the Kitchen Workers Union. So far they had over three hundred members. She had no idea how they'd done it, but somehow the guys had managed to get the word out while keeping it under the radar. Young people, old people, men, women, they were all coming to see Kenny, full of rancorous stories about how they were sick of lying down and taking it. At last their stoicism had worn thin.

"It's not enough. We have to do more to get people to join up. *Faster.*" It was a cloudy night. Kenny's face was immersed in darkness.

"Why does size matter so much?" Akira asked.

"Yeah, it's better if we keep things small and tight." This was Shig now. He was standing beside Lily, too close, his rancid scent wafting over her. "We're a secret tribe, right?"

"Can't you understand?" Kenny sounded exasperated, like he'd explained this a thousand times before. "The whole point of a union is to encompass *everyone*. That way, when the shit hits the fan —"

"Everyone'll be on our side." Kaz. Finishing Kenny's sentences, as usual.

The doleful wind filled her head with a desperate feeling. If Shig and Akira still had reservations, they certainly weren't voicing them. Yet if Lily opened her mouth, they'd only gang up on her — call her a stick-in-the-mud, a priss, a scaredy-cat girl. Her objections would only serve to draw the gang closer together and push them to greater heights of foolishness.

"We have to do something to get more people pissed off," Kenny continued. "Sure, they're mad about the missing food and crap wages, but we have to make them really feel it. Make them fucking livid. So even nice old ladies like Mrs. Okada'll see *we're* not the enemy — the camp bosses are."

"Like what?" This was Kaz or Shig or Akira. Lily couldn't tell in the dark; all their voices were starting to sound so similar. "Another sabotage prank? The net factory — that was a good one!"

Last week, someone had snuck into the net factory during the night and torn a good deal of the weaving to shreds. Although Lily hadn't been made privy to the plans, she'd known in her gut these were the guys responsible. The next morning, scores of people had been taken aside for questioning by the FBI. She'd been terrified, but by some miracle she'd been overlooked.

"Can you imagine the look on Howells's face when he saw all those massive, busted cobwebs?" Shig couldn't contain his glee. The whole thing had been his idea, Lily was sure of it. He'd probably carried it out single-handedly. The guy was fearless when it came to tearing and smashing stuff.

"Howells must've crapped his pants. The army needs those nets. Not gonna make their quotas now. Howells'll have some serious explaining to do."

"Might not get his Christmas bonus after all."

Chuckles all round.

All except from Kenny. "You guys think you're so smart to be pulling this prankster bullshit? It can backfire — it *will* backfire. Makes people think we're the problem. While nice old Mr. Howells is out savin' the world, we're just a bunch of punks and lunatics."

Silence. If anyone raised a word of objection, Kenny was bound to go off on a diatribe.

"Well, what d'you have in mind, Ken?" Shig asked.

"We need a different approach."

"Like what?"

"That's what I'm trying to figure out. No help from you idiots." A beleaguered sigh. "Something smarter, bigger."

AQUEDUCT BY NIGHT, hospital by day. It was a strange, starkly split existence. Thankfully, her responsibilities at the hospital weren't arduous. She made tea and toast for the old folks and sat at their bedsides as they stared into space and sipped and chewed for so long they might have forgotten how to swallow. She rubbed lotion on the backs of their venous hands, discoloured like diseased leaves. If things weren't too busy, the doctor would get chatty, telling stories about the old days. He never talked much about his childhood back in Japan. It was as though his life had begun the moment he got off the boat in Seattle, hardly speaking a word of English. He'd had to enrol at an elementary school to learn his ABCs. Lily giggled in delight at the thought of him as a teenager, surrounded by the apple-cheeked faces and golden heads of kids a third his age. By working hard, he'd managed to skip several grades while earning his keep as a houseboy. She wondered how he'd had the energy for it all. How had he managed to get into med school? And pay for it? But the doctor didn't like to answer questions, so gaps in his life stretched open, years of exhaustion flying by in a blur of aching muscles that no one would ever be able to account for — least of all him.

Now and then, there were children who needed to be cared for while the doctor tended to their parents. Lily set up an arts and crafts table where she taught origami. The little unformed faces looked up at her with such guilelessness. They filled her with joy, these moments she didn't deserve, yet the aqueduct and all its goings-on loomed up and overshadowed everything. It was as if there were two Lilys, another version of herself slipping in and out of the nocturnal shadows.

It started to irritate her when the doctor would ask questions. Maybe she'd spent too many nights listening to Kenny rant; no longer did she feel quite so sure where her loyalties lay. The worst part was that sometimes she couldn't remember what she'd already revealed. In a burst of allegiance to Kaz and Kenny, she'd tell the doctor that things were calming down: they hadn't been out to the aqueduct in ages and nothing much seemed to be going on — could it be possible that Kaz was straightening out at last? Rather than looking relieved, however, the doctor frowned and shook his head.

"You just told me yesterday that Shig pulled another stunt. He's responsible for those obscenities in red paint outside the mess hall, isn't he, Lily?"

"I told you that?"

"That and much more!"

Although she nodded, she didn't understand at all: she didn't understand why memories were constantly slipping away from her.

At times she felt unsure whether she could even trust the doctor. She'd seen the husky men coming and going from his office, their shadows casting grey stains into the hallway. It was no secret that the place was crawling with FBI. As soon as anything happened, no matter how insignificant — some scrappy fight — the G-men could be called in. Not that they did much. They asked a few questions, filed a report. That said, they had become pushier in recent days. Maybe they had quotas on the number of informants they had to recruit, pressure from on high to root out those bad apples. Was that why they'd been doing double duty, showing up out of the blue, swaggering around in their boxy suits, even when nothing much had happened? They hung around the hospital smoking, drinking coffee, and the soapy, waxy whiff of Brylcreem lingered in the air. "Hey, doc," they called out, "you got a minute?"

At first Lily didn't think anything of it, because it stood to reason that if some G-man lackey wanted a quick rundown of the week's events, the doctor was an obvious source. He overheard things; he was privy to conversations when people were at their most weak and vulnerable. It never seemed they talked for long, though his office door was always closed.

But what was the doctor telling them? Indignation rose in Lily's chest. What had he disclosed? Queasiness overtook her, deepening into panic. Had everything that passed through her lips made its way to their ears?

The doctor had worked out a nice situation for himself — that was what some people were saying. He'd cozied up nice and tight with the higher-ups. People were jealous that he still had his car and was allowed to leave camp whenever he wanted. They didn't like it that while they were stuck in the barracks, the doctor lived in a proper house at the edge of camp, and at the end of the war, he'd have money in his bank account, thanks to the handsome salary he was paid here. The rumours were so ridiculous that some people said his house in Little Tokyo was being protected from looting. "What's he doing in return for all this?" the old men gossiped. "He must be doing favours for the camp bosses, informing on everyone, saving his own skin."

Lily didn't buy it. Not really. The doctor was just doing his best to protect his family, and wasn't that what any man in his position would do? And then anger would bubble up inside her. While her own father was being held God knew where, the doctor was putting on his best suit and driving into town? What had he bartered to ensure his comfortable position?

Maybe it didn't matter. Not that he was co-operating with the authorities, but if he *were*, would it be such a big deal, really? A burst of gratitude, mixed with something stronger and more confusing swept over her. It wasn't like he'd ever inform on his own son. The doctor had reached out to her in order to protect Kaz. And now she was linked at the hip with Kaz, practically a member of the family.

AFTER THEIR MEETINGS, they never left the aqueduct together. Safer that way, Kenny said.

Lily was usually the first to leave. It was colder now, especially at night; she could see the white plumes of her breath trailing behind, the chill penetrating her bones through her thin jacket. The ground shimmered like a moonlit lake, slick with the first dusting of frost crystals. Her feet sped up and slipped as she darted through that first stretch of bare desert, always the worst part, and then stuck close to the barracks. She counted one mess hall after another. Cut down an alley, rushed past several dumpsters, moonlight and shadows playing on the loose debris. Hands on knees, chest heaving, she paused to catch her breath.

Footsteps from behind.

A night guard.

Her body froze up, adrenalin shooting into her head.

The only place to hide was in a dumpster, so Lily held her breath and clambered in, crouching down amid the rotting potato peels and chicken carcasses. The rank odours cut off all air to her brain, the weight of her body rustling against the bags, each crackle like lightning.

A meaty hand grabbed her by the hair — needles of pain shot through her scalp, skull, brain. Her body, limp as an old pillow, lurched forward, and a punch landed in her gut, a thud of pure pain. Now the ground was careening toward her face, and all her meticulous preparations for the beauty pageant passed before her in slow motion: the nylon tied around her thighs, her humiliating, mincing steps — *so silly, so vain,* the words of Aunt Tetsuko, who'd cautioned against the pitfalls of vanity, echoing in her head.

Her face hit the dust and gravel gouged her cheek, elbows, knees. A kick landed in her rib cage and something horrible cracked within her. Aftershocks rippled through her core.

"What've we got here? You know what happens to little girls who sneak out after curfew?"

Daring to look over her shoulder, Lily glimpsed a fleshy face fringed with red hair. That guard. How terrified she'd been that first night she'd snuck out and seen him making his rounds. Tufts of hair stuck out the front of his uniform, open a couple of buttons. His cheeks were swollen with desire or something more awful, as though he'd been stung by a hive of bees.

His gaze softened as he recognized her.

"A family emergency — I had to —"

He crouched down and peered in, flashlight in hand, and the beam of light licked her skin. "Don't even think about screaming, sweetie." His damp fingers played with the hem of her skirt.

She struggled to get away, pull herself forward on her bleeding elbows. A strange laugh filled her head, and it had been years since she'd heard that laughter — if it could be called laughter at all. When she was a kid and her father started coming to her room at night, the sound would fill her ears, gently at first: nothing more than a cat mewling, gradually growing louder until it was strident and hysterical, like a donkey braying or a pig squealing. Strangely, there was something nice about how the noise — the laughter — overtook her mind, blanketed everything. She didn't know who or what was laughing, but it surrounded her like an imaginary friend that would always be with her, no matter what.

A hint of movement down the alley.

Kaz. She recognized him in an instant. He always left the aqueduct a few minutes after her. Relief washed over her: he was coming to her rescue. The pain in her gut suddenly felt exquisite, crescendoing in time with her heart.

But he just kept standing there, his body pressed against the wall. *Why wouldn't he come over? What was taking him so long?*

She stared down the alley, silently implored him. He just stood there, paralyzed, his face oyster pale. A soft belly pressed into her from behind, the big hand like a vice on her hip.

"What the hell?"

This voice was familiar. Through the fuzz of her battered ears, Lily recognized Kenny, could it be? Yes, she could see him on the periphery of her vision now. His steps pounded toward her head.

A whack — the creature on top of her spasmed. As she rolled away, pushing the body off her, she saw that Kenny had managed to get a hold of the guard's club. Lying on the ground, she watched a thunderstorm of blows come down. The body had curled into a fetal position, jacket and shirt scrunched up, a layer of blubbery flesh around the lower back and bum exposed, sickly white.

Kaz jumped forward now. "What the hell are you doing?"

"This sicko attacked your girl. You wanna let him get away with it?"

"Christ, Kenny! Don't you think the guy's had enough?"

"Are you gonna help or just stand there?"

The reluctance — the fear — in Kaz's voice was the last thing she'd remember, as she clung to the edges of consciousness. The guard's moaning, the squeal of a dying animal. It echoed the animal laughter pealing across her insides, outer and inner worlds mixing in chaos. After a while, everything was lost in the black river through her brain.

Archive
Fever

Eight

"If you got to be a dinosaur, Mommy, what would you be?"

"I don't know, a brontosaurus? Those are the nice ones that eat plants, right?"

Rita fiddled with the antenna of the cordless; it sounded like Kristen was talking through cotton batten. Something barrelled by in the background. What she'd thought was static was actually the whoosh of traffic, past a roadside pay phone. Sighing, she tried to concentrate on what her daughter was saying: they were on a camping trip, headed to some park where dinosaur footprints had been discovered. Ever since her class had gone to the ROM last year, Kristen had been fascinated by the dinosaur kingdom. It was nice of Cal to indulge her.

Nevertheless, a jealous pang: why did he always get to be the fun parent who swept in for summer vacations while she nursed Kristen through ear infections all winter long? He treated fatherhood like dating: pack your time together into short, fun bursts. And the cavalier way he'd announced that he was selling his practice in order to move to Vancouver, where UBC's dental school had offered him a faculty position, still rankled. As if divorce weren't enough for a poor kid to handle. Yet Cal wanted a fresh start — who didn't? — and when he wanted something, nothing got in his way.

"What kind of dinosaur would you be, Pumpkin?"

"A triceratops."

"Why's that?"

"They have eight hundred teeths. And when their teeths fall out, they can get new ones, just like me. Plus they have three horns to protect them from the meat-eating dinos. So they're pretty smart."

"You're pretty smart."

A wobble of emotion. The sheen of soapy bubbles about to pop amid crusty dishes. Pop, pop, pop. Everything went blurry. Rita rubbed at her eyelids.

Oh, God. Where *was* Lily?

Should she say anything to Cal? Best not to ruin his quality time with Kristen. The prick.

"Do you know that birds come from dinosaurs? So the dinosaurs aren't really dead. Birds are mini dinosaurs. Can we get a bird again, Mommy?"

"We'll see. You remember what happened to Popsicle?"

A solemn silence.

Popsicle had been their beloved budgie, which used to chirp and trill all day long, particularly when the phone would ring, like a mating call. One day they'd returned home to find Popsicle face down at the bottom of her cage. It had been Kristen's first experience of death. Although she'd been sad, she'd been too young to understand death's irreversibility. Only as the weeks went by did the truth settle in, and so many questions began to trouble her.

Rita had dealt with the situation the way she always did: by buying a book. *The Big Goodbye: Fifty Ways to Help a Grieving Child.* When it came to motherhood, she was the Self-Help Queen. She was the target audience that all those pancake-makeup shrinks on *Donahue* were hawking their wares to. She didn't know the first thing about being a mom — just look at her own mother.

For years, she'd thought she didn't even want kids. Cal had been the one who'd pushed for it. And then something kind of melted inside her, and every time she'd pass a baby carriage on the street, this hormonally driven flutter of longing would take flight in her belly.

Not that she ever became one of those women all gung-ho about motherhood. It was bound for failure. Of course it was. Way too much pressure to put on a poor kid, to expect her to somehow redeem one's own train wreck of a family.

Still, if they were going to do this thing, they were going to do it right. Cal signed them up for a Lamaze class, where the instructor explained how pregnancy was all about *gestation*, which was as much about developing a body of ideas and attitudes about parenthood as simply carrying the fetus to term. While purging all trans fats from her diet and stocking up on garlic and brightly coloured veggies, Rita read countless books on how to bond with her unborn baby by listening and responding to every kick and reading stories that could be heard through the walls of her distended belly.

It didn't matter how much she read or did, however. She still feared that she'd missed some crucial lesson, that she'd fail miserably in the end.

"Did Daddy pack enough warm clothes for you?" It would be cold at the campsite at night. Men didn't think about these things.

"Jodi did."

"Jodi?"

"Yeah. She's Daddy's new friend."

A strange, unsteady sensation passed over Rita. Sure, she'd assumed that Cal was dating, but this was the first woman he'd introduced to Kristen. Not that Rita hadn't sensed this moment was coming. Still, couldn't he at least have the decency to give her a heads-up? And was it really appropriate for this woman — his new girlfriend — to accompany them on a camping trip? After all Cal's moaning about how much he missed Kristen, how about a little one-on-one father-daughter time? Rita pictured the three of them — Kristen, Cal, and Jodi, the impostor mother — sitting around the campfire, roasting hot dogs. Staring at the scratched up walls of her apartment, she'd never felt quite so alone, pathetic.

"Well, what's this Jodi like?"

"She's nice. She painted my toenails red."

So that was all it took to win a little girl's favour? And what kind of woman thought it was appropriate to paint a six-year-old's toenails fire-engine red anyway? What next — she'd be perming Kristen's hair? And where was Cal in all this? Rita had to struggle to keep her voice from quivering. "Honey, do you mind putting your father on?"

Cal sounded totally relaxed as he greeted her.

"So Kristen was just telling me about the new woman in your life."

"Yeah, the girls have been hitting it off."

The girls. Cal used to refer to her and Kristen as his girls. It hadn't bothered Rita at the time, but now — hearing this reference attached to her daughter and another woman — it made her skin crawl. "How old is this Jodi woman, anyway?"

An irritated sigh. "Relax, Rita. She's thirty-one."

So she was older than the twenty-two-year-old flight attendant he'd dated during their separation. Cal had long had a roving eye when it came to pretty young things. Though he claimed he'd never acted on his desires before they split up, Rita suspected otherwise.

Just because Jodi was a respectable age didn't mean she was fit to be taking care of a small child. "What exactly does she do?"

"*Do?*"

"For a living."

"She works in international development. Now are we done with the third degree?"

For a moment, Rita almost wished he'd said an aesthetician, a cocktail waitress, a stripper. "Well, what does an international development consultant know about kids? I thought this was supposed to be *your* time with our daughter, Cal? Instead, you're getting a perfect stranger to babysit her all the time?"

"Christ, Rita. Jodi's a part of my life now, so of course I want her to be a part of Kristen's life, too!"

"Oh, nice. As always, you've got our daughter's best interests at heart."

"It *is* in her interest to see her parents happy. With other people. You, too, Rita. You should move on, start dating."

"Oh, yeah?" The gall of him. "And who says that I'm not?"

"Look." His tone softened. "I realize this can't be easy for you. It isn't easy for any of us."

"Oh, *really?*"

Cal didn't make it appear very hard at all.

RITA FLOPPED DOWN on the bed in Kristen's room and stared at the ceiling for a long time. Fighting with Cal had left her drained. As if she hadn't already been feeling utterly drained.

Although she'd given Kristen the larger of the two bedrooms, it was still only half the size of her old room, back in the days when they all lived together as a family. And the windowsill was cracked and mouldy, the screen in tatters. Painting the walls robin's egg blue — Kristen's favourite colour — would help. A bit, at least.

What kind of mother let her child live in these derelict conditions?

All her life, Rita had resented Lily for letting them grow up in poverty. *You've had a good life, haven't you, dear?* Rita still had no idea what her mother had wanted to hear in asking that strange question. Absolution, perhaps. Well, the truth was that Rita didn't feel like she'd had the greatest of childhoods.

Would Kristen one day feel the same way? Would she hold Rita responsible for not being able to keep their sprawling house on Golfdale Road? She probably resented Rita already. Yet poverty was a relative thing. In Lily's mind, they'd never truly been poor because they'd owned their own house — even if it had been mortgaged to the hilt and crammed with all those weird boarders. So many different types of hair all woven together in the giant hairball that had clogged the bathtub. Red pubes, grey pubes. Mismatched, multicoloured dishes on the counter, vestiges of foul-smelling foods. The constant rise and fall of husky voices through the thin walls, a waterfall of piss into the toilet. No matter how familiar these men's intimate sounds became, they remained absolute strangers.

The walls of this place were thin, too. Last night, the kids upstairs had thrown a party and later Rita had heard staggering around and ecstatic moaning, as two — or several — of them went at it until the early hours of the morning. What was she going to do when Kristen got back? Knock on their door and say, "Excuse me, I don't mean to be a killjoy, but would you mind keeping the orgy down so my daughter can sleep?"

Funny how she'd never thought of Lily as a single mom until now. Why was that? Maybe because Kaz had never been around to walk out on them. At least, Rita had no memory of that. She'd been too young to remember anything. Had she been older when Kaz ran off, she would have seen Lily's aloneness as a distinct change from an earlier, happier state, rather than just the way things had always been. Struggling to get by, for Lily, was simply the norm. Because that's what single moms did. As if Rita had time to date anybody. Cal had some nerve giving her dating advice.

She'd promised to go over to Gerald's house again today, and now she was late because Cal and Kristen had called later than scheduled. They'd probably lost track of time because they were having so much fun with Jodi, all three of them lounged back in the car, listening to Beatles tunes and playing licence-plate games.

If Lily were here now, Rita would ask: How on earth did you manage to do it? How did you make a home for us from a crumbling old house, furnished with battered castoffs? How did you not drown in self-pity as you saw all the happy families around you?

But Lily wasn't the sentimental, self-pitying type. She was a survivor who rolled up her sleeves and did whatever needed to be done. Rita prayed that her survival instincts were serving her well now.

MAIL HAD PILED up at the house. A bulky stack of bills interspersed with *Cosmo* and *Glamour*, the puckered, painted lips jumping out like wounds. As Rita sorted through it all, stacking magazines on the coffee table, she noticed that some back issues had scraps tucked inside. She'd forgotten about this old habit. For a while Lily had carried around a notebook to jot things down in, as an aid to her memory. Although that hadn't lasted more than a month, she'd improvised another system: things furtively scribbled on napkins and discarded envelopes, shoved here and there.

They were just lists. *Bread, wine, aloe vera, hair dye. Rice vinegar, dashi, nori, pickled ginger. Pick up dry cleaning, vacuum, eggs. Sweets for Nisei Women's Club, fibre for Gerald, 2:00 Gerald Y-E. Plums, meringues, Ted F., Folgers, pork chops, Ted F., 3:00 Fri. Drano, if not call plumber, Polysporin, prunes.*

On they went, all in Lily's messy, curvaceous hand. Some had dates at the top; others only had *Thurs* or *Mon*. Perhaps the month of the magazine in which each note had been stashed comprised Lily's system of cataloguing her life. Her brain probably wasn't that methodical. But what did it matter if she wrote *Maxwell House* instead of *Folgers*? None of these chicken scratches were terribly illuminating.

The only thing that seemed at all out of the ordinary was "Ted F."

Years ago, Lily had dated a man named Ted Fujita. His freshly bleached dentures gleamed whenever he smiled, an eerie contrast to his liverspotted skin. He was one of those men who always seemed to be trying to give the impression he was happier and more successful than he actually was.

What could he be doing on her mind after all these years?

Just as likely, however, that "Ted F." referred to Lily's hairdresser or plumber. Besides, Rita didn't relish the thought of cold-calling her mother's ex; the news of Lily's disappearance would throw him into a panic. It was exhausting always having to deal with other people's frazzled nerves.

"THERE'S A LADY on the phone. I think you better talk to her," Gerald hollered up the stairs.

Rita picked up the bedroom extension. "Hello?"

"My name is Aya Yamamoto. Your mother and I know each other from the Nisei Women's Club."

A rise of excitement in her gut. "Thank you for calling — we've been wanting to get in touch with the club."

"As soon as I heard about Lily, I had to call to see if there's anything I can do to help." Perfect English, not a trace of an accent, a typical nisei. Mrs. Yamamoto's words were almost too perfect, too carefully formed.

"How was my mother at your last meeting?"

"Actually, Lily didn't come."

"But my mother always attends, doesn't she? She speaks so fondly of your activities at the club." In truth, Rita had no idea what they did there. Flower arranging? Tea ceremony? Sewing tiny Japanese angels with black yarn hair for the Christmas bazaar?

"I also thought it a bit odd that we didn't see her last Thursday."

Thursday. The day before Lily disappeared.

A light purring: breathing, hesitating. Was there something else Mrs. Yamamoto wanted to say?

"I'm not talking about the Nisei Women's Club, Rita." The voice dropped to a whisper. "I'm talking about our *other* meetings."

"Other meetings?"

"So Lily never told you."

"Told me what?"

"Oh, she wouldn't have." A peculiar excitement — the thrill of secrecy, a girlish note — animated her voice.

"Mrs. Yamamoto, what *exactly* are you referring to?"

Silence.

Rita flushed at her own brusqueness. "I'm sorry. I just ... I haven't been sleeping well."

Shuffling on the other end. Mrs. Yamamoto was pacing around, emitting a nervous, bristling energy. "Better if we discuss this in person."

That edge of paranoia. It was the trademark of folks of that generation. They believed that the government and police were spying on them constantly. It was absurd — pathetic, really. Did they honestly believe they were important enough to merit phone taps? What was this, Watergate? Yet they lived in a world of government conspiracies and men in dark suits out to get them.

Evidently, Mrs. Yamamoto had no intention of saying anything further unless Rita paid her a visit. Well, it wasn't like she was getting a lot accomplished here anyway. "Shall I come over to your house right now?"

"Tomorrow morning would be better, dear."

Rita jotted down the address in Don Mills, wondering whether Mrs. Yamamoto was some batty old lady in need of attention, neglected by her kids. Maybe that was what the Nisei Women's Club was really all about.

RITA FILLED HER GLASS yet again, kicked off her flip-flops and lay back on the lumpy couch. The good thing about buying French Cross in four-litre cartons was that it allowed you to lose track of how much you'd drunk and not feel guilty about having polished off a whole bottle.

The wail of a baby rose up through the floorboards from the basement apartment. A guy with a shaved head and plenty of intricate tattoos lived down there. Had an ex-girlfriend showed up out of the blue with their offspring in tow? While Rita didn't relish the thought of a crying infant in the building, the guy was lucky, really. Having a kid around forced structure and discipline on your life. If Kristen were here now, no way would Rita be staring at the wall, slowly getting wasted.

She used to have friends she could talk to when she got like this. A few years back, her best friend from art school, Meryl, had hooked up with a Mexican potter, and now the two of them lived at an artists' colony in Oaxaca. The place didn't even have a phone. These days the extent of Rita's contact with Meryl was an occasional postcard: "Come visit me — mi casa es tu casa. It'll be like the old days. You can get back into your painting. And there are plenty of beautiful men wandering around half-naked." It was a lovely idea, but she'd never make it out there. If she ever had enough money to go on vacation again, she'd want to take Kristen, so it would have to be somewhere more child-friendly. At times like this, though, she desperately missed talking to Meryl.

Sure, Rita was friendly with a few colleagues at her school, but they weren't old friends. They were fine for a lunch out or a coffee in the staff room but that was about the extent of it. Besides, most of them had picture-perfect lives. They probably weren't even in town, off at their cottages for the summer. And she had one or two single girlfriends who were good for a night on the town and wretched hangovers the next morning (exactly where she was headed anyway, unless she eased up on the French Cross). They were the sort of friends you could chat with about guy problems, sex. Not your mother having gone missing. Was it really possible that she had nobody she could call up to talk to? How had she let herself become so isolated? Somewhere along the way, Rita had managed to lose touch with every single living soul who'd once cared about her. How the heck had that happened? Was this why people got dogs? A dog would nuzzle his furry head against her thigh, every hair breathing warmth, affection. At least with a dog around, she'd be assured that if she hit her head in a drunken stupor, she wouldn't die all alone on the living-room floor with nobody even noticing.

GRANDPA ALWAYS KNEW how to cheer Lily up. "Your mother came *this* close to winning the Cherry Blossom Pageant." His words had confused Rita, because she'd thought all pageants were like the Miss America contest, and she'd never seen any Asian participants on TV. This had been a different kind of beauty contest, Grandpa explained, one that was only for the Japanese immigrant community.

Back then Rita must have assumed her grandfather would live forever. He was like that old elm tree in their front yard: a bit gnarled, its branches twisting off in tormented directions, but perfectly solid, its bark so comforting to touch.

Until one day the tree had to be chopped down. Grandpa's heart attack seemed just as sudden and brutal.

His death left Rita panic-stricken, numb. Like she was lying in a tepid, murky bath and couldn't muster the energy to pull the plug if her life depended on it. How empty, how devoid of anything, the house now was, with just her and Lily. Listening to the crunchy-mushy sound of each other chewing, a yellow cereal-box wall between them.

Weightless. That was how she felt most of the time. With Grandpa gone, the sensation was more extreme than ever. He'd been her only connection to her father, and now he was gone, gone, *gone*. They were both gone, and nothing could ever change that.

Since there was no one to keep house anymore, with Lily in her debilitated state, the two boarders moved out quickly. And Tom had left a long time ago to live with his girlfriend.

So everything was going to fall to Rita. It didn't matter that she'd just graduated from high school and had her whole life ahead of her — "most likely to travel the world" written under her self-consciously vivacious smile in the yearbook. What did it matter? She wasn't going anywhere. She'd be forced to be the saintly one. Every Asian family had one: an unmarried daughter who got stuck at home caring for the ailing mother, fixing tea and doling out pills and massaging bunioned feet. Perhaps at first it would seem to be just a temporary situation — just keeping Mom company until she got back on her feet — except in Lily's case that was never going to happen. While Tom would be grateful at first, soon he'd take everything she was doing for granted, and since she'd never have time to get drunk and meet guys to dance the night away with, she'd never fall in love. The years would slip by, and before she knew it, she'd have gone from being the good daughter to just another lonely spinster, staying with her mother as much for her own sake.

So Rita rebelled. If Lily was a mess, Rita had to show everyone that she could become even more of a shit show. It wasn't something she planned, yet maybe there was a vague sort of premeditation in her attempt to out-Lily Lily, as she slithered into her tight, fringed miniskirt and brushed silvery soot over her eyelids, particles getting stuck on her trembling lashes such that she saw the world through a haze of stardust — more so, inhaling deeply, holding that first hit in her lungs for a moment frozen in time. And then she and her best friend, Eve, were out the door, their pulses thrumming, heading to Yonge Street to hear some group that Eve adored play at Friar's Tavern or Le Coq d'Or. The music sounded folksy but more upbeat than what Rita was used to, and she couldn't really get into it, woodenly bopping her head and hanging back from the stage. Things got easier after that guy who looked like Jesus bought them drinks and gave them a tiny white tab. Then something seemed to loosen or open up in Rita's body — distinct and actual enough to have its own colours and luminosity — and soon the music was whooshing through her heart, a magnificent sense of freedom taking over.

She didn't feel like she was looking at herself as she leaned toward the watery mirror at some guy's apartment later that night, tracing the feral shadows around her twin's eyes.

This other Rita, the bad daughter.

WHEN SHE GLANCED in the bathroom mirror the next morning, her skin appeared thin and weathered, splotched by sunspots and burst capillaries. Lily had always warned about the dangers of the sun and too much drink, but of course Rita hadn't paid any attention.

She resolved to be a better person, if only for Kristen's sake. Forgoing her morning cola, she walked to the mini-mart and bought a jar of instant coffee and a pale green banana that left behind the taste of wood chips.

Then she put on one of her better dresses, the navy blue one with white polka dots that she usually wore for teacher-parent interviews, and drove out to Don Mills. The streets were wide and empty, flanked by trees that were so healthy-looking they almost appeared fake, as though they'd been made out of plastic.

Mrs. Yamamoto's living room resembled one big crib. Knitted stuffed toys — puppies, kittens, elephants — crowded every surface in multiple pastel shades. They were perched atop the fireplace and the credenza and tucked around cushions on the cellophane-covered sofa. Rita had to extract a duckling wedged beneath her butt.

For the first twenty minutes, all Mrs. Yamamoto could talk about was her dog. A tiny blond poodle — a *real* poodle — which she was feeding cream wafers. "The vet tells me I shouldn't let Momo have people food, but I figure he's getting older — you only live once!"

Mrs. Yamamoto was getting older, too. Her white tresses looked vampiric, her skin like rice paper.

"So you were going to tell me about these *other* meetings Lily attended?" Rita began yet again, in as calm a voice as she could manage. Each time she circled back to the point of her visit, Mrs. Yamamoto seemed to miss the urgency of the situation, insisting that Rita have a cup of tea and choose a toy for Kristen.

"Other meetings?"

"Some meeting other than the Nisei Women's Club?"

Bony fingers touched the gold locket around her neck. "The house meetings. Oh, yes."

Rita bit into one of the butter tarts she'd brought; it exploded in a flaky mess, crumbs snowing all over the lime-green brocade of the armchair. She tried to clean it up, only making the pastry dandruff worse.

"It was at Mavis Okawara's this time."

"What do you do at these meetings?"

"Oh, you know. We drink tea and chat about this and that. The old days."

"The old days?"

"Well before your time."

"These meetings aren't part of the Nisei Women's Club?"

"Gosh, no. Men are allowed, too. Most of them are men — you know how men are about speaking up!"

"Speaking up about *what*, Mrs. Yamamoto?"

She pulled at a lint ball on her skirt, downturned eyelids like seashells. "An apology from the government. For what happened."

"You mean the internment?"

A slight bob.

"Lily was getting involved in *redress*? You can't be serious."

"I wouldn't say *involved*. She's just interested in learning more."

"Are you sure about that? My mother refused to talk about the internment — practically denied it even happened."

The Redress Movement would hardly be Lily's thing. Nor was it Rita's, to be honest. Occasionally, an article would show up on the back page of the paper, quoting the Minister of Multiculturalism, full of grand promises that never seemed to amount to jack shit. And she'd received a phone call from some organization with a fancy title, asking if she'd like to donate or volunteer. They were the activist set, intent on raising awareness about the injustice that had been committed. Good luck with that. Rita had given a bit of money simply in order to get off the phone — not that she didn't believe it was worthy and all; it just made her uncomfortable to throw money after a lost cause. Besides, what good could come of thinking of yourself as a victim? That had always been Grandpa's view, in any case.

"Things are changing, maybe," Mrs. Yamamoto murmured. She stared out the window at a massive maple, leaves lit up with blotches of sun. She didn't say anything for a long time, her thoughts receding to a time she didn't want to — or couldn't — explain. "Shikata ga nai. Why talk about something that can't be helped? That was how we all thought back then."

"But not anymore?"

Her lips twisted slightly. "Now, we just want to learn more. So we go to the house meetings, drink tea."

"What is it you're hoping to accomplish?"

"Well, for one thing, my son tells me it'd be nice to pay the mortgage off on this place."

Rita wiped her fingers as her impression of this frail, white-haired lady resolved like through the lens of a camera. If the government makes an apology, who knows how the money will get divided? That was what was going through these people's minds. Lily had the same steely, practical side to her; maybe it had something to do with having shopkeeper fathers. The prospect of compensation — and getting her fair share — now *that* might catch her mother's interest.

As if she could read Rita's thoughts, Mrs. Yamamoto buttoned up her cardigan and crossed her arms.

"Who organizes these house meetings?"

"The JCNA."

The organization that had called to ask for a donation. "What does that stand for again?"

"The Japanese Canadian National Alliance."

"How many of these meetings did my mother attend?"

"I saw her at a house meeting about a month ago. And when we chatted at the last Nisei Women's Club, Lily said she planned to come to the house meeting last week. She never made it, I guess."

"How did she seem to you at these meetings?"

"She just stood by the wall, listening. You know how it is. We don't want to stir up trouble. Maybe it's best to let sleeping dogs lie.

That's what my husband thinks, so he doesn't come. And maybe he's right" — her eyes dropped, but not before Rita had caught the flash of fear — "if this is what's happened to poor Lily!"

That old morass of paranoia. Rita laid a hand on Mrs. Yamamoto's arm, suddenly overcome by sympathy. "You think Lily's disappearance has something to do with the fact she went to a redress meeting?"

"The government keeps an eye on us all the time."

An uneasy chuckle died in Rita's throat. Yet folks like Mrs. Yamamoto had had relatives secreted away in the middle of the night, dragged off for interrogation, so maybe it wasn't so absurd that they'd forever be watching over their shoulders. They'd lived in those dusty camps no one talked about. No amount of compensation could change that fact.

"Who leads these meetings?"

"That professor." Mrs. Yamamoto looked tired. She brightened as the poodle jumped on her lap. "If you don't mind, Momo's due for his walk soon."

"What's this professor's name?"

"Mark Edo. I believe he works at U of T."

Momo must have sensed the hesitation in his mistress's voice; he began growling at Rita and nipping at her ankles. She grabbed her purse and jumped up to leave.

THROUGH THE GLASS wall of the phone booth, Rita watched a couple of teenage girls perched on the curb. They were passing a cigarette back and forth, holding it like a joint, a smoke swirl around their desultory expressions. She missed her students; she missed her regular life. She missed her mother. A lawn across the street was the most brilliant green — so bright it almost hurt to look at it — and it seemed all wrong that the patch could be so lush and alive while Lily was still out there missing.

Gerald sounded excited when he answered the phone. The note faded upon realizing it was only Rita. "So what did you find out from the Yamamoto woman?"

"Did my mother ever say anything about getting involved in redress?"

"Did she ever say what about getting a new dress?"

"*Redress.* The Redress Movement."

"What the heck's that?"

Just as she'd suspected. "Did Lily ever talk about being interned during the war?"

"Interned? What're you talking about?"

Rita explained how her mother's family had lost everything and been thrown in camps. She shared with him what little else she knew about the internment and Redress Movement. "Lily never told you anything about this, Gerald?"

Ruminative silence. "She mentioned that her dad had lost his shop during the war. She was mad as hell because it would've been worth a crap load of money now. But I had no idea she had to go live in a camp." A disgusted snort. "Well, that's the U.S. government for you. Ignorance is, ignorance does."

"It happened in Canada, too."

"Not surprising." It was clear from the frog in his throat that he found it very surprising indeed. Gerald was one of those guys who liked to go on about being a proud Canadian. "Well, what does any of this stuff have to do with Lily's disappearance?"

"Nothing, probably." She was just killing time, in some lame attempt to feel useful, because what else was she supposed to do? And yet, as Gerald prattled on, the conversation with Mrs. Yamamoto continued to replay in her mind.

DON MILLS CENTRE was dead. The few people there had arthritic hips and dandelion-ball hair and they pushed walkers. Rita carried her tray to a table in the corner of the food court. She squirted ketchup all over her fries until the whole thing looked like a bloodbath. Normally, she was more careful about what she ate, but what the hell. A bit of grease might revive her senses.

She opened the spiral notebook she'd just bought at Zellers and jotted down a bare-bones summary of her conversation with Mrs. Yamamoto. *Why would my mother get involved with redress?? Follow up with Mark Edo, prof at U of T,* she added. Officer Lee had told her to keep a log of all communications surrounding Lily's disappearance. He'd said it as though Rita's notes might actually be useful to the police investigation at some point, but she suspected he was just giving her something to do.

After she'd finished her cheeseburger, everything settling in her stomach like a cement block, she pulled out the list of people whom she was supposed to be getting in touch with. Most names had been crossed off, though a few remained. One name in particular weighed heavily on her heart now that she was surrounded by old folks.

Aunt Haruko.

It wasn't likely that Lily would have contacted her, but someone needed to call and check. Rita had been dragging her heels.

She couldn't remember much about the old lady beyond a few lone images. That tiny shrine inside her bedroom closet. The delicate crunch of tatami beneath bare feet. A small brass box emitting a stream of gritty, aromatic smoke that made Rita's throat tickle. Aunt Haruko chanting something, some magical incantation, in a soft, mysterious language that sounded nothing like English or Japanese. Rita recalled kneeling and closing her eyes as raindrops peppered her cheeks. When she had opened up, she was looking at a dripping wand. "You're a Kirishitan, now. Just like me and your bachan, ne?"

Rita had never met her grandmother, her bachan. The Hidden Christian thing had something to do with some religious sect that her grandmother and Aunt Haruko had belonged to back in Japan. Tiny white paper crosses would fall from the wide sleeves of her flowered housedress and flutter to the ground. Aunt Haruko stashed the crosses all over the house — under mattresses, at the backs of drawers, in the cookie jar. They honoured the many Christian martyrs who'd died in Japan over the centuries. One morning, Rita had stumbled upon a figurine of Christ on the cross tucked away behind some soup cans — she'd screamed, thinking it was a dead mouse.

That had been back when Aunt Haruko lived with them. Around the time of Rita's seventh birthday, Aunt Haruko had moved away. The Buddhist church was opening a Japanese nursing home for the issei widows and widowers. Some deceased patron of the church had bequeathed his property out in St. Catharines, where Yoneda Home would be established. They desperately needed people who spoke Japanese and could interpret for the old-timers. Aunt Haruko said it was God's will that she help out.

Her departure had upset Rita terribly. Who would teach her how to paint with watercolours now? And Aunt Haruko had promised that down the road she'd teach Rita sumi-e — Japanese brush painting — which was harder because it employed only black ink, diffused into so many shades of translucent shadow. Rita liked watching Aunt Haruko paint this way. Strange, unpopulated landscapes of light and dark. Bamboo shoots. The trunk of a cherry blossom tree, unpredictable in all its knots and curves. It was fun to try to guess what the picture was going to be. As it took shape in deft strokes, Rita felt still and calm inside.

As the years went by and they saw less and less of each other, Aunt Haruko faded into a ghost of another time.

There was something about watercolour that was like exploring a yearning, as though the wistful, translucent colours formed a mirage of something that Rita could barely remember, that she was struggling to hold on to. The back of her head against the old woman's sagging breasts an oddly reassuring feeling, like laying her head on a grassy mound. She wondered if Aunt Haruko had been happy in her life without them.

Nine

A face hovered above, familiar, yet strange. "How are you feeling, Lily?"

Numb and sluggish, lost beneath all these cumbersome layers of flesh. She thought of a collapsed horse that she and her father had passed on the side of the road once. Shapeless as a mound of dirt, left for dead by some farmer who'd given up on beating it back to life. She hadn't realized that the creature was still alive until its dull flank twitched. Through the rear window it vanished in the distance: a dark blotch, a pinprick, nothing.

A similar animal impulse stirred indistinctly, deep in her body. "How did I get here?"

"Kaz brought you. He found you behind one of the barracks. Who did this to you?"

The thick, woolly scent of sweat and desire. Head hitting the ground, body becoming weightless, as though she were sinking underwater. The voices dancing above her seemed to be getting louder and harsher, even as they were floating away.... And then it came back to her: Kaz hiding, immobile, in the background.

The thud of Kenny's feet, his voice thundering down. The stench of the dumpster, that guard's menacing, meaty hands, his endless moaning....

What would have happened if Kenny hadn't come along? Would Kaz have watched her be violated and left her for dead?

"What do you remember?"

"Nothing."

"Are you sure?"

"He was wearing a black mask. I couldn't see his face."

"Your underwear was torn."

"He didn't do anything. Kaz came to my rescue and the guy ran off." It came to her instinctively, as lies often did.

The doctor looked away, like he didn't really believe her.

Her cheeks grew hot at the thought of him examining her. Those bruises weren't from last night. Earlier that week, Kaz had her up against a barrack, in an area of the camp still under construction. The tarpaper wall had rubbed roughly against her backside as he'd thrust into her, and with each jolt, she'd felt herself dissolving into the dusky, vermilion-streaked sky.

"Someone else was hurt last night."

"Who?" She forced herself up.

"A guard named Aiden. Two attacks in one night. There must be a maniac on the loose."

"Was he hurt badly?"

"He's in a coma. We found him beaten — alive, just barely — behind one of the mess halls."

"Is he here now?" An inward shudder. *Please, no.*

"They took him to the hospital in town."

Relief washed over her, trills of that strange, neighing laughter.

The doctor was watching her closely. "There's going to be trouble now."

"Fights break out here all the time."

"This is more serious — he's a guard. He might die. There's

going to be a full investigation. If you know anything, Lily, you must come forward."

"I told you the man had on a mask."

"Kaz doesn't have anything to do with this, does he?"

She shook her head.

THE SMELL OF mothballs rose in her nostrils as she awakened. Peeling wallpaper, a faded rosebud print. If she wasn't in the hospital anymore, she must be dreaming. Being in a real bedroom — even in a dream — was a blissful prospect.

Stepping into the dim hallway, Lily paused in front of a framed black-and-white photograph. The woman's features appeared too large for her smallish face, giving her the look of an overgrown schoolgirl, her braided hair coiled around her head. Even as she smiled, her eyes seemed to glare at the camera, watchful, self-righteous. The man beside her resembled a better-groomed version of Kaz.

The doctor and his late wife.

With a rush, Lily realized she wasn't dreaming — she was in the doctor's very own house. He must have moved her here while she was sedated.

She tiptoed down the creaky stairs into the kitchen, her feet sticking to the linoleum. Sticky with too much lemon cleanser. Tears of homesickness filled her eyes.

The one real house in Matanzas. Leftover from another time.

A real bathroom, complete with a toilet that actually flushed. Such luxury, after months of being made to use the latrines, no partitions between the roughly made seats. The stench, the embarrassed, humiliated eyes.

A mirror loomed above the sink. A sallow, frightened face stared back at her, one cheek turning all the colours of the rainbow: plum red, putrid yellow, all backlit by a greenish tint. Tiny blackish scabs were sprinkled atop the cheekbone amid criss-crossing scrapes.

She staggered into the hall, where a dim silhouette confronted her. Was she dreaming after all? A white dress flowed down to the woman's ankles and her hair was coiled up around her head.

The woman in the photograph. *Kaz's dead mother.*

A scream erupted in Lily's throat.

The woman — the ghost — kept approaching. She touched Lily's arm, her hand inhumanly cool and dry. "What's the matter?"

"*You're — you're —*"

"My name is Haruko Uchida." A formal, stiff bow.

"Kaz's mother?"

"Heavens, no. I'm his aunt. My sister — God rest her soul — refused to leave Japan without me."

"Nice to meet you," Lily said shakily. "Uchida-san." She'd said she was Kaz's aunt, so maybe Obasan was the proper address.... Obasan, Aunt Haruko. She looked more like an Aunt Haruko. Metallic streaks in her braids made her look like an old woman though she couldn't be much older than the doctor.

"Your poor cheek. It hurts, ne? I've a cream for it, Lily-san." With her accent, she couldn't get her tongue around the *L*'s, so it came out more like "Riri-san." The name of a twin self, a demonic double.

THAT NIGHT, LILY dreamt she was back in the alley, crouched inside the dumpster, a massive rat scurrying overhead.

And then it jumped down on her. Its beady eyes glinted and its tiny fingernails rustled her hair, digging into her scalp.

The rat suddenly transformed into the guard — fat, florid cheeks sprouting whiskers. Fury surged into his face. Now he was on top of her, pulling up her skirt with his weirdly humanoid hands, the weight of his bristly belly thrusting into her, pinning her down.

She struggled to get away but couldn't move, so she simply pressed her cheek to the ground, stared at the moonlit litter.

And there was Kaz: just watching, smiling a little.

The rat let out a grunt, as a burning fluid shot into her. She screamed and woke up.

THE DOCTOR WAS right, there was an investigation. Two FBI agents came to his house. The younger one was thin and angular, his freckled skin covered in patches of heat rash. The older one smoked like a chimney and talked while barely moving his ashen lips. They insisted on speaking to Lily alone.

The doctor hovered in the doorway. What was he so worried about? Was it simply that he wanted to protect her from interrogation? Or was he concerned she'd incriminate Kaz?

Reluctantly, he left at last.

The men began asking her questions.

"A mask. He was wearing a black mask. I didn't see anything."

"What did this mask look like?" the younger agent pressed.

"A strip of black fabric tied around the guy's face. Eyeholes cut out."

"Colour of the eyes?"

"I don't know. Brown, maybe."

"What kind of eyes?" the older agent said.

"What do you mean?"

"Slanty, Oriental eyes?" His pudgy fingers stretched out his eyelids. "Or normal, like mine?"

His words hung in the air, bloated and ugly as his fingers.

Something was distracting her, messing up her vision: a moth must be responsible for that slip of shadow flitting about the corner of the room, and it was spreading its wings, speeding up, flapping manically, darkening the ceiling like a rain cloud. As she felt herself being pulled under its shadow, her body was losing all substance. She was a moth — she'd been reincarnated as a moth, just as her mother told her would happen one day. A rustle of wings, a plaintive susurration. A voice. The voice of the moth? Did moths have vocal cords? "Now look what you've done." "Dummy, why did you have to say anything about eyeholes?" These voices weren't gentle and moth-like, they were hard, mocking. If she said the guy had Caucasian eyes, they'd know he was one of the guards — who else could he be? And they'd bring all the guards into a room and force her to look each fellow in the eye, and when she couldn't bring herself to accuse anyone, they'd say she was crazy, that she'd never been attacked at all....

The moth had slipped away. She craned her neck, stared into the upper reaches.

Now the men were looking at her like she'd just said something important. She tried to remember the last thing that had come out of her mouth.

"We appreciate all you've been through, miss. You've done the right thing in coming forward."

But what had she given them? What had she said?

The moth swerved back, closer this time, and she grasped it in her hot palm.

IT SEEMED THAT her whole life had been reduced to a series of fading-to-black moments, contrasted with the reverse: zooming-to-light. Aunt Haruko was sponging her forehead. The doctor was spooning lumpy rice gruel into her lips. The floorboards creaked, the walls breathing their damp, cool shadows.

Her old life under Aunt Tetsuko's thumb had fallen away. Funny how that had happened. After all her griping about the inappropriateness of the doctor's attentions, the old cow was relieved to wash her hands of Lily. One less mouth to feed. No one from the family even came to visit.

Her tongue felt fat and furry, her thoughts equally sluggish. The bottom of the ocean beckoned with every breath.

Then one day, Lily caught sight of a dim apparition behind the doctor. Excitement made her bolt up. Kaz? At first, she thought she was seeing double, until the two faces separated, moved apart. The doctor receded through the doorway.

Kaz kept standing there, hanging back, as though he couldn't believe the evidence of her damaged face. "You have to believe me, Lily — I had no idea this would happen to you. Don't worry. They're just bruises and scrapes. They'll heal."

Turning on her side, she hid her bad cheek, unable to bear the weight of his stare any longer.

"If that monster wakes up, he'll wish he hadn't. We'll finish him off. Should've finished him off the first time!"

A hot coal glowered inside her as she observed Kaz behaving as if he were the one who'd saved her — he who'd simply stood there, like a schoolboy, frozen with fear. Did he think she'd been unconscious the whole time? Yet what should she do? Confront him? He seemed immersed in the little world of his own creation. Maybe he actually believed the lie.

Maybe, just maybe, she could believe it, too. She found herself letting her mind turn inward to envision another, more favourable scenario, one where it *was* Kaz who'd intervened to beat her attacker to a pulp. He could've — would've — wouldn't he? The heat of his passion, yes, she'd felt it before, and she could see it now, her imagination fleshing out the scene, adding key details — Kaz's cheeks awash in fury, the blur of his flying fists — and the more she thought about it, the more she found herself wrapping her mind around the delusion. How much easier her world became if she allowed herself, just for a moment, to believe in this subtly — beautifully — altered reality.

Then the fantasy faded. Panic and anger resurged, though now in muted form. Her head was full of static, like a radio gone berserk. "What if that guard wakes up, Kaz? What if he remembers everything?"

"He won't. And even if he does, he'll be a vegetable the rest of his life, in no condition to talk to anybody."

KAZ CAME TO visit the next day, too. Crouched down at her bedside, his breath a hot tickle against her ear, he told her that the FBI had been asking questions about Kenny. Somehow they'd gotten it in their heads that he might be the attacker. "I don't suppose you said anything that could point them in that direction?"

"I didn't tell them anything! I just said the guy had on a mask."

"So according to that story, it could've been Kenny."

"It could've been *anyone*." But how could she be sure of what she'd disclosed? That awful moth swerving overhead, pulling her under its trembling shadows....

"Maybe you should tell the G-men what really happened. To clear Kenny's name."

He wanted her to say … what? That a guard had attacked her? But would anyone believe her? And then they'd all be implicated in the scandal. "How would I explain that I sneaked out that night? And how … how would we account for that guard being beaten within an inch of his life?"

"Well. I don't know."

"Oh, I have an idea." She propped herself up. "I'll tell them that *you* beat the guy up. That's what happened, right, Kaz?"

"Well. Me and Kenny together."

The two of them together. He sounded so certain.

"So you and Kenny'll share the blame then?"

"I don't know, Lily." Anguish sharpened all his features.

THE THIRD TIME Kaz came to see her, something else was on his mind.

"Listen, Lily, I have to ask you for a favour. Things have gotten bad around here. There's been a crackdown. My photographs have been seized. Everything the police could get their hands on."

"What? Why now?"

"Remember those WRA photographers?"

She shook her head.

"Sure you do. Emily Archer?"

The woman with the deep, woolly laughter and sure-footed stride. That was how people walked when they were used to being listened to. She'd gotten her hooks into Kaz, poisoned his mind with dangerous thoughts.

"On Em's last visit, I showed her some recent photos. Not just sunsets and pretty girls." His eyes narrowed, like he was trying to peer through the slit of a keyhole. "*Real* pictures. Of the stuff *really* going on here. Em was fascinated by what she saw. All the violence and fear she hasn't been allowed access to."

"So?" After all she'd been through, Kaz wanted to talk about this other woman?

"Em thought my pictures ought to be seen, so people'll know what's actually going on. So I let her circulate some of my photos — keeping my identity secret, of course."

"You didn't, Kaz!"

"One of my pictures ended up on the cover of a magazine. A small, arty magazine, the kind no one cares about usually. But these days, the government *does* care. The image got traced back to me. Last night, the FBI found out where I've got my darkroom and confiscated everything. My camera, all my equipment."

"Oh my God."

A vein on his forehead was pulsing. As she watched it throb, like a river about to overflow, her own blood pounded. If it weren't for his father's position, he wouldn't still be here. Not by a long shot. Surely he realized how close he was to being hauled away to the real prison camp or worse.

His fear only seemed to embolden him though, an intoxicant to his nerves. His hands made a rattling noise and extended a small tin box. He looked at her hopefully, sheepishly. "This contains all the photos the G-men didn't get their hands on. The floorboards are loose under your bed. It's the perfect hiding spot. Give me the other pictures I've given you. We'll put them all together in this box and hide them. You've got to protect them for me."

Scraps of sunlight were playing on the far wall, dancing on the periphery of her vision. She thought of that picture of her strolling across the desert under the sun's caress. The very image Kaz had used to seduce her. Perhaps it was for the best it was going to be buried.

A spell of dizziness, as she stood up and let him push the bed aside. She found her little pouch of pictures. Without looking at any of them, she thrust the pile at Kaz.

Two floorboards popped up, revealing a small, dark cavern.

A vault. A coffin.

AFTER HER MOTHER had left them, whenever Lily used to feel sad as a child, one thing could lift her spirits. That blinding light. She first saw it one night after her father had gone out. Lily had been unable to sleep in the muggy weather, so she'd slipped out her bedroom window to the front lawn. A blazing white light was coming down the street, filling the sky with a bright aura, too painful to look at directly, but she didn't want to shield her eyes.

Her mother was coming home — she was sure of it. The light drew closer. Even after she'd returned to bed, she knew it was still out there, hovering and protecting her.

As time went by and it became clear her mother wasn't coming back, Lily found herself thinking back to that mysterious asteroid and the glow it had ignited inside her. For some reason, she remained convinced it had been her mother: the last hot surge of their connection. The light had stayed in her head all these years, flickering, gathering force whenever she felt sad and depleted, giving her the strength to carry on.

A DAB OF CREAM. Shock of wetness, followed by mild stinging. Aunt Haruko's knobby fingers were massaging in the lotion. If this was how a ghost's fingertips felt, Lily didn't mind at all. She might have become a little girl again. POND'S, read the label. She imagined herself slipping into a pond: the cool water rippling up over her skin, washing her hair, healing everything.

The old woman gave a solemn nod. "Genki?"

"Genki." Maybe just saying she felt better would make it true. "Have you seen Kaz?"

"I told you, Lily-san. He hasn't come today."

Despite everything, the afterburn of hope still lingered, softening his betrayal. That monstrous, beautiful face hovering above her, features occluded by shadows. *Maybe it had been Kaz. Not Kenny, but Kaz. Or both of them.* The mantra caught hold in her heart.

LATER THAT NIGHT as she lay in bed, shouting filled the house. She finally got up. Peeking down the staircase into the shadows, she couldn't see much of anything, yet Kaz's voice was unmistakable.

"This is outrageous — what did Kenny do? They don't have any proof. There's been no investigation. They just went ahead and arrested him!"

"It doesn't matter," the doctor said. "He's a troublemaker, one way or another."

"You really don't care? None of this strikes you as the least bit unjust?"

Lily ventured down. "What's happened to Kenny?"

"The police have arrested him, dragged him off to prison! They're saying he's the madman responsible for both attacks. *What did you tell them?*"

"Nothing." The word sliced through the air.

"See? All the police have to go on is what Frank Isaka told them. He has no problem pointing fingers. And the police just take his word!"

"Let them run their investigation and *you stay out of it,*" the doctor said. "The less you have to do with Kenny Honda, the better."

"Oh, no." Kaz backed away.

She searched for some hint of tenderness, submerged affection. All she saw was cold disdain. Kaz wanted her to do what? Come forward? But the moment for that had long passed, and would the FBI believe anything she had to say, anyway?

Guilt stretched across her chest, an image of Kenny's irreverent grin lighting up the far reaches of her conscience. If it hadn't been for that second set of feet pounding toward her, that guard would have had a lot of fun. No doubt, she was indebted to someone. But whose feet had they been? As she reached back through the tunnels of her memory, it was Kaz's face she now saw looming above her — fierce as a warrior, backlit by moonlight, his eyes incandescent. It *had* been him, hadn't it? Kenny had been there doing his part, but so had Kaz. That horrible moaning from the lumpish body on the ground as though the earth itself were trying to offer up some doleful apology. If Kenny was destined to take the fall for both of them, why shouldn't he? Why should they both go down? Was it so wrong of her to be thinking this way? She had to protect Kaz from himself, from his own excessive loyalty. It was what the doctor expected of her. After all the doctor had done for her, she owed him that much, didn't she?

The door slammed with a crack, like a gunshot. She felt herself flinch, stiffen. Kaz hadn't even bothered to look at her on his way out.

Ten

How strange that Chinese people all lived together in Chinatown, Rita used to think. Walking along Elizabeth Street, her hand clasped in Grandpa's, a hush came over her: red lanterns glowed in restaurant windows, dragon-head kites flew in doorways, and the air was rich with fragrant, meaty odours pouring out of Sai Woo and Kwong Chow. None of the kids stared at her or made faces; they just assumed she was one of them.

But Japanese people didn't have their own neighbourhood; they hadn't since the war, according to Grandpa. A long time ago, he'd had his own medical practice in Little Tokyo, but that had been on the other side of the world in some big American city. Now it was all just a bunch of rat-infested warehouses.

This had been a problem when it came time for him to set up his new practice. A Japanese doctor needed Japanese patients. For the longest time he'd worked as Dr. Chong's assistant while studying to take the medical exam that would allow him to practise in Ontario. He wasn't as sharp as he'd once been, Rita suspected. The new procedures and regulations seemed to baffle him as he sat at the dining-room table, night after night, barricaded by textbooks under the watery green glow of the banker's lamp that Lily had salvaged from a church sale.

The prospect of Grandpa becoming a real doctor again was balm to her senses. She loved talking about how he was a great man, a real pioneer, one of the first Japanese doctors in North America. He'd left Japan when he was only fourteen and had five yen in his pocket. God didn't make men like him anymore, Lily would say, by which she meant that Kaz had been a sorry-ass failure.

When Grandpa finally passed the exam, she was ecstatic. At last they could set up his office on the first floor. "A real doctor's office," she kept saying. Lily got all dressed up and they took the streetcar to a used furniture store, where they chose some upholstered chairs and a heavy metal desk. The next day when the furniture arrived, a manic energy came over her and she dragged everything around, trying out different configurations for the waiting room. Finally satisfied, she sat down and crossed her arms with a small, whimsical smile.

Day after day, the room remained empty. Nevertheless Lily continued to sit at the receptionist's desk, long after her face had lost its dreamy quality and frozen over into dogged optimism. After school Rita would find her mother still sitting there while Grandpa stayed in the backroom off the kitchen, his so-called office.

His face lit up as Rita came in, and sometimes he'd pretend that she was his patient. He slipped the stethoscope into her ears so she could listen to that strange thrum inside herself. Then he patted her head or hugged her fiercely before telling her to go do her homework. Once or twice she glimpsed tears in his eyes.

A few months later, he removed the sign from the front door and went back to Dr. Chong's office. Yet the clunky receptionist's desk remained front and centre in the hall for years, in the way, crowding everything.

ALTHOUGH THEY LOOKED more like adults than the brood Rita was used to, they still had that hapless, bewildered air of adolescence. They were crouched down, sprawled out in plaid pyjama pants, or perched atop lumpy backpacks, reminiscent of homeless people.

"D'you get what Turner means by 'betwixt and between'?" a girl with candy-apple hair asked another girl, whose shaved head made her look monk-like. They both munched loudly on chips.

"It's all about thresholds. Bad things happen when you go from one state to another. Life to death, you know, crap like that. It's gonna be multiple choice, anyway."

The smell of mildewed carpet mixed with sour cream and onions was making Rita queasy. But lining up for office hours seemed the fastest way to get face time with Dr. Mark Edo. It turned out that he was a professor in the Department of Archaeology, a rundown Edwardian building at the edge of U of T's campus, barely distinguishable from the frat houses nearby. When she'd called, his phone went to voice mail. So here she was, camped out with everyone else.

The door opened, as a thin kid with a sage-like beard stepped out. The voice inside the office kept right on rattling off titles. "Yup, I'll add it to the orals list," the kid repeated, dazed. Rita had never heard of these authors. Clifford Geertz? Someone who'd written about the savage mind — whatever that meant. Clamminess nipped at her armpits.

"Next."

A jam-packed bookshelf and an Amnesty International poster greeted her. Several masks hung on the wall opposite. Woven out of red, white, and black straw, they appeared to represent some demonic animal with a long snout and tiny, catlike ears.

"They're used by indigenous groups in Panama to establish connections with animal spirits."

"You're not freaked out having them stare at you all day?"

"Naw, scares the kids." A light chuckle.

The guy behind the desk was younger than Rita had expected. More surprising was the fact that Dr. Edo didn't look Japanese at all.

His nose was a bit flatter than a hakujin's normally would be but, that aside, this guy could be a mountain climber or modern-day shepherd. Pale brown hair, longish, scruffy. Stubble all over his chin. Late twenties, early thirties? In an attempt to look a bit more professorial, he'd thrown a linen blazer over his cycling jersey, which, if he were to stand up, would probably reveal nice stomach muscles.

"I'm Rita Takemitsu." She sat down across from him, flustered.

"You're in which of my classes?"

"I'm not in your class. We've never met before." Didn't she look a bit old to be one of his students? She wasn't sure whether to be flattered or insulted to be grouped with the squatters outside.

"Gave up trying to remember names and faces a long time ago. So what brings you by, Rita?"

"I hear you've been pretty active on the redress scene."

"Oh, yeah. My other job. As if teaching a full load isn't enough." He rubbed his eyes, laughing grimly, as though he couldn't figure out what had possessed him. "Yeah, I've sunk my teeth into the whole redress thing. Why? Are you interested in getting involved? Because we need people, big time."

"It's more of a personal matter."

He looked slightly rebuffed.

"My mother" — she passed him a flyer — "I think you may have met her?" But if he couldn't remember his students, what were the chances he'd recall Lily?

"What? Lily's gone missing?"

Rita began talking, stumbling over her own fragmented thoughts. The whole thing sounded so crazy she had to keep reminding herself that this was real — this was the reality of her life right now. *Her mother was missing. Hurt, maybe. Or worse.* Panic filled her throat. All the problems in their relationship suddenly seemed so petty. Hot pressure gathered behind her eyeballs. If Lily could just be found, Rita resolved to let go of all those old resentments, turn over a new leaf.

"Is there anything I can do to help?"

For a heaving second she didn't trust herself to speak. "I was hoping you could tell me about my mother's involvement in redress, Dr. Edo."

"Mark. Call me Mark. Everyone does." He extended a box of tissues.

"Fine, then. Mark." She blew her nose with embarrassing loudness.

"Well, what do you want to know?"

"Did Lily strike you as the type who'd get involved?"

Mark leaned back and blew air through his cheeks, which expanded like balloons stretched to their limit. "I don't know what to tell you. There isn't really one type of person who starts cheerleading for redress. To be honest I don't remember much about Lily, beyond the fact that she was kind of glamorously dressed. I think she just came to a couple of the house meetings and stood at the back, silent."

"Yeah, sounds like her. She was probably uncomfortable being there at all."

"A lot of folks are at first, particularly the older generation. They're scared out of their wits to come to public meetings, worried that if they talk about the past, they'll end up provoking discrimination, like in the old days. That's why the JCNA started holding meetings at people's houses over tea and snacks. Make it more like a social visit."

A social visit. Seriously? These redress types were naive as a bunch of kids running for student council. "You really think a cup of tea'll change anything?"

"We're still in the early days — I'm not expecting the government to cut us a cheque tomorrow. That said, we *are* making progress. Do you know that when they rounded everyone up and carted them off, the government called them 'evacuees'? Like we were being evacuated for our own good to save us from a flood, for fuck's sake. It was systematic *imprisonment*, Rita."

His words touched some place deep within her body where she didn't want to be touched at all — some old fracture that had never healed properly and still tingled and ached. How did he find it so easy to talk about this stuff? Maybe it was because he was only half, or a quarter. He didn't know what it was like to be a true outsider.

"Do you actually remember camp, Mark?"

"Naw. I was born a couple years after my dad got released. So growing up, what did I know? It was like the place never existed. Occasionally, someone on my dad's side of the family would mention the bad old days, but I had no clue what 'camp' meant, not really. I thought it was some place naughty kids got sent as punishment, like reform school, you know?"

He held her gaze for longer than felt comfortable. And now he expected her to open up, too. Her shoulders had clenched into rocks.

"So what's next on the redress agenda?" she said, after a stiff silence.

"We have several projects in the works. Some of the older folks who remember being interned are putting together a book that'll document their memories. The JCNA is going to publish it and get it into the hands of the media and government leaders. Ted Fujita's heading up this initiative."

"Ted Fujita?" She straightened up.

"He's a prominent retired businessman."

"I know who Ted Fujita is. My mother used to date him."

Lily's scrawled notes, tucked inside *Glamour*: *plums, meringues, Ted F., Folgers, pork chops, Ted F., 3:00 Fri.*

"I think she'd started seeing him again, maybe. Not *seeing him*, seeing him."

"They're friends, you mean?" Mark asked.

"Yeah, I guess." Like Lily could ever relate to men purely as friends.

Perhaps they'd run into each other at one of the house meetings and decided to catch up over a drink. Rita couldn't imagine they'd have much to talk about — not after the way things had ended. She wasn't sure how the whole thing had played out, but it seemed that Lily's penchant for bragging about how well the Fujita clan had done financially had ruffled a few feathers. Mr. Fujita's kids had staged a kind of family intervention; maybe they'd passed a conch around in a circle, each taking a turn to catalogue Lily's faults. In any case, their message had been clear: don't walk down any aisles, Dad, not without signing an airtight pre-nup, and keep the silverware under lock. A couple of weeks later, Mr. Fujita had unceremoniously dumped her.

"I can give you Ted's number, if that helps any."

Calling the guy out of the blue would be awkward, to say the least. "Sure. Thanks."

Mark flipped through his Rolodex. "You know, we're having another house meeting Thursday evening. Let me give you the address. There'll be lots of people there you can ask about Lily. Maybe someone knows something useful."

Glancing at the slip of paper, she was startled to see that he'd included his own number, too.

"Or call me if you just want to talk."

A blast of warmth she didn't want to be feeling hit her stomach. But he was probably just being nice because he was that kind of guy. He seemed like one of those tree-hugger, do-gooder types, like the protest leaders she'd known back in her hippie days, so eager to get all worked up and stage a sit-in about anything. That was the last thing she needed right now. Her days of tie-dyed T-shirts and grubby bare feet were long behind her.

NOTHING ABOUT LOU'S office had changed much. It was your basic vanilla doctor's office at Bay and Gerrard. He'd tried to make it a bit homier by laying out a few knick-knacks: a jade Buddha, a rubbery-looking plant, an embroidered scarf stretched out over the radiator. There was a bookshelf crammed with the usual suspects — Freud, Jung, cognitive behavioural readers — but also some surprisingly avant-garde tastes, like Proust and Colette. Rita wondered if he had a soft spot for Paris and the louche underworld.

Lou, Dr. Louis. His chocolatey eyes fastened on her with warmth and curiosity, yet always with that familiar remove, that air of aloofness. She felt sheepish coming back to him after they hadn't seen each other for so long. It was like being in one of those interminable friends-with-benefits things, where the door was always left open a crack, no matter how awkwardly the last tryst had ended.

Whatever the case, here she was, stretched out on his worn leather sofa. The meandering crack across the ceiling looked like a hair on the bathroom floor. As if this whole bizarre day had never happened. She could be standing in her bathroom, fresh out of the shower and snapping in her contact lenses.

When Rita had gotten up that morning, she would never in a million years have believed that Lily could be involved in redress. Now, she wasn't so sure. Lily's sad, searching expression the last time they'd seen each other, her need for confirmation that they'd had a decent life, despite everything. It made more sense in light of the internment being on her mind. What other vestiges of the past had forced their way to the surface?

Rita wanted to run her palms over Lou's bald head, trace the contours of his brain, as though the answers to the riddles of her life lay within. They certainly weren't coming from her. Not today, that was for sure. Come to think of it, though, Rita didn't feel he was pulling his weight either. All in all, the session was going nowhere fast. At the beginning, she'd tried to talk to him about Lily's disappearance, but Lou had no helpful suggestions, or even words of comfort. Rita wanted practical advice that would enable her to find her mother while Lou, as usual, was more interested in yakking about what had made their relationship sour in the first place. Then she found herself getting side-tracked, distracted by stupid, petty stuff. A good deal of the session had been wasted on all her bitching and moaning about how she dreaded that Kristen would fall in love with Jodi, come home gushing about how they'd gone watersliding and done tons of cool stuff together. Lou seemed to think that this suggested Rita had insecurities about her ability to be a good mother and it all came back to her own warped relationship with Lily. Christ. It was like he was deliberately goading her today, trying to get under her skin. If Lou weren't Lou, like hell would she pay money to take this abuse. Then they'd somehow moved on to the topic of Tom, who loomed in Rita's mind, his catch-you-later smile lit up like a hologram. Her brother was a recurring source of irritation she circled back to. How tedious and repetitive Lou must find her rants.

Then again, he had it coming. At the start of their session, he'd said, "Just think out loud. Anything at all that comes to mind."

So there it was: her mental diarrhea.

"If I've understood you correctly," Lou said, sitting back, his fingers interlocked in a teepee, "you resent Tom for treating you like his kid sister who doesn't remember anything about that whole period when you were young. At the same time you're resentful that Tom *does* have more insight into that time." He looked at her for confirmation.

That was what she'd been going on about? Okay, maybe.

"How do you feel when he withholds that information from you?"

"How do you think it makes me feel?" She'd forgotten how therapy made you spit out the most obvious answers, like you were in grade school again. "It makes me feel like *crap*. Like he holds all the cards."

"So you're playing a game? Where one person wins and the other loses?"

Now they were chasing metaphors. "Kind of. But not just your average game. Tom was never into cards."

"Keep going, Rita. What kind of game, then?"

"One Tom invented. One where he made up all the rules. The night stalkers."

It wasn't the first time she'd mentioned this game. If she ever found out Kristen were engaged in anything so twisted, she'd be livid. Kristen was lucky to be an only child. No one would pull her into a dark, cramped closet that smelled of the mildewy depths of the earth, her wrists bound so tightly that her palms had turned tingly, a gorilla-like hand clamped over her mouth until the edges of her consciousness seemed to be fraying, unravelling.... "The night stalkers are here to get you," Tom would whisper, and she could see — thanks to the crack of light that danced over his face — how much he enjoyed her terror. Almost as much as he enjoyed being the one to alleviate it. Just when she thought her lungs would explode, the door burst open, light flooded in, and Tom switched over to his other role. Her big brother, her hero, here to save her from the night stalkers.

Surely, Lou didn't want to hear it all again. On the other hand, maybe he didn't even remember. How many patients did he have, all inundating him with their sob stories?

"I wonder, Rita. You've talked before about how your brother could be mean to you."

"I'm sure the whole experience was character building."

"Character building how?"

"Oh, I don't know." There wasn't enough food in her stomach to sop up all its corrosive acids. "Let's just say I could see where he was coming from."

"How do you mean?"

"Tom was jealous of me, and he had every right to be jealous. Let's face it — *I* was the favoured child. The *good* child. At least, that was the case for as long as Grandpa was alive. As long as I had him, I could keep my shit together."

"You were always your grandfather's favourite? What makes you feel that way?"

"He took an interest in me. Helped me with my homework. If I got sick, Grandpa made me soup. He taught me how to play chess and cards."

Lou's eyes flicked from her to the paperweight on his desk — an insect fossil with willowy legs — and then back again. His nostrils flared like tiny parachutes. It was how he always looked when he was on the verge of some insight, some aha! moment in the puzzle of her life. Although she rarely remembered his radiant conclusions, the thrill of just watching him get so excited made the whole exercise feel oddly worthwhile.

"What makes you think your grandfather never took an interest in Tom?"

"It was different with him."

"Different how?"

"Just *different*, Lou. Because he was a boy, I guess. Tom must've reminded Grandpa of Kaz." The words sprang from her lips, leaving her drained.

When Grandpa had died, there'd been a will, a lawyer. There must have been a reading of the will, which Rita hadn't attended because why should she? She hadn't expected him to leave her anything. And by that point Rita was caught up in the hallucinogenic world of musicians and poets and lovers and the great, overflowing world spirit she'd flung herself into. She couldn't remember how the lawyer had tracked her down. He was a balding guy with yellowed teeth, sharp and crooked. They glinted as he spoke, and his words somehow seemed intrinsically tied to those pointy incisors. *Money.* He said the word in practically every sentence. It turned out that Grandpa had left her a nice bundle. Nineteen grand. The news left her winded. It was more than anyone would have guessed the old man had socked away for a rainy day.

While Lily inherited the house, Rita had been given a nest egg that would put her through art school and pay for quite a few lifestyle excesses along the way.

But Grandpa hadn't left Tom anything.

So maybe it all came down to money, in the end. For whatever reason, Grandpa had loved her more than Tom and attached to that love a very generous cheque that left her forever confused, guilt-ridden.

Lou looked up from his notes. "I'd like to explore this issue further next time."

ALTHOUGH THE CAFÉ was closed for the night, lights were still on. Rita could see through the glass door a large shambling man wiping down the counter. He looked up and saluted before letting her in. Yesterday she'd heard locals joking around with him, calling him Patrón, and she'd wanted to say something friendly as well, though nothing came to her. Today they just smiled at each other while she chose an almond croissant and he fixed her a cup of decaf.

Wending her way into the market, she walked past the vintage clothes shops full of gold lamé dresses and beat-up jeans, past the ethnic curio shops with African masks and beaded headdresses hanging in the windows. She speed-walked down Baldwin. A couple of punks were dumpster diving in the twilight, *NIL* spray-painted in fluorescent green on their leather jackets. She breathed deeply, inhaling the rotting vegetables mixed with cigarette smoke and other earthier, more potent odours, hoping to catch a second-hand high that would provide a moment's respite from her life.

A wild-looking creature was roller skating down the street. She was dressed unseasonably warmly in a matted fur coat that seemed to continue into her tangled blond dreadlocks, bits of fluorescent pink wool woven throughout. She spun around on unsteady, pelican-thin legs. Delicate moons of soot rimmed her eyes, pancake makeup seeped into her wrinkles, giving her skin the look of melting wax, but also a strange, sad beauty. For the past twenty years, she'd been here partying and, though oblivious to the passage of time, time had left its marks all over her body.

She skated over, waggled a half-smoked cigarette butt.

"Can you help me?" Her voice breathy. She snapped her fingers mimicking the flick of a lighter.

"I'm sorry, I don't smoke anymore."

The woman rolled closer, the rot of her breath covered by cinnamon gum. She seemed to think she belonged somewhere else — somewhere much grander, with red carpets and flashing cameras — and was sadly confused to find herself on this dingy street. That glint of hard-edged disappointment mixed with indignation and lost dreams. There could be no reasoning with that look, Rita knew all too well from experience.

Eleven

Fatigue descended, and cold seeped into her body. Veils of clamminess spread down her legs and arms, wrapping around each finger and toe.

It was those pictures stashed under her bed. Sad, wraithlike faces. Smudged apparitions of lives that could have been. Lily wanted to stare them down — strip them of their haunting power. Rip them to tatters and set them free on the wind.

But what was the point of tormenting herself? She thought of Urashima having returned to the land of the living with the three boxes the sea princess had given him. Wouldn't he have been better off if he'd never opened them up? What good could come of knowing you'd fallen out of time, your whole life seized away from you?

Aunt Haruko came in. "Another bad dream, ne?"

Must have been crying out again in her sleep. When she closed her eyes, there was only a blackness beyond all blackness, without a trace of dream residue. Lily shook her head.

"Mou daijobu." You're all right now.

The soft, melodic syllables soothed her senses and she might have become a child again, pressed against her mother's bulky lap.

Upon opening her eyes, though, she didn't feel all right. Her hands were boiling, then freezing. An army of aches was attacking her tender right breast. She wasn't even sure where she was right now, beyond a vague sense that she wasn't where she was supposed to be. This wasn't her childhood bedroom. This woman she called Aunt Haruko wasn't her real aunt.

Lily suspected she'd been overheard retching the other morning. Outside the bathroom, Aunt Haruko turned away abruptly, as though something had upset her. Lily felt confused. It was no secret that the food from the mess hall often made her sick.

"Here." The speckled hand extended a glass of powdered milk.

As the chalky fluid hit the back of Lily's throat, a surge of sour sweetness came back up.

She had to find Kaz. She hadn't seen him since the night he'd stormed off, the night of Kenny's arrest. A mutiny of voices: she could hear them whispering, tittering away, condemning her for being such a coward, Daddy's little girl. She could have helped Kenny, but instead she'd remained silent, just as she'd always kept silent about her father. And now it was too late.

The scabs were falling off, leaving droplets of newborn skin; her bruises had faded to a pale green-yellow aura. If she waited too long, all traces would vanish, her last hope of winning Kaz's sympathy, forgiveness.

A tangle of shoots and flowers spread out on the kitchen table. The delicate, butter-yellow petals splayed back acrobatically, their last triumphant stretch before slackening. Sturdy, leafy stalks curved gracefully. A lush coral flower, paler at the centre. When she was little, they'd called it the drunken-lady flower, because it was white upon first blooming, but pinkened in the final euphoria of its beauty.

And after that there was nothing but death.

Running her fingertips along the kenzan, she thought of falling back — just letting her body go limp and falling upon the bed of upturned needles.

The doctor had left all these materials out for her in hopes that a little activity would help revive her.

Snip, snip, went the steel clippers. Caress of a waxy green skin. Sculpting it, the way she used to sculpt her hair in the morning. Her style had become looser, improvisational — no longer did she care about controlling the height and shape of each branch and leaf. These traditional principles fell from her mind, and now she randomly stuck flowers in, here and there, a riot of colour. A peculiar queasiness, like motion sickness, grabbed at her chest as her fingertips traced the wobbly bright blotches.

And then the doctor was standing behind her. So it was evening already. The colours deepened, drowned in shadow.

She pushed her arrangement off to the side, hoping he wouldn't be offended by her ugly creation. But the doctor had other things on his mind.

"I don't suppose Kaz's come to see you?"

She shook her head and the yellow streak jumped out at her.

"He's been sucked into the secret meetings, I'm sure of it. Have you heard?"

How could she have heard about anything?

Yellow flowers symbolized something wishful, uncertain. They said, *Take my love — won't you please take my love?* Hopeless desires and memories of lost times.

Secret meetings. The doctor was saying things she didn't want to hear. It seemed people had gathered today behind Kenny's mess hall. The same thing had happened yesterday or the day before, or maybe he'd been talking about this for several days now; her capacity for processing such news had reached its saturation point.

"Not just members of the Kitchen Workers Union — now it's also regular folks. Issei and nisei alike."

"Why do they meet?"

"People have been gathering *for days*, Lily. Haven't you been listening? Ever since Kenny was arrested. Each afternoon they scheme about how to bring about his return to camp. Now the crowd's gotten so large the meetings might have to move to the firebreak."

She toyed with an uncut branch that resembled a broken antler.

"You know what else I've heard? The meetings are conducted entirely in Japanese, so the camp supervisors are kept in the dark. They try to break it up, but people keep right on talking."

It was her fault. Her fault that Kenny had been taken away. Because of something she'd said. The FBI agent had stretched his eyelids into thin slits, like buttonholes sewn out of flesh. It had given her quite a fright, that face he'd made, so she'd nodded just to get him to stop. Yes, she'd nodded, she could remember that part now: she'd confirmed his suspicion that her attacker had Oriental eyes. Oh, why had she done that? Why was it always so much easier just to tell people what they wanted to hear? If only she could take it back.

Surely, that wouldn't have been enough for them to arrest Kenny.

"But he didn't. Didn't attack me."

The doctor acted as though she hadn't said anything. Maybe she hadn't.

"Kenny didn't attack me!"

"Not another word about Kenny Honda. You stay out of it, Lily. You hear me?" It was the same cold expression he'd had when saving that poor girl's baby. Bringing life into the world, saving lives, knowing when to pull the plug. When to pluck out a diseased apple. Getting blood on his hands didn't bother the doctor at all.

"What did you tell the FBI? He didn't attack me. It wasn't Kenny!"

"How can you be so sure, Lily? The man was wearing a mask, you said it yourself. Besides, Kenny's a troublemaker. He'd have been arrested one way or another, in the end."

"I *know* it wasn't Kenny. What did you tell them?" Tears stung her eyes.

"They asked for my opinion and I gave it to them. Based on what I know."

That included everything she'd told him on those hot afternoons at the hospital.

More than once, in recent days, she'd seen Frank Isaka sitting at the kitchen table, sipping tea, talking with the doctor softly. Their heads, bent together, formed a dark tent. When Lily hurried past to fetch a cup of water, Frank looked up, his gaze lit with interest. For a second it looked like he wanted to say something to her, but she quickly turned away.

COLD, DRY AIR slapped her skin. A fine white patina on the ground reflected the sun, dust indistinguishable from frost.

How many days had she been tucked away, convalescing? Time itself felt unstable, as though she'd awoken from a coma and couldn't ascertain where the threshold of reality began. The place seemed different now; the front of chilly air had energized people, jolted them out of complacency. They were walking around in small, tight-knit groups, shoulders hunched up under bulky coats, speaking in hushed tones, eyes brimming with secrecy and suspicion. Why were there so many aimlessly wandering around in the middle of a workday anyway?

In front of the net factory, a crowd had gathered. Shig and Akira were setting up signs. They glanced up at Lily and then chose to ignore her. She noticed Kaoru at the edge of the group.

"Where's Kaz?"

"He was here earlier," Kaoru said. "He must've gone to one of the other protest sites."

"What's going on?"

"Didn't you hear? No one's working today. Everyone's up in arms — taking to the streets!"

"Free Kenny Honda, Hero of Our People," read one sign. "Fair Wages for Your Kitchen Workers!" announced another.

"Rumour has it that guard died last night at the hospital, Lily."

"*What?*"

Then a terrible relief swept over her: if he were dead, at least that meant he'd never wake up.

"Yup, you heard me. So everything's getting pinned on poor Kenny! But everybody knows he hasn't done anything. The camp bosses just want him out of the way because he's been pointing fingers, raising a ruckus."

"But the police," Lily said weakly. "The police won't tolerate this."

"What police? Our evacuee police force? Those boys are in the same boat as us and some of them are getting pretty sick of it, too. And the FBI? Well, they'll have their hands full if they try to arrest *all* of us."

When the shit hits the fan, everyone'll stand behind us. That was the whole point of the Kitchen Workers Union, as Kenny had said from the get-go. It almost made her laugh. After all his moaning and railing about how they needed to think bigger, all he had to do was get arrested. In his absence, all Kenny's plans were playing out beautifully. It couldn't have been going better if he were here in the flesh, running around, barking orders. As their martyred leader, he'd turned himself into the heroic cause that could win people's hearts and anchor the movement.

But at what price? Was he going to be blamed for beating that guard to death? Had he? Or had it been Kaz? Their faces blurred together like a ruined photograph in the cavern of her memory.

"Why don't you join us, Lily? That would send a strong message."

"I'm not feeling well. I need to lie down."

In the middle of the circle, Shig had made a bonfire in a garbage can. A gust of ashes blew in her face. She got jostled aside as the crowd gathered around, chanting and shaking their fists.

CROSSING CAMP, SHE couldn't believe her eyes. Garbage cans were burning, full of odds and ends of homemade furniture pillaged from the barracks. Bright yellow signs, bearing the words INU or

TRAITOR, were tacked to certain doors. Guys in black masks —
brandishing baseball bats — darted from door to door, shouting
obscenities in Japanese. A new spirit of wildness and something
frighteningly close to festivity infused the air.

Her story about the man in the black mask must have caught
hold in someone's imagination….

The door of their old barrack had been removed from its hinges.
No one was there. Aunt Tetsuko and her brood must have fled,
salvaging as many of their possessions as possible.

Wind cut against Lily's cheeks. She was walking — no, she was
running — but had no idea where she was going; she just kept moving in circles. No place was safe now, not even the doctor's house.

A STAGE HAD been set up outside. A banner that read JACC
CALL FOR CALM fluttered overtop. A crowd had gathered around.
As Lily moved closer, Frank Isaka ascended to the podium. He
glanced nervously at Ed Howells, the camp director, who stood
on stage beside him.

"Ladies and gentlemen," Frank said, "we're a law-abiding, patriotic people. How can it be that a few troublemakers have managed to
seize control of our camp? I beseech you to think twice before you join
the bad apples in their campaign of anarchy! Don't bring shame to our
entire community by forcing Mr. Howells to call in military assistance, as he'll be forced to do if this outrageous behaviour doesn't stop!"

Frank launched into his usual monologue about the grand history of the Japanese-American people — struggling to overcome
prejudice, but always in a peaceful manner, and if necessary, quick to
turn the other cheek. But where his rhetoric had once brought tears to
old ladies' eyes, a current of jeers and hisses now rose from the masses.

"What have you done for us, you Jackrabbit!"

"You're all just out for yourselves."

"I'd take the Black Dragons over the Jackalopes any day!"

The taunts grew louder, drowning out Frank's voice. He raised his hands, but no one paid any attention and someone yelled out, "Who do you think you are? The Messiah himself?" followed by much laughter. A tremor passed through the crowd, like the first quivers of an earthquake, and Lily backed away to extricate herself from the upsurge.

"That girl, the one who's walking away." Frank pointed, looking at her like they shared a special bond. "The girl with the bruised cheek. Lily. I've heard all about your story."

She froze, speechless.

"Poor Lily," Frank continued, "is evidence of the destructive force overrunning our community. Did everyone hear about how she was attacked?"

"Come up on stage so everyone can see you," Mr. Howells said through his loudspeaker.

Terrified, she didn't budge an inch.

The camp director kept gesturing and someone pushed her forward so she was forced to go up.

How startlingly different it was to be on stage now. What had happened to the sweet rush of all those upturned faces as she'd sauntered across the stage in her rented kimono? How foolish and faraway those girlish dreams seemed from here. She captured their attention for other reasons now. Her battered face had transformed her into a symbol for the entire community: vulnerable, caught off guard, beaten, stupid. That was why the sympathy in people's eyes quickly switched over into wariness and self-loathing.

And then, she glimpsed Kaz. He was smiling at her, a broad, beaming smile, proud to see her up there, perhaps. That smile breathed new energy into her body and her head began to clear.

Frank put a hand on her arm while extolling her bravery in the face of anarchy, but she hardly even heard what he was saying. *Kaz was smiling at her.* In an instant, the light from his eyes seemed to diffuse into the eyes of everyone around him — transforming the crowd into adoring admirers. How desperately she wanted him to come closer, put his arms around her, bury his face in her hair forever. Everything was wavering and trembling through the sheen of her tears, and she might have been on the verge of fainting from pure happiness: the world felt so different under the warmth of Kaz's darkly shimmering eyes.

"THAT WAS BRILLIANT," he said, later that day. They were standing outside the mess hall, after dinner.

There was so much Lily wanted to say, now that she finally had his attention. She didn't know where to start, a whir of excitement in her head. "I feel terrible about Kenny's arrest. You have to believe me, Kaz!"

"Let's not waste time pointing fingers. We've got bigger concerns now."

"Oh?"

"Frank Isaka's really warmed up to you."

She smiled, pretending to follow his line of thought perfectly. The envelope of newspaper clippings drifted into her mind. Her glow faded.

"You can help us, Lily. You can help us even the score."

His words slid past, refusing to line up. *Score. Even. Help. Score. Scorch.* Their meaning constantly slipping away.

An urge to do something unfathomable came over her — spit in his face, claw at his eyes, run away. A quiver of nausea, like a feather was tickling her tummy, but from the inside. Where would she run, though? The desert stretched out endlessly. She'd never get away.

All along, she'd known what he wanted her for. Why did she feel so blindsided? Her bitterness subsided as she swallowed her humiliation, reality hitting with a dull thud. By lashing out, she'd simply outlive her usefulness. Even the doctor prized her as an object of utility, his last tenuous hold over his son.

"What is it you want me to do, Kaz?"

"Take a stroll with Frank. Take a romantic stroll. That's all."

"Why?"

"Why not?" A devious grin.

"You're not going to tell me what's going on here?"

"You can make Frank fall for you."

The challenge worked its way into her head. And then something was coming undone inside her, stirring to life those crystalline peals of laughter, filling her with a current of desirability, rapture. *I've got all the guys wrapped around my baby finger.* Suddenly, she felt ready to bloom like that first explosion of silky, tattered petals in spring.

Twelve

Rita upended a box of shoes and stuffed animals. The mangy panda Kristen had had since her first birthday rolled onto the floor, face down. A jumble of pastel laces clung to her old silver platforms. The thought of matching up pairs seemed exhausting, as she sank to a crouch, knuckles in her eyes, a contact lens grinding across her retina.

Where were those damn officers? Nursing their second double-double of the morning? Why was no one returning her calls?

Last night on the phone, Gerald hadn't been terribly coherent. Lily's car had been found broken into, abandoned. That much he was clear on. But the police didn't seem to think the break-in had anything to do with her disappearance.

Gerald's cheery insistence that they were lovey-dovey newly-weds, not a care in the world, had faded. Now he seemed to be seriously considering the possibility she'd left him.

Rita pushed aside a bag of old winter coats.

Beeping pierced the air.

She grabbed at the cordless, palms spastic — it slipped from her grasp and banged to the floor. "Hello?"

"Uh, Rita, Lee here."

"You got in touch with Gerald yesterday about a breakthrough in my mother's case?"

"I don't know if you'd call it a breakthrough, exactly. A few days ago the guy who operates the parking lot near the bus station reported that the lock on Lily's car had been popped, the radio ripped out. He was about to have it towed, anyway."

"This happened *a few days ago*, and you're only telling us about it now?"

"We needed to process the car: check it for fingerprints, evidence, forensics. Standard procedure."

She'd thought they were buddies, she'd thought Lee liked her. *He* was the one who'd reached out to her, tried to get all chummy and flirty. She expected he'd at least have the decency to give her a heads-up.

"So my mom's car." Rita tried to keep her voice under control. "What did you find?"

"Nothing. It came back totally clean."

"No fingerprints, no sign of a struggle?" Seats splattered in blood? Shattered glass? Too many horrible images were rushing through her mind.

"Nothing out of the ordinary. In fact, as I told Mr. Anderberg, we can release the car to him."

"What? You're not keeping it as evidence?"

"Evidence of …?"

"The guy who broke into Mom's car might have hurt or kidnapped her!"

"Kidnapping's not an option we're exploring, Rita. The car showed no signs of foul play. The parking guy remembers Lily dropping it off. Then she went into the bus station, where a girl at the booth sold her a ticket. Her car wasn't broken into 'til later."

"Where was she going?"

"The girl can't be one hundred percent sure, but she thinks the ticket was for New York."

"Aren't there records?"

"Not if you pay cash. She hasn't used her credit card at all yet."

The six-hundred-dollar withdrawal. Christ.

"Does your mom have any friends or family in New York?"

"I don't think so."

"Did Lily ever visit the Big Apple?"

"Once or twice. Not recently, though."

"So maybe that's it. The old girl got a craving for Macy's, Liza Minnelli."

"Then why hasn't anyone heard from her? She'd have at least told Gerald."

"You yourself said sometimes she needs a little alone time." Lee's voice softened a smidge, suddenly weary. "To tell you the truth, that's what a lot of these missing person cases turn out to be. People want a break from their boring lives. They usually come back if you give them enough time."

She'd assumed that the break-in would escalate her mother's case, but just the opposite seemed true. Who didn't dream about a little New York getaway?

"Don't get me wrong. We're continuing to monitor things. We've passed on her photo to the NYPD. But I suspect Lily'll come back soon enough on her own. Didn't you say she always does?"

"*No*. I mean, yeah, I did, but this time something's different." What was different? It was just a gut feeling, combined with a good shot of guilt. "Isn't there anything more you guys can do?"

"Like what? We could reach out to the community for help searching the 'hood, but that won't do much good if your mom's left Toronto."

"What about the media?"

"They've got our press release. Look, Rita, I don't know how to put this. Most missing person cases don't attract much attention unless the missing are doe-eyed toddlers. It's harder with adults, because people assume they chose to disappear. Which happens a lot, for a variety of reasons. Deadbeat dads, runaway teens, the list goes on."

Crazy mothers. She blinked back tears.

"We need more evidence to surface before we can continue the investigation."

A gust rose in Rita's chest. So this was how it felt to get the brush-off. "What am I supposed to do now?"

"I know it's frustrating, but the best thing you can do is make sure you're taking care of yourself. I could put you in touch with someone to talk to."

"Oh, great." The last thing she needed was another shrink.

"We'll keep you and Mr. Anderberg posted." The guy's mind had moved on to other things, like the important matter of whether it would be a burger or falafel for lunch.

"WELL, MAYBE HE'D enjoy some company?" Rita balanced the phone in the crook of her neck, while wiping her hands on her thighs.

"Thanks for your concern, but Dad's not up to having visitors so soon. He was just released yesterday."

It turned out that Mr. Fujita had taken a nasty fall at the cottage and been rushed in for knee surgery.

The bearer of this news was Alice Fujita. Rita remembered her as a stout, mirthless woman, who wore sensible, round-toed shoes, and had the air of Mother Superior. She was an elementary-school principal, the least successful of the Fujita kids, which said more about her superstar siblings. Ever since childhood, Rita had been hearing about their exemplary lives. The eldest son, Doug, was a VP at CIBC; one of the younger boys was a cardiac surgeon. They were held up as models of how the community had made it despite all the setbacks.

All that model minority crap made Rita want to vomit.

Upon being told about Lily's disappearance, Alice's resolve didn't weaken for a second. "I'm sorry to hear about your mother's problems, but I have to think about my father's health right now."

Alice had never liked Lily. She was probably the one who'd organized the family coup.

Well, the only thing to do was show up anyway. If Alice didn't like it, tough bananas. Stopping by Loblaws, Rita bought a pound cake that could pass as homemade, just barely. During the long drive out to Etobicoke, she mulled over what to say, but there really wasn't any way to gloss over the fact that she was showing up completely uninvited. Mr. Fujita — drugged up on painkillers, in agony — was the only person who might have any useful information about Lily. No doubt, Lee and Davis would consider this a wild goose chase, though they'd probably encourage Rita, just to keep her out of their hair. She wondered how much police work consisted of managing difficult family members. Was that what she'd become? She sighed, idling in traffic.

At last, the congestion loosened and she sped onto the Kingsway. An ash-blond lady honked her BMW as Rita cut her off. Such granny driving in this picture-perfect neighbourhood, with its village-like shops selling overpriced cheese. A lot of things about the place got under her skin — just because it looked like a faux-pastoral dream didn't mean people weren't drunk and beating their wives — but Lily had always yearned to escape to exactly this kind of setting.

On Queen Anne Road, Mr. Fujita lived in a Georgian house that his kids had bought for him. Its large paned windows stared out like mathematical grids. A white door, capped with decorative crown and framed by pilasters on either side. A testament to the perfect symmetry of the universe. It was as though the house aspired to restore the affluent life that had once been nipped in the bud. Mr. Fujita acted the part of the successful, retired businessman so well, but in truth his accounting practice had never recovered after the internment. So Mr. Fujita had started a business called Oriental Gardener, which sent Asian boys dressed like coolies to prune the rose bushes of rich white folks. And now, several decades later, the gardener had left the garden to assume his rightful position at the master's table.

Everything is exactly as it should be, the house seemed to whisper. Rita rang the doorbell and stood on the doorstep, sweating. Alice looked astonished.

"So sorry about your father's accident. I just happened to be in the neighbourhood, so I thought I'd drop this off." She handed over the cake, feeling utterly pathetic.

Alice gave a stony nod, her arms crossed, her lips a stark horizon. She'd be terrifying if you were ever called to the principal's office. Rita had never managed to master anything resembling that expression with her students.

"So you're enjoying the summer break?"

"Hardly. Dad's accident's thrown a wrench in things. But thank you for this." She patted the cake, with a knowing roll of the eyes. "I'll be sure to give my father your regards."

"Who's there?" a voice called out from inside.

"It's Rita Takemitsu!"

"Rita! Come in."

Casting a timid smile at Alice, she slithered past.

Wood panelling, crown mouldings galore, heavy mahogany furniture, knock-off Thomas Cole paintings. Mr. Fujita's late wife must have been a fan of *Masterpiece Theatre*. That said, signs of frugality dotted the house. A stain on the carpet had been covered up with a mat. Mr. Fujita was stretched out like a sultan on the sofa, dressed in an old green jogging suit.

"Sit down, sit down!" He propped himself up, his right leg swinging out from under the afghan, a log, clad in plaster. "I can't handle the stairs, so they have me sleeping down here. Heavens, if we'd known you were coming, we'd have tidied up, isn't that right, Alice?"

Alice receded into the kitchen to rustle up some tea. Not before flashing Rita a venomous glare.

"My kids are so protective." The old man shook his head. "I hurt my knee and you'd think I'd had a heart attack and gone in for a triple bypass. But enough about me. How are you, Rita? And how is your sweet mother, Lily?" A wistful look came over him as he said Lily's name. Just as quickly, the softness vanished.

"That's just it, Mr. Fujita. I don't quite know how to put this. Lily's gone missing."

"*Missing?*"

Keeping things as succinct as possible, Rita told him what had happened.

His jaw jutted forward and trembled in a frozen half-smile. "That's impossible. I just spoke with her last week. We were supposed to see each other on Friday, but after my accident, I called to reschedule."

"How did she sound?"

"Pretty normal, I guess. We didn't talk long. I was very tired."

"Mark Edo happened to mention that you're working on a book about the internment."

"That's what Lily and I were meeting about."

"My mother was helping you with the book?" So redress *had* been on her mind, there was no denying it now. The realization hit Rita like a sharp rebuke. While Lily had come around to support the cause, Rita was the one still burying her head in the sand.

"Nothing had been decided yet. Lily wasn't sure how involved she wanted to be. You know how it is. People want to help, but they're nervous. Oh, God. I can't believe she's missing!"

"You were trying to convince her to come on board?"

"I suppose you could say that. Lily implied she had some photographs that might be useful."

"Photos ... of?"

"Camp. Where she was interned, I assume. A friend of hers took the pictures and asked her to safeguard them."

"Safeguard them? But ... why?"

"She didn't say. Didn't have to, I guess. Easy enough to read between the lines. None of us were allowed to keep our cameras in the camps — that was the first thing the government took away." Mr. Fujita explained that most of the pictures people had given him for the book reflected the decades before and after the war. Japantown, the good old days. And then the slums they all lived in after they'd been forced to migrate east. "So these pictures Lily's friend took — of camp — are very rare. The photographer must've somehow managed to take them on the sly."

"Did she mention the photographer's name?"

He shook his head. "She cautioned me not to get my hopes up either. Maybe the pictures had gotten lost somewhere along the way. She didn't seem quite sure what she'd done with them."

With something as unique as these photographs — if they actually existed, if Lily hadn't fantasized them just to get Mr. Fujita's attention — you'd think she'd at least keep track of where she'd put them.

"Will you please let me know as soon as you hear from her?" he asked.

"Of course. And if she reaches out to you first, you'll contact me immediately?"

"Lily and I don't talk very often…. We hadn't been in touch for years before the book came up. Things were never the same after — well, you know. I've often wondered what would've happened if …" Mr. Fujita looked doubly grief-stricken. "It doesn't matter now. She's a happily married woman."

"Yes, she is."

Was she? What did Rita really know about her mother's marriage?

AT YONEDA HOME, a surprising number of residents weren't Japanese. Maybe they'd gotten a foot in the door by being married to Japanese folks. The old white men made little effort to hide their stares at the cheery Filipina girls bustling around in pink scrubs. Rita could feel their eyes on her own ass as she made her way past the wheelchairs huddled around the TV.

French toast, unwashed hair, and sandalwood incense filled the air. Shoji screens partitioned off a meditation area to the side, but it didn't seem to be getting much use these days; this set was more interested in *The Young and the Restless*.

After signing in at the front desk, she was directed to a room in the new part of the facility, a long *L*-shaped addition that snaked off the end of the stone mansion.

The door was ajar. By the window sat a small figure swaddled in a pink-and-brown quilt. Rita barely recognized her. The last time they'd seen each other must have been at Rita's wedding. Even then Aunt Haruko had looked frail and dozy, but at least her hair had still been gunmetal grey. Now it had turned so white it appeared blond, fine and staticky. Her skin had loosened in crumpled, discoloured folds. A hint of lipstick, applied in a smear. Or maybe it was grape-juice stains.

She seemed so alone, withdrawn. The poor woman had to be well into her eighties. At some point, it stood to reason, she'd go from being a top employee at Yoneda Home to one of the inhabitants.

As Rita leaned over to offer a hug, the shoulders flinched, pulled away.

"Is that you, Mary?"

"No, Aunt Haruko. It's me, Rita."

Her eyes had turned an opalescent blue-grey, milky with cataracts.

"Rita." The lips compressed in a hesitant smile.

A small, sparsely furnished room. At least the violet bedspread matched the curtains. Her view looked onto a Japanese garden: all the miniature trees and bushes were beautifully pruned, black stones jutting up like tiny mountains along the well-swept pathways.

Framed pictures hung crookedly on the walls. Jesus in a meadow, surrounded by a flock of sheep. An ink painting of a wisteria tree. It must have been done years ago, when Aunt Haruko's hands were still agile, capable of turning the brush in so many curves and turns to capture the gnarled solidity of the main vine and the delicate, springy, new shoots.

"You're at art school, ne?"

"That was a long time ago. It didn't work out. Now I'm a high-school teacher."

Failure prickled Rita's skin. She hadn't done much with her artistic talent, but maybe she'd never been that talented to begin with. When had Aunt Haruko last painted? Those arthritic hands would be lucky to hold a toothbrush these days. It was terrible how she'd slipped off everyone's radar. The fragility of their family — all their interwoven, wrecked lives. Surely this wasn't how things were in all families? Kristen had once remarked that her friends had lots of aunts and uncles and cousins and second cousins, everyone running around, singing Christmas carols. Why had Rita let things get like this? When things had been good, why hadn't she signed Aunt Haruko out on a day pass and brought her to their old house for turkey and eggnog?

"How's your mother, Rita?"

"Not good. Not good at all." Each time she told the story of Lily's disappearance, it didn't get any easier. The whole thing came out sounding just as unreal as it had since day one. Waves of exhaustion washed over her.

"Hontou? Lily's *missing?*"

"I don't suppose she's tried to get in touch with you?"

"No." There wasn't even a phone in the room.

"When was the last time you saw my mother? Does she ever come to visit?"

Aunt Haruko straightened up. She still had a certain primness that came through in her posture. "*I* took care of Lily, never the other way. Lily was always too busy ... being Lily. And she was never all there in the head-u." *Head-u.* Soft, upward tails. Her voice had lost its edges, reverted to traces of the Japanese accent. And she still couldn't say Lily's name properly, the *L*'s abrading into *R*'s.

"A pretty girl like her, kirei her whole life, everyone fawning all over her, she expected life to be easy." A hint of envy passed over the old face. "It wasn't, of course."

"The internment, you mean. I was wondering if you could tell me a bit about the camp years?"

"Eto ne, it was all so long ago…. Can't we talk about something else?" A timid, placating smile. "I have chocolate in my drawer."

"This is *important*." Rita hadn't driven all the way out to St. Catharines to nibble on rancid chocolate. Her hands felt shaky and out of control, and her T-shirt clung damply to her back. "These are things that have bothered me for years — for my entire life, actually."

What Rita really wanted to say was: you owe me. It was the least Aunt Haruko could do after deserting them all those years ago — two kids left to fend for themselves in that house of craziness. Hadn't she worried about what had become of them? True, that was before the days of Children's Aid sticking its nose in everyone's business. But still.

She'd been too busy praying to her hidden Jesus to concern herself with the land of the living.

"Please, Rita. I don't remember much. I couldn't have. Better not to remember, ne? In case the police question us. That's what everyone said. Even the doctor."

They sat there in silence. The air between them seemed to tremble with sadness, guilt, disappointment.

"So who am I supposed to ask about these things? Everyone's dead. Everyone except you and my mother."

"Better that way."

Rita placed a hand on the mottled arm. She forced down a sob, her breath heavy. "What happened to my mother at camp? The scar on her cheek …?"

"She never was the same after Matanzas."

"Matanzas?"

"Yes, the name of the camp. Massacre, in Spanish." A hollow chuckle.

"Why didn't Kaz do more to help her get better?"

"Oh, Kaz? Kaz wasn't even here."

"What are you talking about? Of course he was." All those years they'd lived in Toronto, after the war, before she'd been born. How jealous Rita had always been that Tom had at least spent part of his childhood with their father.

A shrug, a noncommittal half-nod. Aunt Haruko was confused, losing her marbles.

"So? What happened to my mother?"

For a second, she almost appeared to be enjoying herself — being in possession of some secret, coveted knowledge. This was the most attention Aunt Haruko had received in years, no doubt. A sad thought.

"You can tell me. I won't tell anyone. It can be our little secret. Like the Hidden Christian prayers, right, Aunt Haruko?"

The dull eyes caught the light. "The doctor tried to stop it, but it was too late — smoke was everywhere. Death in the air."

"Smoke? Death?"

"Destruction of Satan's world was happening even then."

The language of Satan, this was new. When Rita was a kid, Aunt Haruko never said a word about fire and brimstone. According to Grandpa, hell was the hardest idea for Japanese people to get their heads around: the finality of eternal damnation. The notion that there could be a point of no return, without any hope of being reincarnated in a better life.

"'They will throw them into the fiery furnace, where there will be weeping and gnashing of teeth.' Matthew 13:42."

"So back to my mother."

"That was terrible, but I know nothing, don't you see? Ask someone else — don't ask me!" She pulled the blanket over her head.

"Lunch smells good," Rita said at last.

"Oyako don."

Always this same ridiculous dance of one step forward, two steps back.

"Apparently, Lily had in her possession some photos of camp. Do you know anything about this?"

"Hontou? Photos of Matanzas?"

"They were taken in secret."

"I once heard rumours about those photos."

"Who was the photographer, I wonder?"

A cold, rigid countenance.

"*Please*, Aunt Haruko. Lily was going to use the photos to help the Redress Movement."

"Oh, redress." She scrunched up her face. "They were talking about that even in my day. All the troublemakers want is to stir up hatred of us. They don't know what's good for them. Bakatare!"

The ring on Aunt Haruko's hand flashed, as sun streamed through the window. It was her late sister's wedding ring, the grandmother Rita had never known. On her deathbed, she must have given the ring to Aunt Haruko (or maybe Aunt Haruko'd just claimed it as her own). In any case, it had loosened over the years and now slid down so her bony joint barely held it on. Most of the diamond chips had fallen out, leaving empty sockets.

WHAT A COLOSSAL waste of time. Rita's car inched forward in the rush-hour traffic. Flashing lights up ahead: a couple of paramedics carried a stretcher to the side of the highway, where a silver sedan had been crushed in like a Coke can.

In the adjacent car, she could see a cute little girl about Kristen's age. The girl looked tired, her nose pressed against the window while her mother stared ahead angrily and exhaled clouds of smoke from a long, thin cigarette. Rita wanted to shake the woman by the shoulders and shout, "Don't you know how lucky you are? At least your daughter's here with you!" And what kind of mother exhaled smoke in a child's face anyway?

When they'd chatted on the phone yesterday, Kristen had sounded sullen. Her tummy hurt. The first thing that went through Rita's mind, with a tremor of vindication, was that the poor kid was suffering from anxiety, induced by being so far away from her mother. It must be hard on her spending so much time with Jodi. How it irritated Rita, the mere thought of this other woman combing Kristen's hair and helping her with her bath because Cal was bound to duck out of these chores if at all possible, lazy ass. But when Rita tried to talk with him about Kristen's stomach pains, he snapped, "Oh, get over yourself! Our daughter isn't stressed out over anything. She just ate too many cookies, okay? So shoot me. I'm a terrible father — is that what you want to hear?"

Not knowing, that was the worst part. Not knowing what was ailing her baby, feeling totally shut out of her life. That was the sad reality of being a divorced parent.

Rita might as well be living in a black hole. Which was how she felt these days about pretty much all aspects of her life.

At least she'd found out the name of the camp. Matanzas. Some ghost town in the middle of the desert. Matanzas. The name had an ominous ring. "Smoke and death," Aunt Haruko had said. On the other hand, she probably considered just about everything a step toward Armageddon.

Mark Edo might know something about the place. The house meeting he'd mentioned was tomorrow evening. She couldn't ignore a small flutter in her gut: anticipation, hope, maybe. He'd offered to help and something about his warm, straightforward smile made her believe he might actually mean it.

THEY KEPT A KEY hidden in a flowerpot out front. Rita had seen Gerald use it before and the whole thing had struck her as ridiculously dangerous. Maybe it didn't even count if you handed the burglar the key on a silver platter. Now, however, she was glad it was there. When Gerald didn't answer, she didn't hesitate to let herself in.

She headed straight down to the basement. Fumbling around in the dark, she pulled a string that turned on a light bulb. The room was crammed with chairs stacked on top of each other, some country-pine dining-room set that had gone out of style for a reason. Lampshades covered in dust, like old, dejected hats. Margarine tubs brimming with orphan buttons. Evidently, Gerald's first wife had been as much of a pack rat as Lily.

Photo albums were stacked on the floor and a few black-and-white photos had fluttered free. But they were just of a bunch of white folks dressed in frilly bonnets, like actors at Pioneer Village.

What had she been expecting? Muddy roads leading nowhere, snow-capped mountains looming in the distance? Little Japanese girls with fragile eyes, gazing through barbed wire?

She pulled down boxes, her fingers tearing up packing tape, digging inside. Old towels, yellowed and ragged around the edges. Cookbooks with recipes for casseroles that promised wonders with a can of cream of mushroom soup. Yet these weren't the dishes that Rita had grown up with, none of this stuff was. That junk from their old house, which she should have helped Lily sift through, had been dragged off in countless garbage bags, piled high in some dumpster. She reached for more boxes, everything rattling, on the verge of breaking, but she didn't care, something frantic set loose inside her. She had to find those pictures — they had to be here *somewhere*. Where the fuck were they?

Thirteen

Lily waved. Frank sank the ball through the hoop and dribbled down the court, churning up a dust storm. He was showing off, trying to impress her. The sky opened up, a sea of blueness flecked with white foam. Little boys clustered around him. Tim Dewson, tall for his age, one of the few Eurasian kids at camp, got the ball in and ran in circles making a victory sign, his thin frame vanishing in the blur, as though the earth itself were chuffing. Frank clapped the boy on the back and let out a holler. Lily cheered, flashed a smile. It seemed like an eternity since she'd been around happy kids.

"Got a minute, Lily?" Frank said as the game was breaking up.

Just as she'd been debating how to approach him, he made it easy. "Want to take a stroll together?" she asked.

"Sure. Where to?"

"How about past the firebreak?"

"That's the new part of camp."

Lily knew what he was thinking, goody two-shoes. They weren't allowed to wander around the new part. It was a messy construction zone.

To her surprise, he didn't protest as she led the way. They stepped over planks and Frank tripped on uprooted sagebrush. Laughing, he brushed off his knees.

"Have you ever thought about getting involved in the JACC? A girl like you — people would really listen. You could come to conventions with me and make speeches about the horrors of anarchy narrowly averted, thanks to the leadership of the JACC."

So it appeared she wasn't the only one on a mission. Frank talked on, splaying his hands, and all Lily had to do was bob her head a little. The ardour in his voice caught her off guard: was it nothing more than passion for his cause, or was something more interesting driving his desire to spend time with her? But the flicker soon faded. So monotonous, such a good boy, in the end boring. Before she knew it, she was lost in a daydream about how pleased Kaz would be with her for taking Frank on a stroll. In that moment Kaz would know she'd do anything for him, simply because she loved him.

Love.

How bizarre that she was thinking about love. Later when Lily reached for this scene over and over in her guilt-ridden mind, it was the feeling of being in love — utterly, blindly in love — that came back to her, with the force of a slap.

Love led her to take this path, this wrong turn. She couldn't resist walking a few steps ahead of Frank, repeating the very route she'd taken so often with Kaz, her feet following her heart as if lured by a magnetic tug. Even if Kaz hadn't suggested bringing Frank here, she'd have chosen this accursed route.

As they made their way past the half-constructed walls, meandering through this maze that felt like a deserted city, she thought about Kaz pushing her up against the tarpaper, the frictive rub of his unshaven chin against her neck, the tang of his sweat rising sharply.

Rustling somewhere behind. Something was off. Why was Frank lingering so far back? She froze up and called out to him.

A dark, furtive movement. It happened so fast. Three men — wearing black masks — jumped out from behind a wall. One of them brandished a baseball bat, which he used to ambush Frank from behind. Did all three of them have bats? She ducked down behind a pile of plywood and curled up in a ball, knees pressed under her chin, eyes clenched. And yet she somehow remained horribly aware of the movement: the repetitive swing, Frank's rising moans, the men closing around him in a shadowy swirl.

She knew it was them. Kaz had become the ringleader in Kenny's absence. This time there was no doubt in her mind that it was Kaz swinging the bat while the other two looked on. There was something all too familiar about the way the group had contracted, their heads bent together in some unspoken, tribal language. She didn't even need to peek up and see Kaz's shoes or the slight limp Shig always walked with. She knew who they were in her gut. She knew.

She stared at the ground, at the scraggly blades of grass. A snake slithered by and as she watched it vanish, it seemed to be pulling her deeper inside herself.

Kaz kept swinging and the *thwack* started to sound different: more like a *crack* — against bone, against skull. That crazy braying had started up in her head, and it was getting louder, but it couldn't be loud enough. At least her father had known when to stop, sensing how much her mother could take. With Kaz she detected no such restraint. Something had crossed over in him, as if, with every blow, he were breaking free from being under his father's thumb, all those years of enforced civility now giving way to some madness inside.

With a jolt her legs came unfrozen, and she tripped on a rope of sagebrush. She picked herself up and ran, pain shooting through her shins. Yet it wasn't the pain that made her scream. She was screaming without even realizing she was screaming — for help, for someone, for anything.

Fourteen

The meeting was at a mustard-coloured brick bungalow with perfectly spherical hedges out front. Rita stood at the back of the warm, crowded living room. The news of Lily's disappearance had made its way through the gossip circuits. Upon learning that Rita was her daughter, people were full of concern. A couple of ladies from the Nisei Women's Club were particularly anxious, their carefully plucked eyebrows jumping up like Noh performers ("How long did the police stay?" "Did they dust for fingerprints? Take strands of hair from her hairbrush?"). Not that they had much to contribute. Despite having known Lily for years, they didn't seem to know her very well; they'd exchanged recipes for Christmas cookies and that was about the extent of it.

Mark was running around greeting people. Maybe he hadn't seen Rita yet. And then he spotted her. He came over and gave her a hug. "By night's end maybe I'll have converted you. You'll be going door to door handing out redress flyers."

"Ha. Not likely."

"We're about to get started, but you'll stick around after?"

Nodding, she mentioned there was something she wanted to ask him.

Mark looked curious. Then he turned all businesslike and called the meeting to order. He proceeded to discuss quite a bit of JCNA news regarding meeting times, fundraising, media outreach, awareness-building campaigns, petition signing. They were going into another round of negotiations with the Minister of Multiculturalism next month. Rita hadn't realized how much effort and coordination went into the whole redress machinery. It was like someone was running for election.

"All right, now I'd like to get started on the main thing we do here — sharing memories." Mark talked about how any kind of memory was acceptable; it didn't have to be a recollection tied to the internment. Younger folks were welcome to share their thoughts, too. The purpose was simply to open up dialogue about the community and collective past.

His relaxed smile and steady voice were rather disarming. Not long after he'd opened up the floor, a grey head bobbed up. The woman had dressed up for the occasion in a pink silk blouse and pearl necklace. She took a deep breath and began speaking rapidly, afraid that if she didn't get it all out she'd lose her nerve.

"My name is Mrs. Moto and I was interned at Kaslo, a ghost town in the interior of BC. But before we were shipped off, we were held for many weeks at the Exhibition grounds in Vancouver, with so many others in the same boat. I was newly married and expecting at the time." She talked about the shortage of food and crude, smelly living conditions. The humiliation of being compelled to give birth to her first child while confined to a dung-stained stall. Strangers had been standing around on all sides, some trying to help, others just watching. By the time the doctor arrived, it was too late — the baby was already in her arms. "Just like I was a cow, having birthed my own baby in a barn."

Mark didn't look at all uncomfortable. "That must've been a frightening experience for you, Mrs. Moto. Was your baby all right?"

"Oh, yes. I'm that baby." A middle-aged man, balding, with an elaborate comb-over, stood up.

"He never was one for visiting farms, though," Mrs. Moto added.

Laughter pattered across the room.

"Thank you for sharing, Mrs. Moto."

She sat down while everyone clapped.

Silence followed. But gradually, others came forward and told their stories, too. People only ten years older than Rita talked about being pulled out of school and ostracized by kids and teachers for no longer being Canadian, branded as the enemy race. There were stories of terrifying train rides as women, children, and old people were sent to ghost towns and told to rebuild their lives in crumbling, mouse-infested buildings.

Not everyone wanted to talk. Rita could sense the tension rising from the tightly crossed arms of the lady next to her. How had Lily felt as she'd clung to the wall, forced to confront her own unspeakable memories? Rita had never really thought about the full extent of what her mother had gone through — the upheaval, the humiliation, the loss of everything familiar. Heat emanated from people's cheeks as they evaded each other's glances and then timidly, uncertainly, looked back.

Could the tide of memories have triggered emotions Lily couldn't handle? Was that why she'd walked out of her life?

In fact, a couple of people were leaving right now. They edged toward the door and slipped out while someone was in the midst of speaking.

At last things were winding down. Over cups of tepid green tea, people stood around for another half hour, chatting, waiting. Many of them wanted to talk to Mark. All the folks who'd been too shy to tell their stories to the group wanted to tell their stories to him privately so they, too, could be touched by his amber gaze. Rita perched on the edge of the sofa, wondering when she'd get a word in edgewise. Finally, the stragglers left.

Mark flopped down on the couch beside her. "Okay, I'm pooped. Sorry that took so long."

"It's okay. I enjoyed listening to everyone's stories." Enjoyment hardly got at the tangle of emotions she'd experienced, but she didn't know what else to say and now felt like an idiot.

"You mentioned you wanted to ask me about something."

She nodded, tongue-tied.

"Come on. You've had me curious all night."

"What do you say I tell you about it over a beer?"

RITA FOLLOWED MARK'S Jeep to a bar at Yonge and Lawrence, one of those places with a "ye olde" pub sign and worn velvety benches and sports pendants on the walls. They ordered beers, a veggie plate, and basket of chicken wings before she realized that wings would mean licking her fingers and looking disgusting. (Was this a date she'd unthinkingly hurled herself into? It kind of felt like one.) She sipped her beer — not wanting to drink faster than him — and nibbled celery. Then she got worried that Mark would think her a prude, so she attacked a saucy wing with gusto.

So far he'd told her quite a bit about kinship structures among pre-Columbian societies in Panama in the sixteenth century. Apparently, a world of information could be gleaned by excavating the remains of these peoples' dump sites. She pictured Mark, brown as a berry, a baseball cap shading his face, as he sifted through the rubble, eyes alight with childlike wonder. Indiana Jones. But shorter. Mark really wasn't much taller than she was; they were almost eye to eye, standing. Normally, she was attracted to taller guys. *Was* she attracted to Mark? Or was she just falling to pieces and looking for an ego boost in the form of male attention? Could he tell what she was thinking, as she nodded and commented — intelligently, she hoped? Were the same convoluted self-doubts running through his mind?

He was a pretty outgoing guy. He seemed easygoing; though, as they talked further, she began to see another side. He'd grown up in Toronto. Then he'd been away for many years doing his Ph.D. in Pittsburgh and peddling his trade at universities and colleges all over North America. He was older than she'd initially thought. He'd only moved back to Toronto last summer, when U of T hired him on a two-year contract. His job wasn't likely to become tenure-track, so he didn't quite know what the future had in store. Sounded tired of the gypsy life. Maybe that was why he'd gotten involved in redress; the activist work seemed to have a grounding effect.

"But enough about me," he said, suddenly. "You're an art teacher, right?"

"Some days I try to think of myself as one. I go in there and do my impression of one, and the kids don't know any different."

"Not your passion?"

"It's not that…. I really do enjoy teaching. Some of the time, anyway." She rolled her eyes. "But I guess you're right. Not my original passion."

"Which was?"

"Painting. Though I haven't picked up a brush in ages. More important things to do, like paying the bills."

She thought about the stack of canvasses she'd been lugging around for years. Wasn't it time to put that stuff out on the curb? The other day, while unpacking, some masochistic impulse made her peek at the painting on top: a square of pellucid blueness, blurry around the edges, Rothko-like (at least that was what she'd been aiming for). A slip of whimsical sky melting away. A clothesline had been sketched across: pantyhose and lingerie hung down like gossamer wings, dead, insubstantial.

She signalled to the waiter that she needed another drink.

"So did you grow up in the Japanese-Canadian community?" Mark asked.

"What community?"

"Oh, you know, the Japanese Canadian Cultural Centre, the Buddhist church. Didn't they have some annual picnic?"

"You'd know better than I would. My grandfather was involved in that stuff for a while, but after my mother went downhill, we kept to ourselves."

"What happened to your mom?"

"She never was the same after the war, I guess." That was a euphemism, if ever there was one.

"If it makes you feel any better, I only went to the picnic once. I didn't have such a great time. Kids kept asking me what the heck I was doing there. There weren't so many hapa kids, back then. I was a person in a marginal position, whose ambiguous status troubles the lines of demarcation in the social system, as we say in my field. Since marginal figures are credited with having uncontrollable, menacing powers, they're considered dangerous." He made a fearsome face. His tone suggested a playful, ironic distance from the jargon he was using.

It was true that Mark didn't look very Japanese. Was that why he'd jumped on the redress bandwagon? To reclaim some sense of his long-lost origins? Then again, how Japanese was she, really? "Japanese," whatever that meant. Cal had once told her that she didn't know how to cook rice properly. (But he was Korean. Were Korean and Japanese folks supposed to fluff their rice differently?) Maybe she was also a person in a marginal position, whose ambiguous status troubled the lines of demarcation — whatever that meant. She certainly didn't feel like she had any special, menacing powers.

"You're really good at leading the house meetings, getting people to open up. I wouldn't know where to begin."

"All we're doing is creating a safe space. For so long no one talked about anything — it was like those memories of the internment years never even existed. Massive blackouts, collective amnesia. Just put it all behind you, block it all out, pull yourself up by your bootstraps, move the fuck on. The first step in rebuilding community is allowing those memories to surface."

Blackouts, amnesia, repressed memories....

"My mom gets confused sometimes. Ever since I was a kid. She'll look at me at times like she's forgotten I'm her daughter." She searched Mark's face for signs of shock, fascination.

"That must've been frightening for a little kid."

All she saw was gentle concern. Tears smarted her eyes.

As he handed her a napkin, his hand brushed against her wrist. She wondered if he were the kind of guy who often attracted women on the verge of meltdowns.

"It sounds like your mom's had quite the go of it."

"That's putting it mildly."

"How's everything going with the search?"

"Oh, God. Don't even ask." She began telling him about her visit with Mr. Fujita and the photographs that Lily was supposedly in possession of.

"That's fabulous for the JCNA if she has them. They'll be great for the book. Valuable artifacts. Though I'm curious about why the pictures matter so much to you. You really think they're going to lead you to Lily?"

"I don't know." He was right, she was grasping at straws. And yet, her gut instinct that the photos were somehow important persisted — if for no other reason than she needed to understand her mother.

"Where was your mom interned, Rita?"

"Actually, that's what I wanted to ask you about." She couldn't believe she'd gotten so sidetracked. "Do you know anything about Matanzas?"

"The Matanzas Riot."

"What? A riot happened there?"

Mark tilted his head back, inventorying his brain. "Yeah, it was one of the few instances of violent resistance, I think. But most of the stuff I've researched pertains to camps in Canada, not the States. I've read about the Matanzas Riot somewhere, but the details escape me."

"I thought you're supposed to be some hotshot expert, Professor Edo."

She expected a witty comeback, but he kept silent. A moment later, he said, "I can help you find out more if you'd like."

"Yeah?"

"Too bad Robarts isn't open now. Summer hours."

He acted like it would be perfectly normal to head to the library at a quarter to ten, like a couple of caffeine-fuelled undergrads ready to pull an all-nighter.

"How about tomorrow afternoon?" he said brightly.

SHE HADN'T REALIZED that he'd suggested the afternoon because they'd spend the morning lounging in bed, her cheek pressed against the nest of golden down on his chest. If she liked the way morning light streamed through her new bedroom window, she liked it all the more as the rays danced over Mark's sleeping face and illuminated the mottled freckles she hadn't noticed before. She wondered whether he was the kind of prof who slept around with different grad students each week. She hoped not. It was rare for her to meet a guy she could talk to so easily (and who was so skilled, in other ways, with his tongue). But that was the muddling thing about sex: it could make you feel like you'd known someone for a very long time, like you were old childhood friends or something.

Last night, afterwards, her body languid, she'd told him more about Lily's disappearance and erratic behaviour over the years. It was a relief to let go and open up to someone and even indulge in a good cry (under normal circumstances, she was *not* the kind of woman who cried after sex, she let Mark know with a laugh). He just cuddled and listened with his usual calmness, and after she'd exhausted herself, a heavy restfulness came over her limbs and eyelids. The first true rest she'd had in days. Although it was accompanied by a wallop of guilt — since Lily was still out there, lost, God knew where — she luxuriated in that moment of stillness, the cusp of sleep.

Fifteen

The head honcho, Mr. Howells himself, stood behind his desk and lit a cigarette. His pudgy face was damp, wisps of silver hair stuck to his forehead. He was standing close to his secretary, the pretty one with copper curls, their voices so low Lily couldn't make out anything. A handkerchief came out and mopped the upper lip, but his face still shimmered, a massive, dewy peach.

The American flag had been pinned to the wall behind him. Line upon line of blank white stars that confused her with their emptiness, their non-existent glitter, their geometric perfection.

Every so often they'd glance at Lily nervously, as though she were a new breed of criminal they hadn't figured out how to interrogate.

Everything that had come before stretched out like sleep without dreams, black and amorphous, uncertain in duration. A jumble of inchoate, muzzled voices. Humming, humming, always humming. If only that blanket of black vibrating air could be thick enough to swaddle her senses forever.

Running her hands through her lank hair, she extracted scraps of sagebrush. She smelled of oily, matted fur. Fingernails broken, caked with dirt. How awful the way people looked at her now. What would the Cherry Blossom judges say? They wouldn't recognize her — not an unfamiliar feeling. There were times when she'd stare at the eyes watching her in the glass and feel they belonged to someone else: a fleeting friend, a sometimes enemy.

And yet it was that other self that seemed most real, that beckoned to her. As if she could let herself drift away from this dirty, degraded body, and follow that other, more forceful presence....

The door opened and the doctor charged in.

"You shouldn't be here," Mr. Howells said.

"I'm her doctor."

"We need to talk to her alone. We need to get her on the record about what happened."

"What has she said?"

"Nothing. Just keeps repeating she doesn't remember a thing."

Then the images started to surface, like tattered photographs — the masked men, the construction site, Frank's endless moans — but she didn't want to piece it all together. Eyes clenched, memory shuttered. If only everything would fade from her consciousness, recede into the abyss forever.

Flecks of blood congealed around her fingernails, bitten to the quick. *A man was beaten. Frank Isaka.* She couldn't resist putting a finger in her mouth to tear at a morsel of skin. A welcome intrusion of pain, of guilt. *She lured him to that awful place, where Kaz beat him to the ground. Oh, God, what if Frank isn't even alive?* The taste of blood, salty and strong.

"Is he all right? Frank?"

The doctor nodded. "The attacker must've run away when he heard you screaming. You probably saved his life, Lily."

She hugged her arms around herself, trembling.

How she longed for her purple kimono, not the one she'd worn on stage, but the shabby, soft, ruined one, the one she'd practiced in, the one her mother had left behind. She could see it hanging in the empty closet. In the shadows it appeared almost black, and if she buried her nose deep in its folds, a hint of something aromatic and ashy made her remember burning chrysanthemum petals, the incense her mother used to make offerings. It made everything circle back to the same warm, safe place, the girl she was in the beginning....

"You see?" the doctor said. "I can get her talking. She's just frightened. Please give me a few minutes alone with the girl."

"If you were any other Jap doctor, I wouldn't even consider it. You've got five minutes. Not a second longer."

Mr. Howells and his secretary walked out. But Lily couldn't believe they'd truly left; they were standing outside, teacups pressed against the door.

"Who were they?"

"Who were who?"

"*Lily. The men.* When you came to me, you were screaming your head off about some men attacking Frank. You told us where to find him."

She didn't remember that part. It seemed there was nothing there to remember.

"So, Lily, who were they?"

"They were wearing masks."

"Masks? You didn't catch any identifying features?"

The truth would devastate him. Yet she had no more energy for creative lies that risked turning into the most horrible prophecies. "One of them was Kaz, I think. He was with Shig and Akira."

The doctor's eyes looked startled, exposing the fragile geometry of his cheekbones. Yet only a moment later, not so startled, just horrified, sunken, afraid.

Out it all came in a jumble of fragments, whatever she could manage to cobble together. How Kaz had asked her to warm up to Frank. Take him on a romantic stroll. For what reason, she had no idea. Until. Until it was all too late. She felt a wobble of nausea, her breath heavy and sour.

The doctor will know what to do. He'll take care of me.

But he just kept staring into space. Where was the tenacious, self-assured man she'd come to rely on?

"So what do you want me to do with all this information?" he said at last.

"Make things right?"

"You no longer care about Kaz?"

"No … it's not that."

"Are you even sure of what you saw? The men were wearing masks, you said it yourself — they could have been anyone."

She could see by the mixture of hurt and hostility in his eyes how desperately he needed to believe it. She couldn't bear it; she simply couldn't bear to shatter his hopes. Her role was to safeguard that good image of Kaz: a boy who might be full of wayward impulses, but who could still become a great man. The naive optimism that the doctor had often teased her about, that was what had drawn him to her and made him take her under his wing. So now it was her turn to be the Strong One. Tsuyo Ka Ko, as her mother used to call her. The voice of the Strong One gathered force like the bright white asteroid that had descended on their front lawn all those years ago.

"Maybe you're right. They could have been anyone."

A gentle slackening in the air between them. Perhaps he was able to see she was lying. And he was grateful. It was a lie that might somehow benefit the greater good, surely, wasn't it? A hush surrounded them as they watched each other, joined in this new, oppressive intimacy.

VOICES SWIRLED AROUND her, foggy and formless. The room brightened and faded and brightened and faded again. Cool fingers stroked her forehead, lulling her to numbness.

Aunt Haruko hovered above and spooned forth rice porridge, washed down with powdered milk. Sometimes she couldn't keep anything down. Although this woman was taking care of her, Lily could sense her reluctance, disapproval. Her bright, inauspicious stares.

Muffled, singsongy laughter behind. (But how on earth could it be coming from behind? She was all alone in bed, wasn't she?) Nevertheless, someone was talking about her — pointing, giggling. She was sure of it. It didn't matter if they were invisible. The nattering girls gathered around as their ringleader's voice pierced the air with awful clarity: "Our little Cherry Blossom Queen's gotten herself into a bit of trouble. Who's gonna take care of her now?"

The men in dark suits came to see her. Nothing invisible about them. They were the same type who'd come before, the stale odours of their breath masked by spearmint gum and the waxy, medicinal stench of hair cream. Their questions never varied much in content. Despite their efforts to change the way they phrased them — more gently after a while, recognizing that she was, after all, a frightened, traumatized girl — Lily couldn't tell them anything. It didn't even feel like lying. All she had to do was give in to that chorus of voices, and all certainty slipped beyond her ken.

Fighting the weight of her limbs and eyelids, she had an urgent sense of needing to surface, surge up from the black pool. Someone was calling out to her. A child's face, lit by a halo of silver-blue light. The halo swelled and subsided, and the child's face was replaced by a man's.

Kaz.

The way they'd met — the life they were going to have together — soared up in Technicolor splendour. He'd come to her father's shop one afternoon. A photo of Lily, decked out in her finery on stage, had been circulating through the neighbourhood. And he'd seen her, yes, yes, he'd seen her as she'd walked across the stage, yes, that was how it'd happened. She was the one with the giddy laugh that made her cover her mouth — a second too late, after the judges had seen her crooked, discoloured teeth and docked her points for being unladylike. But that didn't matter to Kaz one bit.

All the while, it was a different face that appeared before her, day after day. Or was this face so different after all? The same, only different. Older, gentler: all the sharp edges smoothed over, everything wilted a little. Still, there was something beautifully familiar about those lips and chin and the faint violet hollows held up by the delicate architecture of bones around the eyes that kept on watching her. She looked back while this man — the doctor — spooned crushed-up food into her mouth. "Eat, Lily." As he mouthed these words, it was another face saying them in her mind, but that was all right because she knew that in some strange way the doctor *was* Kaz; they were one and the same person. How wonderful that this man was taking care of her, and at the end of the war he'd marry her, and she'd run his practice from the ground floor of a big white house with a splendid veranda.

The doctor was Kaz, as Kaz would become over the years. If only he could grow into his true self.

"YOUR STRENGTH'S RETURNING, ne? Time to get some fresh air."

So Lily let Aunt Haruko brush out her hair, pulling at the knots like tangled weeds. They got bundled up in several layers.

It was a bright, chilly day, the kind that can seem dizzying, the way the light and cold conspire to assail the senses. Lily clasped Aunt Haruko's arm as they made their way in mincing steps over the terrain, sun reflecting off the frost in silver patches.

Outside one of the barracks, she was surprised to see a tinsel tree, decorated with tarnished brass balls and snowflakes cut from newsprint. Could it be December already?

Beyond that lone effort there were no other signs of Christmas festivity. Most of the barracks appeared more rundown than ever.

What the heck was going on here? That was Cecil Watanabe, with his burly teenage sons, ripping the place apart. The skeletal frame of their house was surrounded by dislodged floorboards, broken apart like toothpicks. Furniture had been thrown outside in a junk heap.

A cluster of people, laden with suitcases and boxes, stood around. Others had already waddled down the dirt road, all their possessions strapped on their backs. Tiny Mrs. Watanabe looked ready to topple over. Vagabond families. Someone's old bachan turned around and looked back, as though a sudden yearning to stay behind had overtaken her heart.

"Where's everyone going?" Lily heard herself ask.

"It's starting. The exodus."

"Exodus?"

"The government's set up a permanent leave program. To start emptying us out."

"A leave program? But why?"

"The doctor says it's because of all the trouble and mischief. Bad publicity for the government, ne? So now they try to separate the troublemakers from the loyal Japanese-Americans. The troublemakers get sent to real prison camp and the loyals have to go back into the real world."

Real world? So this wasn't the real world. The sun's glare had a mesmerizing effect and sent her back into the funhouse of distorted mirrors that lined her mind.

She hadn't seen Kaz since … since when? Where had he been dragged off to? Had he been sent back into the real world already?

"How do they decide who goes where?"

"They have their ways. Some questionnaire. Since all the trouble lately, everyone wants out, but they take their time processing the papers. When the time's right, the doctor'll decide what to do about us."

Behind them loomed the net factory, a giant spiderweb flowing down. But the web was only a ghost of Lily's imagination: green and brown and mustard tendrils weaving up into its intricate texture, brushing like seaweed against her hands, cheeks. The factory was deserted now; nothing was going on there. It resembled the carcass of some long-extinct beast.

She remembered hearing rumours that the war was going to end soon. On the other hand, people had been saying that for ages. Some were convinced that Japan would be victorious, and there were excited rumours that the Emperor would pay twenty thousand yen to every internee who chose to return home. Plum jobs would await them.

"One day we'll go back to Japan, the Land of the Rising Sun," her father used to say. So maybe now he'd seize the opportunity. Would he expect her to go with him? Yet it had been months — years, maybe — since she'd received a letter from him.

"What if I don't want to leave this place?"

Aunt Haruko let out a snort. "Trust me, we want to leave, Lily."

"But where'll we go?"

"God will guide us."

SHE FELT SAFER around the doctor. It was preferable to spend her days with him at the hospital. He gave Lily simple chores to keep her hands occupied, like cutting gauze into tiny squares and refilling bottles. Off in the corner of the ward she sat with her chin down, doing these mechanical tasks for hours.

People looked at her strangely, as though she were cursed; they'd heard rumours about what she'd been through. They knew she was mixed up in the Frank Isaka business.

From the second floor window, she could see in the distance a smattering of tiny, dark heads. So people had started gathering at the firebreak again. Although there weren't that many at first, more folks soon began coming. Each day more heads were clustered there, like an ever-growing black fungus.

Sixteen

Rita's apartment looked more lived in now. Stained wine glasses sat on the coffee table, a vinegary tang in the air. Bed unmade, a crumpled mass that made her think of toppled over sandcastles. A numb ache crept over her. Lily was still out there, and they were no closer to finding her, yet that hadn't stopped Rita from pissing away the morning in bed with Mark, like a horny teenager.

Images of her mother, lost, desperate. On a street corner, panhandling beneath a skyscraper. Wandering past neon sex shops and feral-eyed junkies. If she'd even stopped in New York. Just as likely she'd never gotten off the bus or had slipped onto a connector that sped through the night to Boston, Providence, Chicago. Or she'd hitched a ride along the highway. Had some thug picked her up? Had she been left for dead in a cornfield?

Closing her eyes, Rita counted backward from ten, slowly. She tried to breathe and talk herself down.

Mark had left to teach his afternoon class. He said he'd call later so they could make plans to go to the library. The library. It sounded so ridiculously wholesome.

In these situations she usually immersed herself in blasé indifference. It didn't matter if he didn't call her. Big fucking deal. He had a nerdy laugh and snored as though he were sucking a pillow up his nostrils.

The problem was that she did need to see him. If for no other reason than he'd said he was a kick-ass researcher. Something useful might as well come of their tryst.

She stared out the window at nothing in particular and then wandered out to the porch. The park was empty, beyond a couple of small, pudgy children waddling across the grass. A girl in cut-off jean shorts with a bandanna tied around her hair sat on a blanket, half watching them, half looking like she wanted to get away. Was she their mom? She looked too young to have kids already. But Lily must have been around that age when she had Tom and the whole family moved to Toronto. That had been after the war, after they'd been released from camp. How had they managed to build a new life here? What a world of struggle it must have been. When Rita tried to imagine how her mother had done it, every muscle in her body felt heavy with tiredness itself.

IT HAD BEEN three days since she'd heard from Gerald. She wondered if he'd received any updates from the police. When no one answered the phone, she waited twenty minutes and called again. Nada. Finally, she decided to go over and wait until he got back.

Rita let herself in using the key under the flowerpot. In the kitchen, dishes were piled up, smeared with bright orange sauce and pellet-like bits that looked disturbingly like mouse droppings. A twenty-sixer of Crown Royal — half empty — had been left open on the counter.

Gerald's wallet lay on the ledge by the door along with his car keys. At least he'd had the sense not to jump behind the wheel. But why wasn't he responding to her shouts? Had he fallen and hit his head? Bleeding to the brain, that could really do you in. Or maybe he'd gone missing just like Lily — this house had the tendency to swallow people whole, push them down rabbit holes to the other side of the world.

Rita ran upstairs two steps at a time. She felt like she'd slipped into *Murder, She Wrote*, some minor, clueless character about to burst into the master bedroom and discover a dead body.

It was empty. The ensuite, too. A peculiar bumping was coming from somewhere up above. A repetitive thud, not the scuttle of squirrels you'd expect in the attic. She rushed to the rear of the house. In a little office room, a pull-down ladder dangled mid-air.

"Gerald?" she called up into the black pit as the rungs creaked and a flurry of silver moats floated down on her forehead.

Diffuse, watery light spread across the sloped ceiling from a flashlight on the floor. He was slumped against the back wall, his head rolled forward, long white strands curtaining his eyes, the look of a mad composer. Rita ran over and shook him — the hair flew back as his head banged behind. His eyes clenched and then sprung open: piss drunk, mocking, sad.

"Hiya, Rita — what're ya doin' here? Your ma no longer lives here, haven't you heard?"

"Gerald." She touched his forehead. At least, his skin didn't feel too cold. She remembered when one of her old roommates had nearly died of alcohol poisoning — her skin had been icy, like defrosting chicken. "Lily hasn't left you. Don't be silly. She's just … away. For a little alone time. Remember what Officer Davis said?"

"Sure." His jack-o'-lantern grin faded. He pushed a box of doughnuts toward her with his foot. "Have a cherry Danish. Or two. Cherry Danishes always make things better."

That explained the red smear across his shirt — better than blood. "How much have you had, Gerald?"

"Three — maybe four — pastries."

"To *drink*."

"Aw, I dunno, Rita." An empty mickey rolled on the floor. "I was just, I was just, I dunno, tryin' to be a nice husband, so maybe my wife'll come back, ya know?"

"By getting shit-faced?"

A look of mild indignation. His arms made an expansive gesture. "Lily's always wanted this palace to be her sewing room. So I figured, let's surprise her, okay?"

The clunky black Singer sewing machine sat on the floor beside him. Lily hadn't used that thing since Rita was a kid. Now sewing was her hobby, her passion? What was she going to make? Heart-shaped pot holders?

Rita sank to a crouch and nibbled a Danish; the artificial cherry filling was surprisingly comforting, like children's cough syrup. Gerald's feet stretched out, clad in those fake-leather old-man slippers that Grandpa used to wear.

"Ya know, I thought how could a poor sucker like me get so lucky? Why did Lily marry *me*?" His eyes filmed up, his face, the colour of oatmeal, hollowed out by grief. "I mean, I know her first husband was somethin' amazing — a doctor and all."

Grim laughter caught in Rita's throat. "Oh, you must've misunderstood. That's my grandfather. *He* was the doctor. My father, Kaz, might've wanted to be a doctor at one point. But he wasn't. He wasn't much of anything."

"Are you sure 'bout that, kiddo? I'm pretty sure Lily said she was married to a big shot doctor."

"Yeah, Gerald. *I know my own father.*" But she didn't know her own father; she'd never known her fucking father. Anger splashed over her, hot, roiling — suddenly, she felt she might be the drunk one. Why did it always feel as though everything had happened too late? Before she'd been born, it had already been game over. They'd never had a chance at being anything resembling a normal, happy family.

"Then why would Lily lie to me about her first hubby?"

He was about an inch away from using her shoulder as a pillow. "Sure, Mom *wanted* to marry a doctor. She probably wished she could've married Grandpa. Had he been twenty years younger, she'd have been all over him." The last morsel got stuffed into her mouth, mealy and nauseating. "That's the thing about my mother. She's not so good at distinguishing between fantasy and reality. She *wishes* she'd married a doctor, so voilà! She *did*. Only in her crazy-ass mind."

"I guess there's a lot of stuff I didn't realize about my wife. Okay. Everyone has flaws. I just wanna help her get better."

"Yeah, well. That makes two of us."

They sank into silence and Rita draped an arm around his shoulder.

"So who *was* your old man, then?"

"I don't know. Some guy my mother met at camp."

"The internment camp?"

She nodded. "Grandpa and Mom never talked about Kaz. I think he must've been a real bastard, frankly." Maybe Kaz had never wanted to marry her. A shotgun wedding. Maybe they hadn't even bothered to get married; no one had ever seen any wedding pictures. A man who was good with the ladies, a man who liked to dance. Had Lily actually said that? Or had Rita only imagined it, her memory willing to fabricate anything so it would have a fragile scaffolding?

"What happened to this Kaz fellow, in the end?"

"Oh, Gerald. It's way too complicated."

"Try me. Tom mentioned he took off before you were born. Then he died of a stroke, out in California. Where in California?"

"Dunno."

"Well, where was the funeral?"

"We weren't taken to any funeral."

Had there been a funeral? If it hadn't been for that woman who'd called, they wouldn't have even known anything was amiss. Rita had been the one who'd answered. She'd just turned six and found the telephone a great source of fascination — a voice from another realm whispering in your ear through a magical cord — so Lily had let her pick up, finding something cute about a little girl so eager to play receptionist. The voice on the other end sounded husky and mannish at first. Then it softened. A cough or hiccup, as though the woman had been crying. "You must be Kaz's daughter." Or maybe, years later, Rita only imagined the hiccup and cobwebs of emotion. Only in retrospect did everything about that brief conversation seem preserved in minute detail, as if time itself had slowed down and the afternoon light would continue flowing in watery, goldish beams down the centre of their kitchen forever. It was one of her earliest memories. The before moment. Before everything changed. If nothing out of the ordinary had happened, all that would have been forgotten.

But something *had* happened. Rita passed the phone to her mother. Whatever the woman said, it caused Lily to straighten up, jump back. She held the phone away from her ear like it was a scalding iron. "He couldn't — he couldn't have —" Then she sank to the floor, her legs splayed out at weird angles.

As Rita bent down over her mother's heaving body, she noticed for the first time that the linoleum was covered in a pattern of grey-brown pebbles. Perhaps you were supposed to imagine yourself at the edge of an island, looking out, stranded. Those fake, intricately rendered stones jumped out with all their absurdity and from that day forward, a shivering, nauseous sensation would overtake her whenever she set foot on linoleum.

Without realizing it, she must have screamed for Grandpa because he came shuffling along in his slippers. He picked up the dangling phone. While he talked to whoever she was, on the other end, his gaze swept the room and fastened on a crack across the ceiling. "Oh, I see. I see. I see." His eyes bulged. The crack seemed to grow longer each time he repeated himself.

The next day, Grandpa left for California to settle Kaz's affairs. The rest of the family stayed behind. Not that there'd been any discussion about them going with him.

"YOU'RE STAYING AT *Jodi's apartment?*"

"Yeah." Kristen spoke like it was the most natural thing in the world. "Daddy's here with me, too."

"Because …?"

"Something went wrong at his house. Water's everywhere. All my shoes got ruined!"

Cal sounded sheepish when Rita demanded to speak with him. It turned out that he'd been dabbling in a little do-it-yourself reno-vation. ("And who was watching our daughter, while you were doing all this?" Oh right, he had built-in child care, otherwise known as his new girlfriend.) In the course of putting up a wall, Cal had some-how managed to sever a pipe. Should have stuck with what he was good at: root canals. The place ended up flooded. Under other cir-cumstances, it would be quite funny. But poor Kristen. She sounded stuffed up, as though she were coming down with a cold already.

"You sure you're all right, Pumpkin? You don't have to stay there if it's uncomfortable."

"Where'll I go?"

"I'll fly to Vancouver and come get you, of course!"

"Oh, I'm all right. Jodi's making me a grilled cheese sandwich."

Heat flared through Rita's cheeks. With a great deal of effort, she managed to say, "Well, that's nice of her to put you guys up. Jodi sounds like a nice lady."

"She is. I think you'd really like her, Mommy."

Yeah, right. Not in a thousand years. "Make sure Daddy buys you new shoes, sweetie. Something really expensive, okay?"

RITA WAS TRYING not to get too bent out of shape. A couple hours ago, a stream of little kids in sun hats had bobbed past her window on the way home from day camp, and now they were followed by the plod-ding feet of their dads. Normally, she wasn't like this at all. She wasn't the type of woman who sat around waiting for some guy to *maybe* call her. But it was the fact that Mark had allied himself with her endeavour to find Lily, combined with the reality that she was feeling rather old and out of practice when it came to etiquette after a casual hookup, combined with her disturbing conversations with Gerald and Kristen and the thick, fuzzy layer of a sleepless night wrapped around her brain.

Finally, Rita called the number he'd jotted on the edge of a paper towel.

Although she expected an answering machine, Mark answered on the second ring. "The library. I'm *so* sorry. I completely forgot."

"Everything all right, Mark? Have I caught you at a bad time?"

"Not at all. It's just that I got detained by some students after class. It's supposed to be summer term, but these kids aren't your usual slackers. All stressed out over the mid-term. They talked my ear off and left me so exhausted it slipped my mind, our library meeting."

His voice sounded guarded, artificially friendly, yet impersonal, as though someone were there listening to his every word. The mere fact that he said "library meeting," rather than "library date" seemed telling, but maybe she was over-scrutinizing

A strident voice in the background strangled off as he muffled the receiver. Someone *was* there. A woman? Did Mark live with someone? His wife?

She hadn't noticed any wedding ring. That didn't mean shit, of course. Lots of men chose not to wear them. Cal said it cut off his circulation.

Her cheeks stung with surprise, humiliation. "Look, I should probably let you go. Sounds like you've got your hands full at the moment."

"Wait, the library — I really do want to help, Rita. If you don't mind, though, can we postpone 'til tomorrow?"

"Of course, no big deal." She hated how her voice sounded overly bright. "Tomorrow morning, fine. Ten o'clock at Robarts." She might have been on the phone with the receptionist at a doctor's office, rather than the guy who'd licked every inch of her body just hours ago, right down to her baby toes.

Seventeen

Things had been smelling stronger, more vivid. Not in a good way. Normally, Lily loved a cup of tea first thing in the morning, but now disgust crawled over her. The milk was rancid, that must be it. Come to think of it, all food smelled a bit off. Her own loins, too: sickly sweet, fermented odours emanated up from between her thighs.

And yet she was ravenously hungry. No matter how much she ate or drank, however, she couldn't wash the rust taste from her teeth.

Her breasts had grown veiny and bovine, nipples fluttering with an urge to be pulled at, licked, bitten.

Was this how it felt to be …?

She told herself no, *no*. It couldn't be.

The wail of someone's baby filled the walls of the hospital. The wretched cry worked its way into her brain. A tight, panicked feeling wrapped around her womb, her wayward womb….

She'd been ignoring it for days, for weeks, unable to face how her body was changing. But the willful ignorance she'd been wrapping herself in couldn't block the truth forever.

"Aunt Haruko, I think I'm —"

"Yes." Grey cheeks downcast.

"What … what am I going to …?"

"Does Kaz know?"

Lily shook her head. She needed to find him.

"And the doctor?"

"No." Telling him would be even harder, more horrible. Or would it?

Surely, he'd help her. He'd know what to do. Maybe he'd be happy, slightly. Babies gave people hope. *Kaz just needs to grow up and take responsibility.* Wasn't that what the doctor had said?

That evening, she couldn't bring herself to say anything. The next day she geared herself up to pull the doctor aside, but the hospital was so busy she never got the chance.

It was dusk by the time things slowed down. Curled up in a chair against the wall, she succumbed to a wave of fatigue.

Her eyes fluttered open. Creaks. Shifting feet at the end of the hall. Through the gauze of her sleep-crusted lashes, she could see shadows spilling like translucent curtains. A door inched open. It was the little room where she used to do ikebana, where she and Kaz had once made love in the flush of dawn. She never went in there these days.

The doctor slipped out into a wedge of sepia light. He carried a tray of empty dishes and a silver bedpan.

When she jumped up to help him, he looked up and jerked back — a waterfall of shi-shi sloshed onto the floor.

"Who's in there?"

Her first instinct was it must be Kaz. The doctor was sheltering him from interrogation or arrest. Kaz was in hiding. Relief glided over her. She could tell them both the news about the baby right now.

"*Lily.*" The doctor shook droplets from his palm.

"I want to know."

"Keep your voice down."

She made a move to slip around him, but he blocked her way. If she pushed past, everything in his arms risked clattering to the ground.

"It's not what you think." A terrified whisper. "I *had* to keep Frank here. He begged me. The camp bosses said it's for the best."

"Frank Isaka?" Her heart plunged.

"Who else?"

"But I thought … I thought …" What had she thought? Out of sight, out of mind. Hadn't the doctor said Frank's injuries hadn't been that serious? So she'd wanted to believe he'd recovered and gone on his merry way. He was back on the lecture circuit, touring the country, singing the praises of the JACC.

"Frank's been here all along. No one knows. Howells told me to keep it under wraps. Everyone thinks his injuries were so severe he had to be transferred to the hospital in town."

"You're keeping him here to protect him?" It was the first time she'd thought of the hospital as a refuge.

"What choice did I have? The beating stirred things up, all over. A lot of people have it in for Frank."

The doctor felt responsible for his fate, she could smell it in the yeasty, putrid air between them. Because he knew it had been Kaz who'd delivered the beating.

"How long are you planning to keep him hidden here?"

"As long as it takes, I guess."

"As long as it takes for what?"

"I don't know."

She'd never seen the doctor look so unsteady; the feeble, old man he was going to become had emerged in pencil outline all over his face.

SHE KNOCKED HESITANTLY. "It's me. Lily. Won't you please let me in, Frank?"

Something grated across the floor inside, a chair being pushed away.

As she entered, Frank scurried back into bed. The small, pallid face with purple bruises around the eyes startled her. He was like a feral animal — cornered, frenzied, yet oddly resigned. What had become of this guy's confident, arrogant air? The brightness and vigour that used to infuse his cheeks? All those snappy slogans that had sprung from his lips? Now they were slack, crusted with spittle. She'd never noticed the narrowness of his shoulders. In her mind, Frank Isaka had been a muscular, athletic fellow. The room smelled of deadness, decay — all the foul odours of an unwashed, uncared-for body.

In the corner, perched atop a crate, were the remains of one of her flower arrangements: a pile of yellowish slackened leaves. Not so long ago it had been alive. All her greenery had been laid out on this very cot.

She tried to smile. The tray lurched in her hands, cutlery clattering. She set it down atop a stack of books. "You have to believe I had no idea this was going to happen."

"Of course you didn't, Lily. How could you? We were being followed. If you hadn't run for help, who knows whether I'd still be breathing!"

Where she'd expected accusation and distrust in his eyes, there was only gratitude and helplessness. She felt sickened.

"You're a good person, Lily. Not like those masked cowards." He licked his lips and a hint of pinkness flowed back. "It's like Swift says. Ever read *Gulliver's Travels*?" He gestured at the book. "What can I do if, like Gulliver, my crew chooses to mutiny? After all I've done to help them survive, how do they repay me? By turning against me. By holding me captive, by deserting me, by continuing on with their depraved lives as a bunch of pirates!" Saliva ribbons flew outward as the bruises on his cheekbones emitted a crazed glow.

So it seemed he didn't know. Could it be possible that he really didn't know? For he'd made no mention of Kaz, Shig, or Akira. Frank was so cut off from the everyday goings-on that he had no idea who had it in for him.

"Who did this to you?"

"Yahoos, of course. They're all a bunch of yahoos. Base, humanoid creatures — incapable of ruling themselves, of ruling anything!"

She wasn't sure what he was talking about, but he wasn't pointing the finger at Kaz. Or her. He looked at her like he believed she was on his side. Like she was still a nice, pure girl.

And maybe it was true — maybe she really hadn't known what Kaz had been planning when she'd lured Frank to that desolate place. But she had known in her gut, hadn't she? The stillness of the air, touched by the sting of animal potency, of furry, sweaty, musky haunches, a smell she'd become all too familiar with — of course, she'd known it was him, it was Kaz, waiting in ambush, *she must have known* — but, but wasn't it also true that she'd only been there to protect Kaz at the doctor's request? This other, fading voice ribboned through the noise: sweet, innocent, brimming with hope. The voice of the Strong One. Mother's good little girl. The mewl of the baby in her own belly.

"Is there anything I can do to help?"

"Just sit with me, Lily. Read to me, please."

SHE EXPECTED TO see more FBI agents. After all Frank had been through, shouldn't someone be under the gun to find out who was responsible?

Something had changed, that much was obvious. The G-men had been desperate to cast blame on Kenny Honda. This time around, however, they had no ringleader to point fingers at. Yet they didn't even seem to be looking — that was the strangest part. No one hounded Lily with questions. No one roamed the halls of the hospital.

"Why isn't the FBI doing more? Aren't you worried they'll need to pin the attack on somebody?"

"Not really." The doctor gave a weary shrug. "Frank Isaka might like to believe the camp admin will look out for him. Truth is they're quite happy to look the other way, chalk this one up to a fist fight gone too far. They're tired of the bad publicity this camp's been getting. The sooner they empty the place out, the better."

More barracks were being dismantled. It was amazing how quickly these flimsy buildings could be turned into heaps of scrap. So it was all coming to an end. Their life here would soon be no more. And she'd be … where? Somewhere else. Somewhere better. The doctor, Aunt Haruko, Lily, Kaz, the baby. They'd be a family no different than any other family, and her child would remember nothing of this awful place.

Despite the busloads leaving each week, plenty of tired, disgruntled folks remained to gather at the firebreak to scheme and cause trouble. Every afternoon they were out there. Kaz must be in the thick of it, stirring up dissent. While some people were in an uproar that Frank was still alive, others were upset that the camp admin wasn't doing more to apprehend his attacker. Caught up in the whirl of collective action, these differences melted away.

She needed to find Kaz. She still hadn't told him about the baby. Ever since her discovery of Frank, that little life inside her felt insubstantial, unreal.

She hadn't been sleeping well, her dreams turbulent, desperate. Images of great crashing waves, the water lapping at her ankles. As it pulled outward, her toes sank into the mealy sand.

The tide. Before she knew it, the water had crept up to her thighs, hips, womb. And yet she couldn't move, all sensation in her legs suddenly lost, the icy water a strange anaesthetic.

Then she was flapping wildly, trying to propel herself forward, lugging the dead weight of her pitiful, useless body. Waves surged up and pummelled her in the face, knocking her into the undertow, and when she fought her way up for a gulp of air, the last thing she saw before awaking was a small, white dolphin, jumping through a misty spray.

She spent her evenings at Frank's bedside, feeding him soup and reading aloud from *Gulliver's Travels*. The weird, fantastical tales filled her with anxious awareness of how unknowable the world would always be.

"Do you ever wonder what you'll do after the war's over, Frank?"

"What makes you think the war'll ever end?"

"They say it's ending right now. We're going back to our real lives soon."

"Real lives." He snorted, fiddled a finger in his ear, as though he were trying to dig out a long-dead fly.

A LOW RUMBLE in the distance. The rise and fall of shouting voices. Patter of feet from behind. The doctor's once confident stride, now reduced to a scurry. Without even turning around, she could sense his taut posture, his grief-stricken expression.

"Do you hear that, Lily?"

She nodded, surprised he could hear it, too. So these voices were real, not just in her head. They were chanting something in English or Japanese, she couldn't be sure which. "Banzai!" rose above the din. It was getting louder, like a drumbeat.

Lily and the doctor ran upstairs to the windows facing east. People were gathered at the firebreak by the hundreds, possibly thousands. Several thousands? They resembled an army of ants — jostling, roiling black heads packed tightly together. They were swarming around a stage, where several leaders appeared full of energy and rancour.

"There have been more arrests, Lily. People are very upset."

"Was Kaz arrested?"

"No. Shig and his older brother."

"Toyo? That's crazy. He's never had anything to do with this."

"Who knows whether he has? This morning there was another skirmish when some guys attacked a bunch of evacuee police officers. One of the officers is in critical condition. Howells has ordered the military to be on standby."

The military? She tried to get her head around what the doctor was telling her. He might have been talking through the fog of a dream.

"Lily? Are you all right?"

She nodded, shook her head.

"You've got to stay with me. I can't have you fainting now. There's something I need you to do — *Lily, do you hear me?*"

Her brain came unfrozen, everything rebounding with startling vividness. "I'm fine. What is it?"

"You need to wake up Frank and hide him. That crowd is after his blood."

"Where ... where am I supposed to hide him?"

"Look around the ward. See what you can find." Although the doctor tried to keep his voice calm, the note of panic was unmistakable. "The important thing is that you do it *now*."

Gazing out the window, she saw what had him so agitated. The crowd had started moving, heading toward the hospital.

Eighteen

Rita planned to arrive at the library a good fifteen minutes late. At a coffee shop near the subway she killed time, staring out at the sidewalk, blotched with patches of drizzle. Mark was an ass. He probably wouldn't even show up. So she'd better just assume nothing would work out between them and keep her eye on the real target: Lily.

Turning onto St. George, she walked past a hodgepodge of U of T buildings, departments so small and esoteric that an entire faculty could be crammed into these turreted, ivy-covered houses. At the end of the block loomed Robarts Library, a massive concrete building that had always made her think of a Lego castle.

She entered a dim lobby. At the far end escalators zigzagged up and down. Aside from a few grad students, who looked like they hadn't seen sunlight in years, the place was deserted.

Ah, there he was. Hands tucked in the back pockets of his jeans, lost in thought, shaggy tendrils still damp from the shower. From this place of invisibility, she enjoyed watching Mark — but then he saw her. His face lit up as the distance between them closed, and she couldn't help but feel that crazy, half-dead fish in her stomach. He kissed her on the side of the lips: a disturbingly ambiguous kiss that could perhaps pass as merely friendly (if he were European) or be interpreted as a real kiss that had swerved off course at the last second.

"Sorry again about yesterday."

The herbal, lemongrassy smell of his shampoo. The humidity of his skin. It irritated her that she couldn't help noticing these things. "It's fine. It's nice that your students want to hang out and chat."

A pothole of silence. Slight heave of the chest, as though he were summoning himself. But whatever he planned to say, he chickened out.

"Do you, by any chance, live with someone, Mark?" The words burst from her lips.

"I do, actually." Cheeks aflame.

"Okay …? I thought I heard a woman in the background."

A tight, sheepish smile.

"Lemme guess. You're married, but you and your wife have a little arrangement. You just kinda do your own thing, from time to time. You don't believe in being possessive of each other. Possessiveness's part of the whole evil, capitalist ethos." These academic types were all a bunch of new lefties of convenience.

"Not exactly."

"Relax, Mark." She tried to smile, like she didn't much care. "It was just one night. No biggie. I wasn't expecting to wear your letter sweater or anything."

"Maybe you'd look cute in my letter sweater?"

Now he was truly being a prick. "You're *married*."

"I'm not married."

"But you're with someone."

"Not really. It's hard to explain. Tess and I started out as old friends, nothing more or less. We went to high school together." He massaged the crook of his neck. "Then when I moved back to Toronto and needed a place to stay, she asked if I'd like to be roommates. At some point, things got messy."

"I see." Late one night, watching a TV movie together. Telling each other about their shit days. One too many beers or maybe something stronger. Before you know it, there's kissing, groping. Waking up the next morning in the other person's bed, surrounded by crumpled condom wrappers. Rita could fill in the blanks.

Besides, was it any different than what had happened between them?

He blushed, as if he could sense what she was thinking. "But I don't want you to think that you and I ..."

"That what?" The old blasé indifference had returned with a vengeance. "Really, Mark. You don't have to explain anything."

"It's not like that. Tess is moving out. *Soon*. We ended it, like, over four months ago — bad idea in the first place. It's just that it hasn't been easy for her to find a new place. She got laid off a few weeks ago, and I just haven't had the heart to, well, you know, make a friend *homeless*." His hands shoved in his back pockets again, as though he were trying to stabilize himself.

So her first instincts had been right? He was the do-gooder type, seeking out damaged, neurotic women, wounded birds he wanted to save. Hardly a comforting thought. Was he toying with her? Trying to find some creative leeway around the fact that he lived with his girlfriend?

"Maybe we should, I don't know...." He splayed his hands.

"Just be friends?"

He appeared taken aback.

An image of this Tess woman popped into Rita's head: blond curls, beautiful in a high-strung, fragile way. Nastassja Kinski in Polanski's *Tess*. She had an intuition that Tess might have her own ideas about their relationship being kaput. "For now, anyway."

"Until I've got my shit together, you mean."

"In case you haven't noticed, my shit's not together either. Mom vanished off the face of the earth! I'm not exactly prime relationship material right now."

Right now or ever.

A small, pinched look. Maybe he was laughing at her. Maybe he liked that she'd said "relationship material." She felt unsteady, exposed.

"Fine, I'm here to help. As a friend, for now, if that's what you prefer." He gestured at the escalator, suddenly all businesslike. "Shall we?"

It took a moment to recall what he was talking about. Right. Research. The whole point of their visit. Her brain had turned to mush.

The escalator slowly ascended past a tall glass display case full of ancient books and other treasures. Mark began telling her all about the library's special collections — diaries and letters of famous writers and intellectuals, most of whom Rita had never heard of. He, on the other hand, said their names with an awe usually reserved for rock stars. So it wasn't only a nerdy laugh he had.

They passed an empty cafeteria on the second floor and circled around to the next escalator.

"This place is pretty dead in the summer," he said.

"I don't mind deadness."

"Like we're at a museum, the only two people left in the building after closing."

"I bet a lot of kids dream about that. Hiding in a broom closet and having all the dinosaur bones to themselves. Kristen would be into that."

"Kristen?"

Well, what was the big deal? He'd probably seen her toys around the apartment anyway. "My daughter. She's six. She loves the ROM."

"You'll have to introduce us. Chatting kids up about dinosaur bones is right up my alley."

Now he was definitely getting ahead of himself. She never introduced Kristen to any of her sleepover guests. Which pretty much limited her love life to one- or two-night stands while Kristen was away with Cal.

"So where is your daughter? Doesn't she live with you?"

"At her dad's in Vancouver for the rest of the month. Thank God. I don't know how I'd have explained Granny going AWOL."

They'd reached the fourth floor. A sign for the Periodicals Reading Room greeted them. Mark looked so calm and relaxed, his conscience now cleansed, thanks to the fact she'd forced him to come clean with her. So he got to have his cake and eat it, too? She felt very close to saying, "You know what? Let's just not do this." And taking the elevator down.

But they were here, so what the hell. What did she have to lose?

They entered a spacious room with high ceilings. Jaundiced light pooled on tables occupied only by a homeless man bent over a newspaper. A wall of windows displayed an impressive view of the skyline rising into the grey, clotted sky, above the shingled rooftops and turrets in the neighbourhood below.

"Refresh my memory," Mark whispered. "What is it we're supposed to be researching again?"

"The Matanzas Riot."

"Right." He wended his way around bookshelves, checking call numbers.

"What are you looking for?"

"If you want to find out what happened, the fastest way is to check newspaper coverage at the time. So we're looking for … yeah, here it is. *Comprehensive Guide to Periodical Literature.*"

Multiple volumes, thick as phone books, dusty and bound in cracked green leather, stared down at them. Mark pulled down the one that covered 1941–1943, according to its gold lettered spine, and lugged it to a table near the window. A sharp, mildewy odour filled the air as he opened the yellowed pages. The columns of type were so tiny you almost needed a magnifying glass.

"All articles that were published in newspapers and magazines between 1941 and 1943 have been listed alphabetically under topic headings," he explained. "Looking up 'Matanzas,' it says to see 'Japanese in the United States.'" He flipped back. "Okay, so here it is."

He was pointing at an entry that read, if she leaned forward and squinted:

JAPANESE in the United States

Aliens, but good for the economy; shortages in agriculture and business. il Business Week p 42 F 28 '42

American with oriental eyes; responses to the issue of internment. H. Ashikawa. il CS Mon Je 22 '42

Are internees to become pawns? K. Greene. il NY Times p4+ Ja 15 '42

Business in internment camps. il Business Week p 22–23+ Jl 25 '42

Concentration camps homegrown in America. K. Nakamura. New Repub 110:742–3 Je 7 '42

Democracy for Japanese-Americans? R. Smith. Christian Cent 56:624–5 D 16 '42

Educational pioneering at camps in California. L.R. Fairhurst. Sch R 36:65 Ap '43

Evacuating citizens of the United States. M. Duval. Nation 162:652 My 16 '42

Helping Japanese evacuees. J. Burrows. Christian Cent 64:562 Ap 8 '42

The list continued for the rest of the page. Some titles implied sympathy for the internees while others suggested indifference or support of martial law. But none of that political, ideological crap mattered. When she'd reached the end of the entry, she went back to the beginning and tried to discern from the all too vague titles which article might hold the key to understanding her mother's life.

"I don't know where to start. Are all these articles available?"

"Not all, but they'll have a lot of them in the microfilm collection downstairs." Mark had moved closer to read over her shoulder. "At the end of the main entry, there are also entries on the separate camps."

She followed his gaze:

Matanzas camp

Coast Japs interned in the mountains; Matanzas, Calif. il Life 13:16–20 D 20 '43

Crisis at Matanzas. Newsweek 23: 58+ D 24 '43

Seeing the name of the camp in print gave her body a jolt. The place suddenly seemed real, too real.

"I guess we'll try these?" She jotted down the information on a scrap of paper.

They made their way down to the third floor. A black kid with a massive afro and cherub-cute face sat behind the desk in the media office; he went to find the reels while Mark led her to a viewing booth along the wall. A primitive-looking TV monitor perched beside a contraption with many knobs and spools.

"You're okay with the set-up, Dr. Edo?"

"I got it covered, Corey."

Corey gave Rita a long, curious once-over. High-school and university kids were no different, it seemed, always taking a prurient interest in their teachers' personal lives.

It didn't take long for Mark to attach the first reel to the machine. He flicked on the monitor, which illuminated a smudge of newsprint, and adjusted the focus. The guy had nimble fingers. She pushed the tawdry thought aside.

He hit fast-forward and issues of *Newsweek* flew by, a whir of headlines. As they approached the reel's midpoint, he stopped to turn the reel manually while they checked for dates. He kept going: ads for artificial Christmas trees and Hellmann's mayo and Spam went by. At last, December 24, 1943, came up.

Beneath the headline was an inky photograph: crude, dark buildings had been photographed from a distance through a swirl of barbed wire along the camp's perimeter.

Nineteen

Even in his sleep, Frank looked troubled. Lily shook him. The healed eye fluttered open while the other one twitched, like an insect on the verge of dying.

She explained about the crowd of angry protesters headed to the hospital.

"What do they want?"

"I don't know."

But she did know. They both knew.

"You've got to help me. I'm not ready to die!" He bolted up.

She'd found a shawl to drape over his head and knot under his chin. It was the best they could do for a disguise at short notice.

"Where are we going, Lily?"

The main ward on the ground floor was too crowded. The closet in the corner would be large enough, but she'd never manage to get him in without people noticing. It was far too obvious anyway. The second floor — the room at the back, used for storage — had more possibilities.

"Follow me. I have an idea."

The hall was empty. Everyone had gathered at the windows to peer out at the advancing crowd. Lily and Frank scurried to the back stairs and darted up.

"Over here." She grabbed his hand. People were so riveted by the spectacle they didn't notice the two people sneaking by.

The backroom was dark and musty. Boxes of supplies had been piled up, along with a good deal of old medical equipment that hospitals in the region had donated. Much of it, according to the doctor, didn't even work.

She guided Frank around the bulky pieces to the wall. She pointed at a small door that barely reached her waist. It was a strange little closet; when she'd first discovered it, she'd thought it would be perfect for a child playing hide-and-seek.

"Crouch down and crawl in. I'll bring you a pillow and blanket."

Bewilderment shot through his face. Yet he did as he was told. After he'd settled, she closed the door, leaving it open just a crack. One by one, she lugged large boxes over to create a barricade that hid the door completely.

"Are you all right in there?"

"Just get me out of here alive, Lily."

LOOKING OUT THE window, she gasped. The crowd had gathered right outside: a jumble of upturned faces and waving fists. Some clasped signs; others wielded stones. How many people were out there? They seemed to stretch back forever until they faded into the landscape itself.

"Banzai!" people shouted over and over while the old-timers sang patriotic Japanese military songs.

The young men at the front ventured closer. Someone hurled a rock that hit the main door with a crash, followed by a flinty shower. She backed away from the window but couldn't resist peering out a second later. Was Kaz out there on the front line, flinging stones? She scanned the crowd, unable to find him anywhere; everyone blurred into the sea of angry, anonymous faces.

The doctor rushed in. "Christ, they're going to charge the door at any minute — we have to stop them! Lily, round up the other staff and tell them to meet us at the front door. On your way, lock the back."

"But there are only a handful of nurses on duty. We're not going to be able to keep all these people out!"

"We have to try. Howells will send in military assistance soon."

"Military assistance? Are you sure that's necessary?"

"I don't have time to debate this with you — just go!"

She rushed downstairs, too terrified to be upset by his tone. "Yasuko, where's Kimi? Grab her and whoever else is on duty, and meet me at the front door. Doctor's orders!"

The girl remained paralyzed.

"Now!"

Sweeping the wild locks from her forehead, Yasuko sprang to life.

Lily ran through the hospital and grabbed the few other nurses she recognized.

The doctor was waiting near the main door. His eyes were closed and he was breathing deeply, trying to rescue a moment of clarity.

On the other side, the crowd chanted, "*Hand over Frank Isaka! Kill all traitors!*"

The shouting was accompanied by a deep rumble that seemed to come from all directions. It was as though some giant beast were breathing all around her — infiltrating her lungs, spreading up over her skull, filling her with a manic, caged-in feeling. Rustling, murmurs, marauding voices, screams, whoops of angry glee.... Internal and external worlds blended together in this living, breathing, shuddering animal that was, at once, everywhere and nowhere.

The doctor opened his eyes as she approached. "I have to go out there and address them," he said.

"But if you unlock the door, they'll storm in!"

"Lock or no lock, a few men could break down this door easily. No, our only hope is for me to go out there and try to reason with them."

As he pulled the door open, sunlight spanked across her vision. Everyone blended together in the mass face of this creature that reflected only the dazzling sun.

"Ladies and gentlemen." The doctor stepped outside. "You ask me to turn over Frank Isaka, but the fact of the matter is he isn't here. His injuries were so severe he had to be sent to the hospital in town!"

Jeers and hisses rose all around.

"You liar! You inu!" A cigarette arced through the air and sizzled at his feet.

"We know Frank's in there, safe and sound!"

He held up his hands, in a sign of defeat or an indication the crowd should settle down, Lily didn't know which. "If you don't believe me, I'm willing to let a couple men inside to search the hospital. But I can guarantee you won't find Frank."

What made the doctor so confident? What if they discovered Frank and killed him on the spot?

Amid more boos and hisses, someone stepped forward.

Kaz. She caught her breath, unable to believe it was actually him. He'd pushed his way to the front, followed by Akira.

His innocence was what struck her at that moment. His arms were crossed and she couldn't help but notice their graceful curves, two hills dipping into a valley. While he looked at his father, something in Kaz's eyes, shiny as melted ice, made her think he could see the future: a land of beautiful simplicity, of strawberry farms dotted with rice-picker hats, of pretty girls licking ice cream cones, eager to jump forth to have their pictures taken. A world where things always came out right for him. Not because he was the doctor's son — he didn't realize how much slack people cut him on account of that fact — but simply because he considered it his God-given right.

How she wanted to protect him. Bury his face against her neck, like he'd regressed to being a little boy. And maybe he'd start crying, as she was crying now, and his tears would soak through her dress and everything would be washed clean.

But he didn't even seem aware of her presence, his gaze fixed on his father. "If you're lying, we're *all* storming in. You understand, Dad?"

Dad. The word seemed to cut into him. As the doctor turned away, his jaw slackened.

While Kaz rushed past, she grabbed his arm.

"Lily, what are *you* doing here?"

There was so much she wanted to say to him. And yet, she just kept staring at him, waiting for him to speak first. He looked at her like he couldn't trust her. Like she'd crossed over to the other side.

"Don't do this, Kaz. Please, *don't.* You're throwing everything away — our future together —"

"My future? I've never had a future. Not the kind you and my father fantasize!"

His words stung, but she pushed them from her mind, refusing to believe he meant any of it. Once this was all over, he'd grow up, take responsibility.

With every tear that ran down her cheeks, a flutter of life was making itself felt inside her belly. She was going to have a baby, the doctor's grandchild. Her body felt as though it had no boundaries of its own, like nothing more than a collection of so many tingling, coursing sensations....

A flash of movement on the periphery. A band of soldiers had moved in.

"Kaz, there's something I need to tell you —"

But he'd already wrenched away, disappeared into the building.

TWENTY MINUTES LATER, the army had formed a thick line between the hospital and the protesters. A heavy-set man with a florid face and small moustache appeared to be the commander; he repeatedly ordered the crowd back. People continued to surge forward as a new excitement infused their blood, stirred up by the show of authority. The chanting grew louder and more boisterous, and more rocks were hurled forth.

"Stop!" shouted an old woman at the front. "If you don't stop throwing rocks, they'll have the right to fire on us!"

It was Mrs. Okada, right on the front line, feisty as ever.

No one listened, and the soldiers were met with bolder taunts. "Say please!"

"We're through taking orders from Uncle Sam!"

It looked like a small can, harmless as a soda pop. But it hissed and emitted smoke as it arced through the air.

Then people began coughing and doubling over, pushing every which way, rubbing their eyes and noses as tears and mucus streamed down their cheeks. The soldiers volleyed several more cans into the crowd, and the smoke and chaos thickened. Now folks were running blindly, trying to evade a target they couldn't see — bumping into each other and falling to the ground like piles of dirty, dishevelled laundry. Men pulled up their shirts to cover their eyes while women drew up their skirts, flashing flesh, no concern for modesty now. Screaming to the point that no words were distinguishable.

Lily backed into the doorway, her eyes on fire. A burning sensation covered her skin. The more she rubbed, the worse it got, worse than poison ivy.

If it hadn't been for that terrible itch, maybe she'd have seen the car approaching from the rear of the building. By the time she realized it was careening toward them — heading right for where she stood — all she could do was jump away from the impact. Thunderously, the wall shook and pieces of door frame clattered down amid a tornado of dust. The black car backed up to plough into the wall again. She lurched away, and all she could think was that the building was about to collapse and Kaz was inside. She felt her stomach and soul being sucked in after him, even as her feet carried her in the opposite direction....

She had to protect their baby.

As she looked back, everything appeared very still and bright, her sense of time frozen under the weight of the sun's glare. Hope crested inside her upon seeing that the building remained upright.

Gunfire pierced the air.

Soldiers had opened fire on the car. People were falling in puddles of blood — screaming at a whole new level of terror.

She was trying to elbow her way out. A bolt of lightning cut across the side of her face. Blood gushed onto her hands and she couldn't feel anything — the pain was so pervasive it cancelled out everything, a formless, searing coldness — and she sank to her knees, shrieking, the sky careening and covering her with its horribly placid blueness.

The doctor's face swam up and blocked her in shadow. His arms swooped down and carried her away through the smoke and chaos.

Twenty

"Crisis at Matanzas" in *Newsweek*
(December 24, 1943)

Last Friday afternoon, after weeks of dealing with as much rabble-rousing as 15,000 sons of heaven, Edward Howells threw in the towel on saving face for the War Relocation Authority. Fleeing the mob of Japs, the director of the Japanese evacuation center at Matanzas, Calif., put in a phone call to the Army — barely seconds before the mob took over the switchboard and axed all communication. Fortunately, the call got through to Col. Vernon Powers, who swiftly intervened by taking over the camp and restoring order, with the help of 1,000 men, tanks, tear gas, and Tommy guns.

The Army had awaited the call all day. Nevertheless, by the time Col. Powers received the green light, a dozen Japs and a handful of the center's guards had sustained injuries. As Army management moved in and took over, 25 more Japs were injured. An 8-year-old Eurasian boy, Timothy Dewson, died on the spot, while 30-year-old Wendy Ito was rushed to hospital and remains in critical condition.

Thus concluded the bloodiest encounter to break out at any of the WRA's evacuation centers for the Japanese. The problems had been escalating for the past three months, ever since a group of discontent, pro-Japanese agitators got together to organize a "Kitchen Workers Union." These angry young men have been spreading 1,001 rumors about lack of soap and other such amenities and an alleged sugar shortage — supposedly created by camp employees siphoning off supplies. A tall tale, indeed. (A standard lunch menu at the camp includes roast beef, green beans, salad, and coffee, with cream and plenty of sugar available. If only all of us could be so well fed during wartime!)

The real trouble at the camp was caused by bad blood between the old-time Japanese loyalists and the Japanese-American citizens who stepped forward to lead the Japanese American Citizens Confederacy. The loyalists have accused JACC leaders and supporters of being FBI informants who help to identify troublemakers. The result has been an atmosphere of suspicion and bloody confrontation. Beatings perpetrated on these so-called informants have become commonplace.

On Dec. 17, in the early afternoon, 3,000 or more men and women marched out of their barracks and workplaces to the hospital, where Frank Isaka, JACC President, was recovering after such a beating. The angry mob demanded his release (presumably to finish the poor man off) while throwing stones and singing the Japanese anthem and the Imperial Japanese Navy marching song. "Kill All Informers," the crowd chanted and disobeyed the Army's command to move back. When a troublemaker drove a vehicle into the side of the hospital, the Army fired upon the crowd with tear gas followed by a shower of gunfire.

After the Army had restored order, FBI agents immediately arrested and placed in special detention several men responsible for leading the riot, including Kaz Takemitsu, Akira Ogura, Kenji Kano and Thomas Nakamura. In total 15 evacuees were arrested and taken to a Civilian Conservation Corps camp. The Japanese aliens will be incarcerated by the Department of Justice, while the remaining Japanese-American citizens will be sent to a high-security detention camp, where they will be held for at least the rest of the war.

Frank Isaka, who remained safely hidden in the hospital throughout the riot, suffered no further injuries.

Mr. Howells — unarmed with his WRA public relations man who had resigned just before the incident — tried to hush up all news of the riot. His second-in-command, Clark Richardson, covered up the rumors by claiming it was all lies spread by the Germans. Thanks to the perseverance of a *Newsweek* reporter, an eyewitness was located to verify the story.

As this issue goes to press, the WRA faces investigation by the California State Legislature and State Department in Washington. The question of whether Matanzas and other such troublesome camps need to be placed in Army hands is under discussion.

Unpacking

Twenty-One

Rain came down in wild lashes. As Rita ran ahead in no particular direction, the sidewalk seemed to lurch toward her face — grey, wet, never-ending slabs. A mad crack of thunder made her bones jump.

That first spray of gunfire....

Down the street from Robarts was an athletic field flanked by a stone tower that rose into the gloomy sky like a medieval prison. Where was she going? Where was the subway? At the best of times, her sense of direction wasn't good. How had she arrived at Queen's Park Crescent? A steady flow of traffic coursed by — no one stopping to let her cross, no one caring that she was getting drenched each time a tire hit a pothole.

She ran through an arched gateway adjacent to a stone manor house. This led down a winding path canopied by weeping willows that were laden with pearls of water. Sheltered, she paused to catch her breath.

That web of black print, at once too cryptic and too clear — impossible to process. The only words that had stood out were *Kaz Takemitsu*. A name that for so long had filled her with longing and dread. Her father had been a *leader* in the riot? Was that what the stupid article was trying to tell her? All her life she'd pictured him as a loser: a drunk, mean, small-minded man. That was his legacy, not this.

"Hey, Rita!"

She spun around. It was Mark, under a busted umbrella, loose nylon flapping around his head. He was out of breath, a sweaty, rainy mess.

"You forgot this." He held out her shoulder bag. "*Why did you run off like that?*"

The truth was she'd forgotten all about him. Upon reading that article, her brain just kind of froze up. The next thing she knew, she was racing down the hall toward the fluorescent gap of an elevator.

"What's going on, Rita? You look like you've seen a ghost."

"Did you read the article?"

"No, I came after you immediately."

"It said some stuff about Kaz Takemitsu. My father."

"What kind of stuff?"

"He was involved in leading the riot. Then he was dragged off to prison or some high-security prison camp. Wherever they took the shit disturbers." Her words sounded flat, lifeless. She might have been talking about a stranger. She *was* talking about a stranger.

Mark stepped closer, silver droplets beaded to his lashes. He looked like he wanted to hug her but wasn't sure whether she wanted to be touched. "You never knew anything about this?"

"Nope. Kaz walked out on us. That's all I ever knew."

An unexpected upsurge of pride. At least there was more to Kaz than Tom had let on. All those images of Marlon Brando and Alan Ladd had been more than just little girl fantasies. Kaz *had* stood for something.

"You're soaked to the bone. Come on. Let's get you into a cab."

BACK AT HER APARTMENT, she changed out of her wet clothes while Mark heated up a can of chicken noodle soup. Swaddled in her bathrobe, she sat on the edge of the couch, hands wrapped around the burning-hot mug. The salty noodles slipped over her tongue, and her eyelids began to feel heavy, the edges of her little world fading. Thankfully, Mark didn't ask any more questions. She let her head fall onto a cushion and pulled her legs up onto his thighs. After a long time in silence together, he draped a blanket over her and flicked off the lights.

The weight of her body sinking down, down, *down,* into the depths of the earth. Emotions lapped at her borders, eroding the edges of consciousness. Images passed before her: her mother's closet, strewn with bright dresses; a vase of three yellow chrysanthemums, the kind Grandpa used to make offerings to their ancestors; a dish of burning incense, like the remains of a simmering cigarette, the ashes accumulating until the wind carried them away....

She was in the desert at sunset, the horizon a blinding band of orange neon. The sand-like needles shooting into her skin. It stuck all over her, coating, encasing her, and there was something more to these itchy granules — flecks of white. Bone shards. *Ashes! Whose ashes?* She swatted at her body, desperate to fling the muck off.

Kaz.

Stillness came over her. So at last, this was how it felt to touch her dead father? The ashes moistened as tears dripped into her upturned hands.

Out of nowhere Lily appeared. She was young, so young — little more than a teenager, her face touched with uncertainty, adolescent self-consciousness, trapped in that pupal state of waiting, continual waiting. A weirdly protective, maternal feeling stirred within Rita. Lily's hair was pulled up in a messy bun, and she was dressed in a pink leotard and tutu, tattered and grungy. As if Rita weren't even there, she began a peculiar dance, kind of like ballet, but all the movements were disjointed, choppy. She spun in a clumsy pirouette that collapsed into a fetal position; she slithered through the sand, pulling herself by her elbows. Like a girl in a Degas painting, except drunk or high. Then she was running in circles, churning up silvery sand, and she leaped into the air, but it was as though she'd hit an invisible wall. She fell to the ground, dazed, unmoving. A moment later she jumped up and tried it all again. Only to be knocked down all over. She repeated the futile sequence.

Someone tapped Rita on the shoulder. Turning around, she gasped. The young Marlon Brando. Except it wasn't quite him. The man's hair was pitch black, slicked back, his eyes slanting upward in the shape of raindrops.

"Do you know who I am?"

She nodded shyly.

"What's going on with your mother?"

"She gets like this sometimes."

"Don't I know it." Moody circles glimmered beneath his eyes, mirroring his heavy brows. "It's probably my fault. It wasn't easy on her after they took me away."

"I know." And then, if that might have sounded too accusatory, "It's okay. She's going to be okay, isn't she?"

But before Kaz could answer, the wind picked up speed. She had no idea of his reply, if he replied at all.

"Do you ever wonder what might've happened if things hadn't been stacked against you?"

"But they weren't, Rita. I was the doctor's son. I had it better than most guys."

"Then … why?"

"Why what?"

"Why did you throw your life away? *Why did you leave us?*"

Whatever his answer — if he answered at all — it was drowned out by the hissing gust.

SHE PUSHED HERSELF up with an abrupt, startled movement. Shadows spilled from the sofa to the floor; bars of light cut through the venetian blinds. The air, after the rainfall, felt heavy, sticky.

She had an indistinct sense of some dream about Lily, but when she tried to grasp for it, all she could see were swirls of dust.

How long had she slept? Mark must have slipped out a while ago. How embarrassing that he'd seen her falling apart.

The front door creaked open. Lights flicked on harshly; she blinked, still in the process of waking. He was standing there, his arms laden with grocery bags and a bottle of wine.

"Hope you're hungry."

Prickles of nervousness took over, followed by an irritated sensation. She could deal with someone walking out just fine, but chasing her through the rain and making dinner — whoa, that was a whole other story.

"You really don't have to go to all this trouble."

He put down the bags and stepped back onto the veranda for more. How much frigging food had he bought?

"I took the liberty of looking in your fridge."

"Kensington's great for takeout."

"It's also great for fresh ingredients."

After unearthing a knife and cutting board, Mark set her to work slicing a fennel bulb, which got stuffed inside a red snapper, along with a handful of torn-up coriander. He'd even bought a ball of string to tie the shimmery silver-rose skin back together. While it was in the oven — an aromatic, licorice scent filling the air — he threw together a tomato and bocconcini salad. Crisp, grassy white wine. It cut across her palate, cleansing away the scummy taste of sleep.

Getting some food into her body was a good idea. They hardly even talked while eating.

After dinner, as they polished off the wine, he flipped through her record collection. They reminisced about Gordon Lightfoot, Muddy Waters, Sonny Terry, and all the other musicians who used to do shows at the Riverboat and coffee houses in Yorkville. Mark strummed away at an imaginary guitar with a look of reverie that seemed to verge on parody. Joni Mitchell's voice came on, delicate and strong, dancing through the dimness like silk ribbons. The record reached "Little Green." Rita hadn't listened to this music in years. It was amazing how this woman never shied away from finding words for her most intimate memories and deepest pain — the pain of giving her daughter up for adoption. All the ordinary fears and yearnings of a young mother refracted through the song's poetry. Had Lily ever felt that way, too?

As they fell into silence, Rita's head dropped back on the sofa. She edged forward so Mark could come closer and settle himself behind her; she leaned back against his chest, his fingers locking around her. The aroma of herbs and salt water and crushed garlic wafted off him as he held the weight of her against him. They were just being friendly, she reminded herself. Friends could do this, couldn't they? Like hell they could. But for now maybe it was all right to lie back and luxuriate in this state of half-drunken whateverness. She closed her eyes and tried not to think about chaos and clouds of tear gas and Lily being caught in an upsurge of screaming bodies.

"You know, I always assumed my father left because he couldn't handle my mom. How she was, after the war."

"Sounds like he had his own problems to deal with. What do you know about the guy?"

"Not much. Most of the time, no one breathed his name. He and Grandpa never got along."

"Why's that?"

"Grandpa was such a conventional, rigid man. Don't get me wrong, I loved my grandfather, but he could be self-righteous as hell. Saw himself as a pillar of the community. Except, after the war, there wasn't much community, but that didn't stop him from trying. His son leading a riot? It would've broken his heart."

The stoop of Grandpa's shoulders. The way he'd always kept his distance from Tom, as though even looking at the boy's face were a painful reminder of someone else.

"What about your mom? Would she have been on board with Kaz's resistance activities?"

"Hardly. She idolized my grandfather. It must've horrified her that Kaz ended up getting involved with the shit disturbers."

No sooner had she spoken than her certainty faded, however. The rare times Lily had broken her silence about Kaz, her face had frozen in a numb, blank expression that Rita had interpreted as disappointment, anger, hate. But might there have been a trace of something else — wistfulness, regret? A man who was good with the ladies. Had Lily been referring to herself, in the bloom of her youth? Perhaps she'd been drawn to his rebelliousness, his principles. Kaz, the biggest shit disturber of all. Her mind was a kaleidoscope of so many contradictory whims and desires, who could say what her true feelings about Kaz had been at all?

Mark was watching Rita brood, space out.

"Sorry," said Rita.

"I lost you for a moment there."

"It's just … I don't know. That whole period. How little I understand about what happened."

"What are you curious about?"

"My mom's feelings about my dad. How they got together in the first place. How they ended up in Toronto, of all places." Whether they were ever in love. But she wasn't going to say that aloud.

"Did you ever ask her about any of this?"

Rita shook her head and tried to let all the questions drift away. But it was impossible. Even basic things puzzled her. "I wonder if Kaz would have been released at the same time my mom and grandfather got out of Matanzas. Did they all move to Toronto together? Or did Kaz come on his own later?"

"From what I understand, people got out in waves, depending on whether they were deemed a security threat. So it's entirely possible that Kaz wasn't released until later."

By the time of the riot Lily must have been pregnant since Tom was born in '44. How horrible it must have been for her to be left all alone in the aftermath of that violence.... Who'd taken care of her? Had Grandpa stepped forward? Was that the origin of their peculiar closeness?

Twenty-Two

Going about her day was an elaborate game of connect-the-dots. There were certain things she needed to get done, and if she could just make it from one chore to the next, everything would be all right. Yet the minutes risked slipping away, so she had to work fast: wake Tom up, comb the knots from his hair, get dressed, avoid the silver flash of sunlight swooshing off the mirror....

It wasn't that she was vain. She didn't even wear makeup. No, no, she wasn't that kind of woman.

Sometimes when she'd look at strangers on the street, she'd find herself entranced by the hue of their lips: poppy, magenta, a blackish-red so deep it made her think of dried blood. But when she went to the drugstore to examine the enamel tubes, her elation vanished, disgust sweeping over her.

The doctor's wife was a clean-scrubbed, respectable woman.

Lil.

For some reason, ever since they'd moved to Toronto, she'd started to think of herself as "Lil" more often than "Lily." A simple, no-nonsense name, better suited to a woman of her ilk, far better than the silliness of "Lily." Lil dressed in boxy cream shirts and brown wool skirts that came down well past her knees, hair pulled up in a bun as tight as Aunt Haruko's. Not making any attempt to conceal the scar on her cheekbone. People probably thought this was the reason she avoided mirrors, but only if she were vain could things be so simple. It looked like a birthmark, which it was, in a sense: she thought of it as a boundary that marked her second birth, like a wall in her brain that blocked all the unruly voices from crossing over. Sometimes she could hear them getting louder, and then the borders of her body were losing weight, shadows and blackness closing in....

So she had to be quick. Get dressed, pack Tom's school bag, walk him down the street to school. This was the goal, the whole point of the morning rush, so why did every fibre of her being pull in the opposite direction?

That inevitable moment of parting. Her lips lingered on her son's cheek as she tightened her grip, mesmerized by how the baby fat was falling away, revealing the blueprint of a face that was going to be strikingly handsome. Tom didn't look like the doctor, whose wrinkled face curled inward, and it wasn't possible she'd known him way back in that boyish phase of his life anyway — though she often had an unsettling feeling that she had. Some days, she was haunted by an image of the doctor as a young man: filled with laughter, something teasing about his lips, his face wavering like a lake hit by a skipping pebble. That murmur of terror and loss she didn't understand gathered force all over.

It was just the house making her jumpy. Bricks crumbling, porch sagging like a waterlogged hammock. She sensed it was a fair bit larger than anywhere she'd lived before, but for all the space — the dark corridors and boarded up rooms on the third floor, where the only sign of life was the rustle of mice — it didn't feel anything like home. It swallowed her up. All the battered, unloved furniture had been left behind by the previous owner: upholstery dotted by moth holes and cigarette burns, wooden arms carved up with graffiti, lampshades with ratty fringes, wallpaper faded to the ghosts of peacocks and palm trees.

Best not to think too much about how she'd ended up here, in this damp, decrepit house on Margueretta Street.

Today wasn't a day to sulk. *Save your tears, time to get moving.* People were coming to supper tonight. Dr. Chong and his wife. She'd never met them before, and nervousness nipped at her finger-tips. Somehow, in the course of his excursions, the doctor had managed to befriend the Chongs, and maybe Dr. Chong would help him re-establish his medical practice. She tried to remember why the doctor didn't have a practice of his own anymore. He must have explained it to her ten thousand times.

Trudging upstairs, she sighed. At the top of the stairs, the latest vagabond could be heard snoring. With all these strangers living here, how was she supposed to turn the ground floor into a proper doctor's office? But the doctor seemed content just running this flophouse, where no one paid a cent of rent.

She wandered to the end of the hall and shook her son by the shoulder. He squirmed and scrunched up between the eyes, trying to get away from her even in his sleep, and a blurry impression of someone else edged into her thoughts.

"Rise and shine, handsome."

The boy blinked and looked up, as if she were part of his dream. "It's already morning, Mommy?"

"Get up, Tom."

"Can I have pancakes?"

"No. You'll be late for school."

SOME AFTERNOONS, SHE'D go on long walks. Shoe repair counters, little hardware stores. East along College, street life became busier: portly men sat outside the cafés smoking; store-fronts showed off shiny pots and pans, sensible, clunky shoes that could support a two-hundred-pound matriarch, bolts of jewel tone fabric bursting across the glass. But the way the shopkeepers looked at her was enough to keep her at bay. Maybe they'd never seen an Oriental before. Often, there'd be two of them, a mother and daughter, chatting behind the cash register in some undulating language, and how surprised they'd look when English words sprung from Lil's lips. According to the doctor, they were a hodgepodge of Italians, Portuguese, Jews, Greeks. If they were all strangers from different countries, why did they appear to get on so well together, their tanned, Caucasian faces set against her?

Men were another matter, of course. The single ones lived in boarding houses with large verandas out front, where they'd lounge on the steps drinking beer in the late afternoon after the day's work of laying bricks and spreading tar. They were coarse, oxen-like guys who always managed to look dirty. When it came to a pretty girl, though, a softer side took over. They'd smile and call out "Konnichiwa," followed by sweet, semi-obscene things that she tried to shut her ears to as she rushed by, her bad cheek turned away.

Yet if the experience were so unpleasant, why did she keep walking past? Why did a tremble of a swagger overtake her hips, a faint melody ribboning through her brain?

Perhaps there was a hint of something nice in all their coarseness — something that evoked a shadow of a memory. The limberness of her sapling limbs. Her cheeks blossoming, under the heat of an audience's gaze, every fibre and nerve in her body twitching to life.

It confused and frightened her when she felt this other side of herself awakening. And yet, how invigorating to know that girl was still alive.

LIL DIDN'T REMEMBER much about where they'd lived before Toronto, beyond some discontinuous scenes of another cold, unfamiliar city. The jagged grey skyline. Snow was beautiful and ethereal if you watched it falling from indoors, but she hadn't been prepared for the acid sting against her cheekbones. They'd been staying at a rooming house full of other Japanese folks. While the doctor slept down the hall in the men's quarters, she and Aunt Haruko shared a room with two other women, who were surprisingly good-natured about the colicky baby. "We're lucky to be here. We're lucky Chicago would take us." They rubbed their chapped hands above steaming bowls of udon at night. Most of these folks were used to a warmer clime, yet going back home wasn't an option. It had something to do with the fact that the west coast wasn't part of the clearance zone, whatever that meant.

The doctor was looking for work. How much easier things would be if he were a butler or chauffeur. Not many people these days were willing to put their health in the hands of a Jap doctor. Yet he kept going to interviews and job-placement meetings run by church groups that had taken it upon themselves to help the Japanese. That was how he met Father Hughes, who put him in touch with Mother Saint John in Toronto. She had piercing blue eyes and a small, pale face, so pale that her skin appeared translucent, like the inner layers of an onion. Lil still couldn't quite grasp what it was they were trying to accomplish. It had something to do with helping people who'd been released with nothing from some place called "camp," and the doctor insisted that Lil had lived there, too, though none of the people who came to stay looked the least bit familiar. The doctor said they'd lived in different camps. It didn't matter, he soothed her, the important thing was that they were here in Toronto now, helping Mother Saint John make everyone's path a bit easier.

Initially, the plan had been for him to work at a church-run medical clinic, but it turned out he needed to take an exam to practice medicine in Ontario, and he never seemed to have time to get around to it, thanks to all the other important things he and Mother Saint John were up to.

Whenever some lost soul couldn't find work or got evicted, there was no shortage of spare rooms here. They were old, single men, who didn't have anyone. According to Mother Saint John, some of them did have families, but they'd fallen out of touch during the war, or were so ashamed of having been left with nothing that they preferred to live the rest of their lives in exile. Some were bitter, their lined faces flushed with booze, as they paced around the house, muttering under their breath in Japanese. Others seemed confused, having succumbed to a childlike helplessness. Lil felt sorry for them and wondered if this was how she'd end up, too, if she didn't have the doctor. So she and Aunt Haruko prepared big vats of Japanese curry that filled the house with savoury, nostalgic smells and at least made the men smile in anticipation of a good meal.

WHY DID IT HAVE to be so hard to get a little boy into his snow-suit? Jammed zipper, sweater bunched up, endless squirming. Boots on the wrong feet — Tom kicked them off angrily.

"Why do I have to wear all this? Look at you!"

He was right. She was still in her thin, flowered nightgown, which trailed down below her taupe wool coat (a real find — who'd believe what was at the Salvation Army?). She shoved her bare feet into her boots, still damp from yesterday. It was all wrong: she didn't feel like Lil at these moments, forehead sweating, limpness taking over. Why did Tom keep staring at her as though she weren't up to the task of being his mother? Something crossed over in her, and that current of maternal anger and strength surged back. She'd teach him who was in charge here.

Before they could have it out, however, the doctor came sailing down the stairs, headed for the door with a sense of purpose. Time, for him, always progressed at a steady clip.

"You're cooking something nice for the Chongs tonight?"

"Yes, the Chongs." She searched his face distractedly, suddenly

struck by how he'd aged, the lines around his eyes like rivulets leading up to some unknown territory.

"You won't forget the Chongs are coming to dinner? What are
you making?"

"I was thinking Japanese food. Tempura, chawanmushi, rice,
pickles?"

As the doctor shook his head, worry deepened the wrinkles.
"Let's not rub it in their faces that we're Japanese, all right? The
Japanese did some pretty nasty things to the Chinese during the war."

The war? Hot air stirred at the back of her brain, a dust cloud
gathering force. What was the doctor saying? Did he expect her to
make Chinese food? She didn't know how to — she didn't even like
Chinese food, with all its greasy, brown sauces — and there certainly wasn't time to learn. *Time.* Why was it always slipping away
from her, conspiring against her? And why did she feel in the queasy
depths of her bowels that something had happened to them during
the war, despite the doctor's insistence that it was the Chinese who'd
suffered mercilessly?

He was talking about other dishes she could make, but his words
skimmed the surface of her consciousness, registering nothing.

"The war," she blurted. "What happened to us during the war?"

"I don't have time for this now, Lily. Just remember: don't bring
up the war at dinner. *Please.*"

Tom had seized her leg. "Mommy, I'm gonna be late for school."

"Say goodbye to your father, Tom."

"*Grandfather.* You mean grandfather, of course." An exasperated sigh.

"Grandfather — yes, of course." Of course nothing. Her mind
frantically traced a pattern that followed a dark, contorted maze,
never arriving anywhere. It wasn't the first time they'd reached this
impasse. This humiliating act he expected her to put on. *Why?* Why
was it so important to keep the true nature of their relationship
secret? (Did it have something to do with eluding the authorities?

Was it one of the conditions the church people had imposed upon helping them to move here?)

The doctor was Tom's father; he had to be, she felt sure of it. He'd always been there for her, taking care of her, bandaging her wounds. She knew they couldn't have known each other all their lives, yet that was how their relationship felt, like a long, dark road that sprang out of nowhere and faded in both directions into the horizon. It didn't matter that her face had been marred. The doctor had stood by her throughout that long stretch she could only remember as endless night. And things were better now: they had each other; they had this leaky, tumbledown house; they had their son, and he was everything.

It came and went, his desire for her, like a fluttering, frightened moth. Sometimes he'd creep into her bedroom, night after night, stealthy as the shadow he cast over the blankets. There was love and comfort in his smooth palms cupping her flesh and there was a wellspring of healing power in his body, which, although no longer sinewy, was still warm and inviting. She thought of tender ocean colours at sunset: orange, mauve, pink, blue, purple.

And then, quite some time ago, the visits at night stopped abruptly. His behaviour toward her became jumpy and guilt-ridden; he avoided her eyes at breakfast and addressed her in such cool tones she might have been the housekeeper.

He was Tom's *grandfather*, he insisted, which didn't make sense at all. For how could the seed of life skip a generation?

If only he'd let go of this silly charade. If only he'd give in to the pounding of his blood, which she felt all the more strongly whenever he'd push her away — hands trembling, eyes downcast, cords of his neck taut as kite strings about to snap…. One of these days, he was going to give in to her.

"Are you listening to me?"

She blinked. The doctor's face appeared flat, devoid of passion. "I'm sorry. What did you say?"

"Just cook some nice Canadian food, all right?"

She nodded.

"Now run along, you two. See you tonight."

Canadian food.

What on earth was that?

THE SCHOOLYARD WAS empty. Snow swirled across the asphalt, a red candy wrapper caught in the upsurge. The two-storey brick building loomed behind, its windows laundromat bright. The place appeared about as welcoming as a prison. Still, Lil ought to be setting a better example for her son, teaching him to get where he needed to be on time. *Tom'll be just as messed up as you are.* She squeezed the little mittened hand as she imagined a good mother ought to.

"I'm late. I'll get in trouble if I go in now."

"We'll just have to face the music, won't we?" Icy wind crept under her coat and nightgown.

"Can't I just stay home with you today?"

"No, Tom. You have to go to school."

"Why?"

"Is something the matter?" She knelt down so they were eye level. Recently, she'd become worried that boys in his class were picking on him. He was the only Oriental child.

"No." Yet his eyes appeared transfixed, staring off into the far reaches of the playground at nothing at all. Something secretive and fearful held within.

"Are kids bullying you? I can speak to your teacher."

He shook his head. Snowflakes settled on his nose, melting, like teardrops.

"Are you sure? What's upset you then?"

"It's just that … there's a man who comes here sometimes."

"Not the principal?"

"No, a stranger. He stands over there." Tom pointed to the corner of the playground. "Watches me at recess."

Kids were known to have vivid imaginations. "What makes you think he was watching you in particular? Maybe he's just a nice man out for a walk."

"We talked. He said he knows you, Mommy, but I can't say anything."

Her hands sprang to her cheeks — flushed, embarrassed, though she didn't know why. Her fingertips grazed her scar, incapable of reading its intricate meaning. "What did this man look like, Tom?"

"Tall. He needed a bath."

That didn't say much. "Oriental?"

"Yeah."

"Well, I don't want you talking to him anymore. You hear me, Tom?"

The truth was that she, too, had the unnerving sensation of being watched from time to time: a shock of jet-black hair on the periphery of her vision, a gaunt cheek that seemed all too familiar, a dim version of someone she'd once known and cared for deeply. But by the time she'd turned around, the face had always vanished.

Although it wasn't an unpleasant feeling to have an admirer, it was more than just admiration or desire she'd glimpsed. Something sharper — accusing — that left her weak and unmoored, as if her little life here were a conjurer's trick. Of course, it was probably just her own mind playing tricks on her.

WHEN THE DOCTOR asked for Canadian food, what he really meant was that he wanted her to make something from the cookbook he'd given her for Christmas. It was a hefty, black book with a picture-perfect family on the cover; they were sitting around the dining-room table, a succulent roast in the middle. Father at the head saying grace, his little daughter smiling up at him adoringly. The book offered "recipes to delight the whole family," everything from carrot Jello salad to Spam hash to chicken pie deluxe.

Unloading the bags of groceries made her back ache. Poor chicken: naked flesh covered in goose pimples, loose skin flopping over the cavity where its head had once been. She wondered what had been running through its mind when the cleaver came down. Did chickens have memories? What did a chicken's life consist of, anyway? Depositing the bird on the cutting board, she splayed open its wings and legs and began chopping, struggling with the joints that stubbornly held the creature together, the meat slippery and cold.

At last she'd placed all the pieces in a casserole dish. She stared at the slimy, pink bundles and yellow pockets of fat. The minutes dripped by and she knew she was teetering on the edge of a black spell, so she had to pull back — she didn't have time to go under. Not today of all days. *She was in the desert, trying to run, but every step was a world of struggle.* She blinked, rubbed her eyes. The recipe said to pour cream over the chicken. It fell like a shroud over the broken bones, oddly comforting to watch. And then she could feel herself slipping away on its velvety folds. *The heavy layers of her kimono were dragging her down, something tight binding her knees together, an ache cutting in. The tightness jumped up to her chest, her throat. Sand surged up — spraying her eyes, filling her mouth with salty grit. A shower of bullets, a blast of fire across her cheek. Dogs barking across her brain. A puddle of blood, wilted petals congealed on the surface.*

Twenty-Three

They slept mostly clothed on top of the crumpled duvet, their bodies full of strange electric twitches. At some point Mark spooned her in his sleep, and she surfaced to the warm, tickling mist of his breath against the nape of her neck.

When she awoke the next morning, he was up already. The aroma of coffee — *real* coffee — filled the air. A belated flush of embarrassment about being such a mess last night. She worried he'd want to keep talking about it all. But when she ventured into the sunny kitchen, he had other things on his mind. He was up on a stepstool organizing her rows and rows of wine glasses, a throwback to the days when she and Cal had big, boozy dinner parties.

"First deal with the things that are easy to fix, right?" he said.

It was weird to see him touching all her things, relics from her life with another man.

Perhaps he realized he was being a tad presumptuous. "Don't worry, I'm not moving in or anything."

"I didn't say that you were."

He was wearing plaid boxers and a T-shirt, one foot perched

on the counter, an arm extended overhead in an almost balletic motion, tufts of middle-aged body hair and the beginnings of love handles exposed in the morning light. A Rodin sculpture he was not. The awkwardness softened into a rush of sudden, ridiculous joy. Was he always this fucking energetic in the mornings?

"Mind passing them up?"

"Mark, you really don't have to —"

"The glasses?"

By the time he left in the early afternoon, the place looked a lot more livable. They'd managed to unpack most of her boxes. The coffee table was crammed with scented candles and a mermaid-shaped ashtray she couldn't bear to part with. Towers of books teetered on the floor. Tackling the bookshelves would be her next task, but just now she wasn't up to it.

With Mark gone, the silence thickened. She surveyed all her junk. What a pack rat she was, no different than her mother. As she fanned herself with a magazine, her thoughts drifted, ruminations creeping in.

What had become of Kaz at the end of the war?

What happened when he arrived in Toronto?

Who *was* he?

She called Tom's office. She still wasn't quite sure what her brother did for a living, something complicated and obscenely lucrative in the finance industry. His secretary had been given her message to deliver: Tom was in back-to-back meetings all day. It was a family emergency, Rita said. But no one, not even family — especially family, maybe — was to get through.

The afternoon passed in a blur of chores and explosive emotions. The cheap-ass washing machine at the laundromat mangled her favourite pair of jeans.

THE STREETCAR WAS packed with sweaty bodies. As a kid, Rita had developed a habit of searching the faces of strangers. Maybe

Kaz was out there somewhere, riding streetcars, strolling down the sidewalk, and maybe one of these days he was going to walk back into their lives. "I don't *know* — he was a bum." Was that all Tom was ever going to tell her? Was that why she couldn't bear to make eye contact with the greasy old men who seemed to follow her everywhere, lugging their trundle buggies? That gnomish guy with a matted beard, hunched down across the aisle right now. Layers of dirt gave his skin a silvery patina, as though he'd just climbed out of a chimney, the surliest of Santas.

They pulled into Spadina station. She got on the eastbound line to Bay.

In the sunset, the cement overhang of the Manulife Centre looked like a cliff, bleak and desolate. Aside from a few pinstriped men running to catch their trains back to the suburbs, there weren't many people around. The sleek bank towers that dominated these blocks filled her with awareness of her own smallness, aloneness. At least Round Records was still here to liven things up. A punk from the old days hung around outside panhandling, yet he was likely to get spit on now. Rumour had it the shop was about to be closed, thanks to some luxury department store that had bought up the entire block.

Speed-walking across the street, she headed into a building that looked no different than an office tower. Who in their right mind would want to live in the heart of this cement jungle? She called up on the intercom.

The beeping went on forever. She hung up and tried again. Stared at the broken veins in the marble tiles.

Just as she was about to leave, in he strolled — looking all too relaxed, a bag of takeout in hand.

Then Tom saw her. "Uh, Rita, what're you doing here?"

"Did they cut off your phone line at work?"

"Oh, sorry I couldn't get back to you. You have no idea the shitstorm I've had to deal with today."

"That makes two of us."

A look of mild amusement faded to irritation. Tom was assessing the best way to get rid of her. But then, in his usual Jekyll-and-Hyde fashion, his face broke into a casual smile and he hugged her. One of those weird, businesslike hugs that never felt like a real hug, more like a clap on the back.

"Any news about Mom? Want to come up for a drink?"

His detached, moderately concerned tone turned her stomach. Tom had shoved the whole matter of Lily's disappearance right to the back of his mind so he could get on with his life. Well, Rita wasn't going to let him. Like it or not, he was a part of this family, too.

His unit was up on the twenty-third floor. She wasn't so good with heights, and a vertiginous sensation grabbed at her stomach. So many grey, tumescent forms shot up out of nowhere, and the farther off you looked, the more ominous things appeared, the CN Tower like a sword in the distance. Beyond that there was only water: a dull, blue-grey smear stretched out into eternity. That was where even homeless people didn't want to live, where dead bodies got dumped.

Tom handed her a beer. "So what's up, kiddo?"

Fizz burned the back of her nostrils. She didn't know where to start. Mr. Fujita's photo project? Gerald's bender? The *Newsweek* article? Like he'd care about any of that. Oh and by the way, Tom, did you know our father led a riot that landed him in prison?

His apartment was virtually empty even though he'd been here five years. There wasn't a single painting or even a poster on the gleaming white walls. No framed photo of a girlfriend smiling at him teasingly. She couldn't remember the last time Tom had introduced her to anyone.

A guilt-ridden feeling wrapped around her: she was complicit in condemning him to this strange, solitary existence, simply by being part of the family that had made him this way. While he'd borne the brunt of Grandpa's coldness, she'd gotten off easy, perhaps.

"So some stuff about our father's come to my attention."

"Oh?"

She explained about the article, the riot. This was the first time they'd really talked about the internment, let alone their father's fate. Pumped up on nervous adrenalin, her heart began galloping. Her hands chopped through the air, as though she were refuting his constant objections. But Tom was silent — nodding even, after a while. A small, tight expression, a sheen of fragility. He appeared shaken, but not altogether surprised. Not surprised enough.

"Did you know about this already?" It would be just like him to hoard the information.

He moved over to the window. At last, he said, "Not exactly, but I always thought Kaz had been incarcerated for something. Where else could he have been all that time?"

"All what time?"

"Kaz didn't live with us."

"What? Sure he did. He must've lived with you guys before I was born."

"No, Rita. You always asked me why there were no pictures of him around the house. He was never there."

"What? Where *was* he then?"

"Maybe he had to stay at the prison camp longer than the rest of them. Or maybe he chose to remain out west after the war and keep his distance. Wouldn't surprise me, considering Grandpa would've disowned him after that riot."

Things in her head were shifting, like layers of sediment about to cleave and crack.

"Kaz must've knocked her up when they were at camp, I guess?" he continued. "Who knows whether he even knew I was on the way when he got hauled off to prison." Tom spoke so calmly, matter-of-factly, as his brain drew a Gantt chart around the new data.

"Kaz — never — came to Toronto …?"

"Of course he did. You think you were born by immaculate conception? Yeah, Kaz came to find us when I was five. Stayed for a bit. Knocked her up again. Then took off. And that was it. That's the only time I ever met him."

It was as though someone had slapped her so unexpectedly the pain wouldn't register. "How ... long did he stay?"

"I don't know. Two weeks, two months? I was just a little kid."

It didn't make any sense. "Why would Kaz track the family down, only to up and leave?"

"Search me. All I can say is the guy looked like a bum. He probably needed money and thought Grandpa would take pity on him. Maybe things had gone south out in California. Take your pick. But in the end, whatever hell his life had become, he found that preferable to living under Grandpa's thumb on Margueretta Street."

Grandpa and Kaz at each other's throats all the time. Lily caught in the middle, unsure which man had a greater claim on her affection. She would have waffled, wanting to have it both ways. And in her own little demented world, maybe she could.

"Hey." Tom placed a hand on Rita's shoulder. "What's the big deal? I wouldn't have wanted to have that loser in my life anyway."

"Well, that's *you*. What about *me*?"

She was determined not to cry, yet her throat seized up. Kaz had never been here at all. They'd never been a family — there hadn't been anything for him to wreck in the first place. He'd breezed into Lily's life when it suited him and then left her high and dry, not once, but *twice*. The whole thing was just too humiliating.

"What was Kaz like when he came to Toronto?"

"God, Rita. I can't do this anymore!" Tom's eyes bored into her, drifted toward the window and ricocheted back. "What do you want me to say? That he was some kind of TV dad? Just tell me what you want me to say and I'll fucking say it."

She tried to respond and failed, her chest heaving.

"I know nothing about the man," she said at last. "I ... I don't even know how he died. What kind of daughter doesn't even know how her own father died?"

For a second, Tom's eyes softened, as though he wanted to tell her something, something that might be balm to her nerves. Or make the situation that much worse. Whatever it was, he brushed it aside and turned away. "Look, Rita, I have a lot of work to get through tonight."

Twenty-Four

The man on the porch was smiling at Lil knowingly, like she ought to recognize him. The street lights cast a wan halo about his head. He'd combed his hair, slicked it back with too much oil that was probably just the natural secretion of his unbathed body. The smell of something faintly rusty, like dried rain on an old car, stirred an impulse that made her feel she might start crying at any second.

"Lily." He leaned in to embrace her. The collar of his shirt oily against her cheek.

She didn't back away — didn't do anything. Just stood there. Paralyzed. Rustlings in her head.

"Kaz."

He smiled at the sound of his name on her lips.

THINGS WERE GETTING a bit easier for the Japanese. Employers were more open to giving them a chance since they were, after all, willing to work for lower wages. So Mother Saint John had fewer people to send them. After wishing to have the house empty for so long, Lil found its quietness now haunted her.

One day after breakfast, as she flipped through the newspaper, her eyes fell upon an ad in the classifieds: *Clean, furnished rooms for rent in respectable boarding house.* The price per room wasn't very much, but multiplied several times would make a nice bundle. She thought of the boarding houses farther east, full of greasy, leering men. Surely, not all houses were like that. The keyword was *respectable.*

She called over to Aunt Haruko, who was dusting a potted plant, and showed her the ad.

"Oh, no." A grey tendril slipped out from under her handkerchief. "Strange men under our roof?"

"We've already had strange men living here."

"That's different. They're Nihonjin, ne?" She dragged her rag along the mantle. "Why should we take in boarders?"

"We need the money." Sometimes Lil felt like she was having a conversation with a two-year-old.

"God will take care of us."

"God'll pay our bills?"

After he'd put the down payment on this house, the doctor hardly had any savings left. Although he'd started helping out at Dr. Chong's office, he still wasn't a licensed doctor; the pay was a fraction of what they needed. And the pittance Mother Saint John gave them was barely enough to cover the utilities and groceries, let alone the mortgage. Now that she hardly sent anyone to stay, would that money dry up, too? Clearly, they needed another source of income and if Aunt Haruko couldn't see that, she was as dumb as a doorknob.

I DID KNOW *him once, from somewhere ... before ... before what? Before everything. Just before. What a beautiful word,* before. *Turning back, always turning back to a state of bright white blankness. Like the flash of a camera — that yellow-white chrysanthemum of light hovering in the mind's eye, blinding, promising everything. To the Cherry Blossom Queen. That was who she was destined to become. The girl she was in the beginning.*

THE AD LIL posted on the message board at the Buddhist church only received one response. Daniel Sugimori was a stout, shiny-faced man in his fifties; an easy, dreamy smile framed his chipped front tooth. He was a shoe salesman who specialized in women's shoes — or perhaps, more accurately, in charming women.

The day after he moved in, he came home from work, carrying a shoebox. Gesturing at Lil to sit down, he kneeled in front of her and his callused hand cradled the arch of her foot.

It was a high-heeled sandal made of burgundy alligator skin; the narrow heel curved like the stem of a wine glass. When Lil stood up — a wave of vertigo — she might have become Rita Hayworth.

Tears sprung to her eyes: she felt ashamed of the old brown pumps Mr. Sugimori must have seen her wearing, heels ground down into nubs. She sauntered around the living room, humiliated at how intoxicated she secretly felt.

"YOU LOOK DIFFERENT, you know." Kaz ran his thumb along her cheekbone, lingering on her scar, and then his hand continued up through her hair, loosening the pins with a soft clatter.

And just like that, as she raked her fingers through her hair, it was as if every knot she unfurled was bringing her closer to her true self. The past they'd shared. The risks he'd compelled her to take. She shuddered, a sob caught in her throat, and as it surged up, other sensations and memories came free, too…. Her hand digging into his arm, the feeling of him pulling away from her, the seconds ticking by as she tried to find the words to stop him from going into that doomed building, her tongue frozen, the cacophony of gunshots, and always that feeling of Kaz pulling away from her, like the act of breathing or sleeping itself. For the abyss was inside her now.... How desperately she wished to be back on the other side, the before side. If she just let herself drift away on the current, she could still feel that flush that always came over her whenever he so much as looked at her, that snake of heat winding its way up through her belly. "My, my, if it isn't our little Cherry Blossom Queen." In calling her that, he'd made her so, his hands and words reshaping her flesh.

THE OTHER BOARDERS she found through an ad in the paper. The doctor was none too pleased by the prospect of hakujins under his roof, but who could deny they needed the money?

Mr. Dobson was a retired widower who sat in the living room reading the newspaper day after day. "Coal mine explosion in central Illinois, one hundred trapped," he'd mutter when Lil came in with a tea tray. Some days he claimed he'd been a professor emeritus of world history, while other days he alluded to having worked for British Intelligence during the war. Although the doctor thought Mr. Dobson was full of baloney, Lil believed every word he said. He looked as though he could have been a man of great importance in his heyday, with his well-trimmed moustache, neatly pressed shirts, proper English raincoat, and galoshes.

There were also a couple of boarders who worked as day labourers. They were gruff young men who kept to themselves, happy to rent small rooms on the third floor for less than they'd have to pay if they lived a few blocks over. Since they cooked on hot plates in their rooms, no one saw much of them anyway.

The boarders generated a considerable amount of work, but Lil didn't mind. Imagining herself the owner of a swanky hotel, she sewed new satin drapes. At a rummage sale, she found a gilt-framed mirror to hang above the table where she laid out her guests' mail each day.

KAZ'S FACE LOOKED different. His nose larger, askew. Had it been broken? She wanted to run her fingertips down the bridge to feel the knobby point where the bone had cracked and sutured back together.

Before she could figure out what to say, a little pair of arms clasped her thigh. Tom had run down in his pyjamas. He must have been watching them from the top of the staircase.

"Mommy, it's that man."

"Which man, Tom?" Her hand brushed the top of his head.

"The one you said I shouldn't talk to," he whispered.

Kaz kneeled down so he and the boy were eye level. "But you did keep talking to me, didn't you, Tom?"

Mischievous smiles on both sides. Conspiratorial silence.

"We've been getting to know each other real well, son. I'm gonna take you on a fishing trip."

Kaz stepped into the hallway. He looked up the curved banister to the shadowy, upper reaches, as though not used to being in a house with more than one floor. "So this is where you and the old man set up shop."

KNIT ONE, PURL one. The needles clicked back and forth, a skein of brown wool unravelling in a muddy river. She was helping Aunt Haruko knit blankets for the poor orphaned children of Japan. Some Christian organization had opened an orphanage for all the kids who'd lost their parents during the war. Lil had seen photos in the paper of whole cities reduced to nothing but rubble and blackened landscapes — strange, lavalike scars burnt into people's flesh. Was that what had happened to her own family? She shuddered, an ache loosening inside her. She couldn't remember much about her childhood, but she knew that her mother had gone back to Japan and never returned.

Japan wasn't the only place full of orphans these days. Each evening Mr. Dobson liked to sit in the living room and listen to the

CBC, plumes of smoke veiling his contemplative expression. John Fisher's exclamatory voice came over the airwaves and brought to life the sea of devastation in postwar Europe. The blackish bread and terrible hopelessness of those living in squalid conditions in Paris and Brussels. Roads being rebuilt in Warsaw by folks going at it with picks and shovels. Babies languishing in orphanages, incapable of responding to the word *Mommy* in any language. The stories left Lil numb.

"Mommy, what's an orphan?" Tom looked up from the floor.

"Never mind."

"An orphan's a kid who's lost his parents," Mr. Dobson said.

"Parents can get lost? Like my father?"

"Tom, your father's right here." Lil gestured at the doctor, shielded behind a newspaper.

"Your father, Tom?" The doctor peeked up, frowning. "He lives in California. I've told you that dozens of times."

"Why does he live in California?"

"Because he just *does*."

"WHO IS THIS man?" Mr. Dobson came downstairs, alarmed. "Is everything all right?"

"Of course everything's all right." Kaz let his bag drop to the floor. "I'm Lily's husband — or soon to be husband, that is. The man of the house."

Pleasure jolted into her blood. How long had she been waiting to hear those very words?

Mr. Dobson looked astonished. So did Mr. Sugimori, hovering in the doorway of the living room.

"Who are these people?" Kaz demanded.

"They're my guests."

"Guests?"

"Well, my boarders, I suppose you'd call them."

"So this place is a flophouse?"

"A rooming house, Kaz. It's a respectable rooming house."

He rolled his eyes and came closer, the cedar whiff of whiskey unmistakable now. "I can't believe my father would let you live under the same roof as this bunch."

"It's just that, well, we need the money right now. Just until your father starts up his practice."

Kaz shook his head, looking disgusted, and stepped into the living room. She might have been seeing the place for the first time as he was seeing it now: the uneven hem of her homemade curtains; the yellowed lace cloth placed over the coffee table to conceal its missing leg; the glass clock always ticking — mocking her — atop the boarded-up fireplace.

The front door screeched open. A briefcase hit the floor. Feet padded in. The doctor's feet. How intimately she still knew all his bodily sounds and rhythms. Her heart flew up into her head — thumping out of control as panic crested over her flesh.

A dip into blackness sucked her in. Past and future merging in this lava pit, the one place she could be sure she'd always return to.

Twenty-Five

Hard to believe Kristen had only been gone two weeks. She looked different somehow — maybe she'd grown. Her hair had for sure; it was blowing wildly about her shoulders, giving her the look of the Little Mermaid. Rita pulled it back and fastened it with a strawberry bauble then petted the small, silky head.

Kristen sounded different, too. She'd picked up new sayings, like "oy vey," which Jodi was apparently fond of saying. And when Rita asked what song she was humming, it turned out Jodi had taught her "Girls Just Want to Have Fun." What next — they'd be going to rock concerts together? But Rita didn't even care. Nothing could get her down now that her daughter was back home.

What a delightful surprise. Just when she'd thought things couldn't get any worse, Cal had called yesterday in a panic. It turned out that Jodi had two cats. Kristen was severely allergic — a fact that had somehow managed to slip his mind. Although Jodi had tried to keep the cats in her study, it hadn't made any difference; their dander was everywhere. After one night in that apartment, the poor girl was stuffed up, sneezing. It was going to be at least another few days before the water damage at Cal's house could be fully repaired. So he'd swallowed his pride and asked Rita whether it would be possible to put their daughter on the next flight back to Toronto. In her elation, she'd forgotten to act annoyed in order to maintain leverage for next time.

As soon as she'd hung up the phone, she'd flown into a cleaning frenzy, which had lasted the rest of yesterday and all this morning. Kristen's room was now totally unpacked, her bed made up with freshly laundered sheets. What a paragon of efficiency Rita could be when she was motivated to get her shit together. It felt good — great, actually — to be back in mother mode.

They were sitting on the patio of a little Chilean restaurant around the corner from the apartment. Perched on Kristen's lap was Melanie, the latest gift Cal had given her. While Melanie had a chocolate complexion and thick, black yarn braids, she had exactly the same near-set eyes, dimpled cheeks and sickeningly sweet smile as every other Cabbage Patch Kid. Rita didn't get why everyone found these dolls so irresistible. Maybe it was simply the fact that they'd been born in a cabbage patch. Who didn't fantasize at times about originating out of nowhere, with no crazy family to answer to?

Although it was still morning in Vancouver, it was past lunchtime here. So Rita ordered a chicken empanada.

"It's like a pizza pocket but tastier," Kristen said, slurping her mango juice. She seemed to like their new neighbourhood, with all the tables full of retro sunglasses and floppy straw hats right out on the sidewalk. Still, Rita couldn't help but wonder if there was something a bit forced about her daughter's cheeriness. Her eyes had a dazed, disoriented look, bright with exhaustion.

"You tired, Pumpkin?"

"Nope."

"Well, *I'm* tired then." A terrible pressure was suddenly expanding across Rita's temples, relief mixed with persistent terror. Relief that her daughter was here with her now. Terror that Lily was still nowhere to be found. She pulled Kristen close, fiercely hugging the little shoulders.

"Is everything okay, Mommy?"

She took a deep breath, searching for the right words. "Actually, some things have happened since you've been away. Some not so good things."

"Like what?"

"It's your grandmother. She went off somewhere."

"Where?"

"I don't know.... She's kind of gotten lost."

Confusion clouded the little face. "How'll we find her?"

IT WAS EASY to forget how close the city was to the countryside. Rita didn't even really think of St. Catharines as the country — not with all the strip malls and donut shops — until Kristen pointed out the orchards and vineyards through the car window. There was even one sad-looking cow grazing in a meadow that abutted an empty parking lot. Kristen wanted to know if they could go apple picking, like they'd done on a school field trip.

"Maybe another day. Right now we're going to see your Aunt Haruko."

Nothing Tom had said about Kaz's utter absence from their childhood had faded. Rita couldn't stop replaying their strange conversation in her mind. How could he be so blasé about the fact that Kaz had never been a part of their lives at all? It was an act, she felt sure of it. There were things Tom still wasn't telling her. So it was time to talk to somebody else.

"Who's Aunt Haruko? I don't have an aunt."

"Sure you do. Well, she's not exactly your aunt. She's my great-aunt. Which would make her your great-*great*-aunt."

Kristen wrinkled up between the eyebrows, squinting in the harsh glare of the sunset. Rita tried to explain the peculiar shape of their family tree, not very successfully.

"Why've I never met her, Mommy?"

"Aunt Haruko lives far away in St. Catharines." Yup, a whole hour-and-a-half drive.

Kristen nodded and fell into silence. Then she was reminded of the fact that she needed to use the bathroom. The kid had a bladder the size of a pea.

HUNCHED OVER BY the window, Aunt Haruko didn't seem to have budged since Rita's last visit. Bones poked out the back of her mint-green pyjamas like a half-collapsed tent. The nurse at the front desk had informed Rita that visiting hours were over, but it hadn't been difficult to slip by when the girl got a call from her boyfriend.

"It's me again, Aunt Haruko."

This time she didn't back away. Even leaned forward to be kissed. Her face seemed different tonight, softer, somehow. Despite the unpleasant note their last visit had ended on, Rita suspected Aunt Haruko was glad just to have a visitor. Beneath her flinty words of hell and damnation was a lonely, unloved soul.

"I've brought my daughter with me this time. Kristen, this is Aunt Haruko." Rita beckoned that it was all right to come forward and hug the old woman's shoulders.

Complying, Kristen appeared at once fascinated and frightened. "Mommy, why isn't Aunt Haruko looking at me? Is Aunt Haruko a witch?" she whispered.

"No, of course not. Her eyesight just isn't the greatest." Rita hoped Aunt Haruko hadn't overheard. Kristen was right though: there was something kind of witchlike about her secretive, sombre demeanour. If she was a witch, Rita believed that she must be a good witch. "I brought you some pastries. Would you like to have one?"

"Not much appetite these days."

Orange crullers had once been Aunt Haruko's favourite. Rita put one on a napkin and tore it into pieces. Hesitantly, the old lady toyed with a morsel and then greedily ate it up, flakey crumbs all over her chin. She lightly belched, like it had been years since she'd had anything so good.

Kristen wanted one, too, of course. Rita gave her half on the condition that she play quietly at the table in the corner so the adults could chat privately. They'd brought her set of pencil crayons and a colouring book. Rita got her settled and showed her the paintings on the wall that Aunt Haruko had done years ago. Kristen said she would draw a flower tree, too.

Aunt Haruko started coughing, so Rita fetched a glass of water. Then she noticed a kettle and box of green tea on the dresser. Making tea gave her hands something to do while she mulled over what to say. There really wasn't any way to ease into it.

"There are some things I need to ask you about. Things I've discovered about our family."

"They've found Lily, ne? She's been talking?" A look somewhere between guardedness and resignation.

"No, Mom's still missing."

Although the withered lips had pinched into a knot, she didn't seem surprised that Rita was back, asking questions. Maybe there was something Aunt Haruko wanted to tell her, something that had been weighing on her for years. "Eto ne, what do you want to know then?"

"There's so much I don't understand about the end of the war. How we all ended up in Toronto for starters. Tom's been telling me weird stories…." Tread lightly. It wasn't too late for Aunt Haruko to get upset and drift into stony silence.

Now it made more sense that she'd been so desperate to leave them. Was it any wonder that after all the craziness she'd witnessed, she'd hightailed it at the first opportunity to get as far away from Margueretta Street as possible?

"What are you asking, Rita?"

"After the war, when Kaz showed up, I'm curious about what happened between him and my mother. And how Grandpa reacted to Kaz's reappearance."

The old hands crumpled a napkin, twisted it into a rope. In that moment, as those fragile eyelids remained downcast, twitching slightly, Rita felt sure that there was some secret Aunt Haruko had held inside for far too long.

"Please, Aunt Haruko," she whispered, waiting. "You can tell me."

Twenty-Six

The next morning, she awoke late. Standing shakily, she felt different. All Lil's calmness and self-assurance had been sucked out the soles of her feet. The air was chilly, unwelcoming. Even the floor felt peculiar: the uneven tilt of the floorboards stabbed at her stomach like she was on a boat, sharp edges offering up slivers.

Creaking steps, a knock on the door. She stiffened, held her breath.

"Lily, are you up yet?" Aunt Haruko's anxious voice.

She murmured something inaudible to even herself.

"May I come in?"

"No, don't. I'm not dressed."

"I took Tom to school."

Oh, God. What time was it? Lil would have never overslept and forgotten all about her chores. But that woman felt very far away. Squinting at herself in the mirror, she adjusted the dishevelled tendrils, surprised to discover something sensuous and freeing about barely recognizing herself. Never again would she sleep with her hair bound in a braid. Lily, yes, yes, *Lily*, she repeated the name.

Her name. It felt right again. A sudden tingling ran throughout her body — this mad feeling of being alive, coming awake after so long in a coma, some wild creature exuberantly racing in circles, gathering speed, the wind blowing through her hair....

"Thank you, Aunt Haruko," she managed to say.

"You sure you're all right in there?"

"I'm fine. Really."

The feet creaked away. Lily stared at the wall for a long time, afraid to let her eyes wander. It was terrifying, this rush of sensation, emotion. Her skin prickled, blood coursed through her limbs, right to the extremities of her fingers, toes, lips. She swept a stray lock off her cheekbone, fingertips tracing her scar. At last, she could remember its origin.

THE LIVING ROOM smelled bready and stale; muted whispers called out to her from its dim reaches. Her old self barely audible now, cast to the periphery, the other side. Her eyes fell upon a figurine of the Virgin Mary that Aunt Haruko had put above the fireplace. Now Mary's face appeared empty of emotion — bored, almost — glossy waves around her shoulders heightened with sensuality. Lily shivered, looked away.

Where was Kaz? Where had he spent the night? She thought about his thin body curled up under a dirty awning, indistinguishable from any other derelict lying around the neighbourhood.

The din of last night: harsh, cruel voices. The doctor and Kaz had been fighting, she could remember that much. A cloud of hot, oppressive energy had filled the room. Cheeks florid and taut, the whites of their eyes like full moons. Fear and confusion swept over her, as she looked from father to son: each face but a wavering reflection of the other. Time was pulling away from her in every choked-up breath of every second she failed to distinguish the original face that had laid claim to her heart.... Vile words were flying from the doctor's lips and in one swift move, he'd grabbed Kaz by the collar and thrown him up against the wall. After the initial shock had passed, Kaz smiled tolerantly, as though he were amused by this show of force and had all the time in the world. Sure, Dad, slap me around a little. They all knew it wouldn't take much for him to overpower his father.

The doctor tried to banish him, and Lily started crying, begging him to stay. But Kaz was much too proud for any of that.

MR. DOBSON'S EYES shone with a new interest. This woman has a lot more to her than I gave her credit for, his eyes said.

"Did Kaz come back last night?" she asked.

"No. His bag's still here, though. The doctor put it in the hall."

It was a rough canvas satchel, barely more than a gunny sack, stained and coming apart at the edges. Maybe it would hold some clue to what Kaz had been doing all these years, why he hadn't come to find her sooner.

A comb. A razor, dull to the touch. A scruffy toothbrush. A bar of soap, cracked and yellowed. A couple of shirts. A pair of grey trousers, crumpled as dust rags. When she buried her nose in the fabric, she inhaled a hint of wide-open skies and the sun's hot breath.

Something rocklike at the bottom. A clunky black camera, scratched up as though it had been dropped many times. She ran her fingertips over the matte silver dial, wondering how all its intricate parts worked. Strange to think that this little box was capable of making pictures, capturing life as it really was, or how the photographer so ardently wanted it to be.... But this camera had no film in it; the hatch was empty.

Her fingers searched the bottom of the bag, so sure they'd find a photograph. An image of herself, as she'd been back then. *As she still was.*

There was nothing.

THE SKIRT FELT wrong, all wrong. Too loose, too frumpy — it

bunched up at the waist in elephant wrinkles, making her feel like an old woman. Funny how she'd never noticed that before. Now, all Lily could think was she needed to change out of it. Yet everything in her closet was equally schoolmarmish, hideous.

The next thing she knew, she was walking down the street, the cool, spring air invigorating her senses. She had a faint sense she was supposed to be headed to the supermarket, but her feet pulled in another direction. Her heart thrummed with images of silk lingerie and crystal bottles, full of the most heavenly fragrances.

She got on the eastbound streetcar. Getting off at Yonge, she walked south a few blocks, until she could see Eaton's rising majestically above all the little shop awnings. She lingered in front of the massive display windows, entranced by the unblinking eyes and self-satisfied smiles of the mannequins, their willowy limbs frozen in poses no ordinary woman would assume.

Inside, so many mirrors and bright lights. Trying to act casual, like she'd been here countless times before, Lily made her way to the ladies' apparel section.

Disembodied heads sat on a glass table sporting the latest hats. How deliciously soft the fine wool felt against the back of her hand, the tickle of a sapphire feather. She almost expected the concoction to spring to life and rub itself against her palm.

DINNER WAS A solemn, strained affair. Mr. Dobson and Mr. Sugimori were quiet and attentive, like audience members watching actors on stage. The doctor dealt with the situation by eating more heartily and noisily than usual, lavishing praise on Lily's casserole and salad.

"So how was your day at school, Tom?"

"All right, I guess."

"You look pale. Are you feeling all right, honey?" Lily placed a hand on his forehead.

"That man came back again. He spoke to me at recess."

"What's that, Tom?" the doctor said.

The boy's gaze remained fastened on his hands, folded tightly in his lap like little birds; he looked afraid they might fly away at any second.

"Kaz came around the school again. Oh, God." Lily lowered her voice, with an anxious glance at the boarders. Family business was private business. A car rushed by outside, the sound of a seashell held up to the ear. "We have to reach out to him. We have to let him know he still has a home here."

"He *does*? As far as I'm concerned, he gave up that right a long time ago."

"He's your son. We can't let him sleep on the street."

"So it's true?" Tom looked up. "That man's my father?"

The doctor's fork had frozen mid-air. A blob landed on the table like a splat of dung.

"What's wrong, Mommy?"

"Nothing, baby." Her face cold, wet.

"Your mother's just been under some stress," the doctor said. "Maybe she should go upstairs and pull herself together."

A hint of the old affection — Lil's pedantic voice — wrestled with her conscience. The doctor was being so stiff around her, chewing his food mechanically, barely looking up. But he'd come around, surely, wouldn't he?

Everything was exactly as it should be. There was no other way.

AFTER EVERYONE HAD gone inside, Lily lingered in the schoolyard. She watched the little yellow and purple crocuses peek up, tentative and new. Unsure whether they wanted to bloom at all.

A little girl was still playing on the swing set. Wasn't she going to get into trouble? A bright red dot bobbing up and down, higher and higher. *I ought to go over and make her slow down*, Lily thought, but she couldn't bring herself to break out of this stillness, entranced by the dabs of colour and flickering sunlight and bright white splotches of unmelted snow.

After a while she could feel his gaze. Just as the crocuses could feel her watching them, willing them to bloom, she sensed him willing her to turn around.

There he was, on the other side of the fence. He looked gentler than she remembered, his expression rising, falling, constantly changing: humble one moment, yet mocking the next. Like the men who'd call out to her from the doorways of boarded-up storefronts — "Pretty lady, can't you spare me a nickel?" — and sometimes she'd give it to them simply because it was reassuring to know there were people worse off than she was.

Yet Kaz wasn't one of those folks. As their eyes met, she felt the old warmth and excitement light up her skin. "I thought you might come here...."

"Did you."

"You have to come back to us. You belong with your family."

He stepped around to the other side of the fence. A frown had emerged between his eyebrows, two deep lines that might have been cut with a scalpel.

"Tom knows you're his father. We can be a real family, at last."

"*Family.* That's an interesting word for it."

The little girl on the swing kept arcing through the air, brown pigtails streaming behind. Lily's heart rose and plunged in tandem. "Because of your father? He's taken care of Tom and me. That's *it.*"

"I don't give a rat's ass what my father's done."

Now she'd planted suspicion in his mind — the very suspicion she'd hoped to allay. Her hands sprung to her burning cheeks. But there was nothing to allay.... There'd never been anything between the doctor and her. Truly, at that moment, she thought she believed it. So the future was wide open, wasn't it?

"Why can't we start over, Kaz?"

Ripples of emotion broke through. "Frank Isaka. Do you know what's become of him? Do you know where he is now?"

All she knew was that he'd been all right. The hiding place she'd found for him had done the trick.

"He's at law school. Frank's going to be a big-time lawyer. Thanks to all his friends in high places. Meanwhile, Kenny's rotting in jail." His voice dripped with bitterness. "You were always on Frank's side. *My father's side.*"

Was that true? She began shaking her head. Yet it was hard for her to say what she'd felt, back then. One thing was for certain, though: she'd done wrong by Kenny. He'd tried to save her, and she'd repaid him with her betrayal. Oh, God. Poor Kenny. His name sent shivers of regret through her soul, like the rustle of mice scurrying through dead leaves.

"It's over, Kaz. The war's over. We all have to move forward."

"Do we."

"What choice do we have?"

"Plenty of choice." Something quivered in his face. Then he got a hold of himself, trying to preserve a veneer of calmness, casualness. "My pictures. What did you do with them, Lily?"

"Your pictures? What pictures?"

"The pictures we hid under your bed for safekeeping. Don't you remember? You must've taken them with you when you left camp."

That little space under the floorboards. She'd buried a piece of her soul in that coffin. Why did Kaz have to bring up that business, now of all times? Just when they were being offered a second chance. Were those miserable pictures the whole reason he'd come looking for her? A wave of resentment, thick and suffocating. He had stepped closer to her and placed a hand on her shoulder. As he looked at her, she felt herself melt a little, but then she noticed how his lips had aged, lost their colour. For a second, they reminded her of her father's lips, the way his mouth collapsed in on itself at night after he'd removed his dentures, the skin greyish pink, reminiscent of dead worms.

"What on earth do you want those pictures for?"

"I need them because they can still do some good. Don't you see?"

The tremor in his voice filled her with a strange rush. She wasn't used to having power over him. "The war's over, Kaz. Those pictures aren't worth a hill of beans."

"That's not true! I'm still in touch with people who are interested in what I documented. Emily Archer, my WRA friends."

Flash of apricot hair, sheen of the sun. Cyclops eye of a camera never blinking, never flinching at anything. Was that where he'd been all these months and years? Living it up in San Fran, amid hakujin girls fawning all over him. "Fabulous pictures, Kaz. A true record of the internment." Glasses clinking. Endless babble about revolution and the struggles of the underclass. It made no difference which face they used: a Mexican peasant on the side of a dirt road, a little Oriental girl raking mud.

She didn't want that record to follow them around forever, casting a stain on their new life together. This new life that for a brittle, fragile moment, she wasn't even sure she wanted. Yet what choice did she have? What had she been struggling for, all these years, if not *this?*

"I don't have those pictures anymore, Kaz. I got rid of them a long time ago, I'm afraid."

"Really. I'm not sure I believe you, Lily."

She liked the proximity of his heaving chest and imploring eyes, fastened upon her so intently you'd think she alone had the power to give his life meaning once more. "Come home to us, won't you?"

His lips yielded to her kiss, reluctantly at first, but soon full of the old urgency. As though he were kissing her in hopes of sucking the information right from her tongue. She didn't even care. Soon he'd be so happy he'd forget all about those damn pictures.

Return Trips

Twenty-Seven

Sugar kept burning on the pan, sticky brown goo. Rita was trying to make French toast with caramelized apple slices. How was it that some women made this whole cordon bleu mother thing look so frigging easy?

Kristen was perched on a stool by the counter, quiet and watchful. She'd been like that ever since last night when they'd left the nursing home. On the long drive back, Rita had sensed that her attempts to act normal and cheerful were failing miserably. Kristen knew that Mommy was upset, thanks to something Aunt Haruko had told her. Something that Rita couldn't even begin to process. All she knew was that she felt numb, shell-shocked, but it wasn't the time to fall apart, not with her daughter in the passenger seat beside her.

"Mommy?"

"What?"

"I said 'Can I have Cheerios instead?'"

Rita had been staring at the burnt pan, lost in thought. Blinking her eyes, she tried to snap out of it. "Sure, sweetie." She fetched a bowl and the yellow box. She dumped the ruined pan into the sink with a clatter and sizzle.

She hadn't slept much last night. As soon as she'd tucked Kristen into bed, she'd poured herself a mug of French Cross and flicked on the TV to a horror movie. At some point doziness took over.

When she awoke this morning to a flurry of butterfly kisses, for one blissful second Rita forgot everything and felt like a normal mom, a mom who had it in her to get her hungover ass off the couch and cook amazing French toast.

"We have messages," Kristen said. The light on the answering machine was flashing.

It was Tom. He muttered something about being sorry if he'd been a dick the other night. Unusual for her brother to apologize for anything. His voice sounded tense; he said he'd been thinking more about what they'd discussed. There were certain things about Kaz's life that he'd pieced together over the years and maybe it was time that Rita knew, too. A long, strained pause. She almost thought the message had ended when his voice continued. Apparently, one of Kaz's old friends had reached out to Tom a number of years ago. Emily Archer was the woman's name. Tom left a phone number with an unfamiliar area code, which Rita jotted on the back of her hand in red marker. So he expected her to call this woman, a perfect stranger, out of the blue? And say what? God, why couldn't he just pass on the information himself, like a normal human being? She was about to call him up, when the second message came on.

Davis. The message had gotten cut off partway through.

Returning the call, Rita waited on hold for several minutes.

"Right. Well, guess what, Rita? Your mom's finally started using her plastic. About time, wouldn't you say?"

"Oh my God." Her grogginess crossed over into extreme alertness. "So she's all right? *Where the hell is she?*"

"California. Lily purchased a pair of sneakers in Sacramento a few days ago then charged a motel room in Lone Pine yesterday.

Looks like she's making her way up Highway 395. Any idea what she'd be doing out there?"

California. Camp. Christ.

"My mother was interned there during the war."

"Interned?"

Rita lacked the energy to go through the whole spiel again. Nevertheless, she launched into it.

"So if Lily used to live out there, she might still have friends, right? Someone she'd like to visit?"

"It's possible, I suppose." She didn't think it at all likely. Did anyone still live out there, in the middle of the desert? Her head felt like muddied water, all her thoughts stagnating around islands of muck. "My mom never mentioned keeping in touch with anyone."

After all the miserable, wasted years she'd spent out there, what on earth could possess her to go back?

"You never know. Maybe Lily has fond memories?"

Fond memories? Had Davis listened to anything Rita had just said? People heard "camp" and thought of fun times. But this had been an internment camp. No one had been there by choice. There hadn't been cookouts and beach volleyball and beer-filled coolers. Everything Mark had said about the need for redress echoed in her head with a new urgency. Maybe he was right: redress *was* worth fighting for. If only so they wouldn't have to listen to blockheaded comments about their folks having fond memories of camp.

Now wasn't the time, though, to set Davis straight. They had more pressing matters at hand.

Rita inquired about how the police were even sure that Lily had been the one to use her credit card. "Somebody could have stolen her purse, couldn't they?"

"The department store has a video camera behind the cash. That woman was definitely Lily."

A rush of relief, elation, still tinged with disbelief. So her mother really was out there.

"What now? You guys are heading out to find her, right?"

"Me go to California?" A cough that sounded more like a stifled laugh. "It's not like your mom's a dangerous criminal, and even if she was, we wouldn't be flying out to Cali. I *wish*. Wouldn't mind a few days on the beach. But no. We'll be working with the local police to do whatever's necessary."

"Which is what, exactly?"

"Look, Rita, as I've told you before, it's no crime to go away on vacation without telling anybody. I just thought you'd like to know your mom's okay."

"She's *not* okay!"

"Okay enough to go shopping for sneakers."

"That doesn't mean shit!"

"I can pass along her photo to the local police so they'll be on the lookout. We're not swimming in taxpayers' dollars here. Of course, if *you* want to drive out west, nice time of year for a road trip."

A canned line about keeping everyone posted. Just like that, the call had ended. So that was it. No one was going looking for Lily.

Rita had an image of her wandering along the edge of the highway, face caked with dust, thumb pointed upward. A hopeful, coquettish glance thrown up at some truck driver. Why had she gone out there? Did Lily herself even know? Or had she regressed to some confused, little-girl state in which the laws of reason didn't apply?

Rita called Gerald. No answer. She wondered whether Davis had told him the news already. He'd take it as a sure sign that Lily had left him and was now blithely shopping for new sneakers. Hopefully, he'd have the sense to go to an AA meeting or call his sponsor. She had no time to worry about him now.

Her old black backpack had disappeared in the move. Rifling through her bedroom closet, she unearthed the duffle bag she used for the gym. She dumped in a mass of Kristen's T-shirts and shorts, along with some bottles from the bathroom, and grabbed a pair of her own jeans off a chair. Heart pounding, hands spastic, a toothbrush clattered to the floor. She had no idea what the weather would be like in the desert — might as well throw in sweatshirts.

"What's going on, Mommy?" Kristen poked her head into the hallway, her upper lip rimmed with milk.

"We're going on a trip. To California."

"But I just got back!"

"Well, lucky you. Two trips on an airplane in one month. You'll be a world traveller."

"Why are we going to California?"

"Your grandmother's out there. That's where she ... got lost."

Rita raked her hands through her hair, secured it in a sloppy ponytail. The whole thing sounded so absurd. Were they actually going to do this? She felt like she wasn't thinking straight, but what choice did she have? The longer they waited, the less likely that anyone would ever find Lily.

"Come on, Kristen. Help me, *please*. Grab your pyjamas and at least three pairs of clean socks and underwear."

The doorbell rang. Rita's first thought was that Davis had come to her senses. She was here to interview Rita before heading out to California to continue the investigation.

"Mark! What're you doing here?"

His hair was a mess. He looked so relaxed and happy and wholesome. She was the last thing he needed in his life. To go from Tess to her would be like jumping straight into a frying pan.

"I was in the 'hood, thought I'd drop by. Gorgeous day." He looked up at the bright, cloudless sky, the skin around his eyes crinkling. "How about brunch on a patio somewhere?"

"I'd love to, but I have to get to the airport."

"The airport?"

"They've found Lily."

"What? Where *is* she?"

She gave him a capsule version of her conversation with Davis.

"You're trekking out to Matanzas to find her?" He looked astonished.

"Yup."

She thought he was going to try to talk her out of it. Convince her how insane it was to head to the middle of the desert with no plan, no map, nothing.

Just then, Kristen appeared in the doorway.

Heat rushed up Rita's neck. "Pumpkin, this is my new friend, Mark."

Smiling, he crouched down to shake her little hand. "So I hear you guys are going off on a big adventure in the desert."

"Yup. I like flying on the big plane."

Looking up at Rita, Mark's face opened up with that all too familiar look of camp counsellor vigour. "Don't suppose you guys would want some company?"

"You can't be serious. Why would you want to?"

"What are you talking about? I've always wanted to see the Sierra Nevada."

"To tour an internment camp? To go on a wild goose chase looking for someone's crazy mother?"

"Hey. I'm an archaeologist. This kind of thing's right up my alley."

"You guys go searching for the remains of extinct peoples. My mother is *not* extinct."

Twenty-Eight

At the beginning of the flight, they played a few rounds of fish. Even though Kristen kept winning, she said, "I'm bored. Doesn't anyone know any other games?"

But Rita wasn't about to teach her old maid; some games were best left as memories of a bygone era. The next thing she knew, Mark was shuffling the deck, the cards flowing like a waterfall between his hands.

"Choose a card, any card, look at it, and put it back."

Kristen's cheeks glowed with awe when he magically retrieved her card from deep within the pile. More tricks followed, cards turning cartwheels over Mark's agile fingers. It was cute to see him trying to impress. As Rita lay back, her eyelids began to feel sluggish.

When she woke up, the cabin was dark and a movie was on, some adventure flick in which Kathleen Turner runs around the jungle to find her kidnapped sister.

"Are we going to the jungle, too, Mommy?"

"No, we're going to the desert."

"Can we take the Mystery Machine?"

"Mystery Machine?"

"You know, like they do in *Scooby-Doo*!"

Scooby-Doo. It was Kristen's favourite show, how could anyone forget? Rita smiled at the thought of the three of them running from monsters and ghosts, getting locked in wax museums, and unmasking criminals. Everything solved within half an hour. If only finding Lily could be so easy.

They made it out to arrivals quickly since they hadn't checked any luggage. Such drama, being immersed in crowds of these rowdy, sunburnt Americans. They weren't the least bit embarrassed about displaying their family reunions, complete with bear hugs that could knock down a house. Yet if Lily were to step forward, Rita would put them all to shame.

Watching Mark from the corner of her eye was rather calming: red backpack slung over his shoulder, green baseball cap shading his eyes. Sturdy hiking boots. Must be what he wore when he went on digs. Her canvas sneakers felt flimsy in comparison.

It was nice of him, no doubt, to drop everything to come with them on this hare-brained trip.

"So what now?" he said. "Sleep or rent a car?"

It was midnight, local time. Three in the morning back in Toronto. Kristen rubbed at her eyes, exhausted.

"Let's get a room somewhere," Rita said.

Upon discovering what a rip-off hotels in the airport were, they ended up on a ramshackle shuttle bus headed to a Super 8. It was a far cry from the Mystery Machine, that was for sure. Humid night air streamed through the open windows, a waxy, gritty haze settling all over Rita's skin. The palm trees on the side of the road looked as dejected as upside-down mops.

The motel turned out to be a taupe stucco job, right beneath one of the runways. As they waited at the front desk, the walls began to shake under the blast of an engine. But hey, she could sleep through an earthquake right now.

A small, cramped room, with two double beds covered in orange flowered duvets, greeted them. Everything reeked of menthol cigarettes.

"Classy." Mark flopped down.

After Rita had helped Kristen into her pyjamas and tucked her into the other bed, she wasn't sure what to do, which bed to climb into. This was all such new territory. Would Kristen feel weird and grossed out if she woke up tomorrow morning and found Rita next to someone other than her father? Yet Cal and Jodi had no doubt shared a bedroom during Kristen's visit. That's what couples did, right? Was that what she and Mark were — a couple?

Before long, the room was full of soft, stuttering snores. Rita lay down on the edge of her daughter's bed simply to rest her head — or so she told herself — and soon she, too, was overtaken by waves of fatigue.

SHE AWOKE TO A CRACK of light scissoring through the curtains and a drone that sounded like someone vacuuming the inside of her brain. Mark was awake. He was lazing on a pillow, his face turned toward her, and it was unnerving to know he'd observed her sleeping. The two beds were so close together that she could see the lines around his eyes pucker with the skin's memory of hot summer days and some sad, solitary times, too. She wanted to lean forward and kiss him, but she was too aware of her daughter's presence on the sheets behind her.

As planes kept landing and taking off, Rita felt like her body was falling through time, lost in some place that had no representation on any map, but was always adrift on the margins of her consciousness.

"Mommy, where are we?" A pair of pudgy arms looped around her neck from behind and woke her up fully.

"We're in LA, at a hotel near the airport. Remember?"

"But I thought it's all a dream."

"I know the feeling."

They bathed quickly and got dressed. As they were checking out, Kristen noticed a complimentary breakfast buffet in the corner of the lobby. It was all sugary crap, but what the hell? They needed energy and there wasn't a diner in sight. Rita grabbed a handful of Twinkies and ripped open the packets.

Once outside, the watery-peach sunlight bleeding across the pale-blue sky helped revive them, along with the sweet-cream sugar rush. The palm trees looked less scraggy in the flush of dawn.

There was a car rental place on the other side of the highway, a bit of a trek down. CAR RENTAL 4 LESS, beamed the yellow sign.

The place looked cheap, that was for sure. Discarded receipts rustled in balls on the dirt-streaked floor. A cheery, bald guy informed them that summer vacation season wasn't the best time to show up without a reservation. All their cars were booked up — all the "A" cars, he added. One or two older models remained available if they were interested.

What he showed them was a mint-green Triumph convertible, edged with rust and scratched up along both sides, long as a boat. The thing had to be twenty years old.

"I've always wanted to drive one of these clunkers," Mark said.

He negotiated a sweet deal while Rita bought a map from the woman behind the counter. The route to Matanzas seemed pretty straightforward. The woman traced a nail-bitten finger along CA-14, followed by Highway 395.

"Going camping?" She raked a mound of bangs off her wide forehead, and they feathered back to exactly where they'd started.

"Yeah, you could say that." Fly-fishing, roasting marshmallows, the whole nine yards.

THE FREEWAY WOUND through hilly desert dotted with clumps of scrub brush on both sides. No palm trees here. To protect themselves from the dust and sun, they stopped and pulled the top up over the old convertible; it wasn't easy to get the old accordion to expand.

The sun flashed blindingly off the chrome parts of a pickup in front of them. Mark sped ahead. Rita fiddled with the radio: a raspy, discontinuous version of "Across the Universe" sputtered on then died a few seconds later.

"My number's nine," Kristen announced. "Nine's my favourite number." She promptly began scanning licence plates.

"And I'll take three," Rita said.

"What's this?" Mark asked.

"We're playing the licence-plate game." Kristen explained the rules. "I wish Granny was here. She's really good at this game. She's lucky."

Rita certainly hoped that was true. Lily needed all the luck she could get.

"Where *is* Granny?"

"I told you, honey. She came out here and ... got lost."

"But *why* did Granny come here?"

Rita had no idea how to answer this question. At some level, she was as much in the dark as anyone; she couldn't decode the bizarre workings of her mother's brain. That said, it seemed likely that Lily's journey had something to do with the internment. But how could you explain that sort of thing to a six-year-old? Was it even appropriate to try? On the other hand, Rita remembered how confused and uneasy she'd always felt as a child when Lily would dodge her questions about the past. Kids could sense when something fishy was up.

"A long time ago, when Granny was a young woman, she had to come live out here with her family." Had Lily come with her family? Rita knew so little about what had happened, she wasn't even sure if this had been the case. "All people of Japanese background had to leave their homes and come live in camps. It wasn't a very happy time for anyone."

"But … why?"

The issues and emotions felt far too complex to explain. Rita couldn't answer, a sob suddenly welling in her throat.

"Japan was at war with Canada and the United States," Mark said softly. "When countries go to war, people do bad things."

"Oh." Silence, still full of confusion. "So why is Granny here now?"

"We don't really know," Rita said. It was the only honest thing she could say. "Hopefully, we'll find her and she'll be able to tell us."

AN HOUR LATER, the chatter from the back seat died down. Kristen had put on the new Walkman that Cal had given her. He was spoiling her rotten with gifts, gifts that weren't even appropriate for a six-year-old. But now wasn't the time to get distracted by grudges. Now was the time simply to be grateful that Kristen had something to keep herself entertained during a very long drive.

After a while Rita noticed that her daughter's eyes had fallen shut.

Mark's hand inched forward. It was resting lightly on her thigh, such a casual, intimate gesture. Although it delighted her, it also made her recoil. She couldn't help thinking this was all a big mistake.

"I'm not sure if friends touch each other's thighs like that."

"You're the one who brought up the whole friends thing. I never had any such delusions."

"But you still live with that woman, Tess —"

"Relax, Rita. She's moving out."

"Oh, really? *When?*" The anxiety — the patheticness — she heard in her own voice made her cringe.

"September first. I've given Tess a deadline. Even if she hasn't found an apartment by then, she's getting the boot."

His words sank in, sending tingles over her scalp. She felt like an ass for being so possessive. So bourgeois, middle-aged, boring. But who was she trying to kid?

Lazy mornings in bed together, the Sunday paper crumpled on top of the sheets. Pet names too stupid to repeat. Painting the walls of her kitchen canary yellow, sunlight sluicing in like a waterfall. Long walks in the rain, the smell of earth and wet dog, his fingers wrapped around hers in the pocket of a parka. Lounging at opposite ends of the couch, feet touching. Her earthenware bowls next to his metal canisters, her hair dryer tangled up with the cord of his shaver, their socks balled up together in the dryer, everything covered in the same snowy down.

She wanted it all, yet it terrified and repulsed her a little.

And what if it wasn't what he had in mind at all?

But maybe all that mattered was that Mark was here with her right now — flying into the desert in this souped-up jalopy. He must care about her, considering he'd dropped everything to go on this madcap trip. Although she had no idea where things were headed, for the time being maybe it was nice to coast in this adolescent buzz, like smoking a cigarette for the first time and getting a massive head rush. That she could deal with just fine.

Wavering mounds dotted with billboards. A giant pina colada poured onto a sun-kissed beach. Mark reached for her hand and then grabbed at the wheel, as they lurched over a pothole.

"You're not going to believe what I discovered about my dad. Turns out he never lived with us at all. I'd always assumed he hightailed it after I was born, but he was never around in the first place."

"But ... how can that be?"

She filled him in on what Tom had told her about the peculiar way their family had reunited in Toronto.

"That's a lot for you to deal with. Are you ... okay with it?"

"I don't have much choice, do I?"

She didn't know why she'd opened this can of worms. It was a relief to let him in, maybe. To an extent, anyway.

By the second orange cruller, Aunt Haruko had been talking her ear off. A lot of the things she'd disclosed Rita still hadn't had time to get her head around. Davis's phone call had pushed her into crisis mode.

Maybe one day she would tell Mark everything — the whole fucked-up enchilada. For now, however, there were limits to what she'd burden him with. She stared out at the brownish, mustardy landscape. Place looked lifeless beyond the rare tree struggling for a foothold.

"I was lucky my grandfather and I were close, at least."

They lapsed into silence and her mind drifted. Grandpa's dress shoes, so carefully polished, the toes shiny as apples. Those boxes of notebooks they'd discovered after his death. Small, black ledgers in which he'd kept track of his weekly lotto numbers, the vitamins and pills for his ever-growing array of aches and ailments, obituaries of people in the Japanese community. So many facets of his life, tallied up over the decades in his elegant, upright hand. When Rita was little, he'd tried to teach her proper penmanship. He'd guided her hand up and down in so many repetitive strokes, warmth emanating from his arm behind her.

They passed through towns, if you could call them that. Some were just clusters of dingy prefabs on the side of the highway. A motel. An aluminum-sided church. A town hall. A post office. A school. Mom-and-pop convenience stores with neon Marlboro signs. A stream of watery, sludgy coffee. The sequence repeated itself as Rita sat back and let it wash over her. Everything appeared to be losing particularity, blurring into the amorphous landscape that pulled them forward as though they were riding waves in the middle of a vast, murky ocean. Her ears felt funny with the change in air pressure. At some point, mountains bled through the sky: a faint, jagged stain hovering behind the layers of mist and haze.

"Can you imagine how it would've been to make this journey crammed on a bus, all your worldly possessions in a sack?"

"It must've been … unreal." She pictured her mother: a small, shocked face pressed against the glass. What would it be like to be driven out into this no man's land, your entire life stripped away?

"Where was your dad interned?" she asked, a moment later.

"Kaslo. This ghost town in the interior of BC."

"Did he ever go back to visit?"

Mark shook his head. "I asked him several years ago whether he wanted to. Offered to go with him. We could fly to Vancouver, rent a car. Make it a father-son road trip." He kept his eyes on the road, forehead creasing. Then he laughed, a bark almost. "My dad thought I was nuts. Not his idea of a fun vacation. He'd remarried by then, and he and Shirley were more Vegas types. And then, three years later, the guy was dead of cancer."

"God, I'm sorry."

"It's fine. It happened a long time ago."

The landscape had flattened into washed-out lines.

Rita thought about the Japanese fairy tales Lily had once told her, all the stories of sudden disappearances and reversals of fortune. Girls who dropped iridescent eggs and accidentally killed their unborn children — their resplendent, palatial surroundings suddenly vanishing. Young men who opened boxes they'd been forbidden to look inside, only to be confronted by clouds of smoke and broken mirrors that revealed faces of old men. None of us are where we think we are. None of us are who we think we are. The present constantly disappears, time violently yanked away. That inevitable process of aging could be mysteriously — tragically — accelerated. So many of these tales were about lives evaporating, futures cancelled in a heartbeat.

Lily's extreme frugality, her refusal to throw anything away. How they'd quarrelled when it came time to clean out her basement. Her eyes ablaze, she clung to a cheap, glass vase and barricaded herself in front of that shaky, battered desk she'd rescued some years ago from the sidewalk. Nothing could be wasted — not a sandwich crust, not an empty bread bag. She carried washed-out margarine tubs and plastic spoons in her purse, for you never knew when you might need them. Once while they were walking past an abandoned house, the front yard clogged with weeds waist-high, Lily crouched down to forage. Some thorny purple wildflower had caught her attention, and she wanted to transplant it to her own garden. She was constantly salvaging these scraps of beauty as though this was the only way she knew how to live.

Rita let her face roll toward the window just as the tears started to prickle and burst. She pretended to be asleep.

With a thud, her eyes popped open.

"Shit!"

"What's going on, Mark?"

"Mommy, who said a bad word?" Kristen bolted awake.

"Sorry, I did," Mark said. "I think we've got a flat."

"*Crap*. Oh, Christ, I didn't mean to say that."

As luck would have it, there was no spare in the trunk.

A truck sped by. The driver ignored Rita's frantic waving from the side of the road. Over the next fifteen minutes, three more cars passed by, no one even slowing down.

Mark insisted that Rita and Kristen stay in the car, where they'd at least have the comfort of shade. He'd seen a gas station ten or fifteen miles back. Hopefully, well before he made it that far, someone would stop to pick him up.

Just as he was setting off down the highway, another truck appeared on the horizon. Rita got out of the car and began wildly flinging her arms around while Kristen imitated from the side of the road. This time, by some miracle, the truck pulled over.

"Where you kids headed?" The face that poked out was tanned, leathery.

"We're looking for that camp you folks put us in," Mark said.

Rita's heart jumped. What was he thinking? The heat must have gone to his head. The last thing they needed right now was a brawl with a redneck.

"The war camp." The man squinted with the effort of reaching a long way back into the pit of his memory. A tense silence. "Well jump in, kids, if you want!"

Under normal circumstances, she wouldn't have gotten into this guy's truck if her life depended on it. Old Dell was his name, he informed them — not to be mistaken with Young Dell, his ten-year-old grandson. It was jackrabbit hunting season; he gestured at the rifle at his feet. Rita jammed in beside him, their sweaty shoulders sticking together like saran wrap. Kristen sat on her lap.

Old Dell lived in a town nearby. Although there wasn't an auto repair for a hundred miles, he'd be happy to find them a spare tire for the price of a song.

"I've noticed you folks makin' yer way up north."

"Us folks?" Mark said.

"Yellow folks. I've seen 'em makin' their way back there."

"To Matanzas?"

Old Dell nodded.

"Why would they be headed up there?"

"That's what *I'm* askin' you."

"Oh. I'm looking for my mother." Rita passed over a crumpled flyer. "I don't suppose you've seen her around?"

"Good lookin' woman, her. But no. I'd be lyin' if I said I had."

By this point, the disappointment barely even registered.

"Did he take Granny?" Kristen whispered. "Is he a bad guy?"

"No, honey."

"Bad guy?" Old Dell said.

"We're solving the mystery of what happened to my Granny. Are you the bad guy?"

The old man chuckled. "Sure, if that's the role you wanna cast me in."

"So you were saying that Japanese folks have been coming out here?" Mark pressed.

"I think it has somethin' to do with protest. Carloads of these long-haired Oriental hippies lookin' to march over stuff, now that Nam's long gone. They started comin' out here, maybe startin' ten years back, wavin' banners with Japanese writing and beatin' them big crazy drums out in the sand. Bonfires, strummin' their guitars. Guess they wanna revisit where their parents did time."

"Redress," Mark said, with a steely edge. "It's tied to the Redress Movement. Getting compensation for what our folks went through. The movement's been getting a lot of traction out west."

"Yeah? I've heard rumblin' about that stuff. Sure, it was bad what happened, but we've all had to take the short end of the stick from time to time. That's how history works — winners and losers. If all the losers wanted the government to write 'em a cheque, where'd the handouts stop?"

"Maybe if the government didn't have its head up its ass so much, it wouldn't have to keep writing cheques."

A sharp, hot sensation, something like pride, like indignation, surged in Rita's chest. Mark was right to speak up.

"Hey, I'm just sayin'!" Old Dell raised both hands from the wheel in an exaggerated shrug. "Me, I had a Paiute grandma once, ya know. You'd never know lookin' at me, but go figure. D'you think her people liked gettin' kicked off their land? That's what Matanzas was, in the beginnin'. For thousands of years, they'd lived here. Had trade routes all the way to the coast. Their ancestral spirits are bound to the land."

She imagined dispossessed spirits wandering along the side of the highway, forever dusty and tired.

"That's another injustice that the government should answer to," Mark said. "One of many."

BY THE TIME they reached Lone Pine, it was afternoon already. She'd been expecting a dumpy little town, no different than so many of the places they'd passed through. But this place was surprisingly bustling. Although it had the look of a small town up in the mountains — with restaurants designed to resemble log cabins and shops with neon arrow signs announcing SPORTING & HUNTING GOODS — there was something too freshly painted about its blatantly nostalgic edifices. A young father in a Hawaiian shirt stepped out of an old-fashioned candy shop, a toddler hoisted on his shoulders with lollipop in hand. A chubby woman with tightly permed black hair waved around a map and called down the street to her friend. Apparently, the town was famous as a location for old movies.

Mark parked at the end of the street. They got out and stretched their limbs.

An Asian family was coming down the sidewalk, everyone dressed in matching hiking gear. She'd hoped that in this hillbilly town, Lily would stick out like a sore thumb. Not during tourist season, apparently.

"So what now, Chief?"

"Let's check that motel we just passed. The police said my mom charged a room to her credit card."

Pastoria Inn. Deer heads poked out from the walls of the low-ceilinged lobby. No one was at the front desk. Rita rang the bell.

It was an old, uncomfortable feeling. Growing up, she'd never quite known what explanation would spring from her lips until she'd blurted it out. "My mother, she loses track of time, sometimes. She's absent-minded. But she's okay, really *she is*. Have you seen a woman who looks like this?" Flash of a photo. People's distantly concerned, fascinated stares. The spectre of craziness was fun to contemplate so long as it remained far removed from your own family.

"Can I help you, ma'am?" The receptionist had a lion's mane of auburn hair, teased out as wide as high.

"I'm, uh, looking for a woman named Lily Takemitsu. I think she may be staying here?"

The woman consulted her records. "Sorry, ma'am, you're outta luck. No Lily Takemitsu here."

"Are you sure? This is her picture."

"Never seen her. And I'd remember a mouthful of a name like Lily Takemitsu."

"Oh. She's my mother."

"And my Granny!" Kristen piped up.

"Sorry, hun. That still doesn't change the fact that this Lily lady's not here."

"Are there other motels in town?" Mark asked.

"There's another one down the street and a couple more off the highway."

They walked out into the blazing, punishing sun. They wandered in and out of shops to make more inquiries. Kristen was getting a burn, so Rita stopped in a souvenir store to buy her a visor. They checked the motel at the other end of Main Street, but Lily wasn't there either. Tired and famished, they ended up at a Chinese restaurant with a sea of red lanterns hanging from the ceiling. Heaping fried dishes covered in gooey bright sauces floated by on the arms of waiters.

"She looks familiar." The hostess glanced at Lily's picture. "Yeah, I remember now. A busload of Japanese tourists was here last week, all the ladies under their white sun umbrellas. That must've been where I saw your mom, right?"

Twenty-Nine

"What camp?" The girl behind the cash register stared back, pimples glistening amid her freckles.

Rita cradled a bottle of water to her chest. The fan on the counter wasn't doing anything to cool her, just swirling hot, sticky air. "You're sure there's no site around here where all the Japanese folks used to live? Matanzas."

"Mom?" the girl called over her shoulder. "A lady here wants to talk to you."

The woman who sprang out from the backroom had the same freckly skin and catlike eyes, yet these features had been stretched over a face twice as wide and unsmiling. "Oh, that place? Maybe there used to be something up past Lone Pine, but it isn't there now, I can tell you that much. Got torn down a long time ago."

It wasn't the first time Rita had been told this story. Store owners and gas station attendants remembered virtually nothing. All anyone would say was that the camp, if it had ever existed, had long ago disappeared. And no one had been comfortable with all those Japs living off the fat of the land anyway while the rest of

America had suffered wartime shortages. So maybe it was for the best that Matanzas had been swallowed up whole, nothing left to remind anyone of what had happened.

Rita returned to the car where Kristen and Mark were munching on licorice.

"Any luck, Mommy?"

"Nope."

While they continued driving down the highway, scanning for some trace of Lily, the sand swept up and danced in ghostly apparitions.

Maybe they were barking up the wrong tree. They had no real evidence to suggest that Lily's return had anything to do with camp. But Kristen's question about why Granny had come out here kept nagging. The only reason Rita could think of was camp. Lily had some unresolved business that had drawn her back here.

The land stretched out in cryptic patterns of sage and scrub grass. It was all there, written in some secret code. If only they could figure out what it meant, they'd have the key to understanding everything.

KRISTEN RUMMAGED IN Rita's purse for a stick of sugar-free gum. What she extracted instead was a tiny flashlight attached to a key chain. Flicking it on, she waved the spotlight over the roof of the car.

"This'll help us. All detectives have flashlights, right?"

"Sure," Rita said distractedly. "It'll be useful if we have to search any deserted buildings."

"We might need it before then," Mark said. "Look at that, isn't it something?"

Dusk was falling. Clouds of fiery red, softening to coppery orange, spilled across the mauve sky. The smell of sage and something pungent — like the earth itself was perspiring — filled the air.

"I still don't understand why Granny had to come out here." Kristen stuck the head of the flashlight in her mouth, her cheeks lighting up like a glow-worm. "She must've come for a reason."

"It's hard to explain, honey. Your grandmother has problems. She gets confused about things sometimes."

"Oh, yeah? Like what?"

"I don't know. I'm not inside her head, Kristen." Rita bristled at the sharpness of her own voice. She *wanted* her daughter to feel comfortable asking about all this stuff, didn't she? "Granny's had a hard life — going back to the time she had to leave everything behind and come live here — and that's made it difficult for her, sometimes, to remember the past and behave like a normal person."

These words were still way too vague and evasive for Rita's taste. It was a cop-out, not much better than the cop-outs Lily flung her way when she'd been the kid asking uncomfortable questions.

"You know what I think, Mommy? Granny lost something here."

And maybe, Rita thought, just maybe, it really was that simple.

THE LAST TIME she saw her mother, Lily had looked tired, so tired, as she had for Rita's whole life. The faint lines on her skin had deepened over the years, so they weren't so faint anymore — they were caked with makeup, badly applied, the look of parched, cracked earth. "You've had a good life, haven't you, dear?"

And this time there'd be no hint of hesitation or adolescent sarcasm in Rita's voice as she'd answer, in the affirmative. "Yes, Mom." Despite everything, yes. *Yes, yes, yes.* What she wouldn't give to be able to voice these simple words.

"Hey, what's that?" Mark slowed down.

"I saw something, too," Kristen said. "Like a tall, white ghost!"

He turned the car around with a grind into the gravel.

There *was* something out there. A spike of whiteness shooting up in the distance. All by itself, nothing around it, just sheer desert. Then a blur of sand and wind had erased it already.

They got out of the car and began walking toward whatever that *thing* had been. The setting sun reflected off grains of sand like ice crystals. A jackrabbit hopped by, its ears like giant antennas. They found a path, cutting off the road, that was little more than remnants of pavement faded into pebbles and dirt, firmly packed, mosaic-like. Clumps of old tamarisk trees spotted the horizon, more dead than alive, trunks branching off in upturned, arthritic claws.

A faint apparition. As they got closer, it materialized, gained solidity. There it was — they hadn't imagined it. It was a white stone tower, beautifully proportioned and simple in design. It narrowed into a pyramid at the top, pointing like an arrow up to the heavens. A couple of Japanese characters had been painted on the front in dramatic black strokes. Rita tried to think of a phrase that could capture what Lily had experienced here.

The land that swallowed me whole.

Crude gravestones were clustered on either side.

"Do you think this is where the camp was?" Rita heard herself ask.

"Maybe. This could be a memorial stone or something," Mark said.

"Looks like this was the camp cemetery then."

"Most people would've wanted their dead moved after the war. These few graves must've belonged to the folks who had no family."

Walking across the colourless expanse, her legs wobbled. There was nothing but wide-open space. She might have been standing at the edge of some extraterrestrial land, void of life for millions of years. The place had no boundaries. They must have taken down the barbed-wire fence a long time ago. Whatever roads or paths had once existed had been covered over, absorbed into the earth. It was impossible to walk in Lily's footsteps, to imagine her life here.

As they got farther in, the land became rougher in texture. The wind settled. Rocks dotted the ground in massive squares. They walked around one of these peculiar configurations, and Rita was reminded of a TV documentary about geometric patterns that had appeared out of nowhere in cornfields. Aliens from outer space were thought to be responsible.

"Hey, what's this?" Kristen held up a beer bottle.

"I guess the old hippies who come out here need to keep hydrated," Mark said.

"Something's written here." She'd crouched down to look at a large rock at the corner of one of the square figures.

"Nice work, kiddo." Mark bent down, too. "Someone's etched something with a knife. DAD'S BARRACK."

Rita came over to examine the block letters, running her fingertips over the rough incisions as though she were reading Braille. They walked around the perimeters of several other phantom buildings and tried to imagine their walls and roofs. More etchings identified them as mess halls, latrines, and barracks.

"It's amazing. People have gone to a lot of trouble. Do you think they mapped all this from old photos and plans?"

"Or memory. Maybe some of the old hippies who come out actually grew up here. It's like the folks who did all this are trying to create a kind of invisible museum."

"God, it's weird being here."

They were making their way around an *L*-shape.

"This was the hospital," Mark said. He was reading another etching.

The hospital where the riot had occurred…. An explosive crack of gunfire, like something had blast open, between Rita's ears. She could hear it, she could feel it now: a mass of bodies rising in an upsurge — so many panting, terrified bodies falling on top of each other, everyone merging into a single creature, slick with fear….

"Are you okay?" Mark was at her side.

"I feel kind of weak."

He held a water bottle up to her lips.

They continued walking around the ghost of a building. Her eyes remained fastened to the ground though she had no idea what she was looking for. She rubbed a bit of dirt between her fingertips, letting it soften, turn velvety.

Kristen and Mark moved on to explore other areas. The flashlight came out, a dot of bright white light dancing like a firefly on the periphery of Rita's vision. Their excited voices began to sound distant, hushed. She lingered behind, still near the hospital.

A tremor of movement over on the right. Behind that pile of rocks and debris at the far corner of the floor plate, under the shadows of a dead tree. At first Rita thought it was just wind kicking up a mound of sand. But the movement was coming right from the ground — dirt was being flung up in an arc, and with each heave the tip of a small shovel or tool could be seen.

As she approached, she felt her insides go very still, as though her body had forgotten how to breathe. A cold, shrivelling sensation passed over her scalp.

It was Lily.

That dark mound, crouched down among the rocks and shadows, was her mother.

"Mom?" The word died softly.

Lily didn't look up, didn't seem aware she was being watched, even. The task of burrowing in the ground completely absorbed her attention.

"Mommy, where are you?" Kristen suddenly shouted through the dimness.

This time, Lily bolted up. She looked thinner than before, her bones lost within the crumpled, stained dress. Skin stripped bare of makeup, blotchy and sunburnt in patches. Hair pulled back in a tight ponytail, a thick band of salt and pepper visible around the roots. But it was the same face that Rita had always known: the high, delicate cheekbones and eyes that never stopped moving. Her lips, without any lipstick, appeared chapped, childlike.

"Mom …?"

The eyes rested on Rita, but appeared confused, cornered.

Mark called out, his voice urgent. Lily's eyes darted over to him — a sudden, shining joy overtaking her face. It was as if she knew him. As if she thought he was Kaz. Glimmering through the shadows, far away, ephemeral. In her imagination perhaps he was beckoning, calling out her name, just as playful and arrogant as the day they first met. And then she was running toward him, plumes of sand obscuring her thin figure, her hands extended like they held something. A small box.

When Lily got closer, though, her smile faded, bafflement taking over once more. She staggered backward, inhaled a slap of dust. A piece of sagebrush roped around her ankle and threw her off balance.

Rita ran over and put her arms around the trembling, sobbing body. She drank in the faint scent of lilac lotion mixed with a dusty patina and the acidic sting of perspiring flesh. A sudden bewilderment of dizziness that encompassed both grief and joy. This living, breathing, troubled woman, who would always be her mother.

Thirty

When the Countess Motel was first built, it probably had swanky aspirations. COLOR TELEVISION, a yellow sign proudly announced, a chandelier visible through the glass walls of the lobby. But now the paint was peeling like a bad sunburn, and every third neon letter didn't light up.

Lily's room wasn't much to look at, but it wasn't as bad as Rita had expected. There were two double beds covered in faded terracotta print, and the wallpaper had a seashell pattern. The place was tidy enough. Lily didn't have anything with her.

Mark had taken Kristen to the diner on the main floor. Rita was going to join them as soon as she was sure her mother was okay. That could take a while. Maybe they should get a room for the night, too. Or maybe the best thing was to get Lily cleaned up and tucked into the car. They'd all had enough of the desert to last a lifetime. Rita wondered if it would be possible to fly out tonight.

"Coffee?" Lily's hands clasped together, as she straightened up in an incongruously hostess-like gesture. "I can make real."

"No, Mom. Thanks though." It sounded surreal. She'd trekked all the way out here for coffee and chit-chat?

A strained smile.

Then Rita's heart relented. "Fine, Mom. A cup of coffee sounds good. Here, let me make it."

She fiddled with the small drip-coffee maker on the dresser, emptying the pouch of grounds into a cylindrical filter. They sat in silence as the machine began to gurgle and drip and steam. Rita poured two mugs. As Lily cradled hers to her chest, wisps of steam made the air thicken, waver. The skin on her right cheekbone, where the scar had once been, appeared smoother and shinier than the rest of her face, like a worn-down patch of velvet.

Lily's hands suddenly shot up, balling in the eyes. Her knuckles were swollen and streaked with blood from all that digging. Rita wasn't sure whether her mother was crying or simply trying to block the world out.

"You must be wondering what happened, Rita. Why on earth I came out here."

Strangely, her hunger for the truth had died down. "It isn't important. You don't have to explain anything. Let's just get you cleaned up so we can all go home, okay?"

"But I want to tell you."

"Okay." Always this out-of-sync dance. "So why did you come out here, then, Mom?"

"It started as a … as a mission…." A snuffle.

"A mission for?"

"Ted started it."

"Ted Fujita?"

A slight nod though she didn't look very certain.

"The photographs?" Rita prodded, excitement spreading up her neck. "I visited Mr. Fujita and he told me about the JCNA's book project. Is that what you're talking about?"

"Mmmhmm. They needed pictures. I told him I had some. But — but — they'd gotten lost. I couldn't remember where I'd left them." Hugging her arms around her rib cage, she stared at the air above her knees. "And then — then — well, it came back to me."

"What came back to you?"

"The pictures. Where they were. I can't explain it. It was like I'd watched a movie of myself — my old young self — burying them. Something I always had a feeling I'd done, but that person never seemed like it'd been me. But now I knew *she was me* — so I had to come out here to find them…."

At first, Lily had planned to tell Gerald about the trip. But she worried he'd try to stop her, and the urgency of getting to Matanzas seemed overwhelming. Reading between the lines, Rita gathered that the stress of explaining about the internment had been too much for her. The next thing Lily knew, she was at the bus station boarding a Greyhound for New York. All she knew was that she had to make it to the States and keep heading west. As she transferred from one bus to another, she'd drift off and wake up to sun-drenched fields and deserted barns speeding by, and sometimes, Rita suspected, she had no clue what she was doing on the bus at all. Reality — memory — cutting in and out, like footage from someone else's life.

Upon arriving in LA, she had no idea how to get to Matanzas. No map, no compass, no scribbled directions. It was a miracle she'd made it at all. Walking and hitchhiking along the highway and taking many wrong turns along the way, she'd finally ended up here.

"I found them." A shy glow. Lily extracted from her purse a dirty, rusty tin. So that was what she'd been so intent on digging up. She held it out like proof. Proof of what?

The tin felt light in Rita's hands, as though it contained nothing more than a single feather. The lid made a screeching noise as it popped off. An array of brittle, discoloured pictures scattered across the bedspread.

All the pale, sombre faces. Her palms began to sweat and she worried that the paper would dampen, disintegrate. A manila tag with a number had been tied to a little girl's coat, fluttering in the wind like a dead leaf. She was standing outside the bus that had brought her to camp. The scuffed toes of a young man's boots. His folded hands appeared still and heavy as rocks. He sat on top of his rucksack and stared ahead at nothing in particular. The puffy, swollen hands of an older woman, who might have worked in a dry-cleaning shop, as Lily's mother had. How fiercely those blunt fingers clutched the handle of her suitcase. Dry, dusty roads. Houses like garden sheds. Some of the people peeking out through the shadowy doorways seemed aware that their pictures were being taken; they met the camera's gaze head-on, their lips set in grim, wavering lines or self-reliant smiles that showed they knew they were expected to play the part of pioneer settlers in this anachronistic joke of history. Other people simply went about their business, waiting in endless lines under the searing sun, plates and bowls tucked under their arms, just another day of being herded around like cattle.

More than anything, these pictures emitted a feeling: a dim, grey, monotonous feeling. Of life having been exposed as something less than the Technicolor dream they'd once expected.

A close-up of a man with deeply tanned cheeks. His bushy eyebrows added emphasis to his defiant stare. A dirty apron had been thrown over one shoulder. He looked at the camera with a familiarity that suggested he was buddies with the photographer. There was a proud complicity between them that had everything to do with the black eye this guy wore like a badge of honour. He was smiling — sneering even. Anybody who knew what was good for them wouldn't mess with this dude.

"Is this Kaz?"

"No, Kaz isn't here."

There wasn't a trace of family resemblance, really. After all these years, Kaz wasn't about to show his face now.

"He's … Kenny. A good friend of Kaz." Something wavered in Lily's expression, like it hurt to keep looking at his image. There was some history, some buried pain between the two of them. But when Rita gently prodded, Lily only shook her head, her lips moving in a silent mantra.

Rita continued sifting through the pile. Curious how these images appeared, at first glance, to offer tantalizing glimpses through some secret window that looked directly onto the past. Chunks of reality, miraculously recorded. Yet the more she examined them, the less certain she felt of anything. Where was the larger narrative that could link all these fragments together?

"Who took these pictures, Mom?"

"Kaz did."

"What? *Kaz?*"

Lily nodded, like the whole thing made perfect sense. She picked up a photo and looked at it wistfully.

It showed a girl strolling across the desert, as the wind whipped her hair into a tangle that concealed her eyes. Still, her mouth remained visible: a dreamy, secretive smile, melting inward. Oh, yes. Rita would recognize that smile anywhere.

"It's you, isn't it, Mom?"

"Kaz took it."

The rumble and whoosh of a truck in the distance. Rita might have been standing at the side of the road, winded, covered in dust.

Kaz was the eye behind this bleak, mysterious, fragmentary world?

"He loved taking pictures." Lily gasped, fell into silence. The skin under her eyes twitched. "He always wanted his pictures to do good. I — I should've retrieved them sooner, but instead — instead — *I stood in his way.*" Her voice dissolved into sobs and she hugged her arms around herself, rocking, like a devastated child.

"What happened, Mom?"

"I told Kaz I'd burned the lot of them. It … it upset him terribly."

"When did this happen? When Kaz came to Toronto — after the war?"

A hesitant nod. "He wanted the pictures. I thought I could make him want me, too."

"Why did you pretend you'd destroyed them? And why did you have the pictures in the first place?"

"I had to hold on to them for safekeeping. Kaz asked me to. But I couldn't keep them in my room anymore — they gave me awful nightmares. So I snuck out one night and borrowed Mr. Murase's gardening shovel to bury them."

Lily began talking about how someone had been coming to seize the photos — that was why Kaz had come to her. That much she seemed clear about. But when Rita pressed about the details of what had happened, she fell into silence or incoherence. Rita sensed that there was more to her mother's desire to have those pictures off her hands. No doubt it had something to do with the shame of being captured on film as an internee, a prisoner. At the time, Lily probably felt that burying the pictures was the only way for them to move forward, as a family, into the bright, harsh future of hard-working immigrants, ready to sacrifice everything to rebuild their lives. Forget everything, turn the other cheek. Pull yourself up by your goddamn bootstraps.

There was still so much that Rita didn't understand. "So Kaz was mad that you'd supposedly burned his photographs. Is that why he left us? Surely, it would have taken more than that. *What happened? What happened to our family?*" The torrent of questions shot from her lips, a restless sensation wrapping around her throat. She was incapable of holding back or speaking more softly.

Silence. Lily stared at her lap.

So that was it, all Rita would ever know.

"Kaz was ... jealous," Lily said at last.

"Jealous? Jealous of ...?"

"His father."

When Rita asked more questions, though, her mother wouldn't reply. She simply turned away, turned off. It was as if all certainty about everything she'd just said had floated away, like a wisp of smoke.

AUNT HARUKO'D HAD more to say about what had happened. When it came right down to it, she was quite willing to talk, as if she longed to get the whole thing off her chest. Apparently, Kaz had shown up on Margueretta Street out of the blue, after no one had heard a word from him since camp days. He just waltzed in off the front porch one evening and proclaimed himself the man of the house, here to lay claim to Lily as if no time had elapsed at all.

"I was surprised she even recognized him," Aunt Haruko said.

"He looked that bad?" Rita said.

"It was more than that. Lily never talked about Kaz. I don't think she even remembered him. After the riot, after her injury, she was confused for a long time…."

"Confused how?"

"Forgetful. Full of ridiculous wishes." Mortified, downcast eyes. "You remember when you were little, Lily was sometimes … not herself around the doctor, ne?"

When was Lily ever "herself"? But Rita knew all too well what Aunt Haruko was getting at. Lily's fantasies about Grandpa. The way she'd look at him with heat and longing, as though they were old lovers who shared a colourful and turbulent history, and his attempts to spurn her were part of some cyclical dance. It was gross and disgusting, so Rita and Tom ignored it, ate quickly, and asked to be excused from the table while Grandpa stared at the mushy river down the centre of his plate.

The doctor's wife. There were times Lily truly seemed to believe it. Still. She'd told Gerald that her first husband was a doctor, with a note of pride, no doubt. She'd gotten what she wanted in the end, she'd landed her man.

So Kaz had been jealous. Who could blame him? Was that the real reason he'd left town, choked up by rage?

Or maybe he'd been relieved that there was another man around to assume the paternal role he'd never wanted in the first place.

Aunt Haruko had spilled her tea.

Rita mopped it up, slowly. "There never was anything between them, was there?" She couldn't believe she'd said it — had she actually spoken aloud? This question that had been buried in her soul. This question she hardly dared to think.

"Between …?"

"Grandpa and Lily."

The old woman's hands jumped to her cheeks and as they came down, knocked the teacup clean off the table. It hit the floor with an egg-like crack.

"I never saw anything." Rasping breath flowed out her nostrils. "So I wouldn't know anything about that, ne?"

Rita got down on her knees to clean up the mess. Her hands felt weightless, spastic — the paper towel clumped and fell apart in brown pulp. She thought about how Aunt Haruko had been so quick to make her escape from Margueretta Street. She thought about her grandfather: the slackness of his ashen cheeks, the slap of his fake-leather slippers against the linoleum floor, the coffee-mixed-with-caramels scent of his breath, sour-sweet, as he would sit beside her at the dining-room table and help her with her homework night after night. He was a lonely, solitary man who devoted whatever extra time he had to being there for her. As if he were trying to repent or fulfill some old duty he couldn't fully face up to.

More fatherly than grandfatherly, she'd always felt.

As she'd told Lou, she'd been the favoured child. Waves of guilt and love and something else she could never put her finger on: something that made her cringe, recoil. It had been there for years, her whole life maybe, this sense that their family tree was a gnarled, diseased creature. The beams of their old house creaked and gasped, like they wanted to talk to her and absolve their conscience; they'd witnessed too many secrets in their time.

LILY HAD EDGED to the end of the bed. Rita hadn't realized that the TV was on, emitting silent light. It was a sitcom that she recognized, but couldn't recall the name of, that one about the hippie parents with the Young Republican son and airhead daughter. The reception was bad and the colour was off, giving the actors' skin an orange tint rimmed by fuzzy shadows.

Everyone, perhaps, had these faint, staticky shadow selves following them around, like degraded clones. Yourself, but not yourself. Things you'd done, but couldn't believe you'd done, would never acknowledge. Parts of yourself you couldn't bear to own.

There was so much Rita wanted to ask her mother. About what had happened between her and Kaz when he'd shown up on Margueretta Street. About whether their passion had reignited, as if no time had passed at all. About how she'd truly felt toward Grandpa, whether he was the man she'd always been in love with. And above all, Rita wanted to demand: How could you have been so weak? How could you have let this happen? Who *is* my father? Father, Son, or the Holy Spirit? Dark laughter filled her head, pushing her to the edge of what felt dangerously close to hysteria. How she longed to grab this woman by the shoulders and shake her until they were both limp as rag dolls and scream in her face: Why couldn't you ever stand on your own two feet? Why couldn't you seize control of your life? Motherhood was supposed to change women — make them fierce and invincible as lionesses. But Lily had simply remained the same wounded, hapless girl. Hadn't she realized that her children needed her to get her shit together? Couldn't she see the way men used and discarded her? Not least of all the men in her own family.

But these weren't things Rita could ask. She didn't trust herself to say anything at this moment; words would fail her. There were no words for these kinds of questions.

Whenever she'd turn on the TV to a talk show about the uncertainties and mysteries of paternity, her skin would tighten, her heart booming in her head. Something compelled her to keep watching the impassioned, makeup-slick faces as they dissolved into tears and rivulets of charcoal and glitter. All the anguish and fluttering tissues and hand waving. *All my life, I thought he was my ole man, y'all, but what did I know?* These people seemed unreal, a world apart from her own life, but they weren't so far removed, in fact.

The room appeared glassy, on the verge of being washed away.

It wasn't like these questions had any clear answers. Not at this point, that was for sure. Both Grandpa and Kaz were long dead, buried in the ground, consumed by maggots, or burnt to cinders, cast away on the wind. Well past the point of offering up a drop of blood or DNA.

And was that all fatherhood amounted to? Spilled sperm and the vagaries of chance?

Lily had loved and been marked by both Takemitsu men, and she yearned for something that neither one, alone, could give her. Perhaps, in the end, that was all that could be said for certain.

A rattling bang.

"It's broken," Lily murmured over her shoulder. She'd gotten up to fiddle with the TV and gave it another whack.

"It's okay, Mom. Just leave it." The screen blurred and shone and shot up like flames, and Rita's eyes overflowed as the room seemed to slide sideways in a deluge of blinding light.

Thirty-One

Rita had always wanted to throw a housewarming party. She'd invited a bunch of old friends from art school: everyone was hanging out in the living room, sprawled out on the faded sofas and beanbag cushions, laughing about old times, eating cubes of wine-soaked fruit from their sangria glasses, Janis Joplin crooning in the background. Kristen was on the floor, playing Clue with the daughter of a semi-famous sculptor, their gleeful giggles rising every so often above the din. The two little girls were high on sugar, chocolate streaked across their lips.

What a surprise that Tom bothered to show up. He came inside only briefly then stood on the front porch, smoking cigarette after cigarette. Still, it meant something that he came. They hadn't talked much since their mother's return; Tom had been travelling a lot on business.

Rita wanted to thank him, actually. The message he'd left on her answering machine, the morning of their departure for California, had yielded some much-needed answers.

"So you talked to the Archer woman?" he said.

"Yeah, I did. I'm glad you put me in touch with her." There was more she wanted to say to her brother, but he wouldn't respond well if she got all touchy-feely.

"Kaz trusted the woman. At least he had one good friend."

"That's all any of us can ask for, in the end."

"Yep. Well, nice seeing you, Rita, and your new digs. Gotta go. I'm flying to Hong Kong later today." He butted out his smoke and they exchanged a stiff hug. Through his T-shirt, she could feel his heart beating madly.

Emily Archer. During their stay in California, Rita had been vaguely aware of this woman's phone number, scribbled in red marker, on the back of her hand. The numbers were still faintly visible, she noticed, while sitting at the airport in LA with Lily beside her. Their flight back to Toronto had been delayed. If she didn't call now, she'd never get up the nerve again. The pay phone in the corner of the waiting room beckoned.

As she inserted coin after coin and dialed, she geared herself up for the disappointment of an answering machine. How startling it was to hear a real, live voice on the other end. Rita stammered something about being Kaz Takemitsu's daughter.

Sizzle of a match, a deep exhale, a smoker's cough. "Yeah, I knew Kaz. We went way back. We were old friends from the Matanzas days." Mrs. Archer explained that she'd had a job as a WRA photographer during the war.

That voice and gentle brusqueness was stirring something a long way back in Rita's memory. "My brother, Tom, mentioned that you'd gotten in touch with him a number of years ago, after Kaz's death."

"True. Kaz left behind a bit of money, you see. Not much, but still. And some old cameras. He told me that if ever anything happened to him, he wanted Tom to have it all. But not right away — when the kid turned eighteen. At that point I was to get in touch with him."

"Wow, the guy had really thought things through."

"I'm sorry he didn't leave anything to you, Rita."

"Oh, that's all right." She felt happy, actually, that Kaz had been thinking of Tom. It seemed to make up a little for the fact that Grandpa had always favoured her.

"Kaz had a hell of an eye. I tried to open doors for him when he moved to San Francisco after the war. He wasn't ambitious enough to get anywhere in the art world, unfortunately. And his best pictures were the ones they'd destroyed."

"The ones of Matanzas?"

"So you know about them."

"Yup. His secret photos." Rita explained about the cache that had been salvaged, thanks to her mother's desert pilgrimage.

"But that's impossible. The authorities seized them all."

"That might be what he told you, but there was always this small set he'd asked my mother to hide."

For a moment, the woman seemed hurt that Kaz hadn't confided in her. "That guy never trusted anyone." Then her voice became impassioned, going off on a rant about Kaz's commitment to justice and the truth and his natural gravitation to the pure, naked eye of photography. She wanted to see the rescued photos.

"You're in luck." Rita explained that she was thinking of organizing a gallery exhibition, with the help of the JCNA, for the following spring. Part of their strategy to raise awareness about redress, the exhibit would hopefully attract some media attention.

Then they chatted more about Kaz's years in San Francisco, when he'd been touring the streets to take pictures of hookers and homeless people and he'd been pretty down-and-out himself. At some point Rita's heart stopped pounding. To her surprise, she was actually enjoying the conversation. It had pulled away from her, it was no longer quite there: that raw, obsessive need to recreate in her imagination every detail of Kaz's life without her. She still wanted to know more about the man, but her interest felt oddly calm. She no longer thought of him as her long-vanished dad. Because maybe he wasn't. Probably, he wasn't. Most importantly,

Kaz didn't *feel* like he'd been her father and never would. It wasn't that the absence at the centre of her childhood had been miraculously filled. That hole, that emptiness, was still there. Yet it no longer seemed explicitly connected with Kaz.

He was just a guy, who'd felt the rebellion of youth boil in his blood. Who'd longed to use his pictures to make the world a better place. Who'd made some mistakes he'd paid for dearly in the end.

"I don't suppose Kaz ever mentioned his family?"

"Not really. Though I got the sense he never got along with his father."

"That's an understatement, for sure."

"What happened between them?"

"Long story. If you come to the exhibition, I'll take you out for a drink and try to tell you what happened."

Just as they were about to say goodbye — just as Rita had almost convinced herself that she didn't need to know — something inside her flipped the other way with violent force. "Mrs. Archer, how did Kaz die?"

A weak rasping.

"It was you, wasn't it? The woman who called us that morning. To tell us that Kaz had died. I remember talking to you on the phone before you asked me to put on my mom." How heavy the receiver had felt in her small hand. That golden river of light flowing down the centre of their kitchen, the way it reflected in dull splotches off the worn linoleum. "It sounded like you were crying."

"Perceptive for a little kid."

Rita said nothing.

"Look, I don't know what to tell you. What did your mother say about Kaz's death?"

"If anyone asked, he'd died of a stroke. That's all she'd ever say."

"A stroke."

They listened to each other breathing. She would be frozen on the threshold of this still, fragile moment forever.

"Yet you knew he didn't die of a stroke."

Rita replied that she'd always had her suspicions.

"Look. He killed himself." And a moment later, "So there you have it. He wasn't a very happy man at the end. I suppose few of us are, are we?"

It was what she'd expected, at some level. Even so. Rita hugged her arms around herself and leaned her head against the wall of the phone booth.

"The last time I saw Kaz, he was pale, thin. We sat at the bar, drinking whiskey, watching the ice melt. He wanted to take my picture, but his hands were too unsteady. I should've taken his picture instead. Always regretted not having a picture of that guy."

"Yeah, me, too."

But she did have a picture to remember him by. His picture of Lily strolling across the desert — so young, so lithe, so light, her entire life still ahead of her. Whenever Rita looked at this image, she felt something take flight inside herself, like some elusive notion of beauty and possibility would always be within grasp.

She'd had this photograph enlarged and framed. It hung in the sunroom at the back of her apartment, the room that one day, in the not too distant future, might become her painting studio. It was the one picture that wouldn't be included in the exhibition because Rita wanted to keep it for her eyes alone.

AFTER TOM LEFT, Rita rejoined the party. On a whim she'd invited a few teachers from her school, and to her surprise, they'd all shown up with wine bottles and cookie tins in hand. They were different people in the summer, carefree as the kids they taught, dressed in tank tops and miniskirts, getting drunk, laughing raucously.

Lily looked younger, too. Her roots had been freshly dyed and the sunburn on her face had nearly healed. A lightness had come over her, the tension around her brow and mouth had dissolved. Sipping a glass of white wine, she appeared remarkably at ease.

"You look good, Mom. Have you started going to the gym again?"

"Just some tai chi classes. It relaxes me, I think."

"You can tell. I should try that."

"I can get you in on a guest pass for free, if you're interested?"

There was a time, not so long ago, when this kind of superficial chit-chat would have annoyed the hell out of Rita. But these days she was grateful just to have her mother back in her life. Out in the desert, Lily had revealed more than Rita would have ever guessed possible. And even if she never understood the full extent of those secrets, that was all right, maybe. The important thing was that her mother had gained some degree of peace.

Since her return, Lily had started seeing a therapist whom Lou had recommended. Rita hoped she'd stick with it. Possibly, down the road, they'd reach the point of being able to talk more about the nether side of their family history. Lily's guilt over having kept Kaz's photographs hidden made more sense now, in light of his suicide. What a load to bear. Rita wanted to help lift that burden from her mother's conscience. It wasn't your fault, she wanted to say; you couldn't have known he was going to kill himself. One day, she hoped they'd be able to have that conversation.

She still experienced bursts of sadness and confusion about the state of their family. Some days were harder than others. Some mornings when she looked in the mirror, she found herself scanning her face for signs of genetic depravity. But all she could see were the features she'd always seen, the features that bore more than a trace of Lily, particularly around the forehead and cheekbones, as if they'd both been moulded from the same skull.

Kristen had frog-walked over in one of Rita's old grey sweaters, the neck all stretched out of shape in order to accommodate both arms and legs poking through the baggy sleeves. She hobbled around, her little body lost in the distorted garment, absurd and adorable. As

Lily bent down and caressed the back of her head, Rita experienced a buzz of warm tingles awakening at the nape of her own neck.

"Impressive turnout. Having a good time?" Mark, having snuck up behind, slipped a finger through her belt loop.

"Yup." And she was, who could deny it? A dizzy sensation had filled her head and heart.

"How about you, Lily? A splash more Chardonnay?" He extended the bottle.

"If I have any more splashes, I just might drown. Or get up and start dancing!" She winked, flirtatious as ever. Gerald wouldn't be joining them until later, after his AA meeting, so what else did Lily have to keep herself entertained?

Fortunately, Mark had gotten used to her idiosyncratic personality. "Now there's an idea." He held out a hand in mock chivalry. The music had changed to one of Nina Simone's more upbeat numbers.

"Now don't you get any ideas, Dr. Mark!"

"Mom, Mark's not a *doctor* doctor. He's a doctor of philosophy."

"Oh, Rita, you're way too picky. Any doctor's good enough for an old broad like me!"

"You're not old. Not *old* old, anyway."

"Yeah, Granny's not old!"

Although Lily was smiling, for a second there was a touch of resignation or relief in her expression. After a lifetime of struggling to remain young, the onset of old age no longer appeared to frighten her so much; no longer did she feel the need to fight it. And still, there was something like quicksilver in her movements as she rose to her feet and swayed to the music, ignoring Mark's hand as if it were invisible. Immersed in a rhythm that was hers alone, Lily danced on her own, surrendering to the moment entirely.

Acknowledgements

In researching and writing this novel over the past four years, I consulted several books and films on Japanese-American and Japanese-Canadian history. Discovering Dorothea Lange's photographs of the internment, published in *Impounded: Dorothea Lange and the Censored Images of Japanese American Internment* (edited by Linda Gordon and Gary Y. Okihiro), proved inspirational. Lange's photographs of Manzanar, California, were particularly helpful. Although *After the Bloom* is set in a fictitious camp named Matanzas, this camp is loosely based on Manzanar and draws, to a certain extent, upon historical events that led to the infamous Manzanar Riot. My descriptions of some of Kaz's photographs were inspired by Lange's photography.

The sections of my novel chronicling Lily's participation in the Cherry Blossom Pageant drew upon key information gleaned from *Pure Beauty: Judging Race in Japanese American Beauty Pageants* by Rebecca Chiyoko King-O'Riain. Two documentary films, Emiko Omori's *Rabbit in the Moon* and Junichi Suzuki's *Toyo's Camera*, helped me better understand life in the camps and the possibilities for resistance, as did the *Final Report: Manzanar Relocation Center*, Volume 1, by Ralph P. Merritt (available online through the University of California). The books *Nisei: The Quiet Americans* by Bill Hosokawa and *Redress: Inside the Japanese Canadian Call for Justice* by Roy Miki fleshed out my understanding of the internment and its aftermath. The parts of my novel dealing with Lily's memory problems and dissociative tendencies were greatly aided by information and case studies in *The Stranger in the Mirror: Dissociation — The Hidden Epidemic* by Marlene Steinberg and Maxine Schnall. My understanding of Christianity in Japan is indebted to John Dougill's fascinating book *In Search of Japan's Hidden Christians: A Story of Suppression, Secrecy and Survival*. In incorporating a fictitious *Newsweek* article, "Crisis at Matanzas," into my novel, I researched 1940s media coverage of the internment; my article quotes the phrases "15,000 sons of heaven" and "1,000 men, tanks, tear gas, and tommy guns" from *Newsweek* article "Trouble at Tule Lake" (published in the November 15, 1943, edition of the magazine). This nod to research sources is not exhaustive; I apologize if I have forgotten to acknowledge any texts that have slipped off the radar of my memory over the years.

I am very grateful to the Ontario Arts Council, the Canada Council for the Arts, and the Toronto Arts Council for the grant funding I received in order to dedicate time to completing this novel.

A big thank you to Sam Hiyate and Diane Terrana at The Rights Factory for championing this project from its inception and helping me to see it through. Your insightful comments on multiple drafts helped make the novel into what it is today. Many thanks to Paul Taunton and Léonicka Valcius for looking at early versions of *After the Bloom* and offering valuable feedback. I relied on Yoko Morgenstern's keen eye as a translator for certain phrases in Japanese. Warm thanks to the wonderful staff at Dundurn for all their dedication and hard work to get my novel to the finish line and into the hands of readers: Shannon Whibbs, Margaret Bryant, Michelle Melski, Cheryl Hawley, and Kate Unrau in particular. Special thanks to Kirk Howard for his warm welcome and commitment to my novel.

I'm thankful to all my family and friends for their continual encouragement, love, and support. Stories and memories about our ancestors that some relatives shared with me over the years provided an imaginative springboard, for which I will always be appreciative.

As always, immense affection and thanks to my partner, Chris Wong.

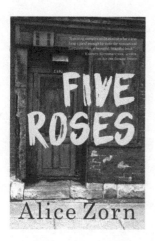

FIVE ROSES
Alice Zorn

A sister. A baby. A man who watches from the trees.
Fara and her husband buy a house with a disturbing history that reawakens memories of her own family tragedy. Maddy still lives in the house, once a hippie commune, where her daughter was kidnapped twenty-seven years ago. Rose grew up isolated with her mother in the backwoods north of Montreal. Now in the city, she questions the silence and deception that shaped her upbringing.

Fara, Maddy, and Rose meet in Montreal's historic Pointe St-Charles, a rundown neighbourhood on the cusp of gentrification. Against a backdrop of abandonment, loss, and revitalization, the women must confront troubling secrets in order to rebuild their lives.

Zorn deftly interweaves the rich yet fragile lives of three very different people into a story of strength and friendship.

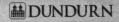